OUR WAY

T L SWAN

ALSO BY T L SWAN

My Temptation (Kingston Lane #1)

The Stopover (The Miles High Club #1)

The Takeover (The Miles High Club #2)

The Casanova (The Miles High Club #3)

The Do-over (The Miles High Club #4)

Miles Ever After (The Miles High Club – Extended Epilogue)

Mr. Masters (The Mr. Series #1)

Mr. Spencer (The Mr. Series #2)

Mr. Garcia (The Mr. Series #3)

Our Way (Standalone Book)

Play Along (Standalone Book)

The Italian (The Italians #1)

Ferrara (The Italians #2)

Stanton Adore (Stanton Series #1)

Stanton Unconditional (Stanton Series #2)

Stanton Completely (Stanton Series #3)

Stanton Bliss (Stanton Series #4)

Marx Girl (Stanton Series – set 5 years later)

Gym Junkie (Stanton Series – set 7 years later)

Dr. Stanton (Dr. Stanton – set 10 years later)

Dr. Stantons – The Epilogue (Dr. Stanton – epilogue)

Lindsey & Linda, thank you for everything you do for me.
It is so appreciated.

To my motivated mofos. I love you to bits.
You know who you are.

To Linda and my PR Team at Forward.
You have been with me since the beginning and
you will be with me until the end.
Thank you for everything.

To my home girls in the Swan Squad.
I feel like I can do anything with you girls in my corner. Thanks
for making me laugh every single day.

This year I'm adding someone new to my list.
Amazon.
Thank you for providing me with an amazing platform to bring
my books to life. I am my own boss. Without you, I wouldn't
have the job of my dreams.
Your belief and support of my work this last year has been
nothing short of amazing.

And to my four reasons for living, my beautiful husband and
three children.
Your love is my drug, my motivation and my calling.
Without you, I have nothing.
Everything I do is for you.

GRATITUDE

The quality of being thankful;
readiness to show appreciation for,
and to return kindness.

I would like to dedicate this book to the alphabet.
For those twenty-six letters have changed my life.

Within those twenty-six letters,
I found myself
and live my dream.

Next time you say the alphabet
remember its power.

I do every day.

PROLOGUE

Eliza

"HELLO, I'm Eliza Bennet. I'm starting my practical experience today," I say nervously to the lady working on reception through the glass window.

She smiles warmly. "Hello, Eliza. Welcome." She punches my name into the computer, and then she stands to retrieve a lanyard before she passes it over to me.

I read the printed name.

Eliza Bennet

Pride fills me and I bite my lip to hide my smile.

"Just wear this for a week until you find your way around so that everyone knows you are new," she says.

"Thanks." I take it from her and put it on.

"Go up to level three to the nurses' station. They will take care of you from there."

"Thank you." My heart is hammering because of my nerves.

I step into the elevator before the kind receptionist has to revive me. *This is it!*

I inhale deeply to try and calm myself down. The elevator doors open, and I head toward the nurses' station.

Just do everything right. Don't mess things up, I remind myself.

Three nurses are talking before I gently knock on the door and their attention turns my way.

"Hi, I'm Eliza. I'm starting my practical today." *Please be nice.*

They each breakout into broad smiles. "Hi, Eliza. Welcome, and come in," the lady with the dark hair says.

"Thanks."

"I'm Marjorie, and this is Beth and Caroline."

"Hi." I grip my handbag with white-knuckle force.

"Follow me. Did I read your resume right?" Marjorie continues as she walks up the corridor with me following her closely. "You've moved here from out of town?" We get to a bank of lockers where she opens one up for me. "This will be your locker." She passes me a key. "And this is your key, but we don't ever lock anything around here; we're all completely trustworthy."

"Thanks." I take the key from her and put it in my pocket. "And, yes, I'm from Florida."

"What made you want to move to San Fran?" She frowns.

"I don't know, I wanted a change and I've always loved this city. The hospital is one of the best in the country." I shrug, it seems like a stupid decision to move across the country on my own now that I've done it, but anyway I'm trying to make the best of it.

"This way, dear," she says as she begins to walk back down the corridor. "Do you know people here in San Fran?"

I trail behind her. "Nope."

She turns to me, clearly surprised. "Where are you living?"

"I got an apartment in town." I shrug nervously, feeling the need to elaborate. "My parents came to help me find a place and get settled. We've been here for two weeks but they went home yesterday."

"How lovely." She links her arm through mine. "Well, you're going to love San Francisco, and you're going to love this hospital. You've made a good decision."

"Thanks."

"Now...," she hands me a pair of gloves, "let's go play drug dealers and hand some painkillers out."

———

Four hours later, I stand and look up at the specials board in the staff cafeteria.

There's so much to choose from, hmm....

"What's good here?" a deep male voice asks. I glance over to see a young man standing beside me, who is also staring up at the board, totally entranced by the selection.

I shrug. "I don't know," I reply. "This is my first day here."

His eyes meet mine. "Your first day?" I nod.

"Mine, too." He seems surprised.

A smile crosses my face. "Really? Where did you move from?"

"Vermont, although I studied in New York."

"Do you know anyone here in San Fran?"

"Not a soul."

"Me neither."

He twists his lips in a semblance of a smile before he holds out his hand to shake mine. "I'm Nathan."

"Hi, Nathan. I'm Eliza." We shuffle forward in the line. "I think I'm going to have the turkey on rye."

He nods as he peruses the choices. "I think I'm going with the ham and pickle."

A lady walks past us with a big slab of lasagne and salad, and both our eyes near pop out."

He points to her plate. "I'm getting that."

"Me, too." I giggle.

"Next!" the server calls. Nathan steps forward. "Could I please have two lasagnes and salads?"

"Drinks?" the woman mutters, uninterested.

"No, Nathan," I whisper, "I'll get mine."

"You can buy my lunch tomorrow." He offers me a naughty wink. "That way, I have something to look forward to."

My stomach flutters.

"What drink do you want?" he asks.

"Oh, Diet Coke."

His brow furrows. "That shit's bad for you, Eliza."

I roll my eyes. "Is it, Dad?"

He twists his lips in amusement. "We'll have a mineral water and a Diet Coke, please." He passes his card to her. "Find us a table," he whispers to me.

"Okay."

I take off in search for a table. This is the best damn cafeteria I've ever seen. Lasagne *and* hot new guys! This is a dream come true.

I take a seat at a table near the window, and I stare over at Nathan as he waits for our lunch. He's super tall and towers over everyone around him. He's wearing a pale blue shirt that's rolled up at the sleeves, as well as a dark tie and navy pants. He has sandy colored hair and big blue eyes. He might just be the most handsome man I've ever seen.

And we're eating lasagne together.

Nerves dance around in my stomach. A few moments later, Nathan sits down with a tray of our lasagne and drinks.

"Thank you." I smile as I take mine from him.

He takes a bite of his food. "So, what are you doing here?" He nods in approval at the first mouthful of lasagne. "This is good."

"Hmm, it is, isn't it?" I begin to chew. "Nursing... hoping to get into paediatrics. " I point to him with my fork. "And you?"

He swallows his food and wipes his mouth with a napkin. "Medicine."

I stare at him as my brain misfires. "You're... a doctor?"

"Resident at this point, but yes. Why?" He smiles as he sips his drink from the bottle, as if he already knows what I'm going to say.

"You're too good-looking to be a doctor." I scoff. "Tell me the truth. Are you a handyman or something?"

He chuckles and holds his hands in the air. "You got me; I actually clean the toilets."

"You moved all the way from New York to clean the toilets?" I roll my eyes as I act unimpressed.

"You're very hard to please, Eliza."

I smile as I cut into my lasagne. "I'm simply saying that I would never have picked you out to be a doctor, that's all."

"What would you think I would be?"

He holds out his two hands so I can look at him and my eyes roam over his perfect physique.

Stripper.

I push my wayward thoughts to the side. "Umm... I don't know. Like a tradesman or something?"

His mischievous eyes hold mine. "Sorry to disappoint you."

"You should be," I tease. "Don't do it again."

He smiles as he focuses back on his food. "You're cute, I like you."

"I'm very likeable." I bat my eyelashes in an over-exaggerated way.

"So, you really don't know anybody in town?"

"Nope." I sigh.

"Me, too. We should hang out."

I bite my lip to try and act casual. "Yeah, that'd be fun." I take a bite of my lasagne. "Just don't fall in love with me or anything," I say sarcastically.

"No chance of that," he replies casually as he takes a mouthful of food. "You're the wrong sex for me."

What?

I snort in surprise. My Coke goes down the wrong pipe, and I choke in a spectacular fashion. "Are you kidding me?" I cough as I slap my chest. "You're gay?"

He laughs out loud. "Why is that so shocking to you?"

This man is the epitome of masculinity. "Because..." I pause as I try to articulate myself. "You give off a very different vibe from other gay guys I've known."

He smiles, clearly amused, and he rests his chin on his hand as he watches me.

I end up smiling too because this is just my crappy luck. "I had plans for us, Nathan," I tease as I rearrange the napkin on my lap.

"I know: lunch, tomorrow."

"No, actually, that wasn't it." I go back to cutting my lasagne. "It was dinner tonight to celebrate our first day together, but you probably have a Grindr date or something and won't be able to fit me into your schedule."

"Eliza..."

"Yeah?" I sigh, thoroughly distracted. He waits for my attention, and I drag my eyes up to meet his, he gives me a soft smile.

"Is that your way of asking me to dinner as a friend?"

"Maybe." I smile.

"I'd love to."

1

Ten years later

Eliza

THE ELEVATOR DOORS OPEN, and I stride out into the grand foyer of the top floor of Nathan's building. "Hello." I smile at the two receptionists.

"Hi," replies Maria.

"Oh, Eliza, hi. You must have a sixth sense, I was just thinking about you," the blonde receptionist says, looking me up and down. "Wow, you look lovely today."

I dust my skirt as I look down at myself. I'm wearing a fitted black pencil skirt and a cream silk blouse, along with high heels and sheer black stockings. My long, dark hair is in a pony-tail. "Thanks. I have a job interview this afternoon with Dr. Morgan, the cosmetic surgeon. I'm making Nathan come with me."

She frowns. "I thought you were happy nursing at the hospital."

"I am, and I will always go back to that at some stage, but I just feel like I need a change at the moment. Besides, I'm not leaving the industry completely. It's still in the medical field, just in a swanky office instead of the hospital."

"Civilian." Maria smiles as she looks me up and down. "Well, you look fabulous, and maybe you can get me a discounted facelift."

I giggle. "I have to get the job first."

"Have you got time to quickly go through Nathan's schedule with me?"

"Yes, of course."

I walk around to behind her desk so I can see the calendar on her computer.

She begins to click through the days, "So you have a charity dinner on Wednesday night. Do you want me to book a car ride home?"

"Where is it?"

"Here in town, at the Fine Arts Museum."

"Hmm, yes, a car would be great, please."

"Okay." She ticks the first thing off on her list. "You have Nathan's father's sixtieth birthday in two weeks. I've booked the flights and transfers. You leave that Friday night and get back on Sunday at 9:00 p.m."

"Okay." I sigh.

She smiles, adding in a naughty wink as if she's reading my mind.

Nathan's parents live in Vermont; it's a trek. "I knew it was coming up, I just didn't realize how quickly. Okay, great." I fake a smile.

"Now, I haven't got his father a birthday present," she

continues, "because I know you like to do all those kind of personal things, but let me know if you want me to get something. I can pick it up tomorrow."

"I'll get it, but thank you." I smile as I rub her shoulders. "What would we do without you?"

Maria smirks as she ticks the second thing off her list. "Let's be honest, you have to approve everything anyway, so I really work for you. I'm actually your PA, not Nathan's."

I chuckle. "This is true."

She goes back to her list. "Ahh, now on the 27th, which is a Monday, in six weeks, Nathan has a breakfast meeting in New York at 8:00 a.m. Shall I book him on a Sunday flight, or would you prefer to have you both on the Friday night flight? He isn't in surgery until the Wednesday the following week so you could make a weekend of it."

"Umm." I screw my face up as I think. "I'll have to try and get the Monday off work but if I get this new job, I'm not sure I can."

"Well, you know he won't go for the entire weekend without you."

"That's fine. I'll take the day off, and if I can't, he'll have to go alone."

Maria ticks her list. "Okay, so I'll book your usual hotel for Friday, Saturday and Sunday night, which will be the twenty-fourth, twenty-fifth, and twenty-sixth?"

"Great. Don't book the flights yet, though. I'll have to get back to you on whether I can go or not."

The intercom comes to life on Haley's desk. She's the other receptionist. "Haley?" Nathan's strong voice snaps through the speaker.

"Yes, Doctor?" She replies timidly.

"Where is the report from Dominque? I asked you to email me it on Monday. I'm looking for it and it's not here."

Haley cringes before she pushes the talk button down. "I'm sorry, I haven't sent it through yet. I'll do that now."

He exhales heavily, and Maria and I wince, knowing what's coming.

"Haley..." he barks.

"Yes, sir?"

"I cannot do *my* job unless you do yours. When I ask you to do something, I want it done immediately. Do you understand?"

"Yes, Doctor."

"Have you sent it yet?"

"Doing it now."

The line goes dead as he hangs up.

Maria smirks and goes back to her list. "Charming, isn't he?"

I smile with a roll of my eyes.

Nathan Mercer is unapologetically the most impatient man on Earth, and understandably so. He expects excellence from everyone because that's what he gives.

He's a cardiovascular surgeon... but not just any cardiovascular surgeon. He's the man who prototyped and patented a new kind of bionic heart: The Viso 220. Five years ago, he had a patient who didn't fit the regular requirements, and Nathan knew how he could fix it. After much deliberation, he used his entire life savings and developed a heart for her.

It saved her life, and it made him a medical rock star.

He now has a factory in Germany that manufactures them and ships all over the world. I'm so proud of him. At the time, when he poured hundreds of thousands of dollars into making the prototype, everyone tried to talk him out of it. They thought he was insane to use his own money on developing a product that had no guarantees. But Nathan had a clear vision of what he could develop, and he did it—he's saved thousands of lives, and in the process he made himself a very wealthy man.

He's handsome, strong, silent, deep... and I won the best friend lottery when we met ten years ago.

We're partners, him and me. Not sexually, of course, but we practically live together, rely on each other and are trusted friends.

"Maria!" his voice blares through the intercom again.

"Yes, Doctor?"

"When Eliza arrives, send her straight in."

Marias eyes flicker to me. "Go away," I mouth to the intercom.

"Yes, Doctor."

Haley and Maria giggle. "Are we done?" I ask.

"He's all yours."

"Thanks... I guess."

I walk down the corridor to his office to find him swinging on his chair as he looks at scans on an x-ray box.

"Hi." I drop my bag onto his couch.

He turns and gives me a broad smile. "There she is."

"Do you always have to be such a grouch with your receptionists? It's embarrassing to listen to."

"Then don't listen." He looks me up and down, and then raises an eyebrow.

"What?" I ask.

"You look a bit sexy for an interview, don't you think? Are you trying to get the job or trying to get laid?"

I roll my eyes. "I'll take that as a compliment."

He stands and comes toward me. Grabbing my shoulders, he turns me away from him and inspects me up and down.

"You like?" I smirk and give a little wiggle of my hips, knowing he's about to lecture me.

He exhales heavily, turns me toward him, and he fastens my top button. "I'm not sure about this job." He mutters, distracted, as he does another of my buttons up. "Why would you want to work for Dr. Morgan when you could manage my office?"

Here we go again.

"You could manage Berlin from here. I could get you a nice office in San Fran."

"Nathan." I sigh. "Will you stop? I am not working for my best friend. We've had this conversation before; it would be weird."

He goes back to his desk and sits down with a huff. "What's weird is that you don't want to work for me." He yanks an x-ray out of the light box. "Do you know how many people would snap up an opportunity like this?"

I place my hands on my hips. "If I worked for you, we would fight every day."

"Why?" He snaps incredulously.

"Because you're a grumpy ass, and I wouldn't put up with it." I undo my top button.

He glares at me. "Do that button back up or I'm not fucking taking you anywhere."

I giggle and do as he says. I'll undo it in the elevator at the interview, it isn't worth the argument with Nathan right now. "You ready to go?" I ask.

"Yes." He closes down his computer. "What am I supposed to do while you are in this interview?"

"Have a drink in a bar and google somewhere new to take me for dinner."

He rolls his eyes as he stands and walks toward me. "I'm not your personal assistant, Eliza."

I smile up at my handsome friend. His hair hangs over his forehead, and his big blue eyes hold mine. He's too good-looking to be this intelligent. He should be a model on the cover of a magazine. I rearrange his tie, and I smile because I know I'm the only person who gets to boss him around. To the rest of the world he's a bastard, but to me he's a big pussy cat.

"Yes, you are." I rise onto my tippy toes and kiss his cheek. "And you know it."

He smirks and holds out his arm and I link it with mine.

"Let's go."

An hour later, I look up at the tall glass building across town. "Here it is."

Nathan's eyes scan the tall building before they come back to me.

I straighten my skirt and smooth it out. "Do I look okay?"

"Yes." He presses his lips together.

"Are you going to wish me luck?"

"Good luck."

"Do you mean that?" I smirk.

"Not at all," he mutters dryly.

I giggle and kiss his cheek. "Where are you going to be?"

"I'll wait in the bar over on the corner."

"All right." I bounce on the spot as I shake my hands in front of me. "Oh, I'm nervous."

He pulls me in for a hug. "Don't be." He kisses my cheek. "If you don't get this position, it's the universe telling you to work for me."

I giggle and step back. "Okay, I'm going."

He smirks and puts his hands in his pockets as he watches me. "Try not to trip over as you walk in. Not a good look."

My face falls. "Why did you say that? Now I *will* trip over. You just jinxed me."

He chuckles. "Goodbye, Eliza."

I hunch my shoulders in excitement. "Bye."

I walk into the swanky building. The foyer has been designed in black marble and beautiful timbers.

I make my way to the lift and read the gold sign there:

Dr. MORGAN, Level 7.

I exhale heavily. *Okay, let's do this.*

I take the elevator up to level seven. Once there, I follow the signs to Dr. Morgan's offices. The glass door is heavy, and his name is etched into the glass. Plush dark carpet covers the floor. This place is... wow! It looks more like a fancy bar or something.

Cosmetic surgeon... of course. It's all about the aesthetics and creating the perfect illusion.

Well played.

I walk over to the desk. "Hello, I'm Eliza Bennet. I'm here for an interview."

The girls behind the desk smile. "Hello, welcome," they say.

The pretty blonde stands. "I'll take you straight through. This way, please."

I follow her down a corridor and into a consultation room. There is a round table in the middle, and a wall-mounted television screen.

"Just take a seat, the doctor will be with you soon." She fills me a glass of water. "Can I get you anything else?"

"No, thank you." She leaves me alone in the room, and I clasp my hands together in my lap. God, I hate fucking interviews. I haven't been to one in ten years. I can almost hear my heart as it tries to escape from my chest.

The door opens, and a young man walks in. "Hello."

I stand to shake his hand, and I'm shocked. He's young... and very handsome with dark wavy hair and brown eyes, not at all what I expected. "Henry Morgan."

"Eliza Bennet." I smile.

His eyes glow as he takes a seat. "Please, take a seat."

He opens a folder that holds my resumé, and his eyes scan through it. "Your resumé is very impressive."

"Thanks."

He closes the folder and his eyes come to mine. "Why do you want this job, Eliza?"

Oh shit.

"Well, I'm looking to move to another field outside of the hospital."

"I see. And what made you want to work for me?"

I smile awkwardly. "To be honest, I don't care who I work for. I liked the position that you are offering."

He smiles broadly and I know he liked that answer. "The position is for a surgery manager. I see you've managed before having worked in intensive care, recovery, and paediatrics."

"Yes."

"Very impressive." His eyes hold mine, and there seems to be a buzz in the air between us.

Is he attracted to me?

"Let me tell you about the position. You will be my right hand. I need you to manage the seven members of staff that I have, while also seeing to the recovery care for my post-op patients. You would need to be on call overnight on the days that I'm in surgery in case the patient is in distress and needs advice or pain management. I operate on Tuesdays and Thursdays. "

I listen intently.

"You would be working out of this office. However, there

will be times when you would need to travel with me to conferences, both interstate and overseas. "

Excitement fills me, this sounds fantastic.

"How does that sound?"

"Great."

"I would need you to start as soon as possible. My manager has become unwell and is currently unable to return."

"I could possibly start as soon as next week," I offer. "I have some paid time off that I could take to allow me to finish earlier."

He sits back in his seat and crosses his leg. "You have an amazing resumé."

"Thank you." I smile.

"However, there is one small problem."

"There is?"

"I'm not sure I would be able to work with you."

My face falls. "Why not?"

"At the risk of being unprofessional, I have to tell you that I'm physically attracted to you."

"Oh." *What the fuck?* "I don't know what to say to that."

"I've never worked with someone I was attracted to before, have you?"

"Umm." Jeez, this guy doesn't mince his words.

"I'm very professional, and I'm in a relationship," I lie. "You wouldn't need to worry about that."

He smiles to himself as if liking that. "Well, that makes things easier. I'm a professional, too."

I clasp my hands in front of me.

He stares at me for a moment, as if assessing the situation. "I have one more person to interview this afternoon. I will let you know tonight, by email, if you have been successful."

"Okay." I smile.

He stands and holds out his hand to shake mine. "Goodbye, Dr. Morgan."

"Call me Henry."

I force a smile. Oh hell, this interview is weird. "Okay, Henry, I look forward to your email. Have a lovely weekend."

"You, too."

I turn and walk out of the room, not entirely sure what position it is that I've just applied for.

Who the fuck tells a person they are interviewing that they are attracted to them? What was that about?

I smile to the girls as I walk through reception. Does he tell them that he's attracted to them, too? "Goodbye."

"Bye." They call.

I get into the elevator and shake my head. "Wow," I whisper to myself.

Maybe he was just being honest. I mean, if he is a serial player or sleazeball, he wouldn't say that to me in an interview, he would just perv on me while I worked.

I shrug. It takes all types, I suppose. I walk out of the building, across the street, and into the bar to find Nathan.

He's sitting at a table in the back, scrolling through his phone with a glass of scotch in front of him.

"Hey." I smile as I sit down.

He puts his phone down. "How did it go?"

I shrug. "I don't know. Fine, I guess. I find out tonight but the job sounds great." I can't elaborate on what Dr. Morgan said to me or Nathan will march into his office like a psycho. He's a tad overprotective.

"What do you want to drink?" he asks.

I glance over the selection. "A glass of red, please."

"Okay." He gets up and disappears to the bar. I take out my

phone and text my two best friends. These ones are my girls—
the ones I tell everything.

> **Just got out of my interview.**
> **The job sounds great.**
> **Doctor was cute, and he told me**
> **that he was attracted to me**

I smirk and hit send. That's something I never thought I'd
write.

A message bounces straight back from Brooke.

> **What the fuck?**

I giggle and another message from Jo comes in.

> **Are you for real?**
> **Serial sleazeball or what?**

I smile as I type.

> **100% Call you later.**

Nathan comes back to the table with my drink, and I stuff
my phone into my bag. "Thank you." I smile. "What have you
been doing?"

He slides into his seat. "I think I finally found an apartment.
I look at it tomorrow."

I roll my eyes into my glass of wine. "You don't need another
apartment."

"Your apartment is too small for us."

"You have your own gigantic apartment across town. If my

apartment is too small, you can always go home, you know."

"Stop it." He gives a subtle shake of his head. "I like to stay with you in your apartment with your things around us."

"But I'm happy where I am."

"What's the problem? Your rent will be the same. Nothing will change for you except you'll get to live in a bigger place."

"Yes, but that means you will lose out financially. Plus, we won't always stay together. What happens when we meet someone? What happens then?"

"Then it's your apartment and I will stay at my place."

"I don't need a bigger apartment."

"I do. I need an office and I need to be able to keep some clothes at your place. I need a treadmill so I can run if I get caught up at work late. Your apartment has one bedroom, Eliza; it's way too small."

"You have all those things at your place." I scoff, how many times do we have to have this conversation? "You can stay there if you want those things."

"Stop pissing me off, Eliza," he snaps. "I'm not having this conversation with you. I'm finding an apartment, and I'm getting it, and you will fucking love it when I do."

I smirk against my glass. Controlling prick. If the truth be known, I really do want a bigger apartment but I don't like the idea of him having to pay for it.

"Oh." As if remembering something, he reaches into the inside chest pocket of his suit and pulls out an envelope. "I got you something."

"What is it?"

"Open it."

"I love surprises."

"Really?" He replies dryly. "I would never have guessed."

I take it from him and tear open the envelope. My eyes

widen. Two tickets to... "Spain?" I gasp as my eyes rise to meet his. "What?"

"Happy birthday, baby."

My mouth falls open in shock as my eyes skim the rest of the booking confirmation. "We're going to Spain?"

"Uh-huh, for two weeks." He gives me a sexy smile. "Next month. I know it isn't your birthday for a few months, but I can only take leave then."

"Nathan." I smile. "Where in Spain?" My eyes speed read the document. "Oh my God, Majorca?" I gasp.

"Pronounced Ma Yorker."

I hold the paper to my chest. "Last year you took me to Italy... now Majorca? You spoil me rotten."

"We can only go if you agree to move into a bigger apartment." His eyes dance with mischief, expecting me to explode.

"You would actually stoop so low to get your own way that you would bribe me with a trip?"

He takes a sip of his scotch. "Undoubtedly."

"Fine, get the damn apartment." I jiggle in my seat in excitement. "We're going to Majorca." My eyes widen. "Oh, but what if I get this job?"

"You tell them before you start that you have a pre-planned vacation that can't be refunded."

I smile broadly as I take his hand over the table. "I have to get it first."

He squeezes my hand in his. "You will."

Half an hour later, we are trolling the aisles of Nathan's favorite bookstore. "It should be here..." He searches the shelves.

"Are you sure it's out yet?"

"Yes, it should be, it released three days ago."

I smile as I watch him search the shelves, Nathan is an avid reader, and his favorite author's new book has just come out. God help us all if they don't have it in stock yet.

"Just ask the shop assistant," I say.

His brow furrows. "If they did their job correctly, it would be here with his other books."

"Just ask. I'm not waiting here all night for you to try and find it."

He turns and looks for an assistant. "Excuse me," he calls.

The woman turns and her eyes light up like it's Christmas when she sees him. "Oh, hello." She rushes to stand beside him. "Can I help you?"

He gives her a charming smile. "Yes, I'm looking for Garaldi's new book. *Into the Woods*. Do you have it?"

"Oh." She smiles sweetly, completely flustered by his good looks. "I'm sure I can find one for you."

I try not to roll my eyes. Honestly, it's embarrassing the way women fawn all over him.

"I'll need two," he tells her.

"Buying one for a gift?" she asks to elaborate the conversation.

"No." He cuts the conversation short and turns back to the bookshelf to continue his perusing.

I bite my lip to hide my smile, Nathan doesn't engage in polite conversation. When he's finished saying what he wants to say, the conversation is effectively over.

"I'll go look in the back," she replies in a fluster.

"Thank you." He replies, distracted by the books in front of him.

"You know it's pretty pointless buying two," I lean in and whisper.

"I need one for your house and one for mine."

"But you hardly ever sleep at your house." I widen my eyes.

"Yes, well... one of these days I'm going to get sick of you hogging the bed and snoring, and I'll return to the peace and sanity of mine."

"Promises, promises." I reply flatly as I roam up the aisle.

Two years ago, I broke up with my boyfriend. Nathan stayed with me for the night because he was worried about me. One night turned to two, two nights turned to five, and here we are two years later. He's still buying two of every book he reads as if he's going back to his house anytime soon.

"Here you are." The sales assistant smiles as she approaches us with two books in hand. "They hadn't been unpacked yet, they just came in."

Nathan smiles as he takes them from her. "Thank you, much appreciated."

He marches to the front counter to pay like the cat that got the cream. Thank fuck they had it. He would have made me search the city for it tomorrow if they hadn't.

He pays the cashier, and we walk out into the street and toward the road. Nathan takes my hand in his.

"I can cross the street on my own. You don't have to hold my hand, you know. I'm not five."

"That's debatable." He mutters as he watches the oncoming traffic. He finally sees a break and drags me across the road.

"What do you think I do when you aren't with me?" I ask as I half run to keep up with him.

"I hate to think."

We get to the other side of the street. He lets me go, and I link my arm through his. Truth be told, I like the way Nathan makes me hold his hand on the roads. He's done it since our very first dinner date, all those years ago.

"When do we go?" I ask as we walk along.

"Four weeks from tomorrow."

"Maria didn't mention it."

"Because it's a surprise." He widens his eyes, as if I'm stupid.

"Oh right." I beam. "I'm going to need new vacation clothes, and oh..." I clap in excitement. "I'm going to get one of those hats I wanted. You know, the ones that match your bikini?"

He smiles, clearly delighted by my excitement. "Okay."

"You're going to need new swim shorts, too."

"I'm good." He smirks.

"Nathan..." I smile up at him. "Thank you, I really needed this vacation. You're too good to me." I kiss his shoulder as we walk.

He leans his head down to rest on mine. "Only the best for my girl. Happy Birthday, baby."

———

It's 10:35 p.m., and after going out for dinner, I watched Netflix, and called my sister April before I googled Majorca all night. I'm now ready for bed. I brush my teeth and tie my long, dark hair in a braid, and then I walk into my bedroom. Nathan is lying on his side, reading his book. The room is dark, the only light from his bedside lamp.

"Is the book good?" I ask.

He turns the page, distracted. "Very."

I turn my blankets down and smile as I watch him. "I can't believe I got the job." The email came in a few hours ago, and I'm still processing it.

"I told you that you would."

"It's so exciting, you know? Something new to learn, and they approved our vacation, so it's all good."

"It is." He replies distracted.

I climb into bed. "Can we go shopping tomorrow for bikinis?" I could ask for anything when he's reading and he will gladly agree, just to shut me up.

"If you want." He turns another page.

I get into bed and turn my back to him. "Let's get up early and go out for breakfast. Then it's shopping all day."

"Hmm," he mutters, distracted. He grabs my hipbone and pulls me back so I'm snug up against his body. This is how I fall asleep the fastest.

"Did I say thank you?"

"A hundred times, now go to sleep." He taps my hip in a silent *shut up now* signal.

I smile into the darkness. "Are you going to read all night?"

"Probably."

"Night, Nathe."

He taps my behind. "Night, babe."

Nathan

"Then I want to go into that new place that opened in the mall," Eliza says as she drags me down the street.

Why the hell did I agree to come shopping all day? What was I thinking? "Yeah, okay." I sigh. "I need more coffee."

"You've had two already."

I look at her, deadpan. "I need more."

She rolls her eyes, unimpressed, and drags me into a lingerie store. "Sit there." She directs me to sit in a large velvet chair outside the changing rooms.

Thank fuck... a chair.

I slump into the seat and wait as she looks around. I take out my phone and scroll aimlessly through it. Eliza eventually picks up a few things before she walks into the changing room. "Won't be a minute."

I exhale heavily. This is the last place I want to be on a Saturday.

I stuff my phone back into my pocket, link my fingers together, and put my hands behind my head.

After a few minutes, she says, "I like this one."

"Show me."

She opens the curtain. I stare at her for a moment and then frown. She's wearing a gold, skimpy bikini. Her hips are curved and her skin has a beautiful honey tone to it. Her breasts are full and voluptuous.

She holds her long, dark hair up on top of her head in a ponytail. "Is this all right?"

My brow furrows as I stare at her. The blood begins to rush around my body, and my throbbing heartbeat echoes in my ears.

"Erm..." I pause as I think of the right thing to say. She looks more than all right. *Fucking hell!*

Eliza flicks her bikini bottom and wiggles her hips. "I think I'll get it."

My cock instantly hardens.

What the actual fuck is going on here?

She puts her hands up and rearranges her breasts in the bikini top, and my dick clenches in appreciation.

Jesus Christ.

I've never reacted to Eliza this way before, and I've seen her in every possible way.

I break into a cold sweat. The room begins to spin, and I stand up in a rush. "I'll meet you outside."

2

Eliza

I FROWN as I watch Nathan practically running from the shop. What in the hell's wrong with him?

I turn back to my reflection in the mirror and smile as I look at myself. I actually look good in this. All those mornings in the gym are finally paying off. I turn to look at my behind and readjust the top over my breasts. Yep, I'm getting it. I try on the second one but it doesn't look anywhere near as good. Gold it is.

I get dressed and take the bikini to the cashier. "I'll take this one, please."

"It's lovey, isn't it?" She folds it and wraps it in white tissue. "It just came in on Thursday. It comes in red, too. Did you see that one?"

"Yes, I did. "My eyes roam over to the others on the rack. "Thanks, but I prefer this color." I glance out through the window to see Nathan pacing back and forth on the sidewalk.

His hands are raking through his hair, and he looks like he's just seen a ghost. What is he doing?

"Have a nice day." The cashier hands over the bag, and I bounce outside.

Nathan's eyes meet mine, and he swallows a lump in his throat.

"What happened?" I ask. "Did the hospital call?"

His face falls. "Yes." He looks around nervously. "That's it, the hospital called."

I link my arm through his. "Everything okay?"

"Yes." He glances down at my hand on his bicep.

"Do you need to go straight away or are we grabbing you more coffee?"

"Umm." His eyes hold mine.

"It's fine." I sigh. "You're off the hook. Come have a quick breakfast with me and then you can go to work. I don't mind shopping alone."

He raises a brow. "If you don't mind shopping alone, why do you always make me come?"

"To torture you, of course." I smile.

"Hmm." He grunts. "It's working."

"Don't forget we're going out tonight."

"Yes, I know." He frowns as he stares out at the people around us, totally distracted. "What time are we leaving?"

"I've got Monica's baby shower this afternoon, and you're meeting us at the bar, remember?"

He rolls his eyes.

I frown up at him. "What's wrong with you?"

"Nothing." He grabs my hand as we cross the road.

"If you don't want to come out tonight then don't come."

"I'm fucking coming, all right." He glances down at me. "Did you get the gold one?"

I smile broadly. "Uh-huh. I'm going to be loving myself sick in that bikini."

"Hmm." He replies flatly. "It was a bit skimpy, wasn't it?"

"Nope, I might even go topless over there. Maybe even nude." I widen my eyes. "The possibilities are endless really."

"That won't be happening."

"Why not?"

"Because..." He frowns. "I'm not protecting you from the sleazy gazes of men. Women get abducted from Majorca all the time, you know."

"They do not." I giggle and kiss his shoulder. "Doesn't bother you here. Being my bouncer is your favorite pastime."

I glance down to realize that we're still holding hands. Nathan seems to notice at the same time. He drops my hand like a hot potato and takes a huge step back. "Listen... I'm going to take a raincheck on breakfast."

"Oh, okay."

"I'm very busy and I can't be loitering around the shops with you all day. Goodbye, Eliza," he announces formally.

Jeez, this patient must be really sick if he's acting crabby. "See you tonight, then?"

He nods and turns.

"Hey!" I call, he turns back toward me. "Where's my goodbye kiss?"

He narrows his eyes before he leans down and kisses my cheek. "Stop fucking nagging me."

I smile up at my handsome friend and fix his hair from hanging over his eyes.

He turns, storms off, and I watch him disappear into the distance.

Hmm, weird. I take out my phone and call my mom. She answers on the first ring. "Hey, Mom." I smile.

"Hello, darling, how's my girl today?"

"Oh my God, I didn't call you last night because it was too late. Guess what Nathan bought me for my birthday?"

"I can't imagine. That man spoils you rotten."

"I know." I laugh. "A trip to Majorca."

"Where's that?"

"Spain."

"Oh my God. Tom!" she calls out to my father. "Nathan bought Eliza a trip to Spain for her birthday."

"Oh, hell, that's great. Can we come?" I hear my dad reply back.

"Can you believe it?" I gasp.

"I can, honey. He takes you everywhere."

"I just bought the most beautiful bikini, and I love it."

"This is great. You have that baby shower this afternoon, don't you?"

I roll my eyes. "Ugh. Don't remind me."

"Listen, honey, I've got to go. Doris is picking me up for tennis in five minutes and I'm not ready. I'll call you tomorrow."

"Okay, love you."

"Love you, too."

———

The waiter pours our glasses of wine. "Are you ready to order?" he asks.

I peruse the menu. "Can we have five more minutes, please?"

"Of course." He gives Brooke, Jolie, and me a broad smile and with a nod of his head he rushes off to serve someone else.

"A toast." Brooke smiles as she holds up her glass. "To surviving an afternoon in the snake pit." She smirks.

"To surviving." We giggle together. God, this afternoon's baby shower was horrendous. "I'm not having a baby shower, and neither are you two," I say before I take a sip of my wine. "Nathan's right, they're a complete waste of time."

"That's if we even have kids," Brooke says casually.

"You don't want kids?" I frown, this is the first I hear of this.

Brooke shrugs. "I don't know. I'm thirty-three and single. Who knows what the future holds. It may not be in my destiny."

"I'm having kids," I tell her. "If I can, of course. Or I want to adopt or foster, but being a mom is something I definitely want to do."

"Well, you'd better get Nathan out of your bed then," Jolie says before she takes a big gulp of her wine.

"What does that mean?" I frown.

"It means just that. No guy is going to want to date a woman who sleeps with another man every night."

"We're friends. And when was the last time you had sex?" I retort.

"A while ago." Jolie sighs.

I look between my two beautiful friends, and something blindingly obvious stands out. "What's going on with us?"

"What?"

"Look at us," I say. "In our thirties, successful, financially independent and happy, yet nobody out there interests us romantically. There's no shortage of men, just none are appealing to us three."

We all stare into space as we each go over that notion in our mind.

"I don't know about you girls, but casual sex has most definitely lost its shine." Brooke sighs.

"For me, too." Jolie nods. "I go to the gym, then work, and I hang with you guys on the weekend. I really don't do much else. I may be the most boring person on the planet."

"Me, too," Brooke agrees.

"You know what the problem is?" I say. "We're too comfortable."

"To be honest, I'd rather eat a cupcake than spend an hour getting ready for a date with a loser. Men just aren't worth the fucking hassle anymore." Jolie shrugs. "Well, let's face it, nobody satisfies us in bed like BOB does, anyway."

We all clink our glasses together. "Amen."

I slump and lean on my hand. "I've had way too many dates with my vibrator. I think I've forgotten what real sex is even like."

Brooke narrows her eyes. "Girls, I think it's official. We're in a midlife rut."

We sip our wine in silence, suddenly depressed by the thought.

"But, how? How did it go from dating all the time and having the time of our lives, to waking up one day and realising that we haven't gone on a date in six months?"

"Continual disappointment in men, I suspect."

"We should shake things up a bit," Jolie chips in.

"Like how?" I ask.

"I don't know." She thinks for a moment, and then narrows her eyes as a plan presents itself. "Step out of our comfort zones. We each have to go on a date and we need to talk to different people—do things we don't normally do. Yes! We could do it. The six of us should go on a date, and then we can reward ourselves with a weekend away... somewhere exotic."

"Oh, please. Nathan won't go on a date with anybody." I roll my eyes.

"Bullshit!" Jolie snaps. "He's fucking people all the time. A man who looks like he does has to be having sex on tap."

"Like when?" I scoff. "He spends every spare minute of his day with me.

"He still has his apartment, doesn't he?"

"Yeah, so?"

"Why exactly do you think he has that bachelor pad, Eliza?" I stare at her. "Nathan's apartment is his booty-call place. He works late some nights, he fucks whoever he wants, kicks them out, and then he goes to your house to sleep."

Brooke widens her eyes as if I'm totally clueless.

I cringe. "You think?"

"I *know*."

"I never thought of it that way. Maybe..." I shrug. "Good for him, I guess." I toast the air with my wine. "At least one of us is getting some action."

"You know," Jolie says. "This little arrangement you and Nathan have going on, is really not good for you."

"Why? I don't care who Nathan fucks."

"Because it's not equal. You can't fuck who you want, or invite men over because Nathan is always at your house. He's got his cake and he's eating it, too."

"We're friends, you idiot. I'm not his fucking cake."

"How many texts have you sent each other today?" Jolie asks.

"We're friends. Friends text each other."

Brooke and Jolie exchange looks. "All right... then put it this way: would you invite a guy over with Nathan there... in his boxer shorts, sleeping in your bed?"

"Absolutely not." I wince. I imagine Nathan strangling some poor man for interrupting his time with me.

"But when Nathan wants to have sex with someone, he has

his apartment to go to," Jolie continues. "He has an out, Eliza. You don't. Why can't you see it? One day, he's going to meet someone special and stay at his apartment with him, and he'll never come back. Where will that leave you?"

I imagine what a horrible day that would be.

Maybe the girls are onto something here. This isn't a normal set up between him and me. The boundaries between us *are* blurred. As much as I adore Nathan, perhaps by spending so much time with him, I'm holding myself back from meeting someone in my future.

Shit.

If I do want to meet someone and eventually have kids, I need to do something different to what I'm doing now.

I *am* in a rut.

Happy, but stagnant just the same.

Brooke and Jolie raise their eyebrows. "So, you do agree that what we're doing isn't working?"

"I do," I concede. "You're right, something has to change or we're going to end up single forever."

"So, are we in?" Jolie asks.

"One date?" I ask. "That's it? No strings?"

"A proper date. Sit down meal and all the trimmings. At least four hours. A kiss at the end of it," Jolie replies.

"Can we leave the boys out of it and make it an exotic girls weekend away instead?" I ask. "I don't want them to know about this." Nathan will never let me live it down if he finds out.

"Of course." Brooke smiles. "This is just the motivation I needed to wear my cute red dress tonight."

"We start tonight?" I gasp.

"No time like the present." Brooke clinks her wine glass against ours. "To operation rut-breaker."

"Whoever gets the first date gets to pick where we go for our weekend away," Jolie says.

"That's going to be me." I smile, and for the first time in a long time, excitement sweeps through me.

What can I wear tonight? I want to pick where we're going away so I need to win this bet. I want to look sexy as fuck.

"You know what?" Jolie says. "I'm going to the bar right now and I'm going to talk to someone."

"You are?" I frown in surprise.

"Yep, fuck this. I'm going to make conversation and everything."

We all giggle, and she looks around as she searches for her unsuspecting target. "See that guy over there?"

We look over to see a cute guy sitting at the bar alone. "Yeah."

"I'm going to go talk to him."

"What, now?" I frown.

"Right now."

She drains her glass, and she slams it down on the table. "Wish me luck, bitches."

"Good luck." We laugh.

She marches over and sits on the stool next to him. His eyes light up when he sees her, and he smiles. When he says something, she laughs on cue.

I smile at Brooke. "And that's how it's done."

"Apparently."

We watch her for a moment as she talks and laughs, and my focus comes back to Brooke. "Do you really think I'm holding myself back from meeting someone by spending so much time with Nathan?"

"Yeah." She sighs. "I do, which really sucks because he loves you more than anyone. I mean, why the fuck is he gay, anyway? He's the perfect male specimen."

"I know." I sigh sadly.

I glance over to the bar to see Jolie and the guy staring at his phone. "What is she doing over there? Are they watching something?" I frown.

"Like what?"

Jolie looks over and bursts out laughing before she raises her glass to us.

"What is she doing?"

Brooke laughs. "Who fucking knows?" She sips her drink. "Oh, tell me about your interview."

"It was so bizarre. We were going through the interview, and I had this feeling that there was something going on with him. You know when you get the feeling?"

"Uh-huh."

"Shots," the waiter says as he puts four shots down in front of us.

"I'm sorry, what?" I frown. "I think you have the wrong table."

"These are from your friend at the bar." He gestures to Jolie, and we look over to see her tipping her head back and doing one, too. She laughs out loud when she stares back at the guy's phone.

"Thank you," we say to the waiter before he disappears through the club.

"What is she doing?" I frown.

"I don't know but she obviously wants to get drunk."

I giggle and pick up my first shot. "Who am I to argue?" I tip my head back and drain the shot glass. "Ugh, tequila." I scrunch up my face in disgust. "She's trying to kill us." I splutter.

Brooke laughs and tips her head back. She immediately picks up her second shot and does it again. "Go on... the interview?"

"Oh." I tip my head back and take the second shot. "Oh God, that's bad." I wince.

"So, we go through the interview, and then the guy says that he's not sure he can work with me."

"Why not?" Brooke frowns.

We hear a loud laugh from the bar. We look up to see Jolie's head is tipped back and she's really laughing.

"That guy must be really fucking funny." Brooke frowns.

"Either that or he's just roofied her drink." I glance at the four empty shot glasses on our table. "And ours. Anyway, so the interviewer then tells me that he isn't sure if he can work with me because he's attracted to me."

"What?"

"I know." I shrug. "Bizarre. Right?"

"Drinks, ladies." The waiter puts down another four shots in front of us.

"What in the world?" Brooke grumbles.

Jolie laughs from the bar and raises her shot glass at us. She tips her head back to drain it, and then goes back to looking at his phone.

"What the hell are they watching on his phone?" I frown.

"God knows." Brooke downs her shot. "This is working, though. I'm feeling buzzed already. So, you got the job. When do you start?"

"A week from Monday."

"So soon?"

"I know."

"What are you going to do about Dr. Flirty Boss?"

"I'm sure it's nothing. Maybe I misheard him?"

Jolie falls into the seat beside us. "Hey." She laughs.

"What are you doing?"

She giggles and gestures to the guy she was talking to. He's currently carrying a tray of eight shots. He sits down at the table with us. "Girls, this is Santiago." She introduces him.

"Hi." We smile. He's *hot!*

"Hello," he says with a foreign accent. "Hello, beautiful ladies."

Jolie's eyes dance with delight as she tips her head back and downs another shot. "We've been watching some movies on his phone, and I thought it was only fair I shared those with my friends."

Brooke and I frown at each other. Huh?

"Ah, ladies." Santiago smiles. "Let me introduce myself." He clicks something on his phone.

"Drink!" Jolie orders. "You're going to need it."

We all take our next shot, and I am feeling very inebriated here. Santiago holds his phone up, and we all look at it. It takes a moment for my eyes to focus, and then I slap my hand over my mouth.

It's him! Santiago is having sex with a woman.

Brooke's horrified eyes stare at the screen, and I burst out laughing at her expression.

He's really giving it to this girl, while her legs are up over his shoulders. He pulls out and turns to face the camera. He's hung like a fucking horse.

I burst out laughing. "What the hell?"

Jolie laughs hard. "Right?"

The video switches to him on a beach, where he's banging two girls who are both on their knees in front of him. He's giving hard, deep thrusts, and he even slaps one of them on the behind.

Brooke's eyes are the size of saucers as she stares at the phone. "W-what the ever-loving fuck?" she stammers. "What am I watching right now?"

Jolie tips her head back and laughs even harder. She's hysterical.

Santiago taps on the screen, and he's soon in the darkness. We each lean in to try and focus, only to see he's fucking another girl on the trunk of a car. The sound of skin on skin can be heard all around us. I hate to say it, but it's actually pretty hot to watch.

My eyes meet my friends, and the three of us burst out laughing again.

"What kind of freak are you?" Brooke blurts out.

"The world's greatest lover," Santiago purrs.

"Where do you meet these women?" I ask him.

"In bars, over tequila." He raises his brow. He's completely serious. He thinks he's the world's greatest lover.

"I find you disgusting," Brooke says, indignant as she drains her glass. "Not to mention offensive."

"And totally fucking hot." Jolie laughs. "We did say we wanted to try something different, girls."

I laugh with her. "Not this different."

Nathan

"And through here is the master bedroom," the realtor says as she shows me through the apartment.

I look over the expansive views of San Francisco. It's a beautiful apartment—the nicest I've seen so far, and I've been looking for a long time. It's the best part of town, close to restaurants and shops.

"Very nice." I walk up to the large master suite, which is

nearly the size of Eliza's entire apartment. There is a large ensuite bathroom off of it. It's not decorated in the colors I like but we can work with that later. There's also a huge walk-in closet. Enough room for both of our things.

This could work.

I look around intently, this is very nice indeed.

I walk back out into the living area, and down the hall.

"There are five bedrooms in total. A loft as the master, two living areas, and a huge galley kitchen with another bathroom on this level," the realtor continues in her sales pitch.

"And garages?"

"Double garage with twenty-four hour concierge."

"And security?"

"Full surveillance."

I turn to the realtor with a smile. "I'd like to make an offer."

———

The bar is bustling, and I'm with Drew and Glen, my two best friends. We're currently waiting for the girls.

"Where the fuck are they?" Drew looks at his watch. "They were supposed to be here an hour ago. I want to eat."

We're not sure if the girls have eaten or not, so we're waiting for them. I take out my phone and text Eliza.

Where are you?

I put my phone down onto the table and wait for her reply.

I look around the room, and over in the corner, I see a familiar face.

I smirk at Glen. "Your best buddy is here."

They look around. "Who?"

"Over by the corner." I tip my beer in the general direction, and Glen catches sight of the guy I'm talking about, and he rolls his eyes.

"Seriously, such a fucking jerk Don't let him see us."

I chuckle as I take a swig of my beer. Samuel Phillips is Glen's archenemy. He's an anaesthetist like Glen, and they often see each other at the hospitals they work at. Samuel's good-looking and confident, and he loves to tell you how great he is at every chance he gets. He drives Glen absolutely mad.

"I'm going to knock that prick out one of these fucking days," Glen murmurs as he takes a sip.

"Why does he get under your skin so much again?" I ask.

"I don't know, he just does. He's flirty, and he has the nurses all giggling like school girls. You're at work, fucktard, put your dick away and just do your damn job."

Drew smirks. "So, you're jealous?"

Glen scoffs. "Of him? As if."

Drew and I chuckle. I pick up my phone and check if Eliza's replied. "Where the hell are they?" I rub my stomach. "I am about to pass out from hunger."

I'm feeling more myself now that I'm with the boys. I've been rattled all day by my little bikini erection this morning.

I was just horny. A good jerk off fixed the situation, and now I can, thankfully, return to normality.

I smile to myself, and I thought it was Eliza...

Stupid fuck.

I shake my head. What was I thinking? Of course, it

wasn't her. I've seen Eliza in next to nothing most days for the last ten years. It wasn't her body... it was mine.

It was just a hormonal malfunction. Nothing more, nothing less.

My thoughts get interrupted by Glen's voice. "About time. Where the hell have you girls been?"

"Watching movies," Brooke says as she tries to keep a straight face.

"More like documentaries," Jolie adds. "Really fucking interesting ones."

Eliza laughs. I look up and catch sight of her and my heart skips a beat. She's wearing a tight black dress. It's off the shoulders and sits just above the knee. Her long, dark hair is down, and her makeup is smokey. She smiles and comes around to kiss me on the cheek, placing her hand on my thigh.

"Hi, Nathe."

She's tipsy; I can tell by her husky voice.

"Hi." I look her up and down. "You look gorgeous."

I feel a twinge in my cock. *No!*

Not again.

She smiles seductively. "Thanks."

"Are we having dinner?" I ask them.

"No, we ate already. We had canapés and tequila."

"Oh, thanks very much. Thanks for telling us!" Drew snaps. "Here we are waiting for you lot while wasting away."

Eliza giggles as Brooke pretends to play the violin.

"Let's get some cocktails," Eliza says, looking over to the bar.

"Great idea."

The girls take off as I grab a menu. "I'm not waiting for

those bitches next time, I'm eating when I'm hungry. Screw this, I'm getting everything."

Three hours later, the boys and I are talking to a group of women when I glance across the room. Eliza is having the time of her life, dancing and flirting up a storm. She has hardly spoken two words to me all night.

And it shouldn't bother me... but it does.

I inhale and shake my head, reminding myself of who I am.

Stop it. Who cares who she talks to? Not me, that's for sure.

"So, are you attached?" the blonde asks as she rubs her hand over my bicep.

"Yes. Very," I answer flatly.

"I don't mind," she purrs. "Makes it more fun. I'm very discreet."

I roll my eyes. *Good grief.*

Glen smirks, clearly amused by her answer.

My eyes find Eliza as Samuel Phillips approaches her. He says something, and she laughs out loud and kisses his cheek in greeting.

I narrow my eyes as I watch the two of them. He's animated as he talks and she's giggling like a schoolgirl.

Oh, please, give me a break.

His eyes roam down her body and then back up to her face. My jaw clenches as I watch him.

Don't look at her like that, dickhead.

Anger begins to roll through me as I feel myself becoming territorial of her.

I snap my eyes away angrily, but before long, they rise to watch over her again.

Samuel's eyes are drinking her in, his attention roaming all over her body.

I know exactly what he's thinking.

I want to march over there and teach him some manners. I need a distraction.

"I'm getting another round of drinks," I say to the guys.

I stand in line at the bar and try to get a handle on myself, stretching my neck to try and release some of the tension.

What do I care, anyway?

It's none of my business who Eliza talks to.

She's a big girl; she can do whatever she wants.

I watch as Samuel takes her hand and leads her to the dancefloor.

He takes her in his arms, and she smiles up at him. I clench my jaw.

Don't. Even.

What the fuck is she doing? She never carries on like this. Actually, all three girls are on the loose tonight. How much did they drink today?

I watch them for a moment, and Samuel's hands are all over Eliza's behind. She doesn't seem to mind.

People block my view until I can't see them. I crane my neck to see that they've moved to the other side of the dancefloor. Frustration fills me.

Fuck this, I'm not waiting in this line. I storm back to where my friends are to get a better view of what's going on.

"Where are our drinks?" Glen asks.

"I'll go back in a minute," I reply, totally distracted.

"Where do you work?" The blonde asks me.

My eyes stay fixed on the dancefloor.

Drew taps me on the leg and gestures to the blonde with a jut of his chin.

"Oh, sorry," I say to her. "I didn't hear you."

"I said, where do you work?"

"I'm a plumber," I lie. Why the fuck is this woman still here?

Drew smirks against his glass as he takes a big gulp.

Will you girls fuck off? I want to watch that douchebag to make sure he doesn't touch Eliza. My eyes go back to them on the dancefloor, and Samuel smiles down at Eliza like he's about to eat her.

I begin to see red.

Don't touch her, fucker, or you *will* die.

I glance at Drew, and he, knowing exactly what I'm thinking, chuckles.

Samuel's hands go to Eliza's ass, and I step forward. Drew grabs my arm.

"Easy," he whispers.

Samuel pulls Eliza toward him, and before I know what I'm doing, I'm beside them.

"Time to go, Eliza," I bark.

"What?" She frowns as she stumbles back in surprise.

"You've had too much to drink. I'm taking you home."

"No, it's okay." Samuel smiles, adding in a sleazy wink. "I'll get her home safely."

"I said no."

He scowls. "Mind your business, Mercer."

I glare at him and pull Eliza from his grip. "Do not fucking piss me off."

Eliza frowns as she looks between us. "Nathan?"

"Don't *Nathan* me." I take her hand and drag her from the dancefloor.

"What are you doing?" she snaps.

"Stopping you from embarrassing yourself."

"*What?*"

I point to the door. "We're leaving."

"Well, that depends."

"On what?"

She narrows her eyes playfully and stops and puts her hands on her hips. "Are you taking me for pizza? Because I'm only leaving for pizza."

"If you fucking behave." I take her hand in mine once more.

"Fine." She concedes. "But I want a whole pizza to myself."

"Don't be a pig." I mutter, distracted.

She waves to our friends. "Bye!" she calls as we walk toward the door. "Why are you such a party pooper?" She says from behind me.

"Do you want pizza or not?" I snap.

She begins to snort and laugh at herself, and I roll my eyes.

Drunk women. Is there anything more annoying?

An hour and a half later, I fumble with the key to get into the apartment. I wasn't joking back there. Eliza isn't just tipsy, she's rolling drunk.

We had to pull into another bar we walked past and have another two cocktails before we had pizza. Now, finally, we're home.

I have her stilettos in one hand, and a vice-like grip on her hand with the other as she sways.

"Stand still," I say.

"Stop bossing me around," she slurs.

I struggle with the key. "I like bossing you around."

"No shit." She widens her eyes at me.

I smile, the key turns, and we stumble through the door.

Before I can say a word, Eliza reaches down to the hem of her dress and lifts it over her head.

She is wearing a black G-string, and when she turns toward me, I burst out laughing. "What the fuck is on your boobs?"

She looks down and frowns with a stumble. "Oh. Nipple covers."

"What the hell are they?"

"They stop you from getting all... nippy."

"Nippy?"

She peels them off and slaps them on my cheeks. I look at her in horror. "You did not just do that."

"Yeah, I did... cause you're a real *boob*." She bursts out laughing and points at me. "Get it, because you got nipple covers on your face... cause you're a *boob*."

I roll my eyes. "Hilarious. Get into the bathroom."

I lead her in and sit her up on the counter. She smiles goofily at me.

She watches on as I put makeup remover onto a cotton pad, and she closes her eyes. She knows the routine; we've done this many times before. She can't sleep until her makeup is taken off. She tosses and turns all night, and it's easier to do it now rather than in an hour.

I wipe the makeup off one eye, and then the other. Her dark lashes flutter as I wipe each of them, and I find myself smiling down as I watch her.

Her cheekbones are high, and her big sultry lips are parted slightly.

My heart constricts in my chest.

"Nathe." Her hands are on my thighs.

"Yeah, baby," I whisper.

"I love you."

I smile softly. She loves me every time she's drunk. "I know."

"Do you love me?"

I lean down and kiss her forehead. "You know I do."

She rests her sleepy head on my chest. "Can we go to bed now?" she whispers. "I'm very tired."

"Nearly finished." I wipe the rest of her makeup off and rinse it clean, and then I lead her into the bedroom. I turn down the blankets, and she flops back onto her back. I lift her legs so that she's lying comfortably, and soon her lashes flutter as she fights sleep.

My eyes roam down her body and a strange feeling washes over me. I've seen Eliza with no clothes on many times before but tonight she feels so... naked.

Raw.

My eyes roam down over her full breasts, then her stomach, her muscular thighs, before resting on her black G-string.

I stare at her for a moment, and my imagination takes me to a new place.

What would it be like to be inside her?

I get a vision of her opening her legs and my body sliding deep inside of hers. The blood rushes to my cock and I lose all coherent thought.

I close my eyes as the air leaves my lungs.

No.

When I open my eyes, I'm unable to help it. I unzip my jeans and take my cock in my hand. Slowly, I stroke it as I drink her in.

She softly moans and rearranges her legs. I can almost feel her movement to the tip of my cock, and I inhale sharply.

Fuck.

I need to get out of here. This is... *wrong*.

I stumble into the bathroom, lock the door and peel my clothes off. I turn the shower on and get in under the hot water. I oil my hand up, and with thoughts of my best friend running naked through my mind...

I fuck myself.

Hard.

3

Nathan

"NATHAN." The voice is gravelly and hoarse.

I frown, my eyes still closed.

"Nathan. Jesus Christ, get your dick out of my back."

My eyes snap open. "What?"

I'm cuddling Eliza from behind. My hand is resting between her bare breasts, and my erect cock is nudged firmly against her lower back.

"Shit." I scramble to my side of the bed. "Fuck, sorry. It's morning..." I splutter as I run my hands through my hair.

"Hmm." She grumbles before she drifts back off to sleep.

I close my eyes in horror.

I get up, go to the bathroom, and then ease myself back onto my side of the bed, lying dangerously close to the edge. I stare at her as if she's a ferocious animal, because at this moment, to me, she is.

This is the unknown to me. This has never happened before.

Why is it happening now?

"Hmm." She pushes her behind toward me.

I stay silent.

She does it again. "Nathe, cuddle me," she mumbles sleepily.

Fuck.

I pull her close and hold her tight as a sense of dread fills my soul.

And it's not about my dick this morning; that shit happens. It's about last night.

Seeing Eliza naked...

Jerking off to the sight of her...

I close my eyes in disgust at myself, and the sick taste of shame fills my mouth.

Our friendship is special. What we have together is perfect. My dick doesn't come into this equation, and it never will. I won't let it.

I can't lie here beside her any longer. I sit up on the side of the bed and run my hands through my hair. Perspiration dusts my skin.

I frown as I try to understand what I'm feeling, but I can't because I *don't* understand it. Ten years of nothing.

Why now?

There's a reasonable answer to all of this, there has to be, and surely this is just a misunderstanding. If I could just decipher what's going on in my head.

Who can sort this out for me?

I think for a moment.

Yes, of course, that's it! I've got it.

. . .

Three hours later, I'm sitting in the waiting room of one of the best psychologists in San Francisco. My elbows rest on my parted knees as I wait. I'm battling an erratic heartbeat, and nerves are coursing through my veins. I've never been to a psychologist before—never needed one.

My eyes roam over the people in the waiting room as I wonder why they are here.

Bet I'm more fucked up than the lot of them.

The office door opens and a man appears. "Nathan Mercer?"

I stand. "Yes."

"This way, please." I follow him into his office, and he closes the door behind us. He holds his hand out to shake mine. "Elliot Hamilton."

He's mid to late forties, distinguished looking, and not what I was expecting at all.

Who it was that I was expecting, though, I'm not sure.

"Hello." I nod. "Thank you for seeing me on such short notice."

He smiles and gestures to a leather chair. "Please, take a seat. When I got your call this morning, I shuffled around a few things to make it work."

"I appreciate it."

His eyes hold mine, and he sits back in his chair. His eyes are assessing, and he shuffles some papers in front of him.

"Tell me, what brought you here today, Nathan? May I call you Nathan?"

"Yes, of course." I inhale deeply as I steel myself to say it out loud.

He gives me a calm smile as he fills the glass in front of me with water. "Take your time."

"I've..." I pause as I try to push the words past my lips.

"I've recently had an unwanted attraction to someone I…" I frown as I cut off my sentence.

"Someone you… what?"

"My best friend."

"Ah." He nods and sits back, as if understanding. "And this is distressing you?"

"Yes." I nod. "Very much."

"And you've never had any attraction to someone of the same sex before?"

"Oh." I frown, realising what he thinks. "That's not it." I puff air into my cheeks. "My best friend is a woman."

He frowns.

"I'm… usually with men." I clench my jaw.

"So, you identify as a gay male?"

"No."

His brow furrows. "How do you see yourself, Nathan?"

"Normal." I shrug. "I don't feel I need to label my sexuality."

He nods. "I see." He pauses for a moment. "You haven't come out?"

"Yes and no. I had a long-term relationship when I was younger, and when we broke up everyone knew that we'd been together. I don't hide being with men, but I don't advertise it, either." My eyes rise to meet his. "I'm a private person. My sex life is mine alone. I don't feel the need to justify my choices. I am who I am. People can take it or leave it."

"I see." He smiles as if contemplating my answer. "And you've never been attracted to a woman before?"

"No."

"It bothers you?"

"Very much."

"Why is that?"

I drop my head. "My best friend and I are very close. I can't fuck this up."

He frowns. "And you think that if you told... I'm sorry, what is her name?"

"Eliza."

"If Eliza found out, you think you would lose her?"

"One hundred percent." I nod. "I know I would."

"How long has this been going on?"

"Just the last few days... but last night..." I frown, too ashamed to keep going.

"Go on, you are in a safe place. This is completely confidential."

"Last night, she got drunk, and when we got home—"

"You live together?"

"Practically. I sleep with her every night."

"In the same bed?" He frowns.

I nod.

He scribbles something down on his notepad. "We'll come back to that. Tell me what happened last night."

I pinch the bridge of my nose as I picture her. "She took off her dress and was wearing nothing but a G-string. And after she went to sleep, I touched myself looking at her."

He rubs his pointer finger over his bottom lip. "Then, what happened?"

"I was disgusted with myself but I couldn't stop. I was too aroused, too far gone, so I went into the bathroom and jerked off imagining I was with her." My stomach rolls. "It was utterly...disgusting."

"Why is that?"

"I betrayed her." I hang my head in shame.

"How long has it been since you have been with a woman?"

"Never."

He raises a brow. "I see."

I clench my hands into fists. His silence is deafening. Fuck this, it isn't helping. "I might just go."

"We're not finished." He fires back without hesitation. "Tell me about your first sexual experience."

I'm not telling him that shit, it's private. "What does that have to do with Eliza?" I snap.

"Everything is connected. Do you want me to help you work this out?"

Our eyes are locked, and I tilt my chin in annoyance knowing this was a mistake. "Yes."

"Then, please." He rolls his hand out. "Continue. Lie back in the chair and relax. We can figure this out but only if we work together."

I hesitate as I go over my options, there aren't any, just tell him. "I was fifteen... at summer camp."

He listens intently.

"I was roomed with a boy. Robert."

"Had you had any attraction to anyone before this?"

"A male?"

"Either sex, boy or girl."

I shake my head. "No, I was into sports and..." I shrug, unable to elaborate.

He waits for me to go on, and when I don't, he prompts me. "Tell me about Robert."

I exhale heavily, wishing I was anywhere but here. "Robert was..." I smile sadly. "Robert was different to anyone I had ever met. He was funny, kind, and he listened to everything I said." I inhale deeply. "At the end of our first week of rooming together, we were tight—good friends. We hung out, laughed all day, and we would talk all night." I hesitate, I hate how this sounds.

"Was there anyone else in the room with the two of you?"

"No."

"Go on."

"There was an undercurrent of a different friendship to what I'd ever had before, although I had no idea what it was. He asked me one night if I wanted to play truth or dare." I smile, remembering it as if it were yesterday. "On the fifth truth question, he asked me if I'd ever kissed anyone, and when I said I hadn't, he admitted that he hadn't, either." I swallow the lump in my throat as my eyes rise to meet Elliot's.

He gives me a reassuring smile.

"He said that..." I frown. Fuck, I hate this.

"Go on."

"He suggested that we kissed just once... to practice for when we were with a girl."

"So... you kissed?"

"Not that night but two nights later. One kiss led to a hundred, and before I knew it, we were making out on the bed."

"How was it for you?"

"Good at the time. Mortifying the next day. I told him I hated him and that it was all a mistake. We agreed to pretend it never happened, but three nights later, it happened again. Only..."

"Only what?"

"It got more heated."

"How so?"

"He went down on me."

"Did you ejaculate?"

I nod. "Yes."

"How were you after that?"

"Confused." I frown. "I never saw myself getting a blowjob from a guy. It just..." I shake my head as the emotions from back then flood through me. "It was never on my radar."

"But...?"

"But I liked it."

"Why?"

"Because it felt forbidden. Like I was being naughty and had this dark, little secret that nobody would ever know of."

"So, it happened again?"

"Every day for a week."

"What happened after that?"

"Feelings started to develop between us. He..." I screw up my face as I remember that time. "He got me, and I got him. We never had labels between us. It wasn't like that because it felt natural, you know?"

Elliot steeples his hands in front of him. "What happened from there?"

"He asked me if I would be his first, and that our time together was over soon and we would never see each other again, but we would always have this. Our secret. I fucked him."

"So, you top?"

"Always." I clench my jaw, angered that I had to say that out loud to a complete stranger.... fuck this, I'm never coming back here again. This is mortifying.

"And that was it?"

"No, we fell in love. It was very special between us."

He smiles softly.

"We began a long-distance relationship where we would spend weekends and every holiday together."

He sits back and crosses his legs with his notepad and pen in his hand. "Tell me about that period of your life."

"It was fucked." I scratch the back of my hair, surprised by the sudden surge of anger that I feel.

"Why is that?"

"I was in a relationship so I didn't screw around. I didn't go out much because I hated how women would hit on me all night and I couldn't give them an explanation as to why I wasn't into them."

"Were you attracted to the girls who hit on you?"

"No."

"Were you attracted to other men during this time?"

I shake my head. "I only wanted Robert. Nobody else ever caught my eye."

The room falls silent.

"The deal was that when Robert finished college, he was going to transfer to wherever I was working at the time. His job was transferable, mine was not." I rub the stubble on my chin as I think back to that time.

"Did that happen?"

"No, he didn't want to come to San Fran."

"And you did?"

"Yes."

"How did that make you feel?"

"Angry."

"Why is that?"

"Because I gave up the best part of my life to be loyal to him. I thought we had a future, but in the end, it was all for nothing. I was done."

"You ended it?"

"Yes."

"Nathan." Elliot's eyes hold mine. "Are you still in love with Robert?"

"No." I shrug. "I was for a long time but not anymore. We're friends. He's openly gay and in a happy relationship."

"Tell me about your relationships since then."

I squirm in my seat, uncomfortable with where this is going. "I haven't had one."

Elliot's eyes narrow. "Not one?"

"I've had sex, obviously, but I haven't met anybody I would want long term."

"So, you have one night stands?"

"What does this have to do with the reason I'm here?" I snap in exasperation. "I don't see why this is relevant. Next question."

"No." Elliot's eyes hold mine. "I'll repeat: do you have one night stands?"

I glare at him. "I have regular casual partners."

"How long do you see the same person?"

I shrug. "A few months."

"Until?"

"Until they fall in love with me."

"Does love scare you?"

"Nope," I push out. "I'm just not interested, that's all."

"I see." He writes some points on his paper.

I exhale heavily as I wait for his next step over the line. He leans back in his chair and crosses his legs.

"Tell me about your best friend." He glances down to his notes to remind himself of her name. "Eliza."

"What do you want to know?"

"When did you meet?"

"We started work at the same hospital on the same day.

We met in the cafeteria. Something clicked, and we became friends."

He scribbles some notes and looks up at me. "This is around the time you broke up with Robert, yes?"

I nod. "That's right. Like two months later or something."

"Tell me about her."

I raise my eyebrows. Where do I start? "She is goofy, clumsy, and she can't cross the street without nearly getting herself run over. She loses her phone and keys all the time." I think for a moment. "She has the most beautiful dimples when she smiles; her whole face lights up." I pause for a moment as I picture her. "She's a great cook. The best, actually." I smile wistfully. "I have leftovers for lunch every day." I twist my fingers in my lap as I try to think of something else to say. "She writes in a diary every night and sometimes, when she's in the shower, I read it."

Elliot rests his hand on his chin as he listens.

"She has the purest heart of anyone I've ever met." I drop my head. "She puts everyone else's needs before her own, especially mine." I smile sadly. "She's a pediatric nurse."

"Nathan," Elliot says quietly. "Why is your attraction to her so abhorrent to you?"

My eyes meet his. "Because she is everything to me. I can't lose her." My heart constricts in my chest. "Just the thought of not having her by my side is..."

"Why do you think you would lose her?"

"We're not... it's never been like that between us." I frown. "She doesn't think of me like that and..."

"And what?'

"I'm a lot to handle... sexually."

"How so?"

"I like it rough. My appetite is insatiable. And I'm..." My voice trails off.

"You're what?"

"Large."

He frowns as he listens intently.

"She's very..." I frown as I search for the right word. "Fragile."

"You don't think the two of you would be sexually compatible?"

"No, and if we ever crossed that line and it didn't work out, we could never go back to where we are."

"You're happy where you are now?"

I smile softly. "Waking up next to her is the best part of my day."

"I see." Elliot begins to scribble on his paper.

"So... how do I turn this off? It can't happen again."

"I don't think I can help you, Nathan."

"Why not?" My eyes search his.

"Because I'm of the opinion that you may be in love with Eliza."

"What?" I snap. "That's ridiculous."

"Is it?"

I stare at him as my pulse begins to sound in my ears.

"Could it be possible, Nathan, that your body is just catching up with your heart?"

"No." The room begins to spin.

"That maybe it's taken this long for you to allow yourself to feel again?"

"You're wrong," I snap, angered that this fucker has wasted my time. "I'm just horny."

"So, why not go and sleep with someone else tonight? If it's that easily fixed, go and take what you want."

Fury begins to bubble deep inside of me. "You don't know me." I sneer.

"How long has it been since you've had sex with someone, Nathan?"

He hits a nerve, and I swallow the lump in my throat. "A few months."

"Why do you think that is?"

I hate this fucking guy.

Our eyes are locked, and anger hangs in the air between us.

"Would you feel like you're betraying Eliza if you were intimate with someone else? If you gave your body to someone else and not her?"

My nostrils flair as tears threaten to fall.

I drop my head, rattled.

Fuck.

Eliza

I wake slowly to the sun peering through the side of the drapes. My head is snuggled into Nathan's broad chest while he's on his back. His fingers are mindlessly running through my hair. He's obviously been awake for a while.

I inhale deeply and pull out of his arms to stretch.

"Morning," he whispers in a gravelly voice.

I smile sleepily. "Hi." I look around for my phone. "What time is it? Where's the alarm?"

"It didn't go off yet. You forgot to close the drapes last night."

I wince against the morning sun. "You mean *you* forgot to close the drapes. Since when has it been my job?"

"Well, if we were at my house,it would be my job, but since this is your house..." He shrugs.

I roll my eyes and climb out of bed. "Just do us both a favour and don't speak today, okay?"

He chuckles, rolls onto his side to face me, and leans up onto his elbow. His eyes slowly drop down to my bare legs. They linger for a moment on my thighs, and then as if remembering where he is, they snap back up to my face.

I'm wearing panties and a camisole. I'm also braless with everything hanging out but that's nothing new. This is my usual sleeping attire so I put my hands on my hips. "What are you looking at?"

"Nothing."

"Did you just check me out?"

"No." He frowns as if disgusted. "Are you kidding?" He climbs out of bed in a rush. "What the hell is wrong with you?" He demands. "Why would you even say that?" He storms into the bathroom and slams the door.

I begin to make the bed. Jeez, I was joking. Why's he so touchy today?

I flick the kettle on and dress into my gym gear of black work-out pants and a black tank top. I put my hair into a high ponytail. I attend the 5:30 a.m. spin class every morning while Nathan goes back to his house and gets ready for work. He does his early rounds at the hospital before he starts his day. It's a comfortable little routine we have. I go to the gym in the morning while he works, and then he goes to the gym straight after work in the evening while I sort dinner.

Moments later, he re-emerges from the bathroom.

"Your coffee is on the counter," I call as I tidy up the cushions and throw them back onto the couch.

Why am I so messy at night?

"Thanks." He picks up his travel mug.

"Are you going to do the online grocery order today?" I ask

as I get his leftovers for lunch out of the fridge and pass them to him. We have a deal. He pays for the groceries and I do the cooking.

"Yeah." He peers into the side of the Tupperware container. "What's on the menu today?"

"Lasagne."

His brows rise in surprise. He worked late last night and skipped dinner with me. "You had lasagne last night without me?" He puts his hand over his heart as if wounded. "How could you?"

"Uh-huh, you missed out big time. It was one of my best."

"Did you give me extra today?"

"I did."

He smiles down at me. "What would I do without you?"

"Starve, I expect."

He kisses my cheek. "See you tonight." He picks up his keys. "Email me the shopping list."

"I already did, and don't purposely forget the chocolate like you did last week. I'll just make you go find it at 10:00 p.m. again."

"Whatever." He disappears out of the door.

I smile as the door closes behind him, and then I remember where I have to go now. I exhale heavily. Ugh, spin class. It never gets more appealing. Every day it's a drag.

One of these days I'm going to wake up fit and hot, and I'll never have to go again.

Until then, though, it's off to the gym I go.

———

I flick through the rack of evening dresses, hmm, I've worn most of these before.

"What about this one?" Brooke says, she is taking a dress off the rack and holding it up.

I look at the red dress in her hands. It's long, fitted, and has a plunging neckline. "Yes, that's nice." I turn back to going through the selection. "I'll try that one on."

Brooke and I are in the dress rental shop. I go to so many black-tie events with Nathan that I couldn't possibly buy a dress for everything. Here, I can rent a beautiful designer dress for next to nothing. The shop is owned and run by two young girls. They buy the latest designer dresses, one in each size, and they rent them out for a fraction of the cost. It's a fantastic idea, and their business is growing. They are opening their second store next month.

"Oh, this one just arrived, too," Libby, the shop assistant says as she holds up a gold dress.

"That's nice." I nod.

"I'll hang it in the change room."

"When is the ball?" Brooke asks.

"Tonight."

"Tonight? You're cutting it a bit close finding a dress, aren't you?"

"Yeah, I kind of forgot about it, to be honest. I've been so focused on this new job that I've thought about nothing else." I pick another dress from the hanger. "What if I can't do it?"

"Do what?"

"The job. I know nothing about cosmetic surgery. What the hell was I thinking even applying for a manager's position there?"

"Stop it, you're just nervous." She hands me a cream dress. "Try this one on."

I take the dress into the cubicle, along with the others, and I pull the curtain across.

"If you couldn't do it, they wouldn't have given you the job," she calls out.

I take my top off. "Maybe I got the job because Dr. Morgan likes the look of me."

"Who cares why you got it? No more shift work, no more cleaning up vomit, and the pay is nearly double."

I roll my eyes as I step into the red dress. "I guess."

"You're just nervous and talking yourself out of it."

I look in the mirror and smile at my reflection. "I like this one."

"Show me."

I step out of the cubicle.

Brooke's eyes light up as she looks me up and down. "Hell yeah, that's hot."

It's a deep red and fitted. The back is lace and the neckline is plunging. It's a perfect fit. "I'll take it." I smile.

"You don't want to try on the others?" Libby asks.

"No, I'll wear them next time. I can't be bothered to try on more." I twirl and look at my behind once more. "What color shoes would I wear with this?"

"Nude."

"Okay, I have a bag that will match," I say as I stare at my reflection. "Hair up or down?"

"Up, to show off the back."

I pull my hair up on top of my head to see what I look like. Aha, looks good. "Done." I smile. "That was easy."

———

I hear the key in the door at 6:45 p.m., and I smile. He's never late.

"Hello?" I hear him call out.

"Hi, won't be a minute. Can you pour us a drink?"

"I bought some champagne." His deep voice calls.

I smile as I put on my lipstick. "There's a reason I love you."

He chuckles, and moments later I hear the pop of the cork.

"How was your day?" he asks.

"Good, although I'm freaking out about this job." I rub my lips together.

"Why?" I hear the cupboards opening as he gets the champagne glasses.

"I don't know." I turn and look at my behind in the mirror. Wow, this dress is gorgeous. I walk out into the kitchen, and Nathan raises his eyebrows when he sees me.

"Wow." He smiles and leans down to kiss my cheek. "You look... hot."

I wiggle my hips and straighten his bowtie. "You don't look so bad yourself."

He passes me my glass of champagne and clinks it with his. "Cheers. We're celebrating."

"We are?"

"I got the apartment." He smiles broadly.

My eyes widen. "You did?"

"*We* did. Now I'll actually be able to fit into your apartment."

I giggle.

"Now, what's this about your new job?" he asks.

"I don't know." I take a sip. "Hmm." I eye the bubbles in my glass. "You got my favorite. I guess I'm just nervous."

"Why?"

"What if I can't do it?"

"Eliza." He gives me a beautiful, big smile. "You can do anything you set your mind to."

"Aww." I lean up and kiss his cheek, and I run my fingers through his stubble. "You're the best cheerleader."

"Well, that's emasculating." He raises a brow.

"You know what I mean." I run my hands down over my body. "Do you like this dress?"

His eyes roam up and down my body. "I love this dress."

"Do we have cheese?"

"Hmm." He goes to the fridge and peers in. "That incompetent shopper probably didn't buy any of the good stuff again."

"I really do need to fire him."

He chuckles as he pulls out some Camembert and places it onto the counter.

"Do we have quince paste?" I ask.

"Yes, Queen Elizabeth, give me a second to find it."

I giggle. "I like that title. You may call me that all the time now, my faithful servant."

He smirks as he digs out the quince paste and passes it to me. I make a little platter for two.

"You know, we should probably stop doing this before we go to these things. I always walk in looking three months pregnant."

He shrugs as he shovels a cracker and camembert into his mouth. "I still look good."

I giggle and take a big scoop of cheese onto my cracker and put it into my mouth.

"What's your new boss like?" he asks.

"Umm." I swallow what's in my mouth and it scratches my throat the whole way down. "Seems okay." I wince.

"Male, female, young, old?"

"Guy, middle aged. Seemed boring," I lie, Henry Morgan didn't seem boring at all but I'm not in the mood for a Spanish

69

inquisition. "Oh my God." I gasp to change the subject. "Did I tell you about the guy we met on Saturday night?"

"No." He frowns.

"Jolie met this guy." I giggle just remembering it. "She met this guy named Santiago who was showing her videos of him having sex with different women."

"What?"

"I'm serious. Like full frontal hard fucking. All different women, all different positions."

Nathan screws up his face. "What did Jolie do?"

"She drank shots of tequila while she watched it."

"What?" He chuckles. "Are you serious?"

"Yes, it was the most bizarre thing I've ever seen."

"You watched it, too?"

I laugh.

"You did?"

I shrug. "It was kind of hot." I offer as an explanation.

"He could have been a serial killer. Guys don't just show women videos of themselves having sex with other people. That's just fucking weird. Like stalker weird."

I laugh. "I know, right?" I shovel more cheese and biscuits into my mouth. "I've never even filmed myself having sex. I wouldn't even want to watch that back, let alone show other people."

"What?" Nathan frowns. "You've never filmed yourself having sex?"

"No." I scowl. "Have you?"

"Everyone's done that."

"Not me."

"Why not?" He seems shocked.

"I don't know?" I laugh. "It's never come up. Nobody I've slept with has ever suggested it."

He stares at me in disbelief. "Eliza, just how vanilla is your sex life?"

I widen my eyes. "Well, very vanilla if this is anything to go by."

He sips his champagne as if fascinated. "And you like vanilla sex?"

"Not really." I shrug. "I've never thought about it before. I guess I'm waiting for a big, bad man to teach me bad things."

His eyes hold mine.

I smile, slightly embarrassed by my lack of experience. "Anyway, I forget what sex is even like."

"How long since you have had it?"

"Two years."

"You haven't had sex for two years?" he gasps.

"Nope."

"Jesus, Eliza." he whispers. "Why not?"

"I guess I'm waiting for Mr. Right this time."

He stares at me for a moment before he speaks. "So, what you're saying is that you're waiting for a Mr. Right to teach you how to be bad?"

"Precisely." I smile. "Do you know anyone?" I tease.

He runs the backs of his fingers down my cheek as if distracted. "Maybe."

I smile up at my beautiful friend. He looks so handsome in his dinner suit. I rearrange his bow tie and run my fingers through his messed-up hair.

"Are you ready to go, Mr. Mercer?"

His tongue darts out and slides across his bottom lip, and I get the feeling he has something else on his mind. "If we must."

4

Eliza

WE WALK INTO THE BALLROOM. The venue is grand with high ceilings and beautiful, low hanging chandeliers. Huge vases of beautiful pink and cream fresh flowers sit on every table alongside lit candles. Glamorous people in black tie are standing everywhere.

"What's this ball in aid of again?" I ask as I scan the room.

"It's a fundraiser for The Children's Medical Research Hospital."

"Looks swanky." I smile.

"I certainly hope so. The tickets were ten thousand dollars."

"Each?" I frown.

"Yes." He twists his lips as he looks around. "It's a good cause."

I widen my eyes. "Jeez." I try to work out how many people are here and how much they are raising.

A bartender walks past with a silver tray of champagne.

"Champagne, sir."

"Thank you." Nathan takes two and passes one to me. He takes a sip of his. He winces and looks at the glass.

"No good?" I frown.

"Not twenty thousand dollars good."

I giggle. "Nothing is that good."

He takes my hand and leads me over to the seating arrangements where he scans the chart.

Hmm, I think there would be at least five hundred people here. I do the math in my head. Is that five hundred thousand?

"If there are five hundred people here, is that five hundred thousand dollars raised?" I ask as Nathan leads me over to our table.

"Five million." He replies distracted as he weaves in and out of the tables.

"Holy crap, that's a shit ton of cash," I whisper.

He chuckles as we arrive at our table, and he pulls out my chair. "You have such a way with words, darling."

He undoes his dinner jacket button with one hand before he sits down. He instantly turns to the woman and man he is seated next to.

"Hello, I'm Nathan Mercer. Nice to meet you." He shakes their hands and then gestures to me. "And this is Eliza."

"Hello." The lady and man smile. "I'm Mario, and this is my wife Alessandra."

"Hello." I shake their hands. Nathan and his impeccable manners. He introduces us wherever we go.

"Lovely ball room, isn't it?" Alessandra smiles.

"Gorgeous."

"Dr. Mercer!" someone calls, and we turn to see a woman smiling and waving. "How lovely to see you."

Nathan smiles broadly and offers a wave. His eyes dart to me for approval to go talk with her.

"Go, I'm fine." I smile and lift my glass of champagne. "I've got company."

She smiles and waves at me, and I wave back. I've seen this woman at a lot of the charity events we go to. She's a doctor and seems nice.

Nathan kisses my cheek. "I'll bring you another one back. Won't be a minute." He nods to our tablemates. "Excuse me." He gets up and goes and talks to her, and they walk over to the bar and fall into conversation.

Mario frowns at me. "That's not *the* Dr. Mercer, is it?"

"Umm." I raise my eyebrows. I get asked this a lot.

"The heart surgeon?"

"That's him." I smile.

He watches Nathan across the room at the bar. "Wow, he's so young in the flesh."

My heart beams with pride. "He is, and his reputation is well deserved."

Another couple sit down at our table. "Hello." They both smile, and we do the introductions and shake hands.

I glance over to see Nathan is looking my way. He doesn't leave me alone for long. He's now talking to three other men, and he holds up a finger as if to say he'll be a moment.

"I'm fine," I mouth over at him.

"Eliza?" I hear someone call.

I turn to see a familiar face, and I laugh. "Gretel." I turn to the people at my table. "Excuse me." I stand and kiss my dear friend on the cheek.

Gretel is my ex-boss. The best damn boss I ever had, actually. If she hadn't retired, I probably never would have even contemplated leaving. She's beautiful with her silver bob haircut and glamorous designer clothes. Her husband is the mayor of San Francisco, and Gretel knows everyone in town.

"Oh, it's good to see you." She smiles as she holds my hands in hers. "Are you here with Nathan?"

"Yes." I gesture over to the bar. "He's talking to some friends."

"Oh my God, what is this I hear about you leaving?"

"Wow." I shake my head. "News travels fast. I only resigned today."

"Where are you going to be working?"

"For Doctor Morgan."

She frowns. "The plastic surgeon?"

"Yes, that's him."

"Boy, he's a dish." She smiles and plays with a piece of my hair. "You sure are a magnet for good-looking doctors."

"Too bad I can't snag any of them." I laugh. "And Nathan doesn't count."

"Speak of the devil." Gretel smiles. "Hello, darling."

Nathan kisses her cheek. "Hello, Gretel, lovely to see you."

Gretel looks him up and down. "Good grief, do you get better looking every time I see you, Nathan?"

I smile as I watch the two of them exchange.

He chuckles and shakes his head. "You're as shameless as ever."

"Gretel!" someone calls.

She looks over. "I'm being summoned." We glance over to see her husband at the bar, obviously needing help. "I'll see you both later."

"Okay, bye."

Nathan hands me a glass of champagne. "Thanks."

"Eliza," a deep voice says from behind me. We both turn to see Henry Morgan.

"Oh." Fuck, what's he doing here? "Hello, Dr. Morgan."

"Henry," he corrects me. His attention turns to Nathan, and he puts out his hand to shake his. "Henry Morgan."

Nathan smiles and dips his head. "Nathan Mercer."

"Ah." Henry's eyes hold Nathan's for a moment, and I can see he's just worked out who Nathan is. "I'm the new boss."

Nathan's eyes meet mine and he subtly raises an eyebrow. "Really?"

"And you must be the boyfriend?"

"Yes," I cut him off before Nathan can answer him. "This is my boyfriend, Nathan."

Nathan's eyes flicker to me in question. "That's right." He puts his arm around me, and pulls me close, smiling sexily. "Well, you hired the best possible person for the job. I trust you will look after her."

Henry smiles broadly at me. "I intend to; don't worry."

His eyes go back to Nathan, and they stare at each other for a moment. Something is exchanged between them, although I'm not sure what it is.

Nathan's eyes come back to me.

Fuck.

"We need to get back to our table. Let's go, baby." I smile as I pull Nathan by the arm. "Nice to see you, Dr. Morgan," I say in a rush. *Go away, now.*

"Henry," he corrects me. "And do come quickly. The sooner you are under me, the better."

Nathan stares at him.

"Working under me, I mean." He chuckles. "That sounded wrong, didn't it?"

"Not to mention deluded," Nathan replies dryly.

"Goodbye." I fake a giggle. "Lovely to see you again." I drag Nathan back to the table.

Oh, crap.

Nathan sits down with a thud. He tips his head back and takes a huge gulp of his scotch.

I smile around my champagne glass. Oh, great.

Nathan's eyes meet mine. "I thought you said your boss was old."

"He is old." I lie as I try to act casual.

He raises an eyebrow. "Why did you tell him I was your boyfriend?"

I put my hand on his thigh under the table. "I tell a lot of people you're my boyfriend," I whisper.

"You do?"

"I do." I smile up at him. "Why, am I ruining your reputation?"

His eyes soften. "You are, actually." He picks up my hand from his thigh and takes it in his. His eyes go over to the bar to watch Henry. "Something feels off about him."

"He seems okay. He's a bit full of himself but that doesn't bother me."

"So, if I'm your boyfriend now does that mean I get to molest you on the dancefloor later?" He asks as he raises his eyebrow.

I giggle. "Go for it."

Over the next four hours, I watch as people try to get Nathan's attention.

He's polite and frank, and he doesn't linger with anyone. His attention always comes back to me. He walks back from the bar and holds his hand out.

"Would you like to dance, Eliza?"

I smile as I take it. "I would."

Nathan is a wonderful dancer. We dance at every event we go to. He leads me out onto the dancefloor and takes me into his arms where we begin to sway to the music. The quartet band is playing *Unchained Melody*.

"Thank you for coming with me to all these things."

I smile up at my beautiful friend who is so much taller than me. "I enjoy them. They're fun, and it gives me a chance to get dressed up."

He holds me close as his hand lingers on my hip, his breath dusting my neck.

He stares down at me, and something feels different tonight. I don't know what it is. It's as if I'm the only other person in the room. His attention is two hundred percent on me. He's always attentive, but I'm really feeling it tonight.

Perhaps it's the fact that I told Henry that he's my boyfriend and I know that he's playing the part.

Yes, that must be it.

I look up at him and run my fingers through his stubble. "I had a great night. Thanks for my ten thousand dollar ticket."

He chuckles and then spins me. We sway to the music once more.

He leans and gently kisses my lips with a little suction and a whole lot of nice.

I frown as my breath catches.

"Your boss is watching," he whispers.

"Oh." My eyes dart over to see Henry standing at the side of the dancefloor. "Right."

Nathan's lips drift to my temple and he kisses me again. I feel myself melting into him.

He's strong, virile, and he's holding me so close. I must be the envy of every woman in the room. God, I love this man, and here he is playing the part of my boyfriend to protect my lie.

We dance and we dance, and Nathan makes me miss having someone for real.

He holds me tight, makes me laugh, and he kisses me softly on the cheek whenever Henry is watching.

If only I could have the closeness that I have with Nathan with a boyfriend—someone who could love me in every way. Someone who could be really mine.

"You ready to go? The car is here," he whispers.

"I am." I return to the table and to the people we were sitting with. "Lovely to meet you all."

"You, too."

Nathan goes around and shakes their hands. "Goodbye. Nice to meet you." He takes my hand and we walk out the front to get into the back of the black Audi waiting for us.

He holds my hand on his lap, and I smile out of the window at the glamorous ball as it disappears into the distance.

"That was a great night. I enjoyed myself."

"Me, too." He squeezes my hand in his lap. "Thanks for coming with me."

I rest my head on his shoulder. I feel so safe, and I'm feeling especially close to him tonight. I don't know why, he just seems different. Or maybe it's me. Maybe all this talk about not dating with the girls has me missing having someone special in my life and I appreciate our friendship even more.

"Are you tired, baby?" he whispers softly.

"Hmm." I smile sleepily.

He kisses my forehead, puts his arm around me and pulls me close. I snuggle into his chest. It's warm and feels so good beneath my head. His aftershave wafts around me. Being inside Nathan Mercer's arms is my favorite place to be.

Twenty minutes later, we pull up outside my apartment. Nathan leads me out by the hand, and we walk inside and into the elevator.

"Did anyone show you footage of themselves having sex tonight?" he asks.

I giggle. "Disappointingly, no."

He smiles down at me.

"What?"

"Did I tell you how beautiful you look tonight?"

"Tell me again."

He tucks a piece of hair behind my ear. "You really did look beautiful tonight."

I smile up at him. "Do we have chocolate?"

He smirks. "So, I tell you that you look beautiful, and you ask me if we have chocolate?"

"And?" I smile. "Your point is?"

"My point is that I'm being judged on my shopping abilities."

I giggle and turn my back to him. His big arms wrap around me from behind.

"That better mean there's chocolate in the fridge, Mercer," I mutter as I put my head against his chest.

He chuckles and rests his chin on the top of my head. The elevator doors open and we make our way down the corridor. Nathan opens the door to my apartment and we walk in. I go straight to the kitchen, flick the kettle on, while he goes to the fridge to grab something, which he quickly puts behind his back.

"What have you got there?" I ask.

"Ah," he teases. "What do I get for it?"

"If it's chocolate... anything you want."

"You really should play harder to get." He raises an eyebrow and produces a box of my favorite chocolates.

I clap my hands together. "Where did these come from?"

"I bought them today when I got the champagne." He opens

the box and pops one into his mouth. "You want?" He holds one up for me. I open my mouth and he puts it in.

"Hmm." I close my eyes at the rich creamy taste. "Delicious."

His eyes darken as he watches me suck on it.

He takes his jacket off, undoes his bowtie and top few buttons. I make us a cup of tea and take another chocolate.

I watch him take off his shoes and then undo his belt and slowly slide it off.

My breath catches. Why am I noticing how masculine he suddenly is?

"So, what did you want?" I ask as I hand him his cup of tea. "For the chocolates."

His eyes hold mine. "I want to get you out of that dress."

I smile. "Well, you're going to have to because I can't reach the zipper."

He chuckles and sits me up onto the counter in front of him. We both sip our tea, our eyes locked on each other.

Something *is* different but I can't put my finger on it.

"Two years." He smirks.

"Are you still thinking about that? Why? When was the last time you had sex?"

He steps forward, in between my legs, and his hands rest on my upper thighs. "A long time, too."

I frown, surprised. "Why?"

His eyes hold mine. "I guess I'm waiting for Mrs. Right."

I smile up at him. "Are you going to teach her bad things?" I tease.

"Fuck." He pauses, his eyes drop to my lips. "I want to."

My face falls.

Our eyes are locked, and you could cut the tension between us with a knife.

Wait, what? I was just teasing.

He pulls me closer on the counter toward him in a decid-edly sexual manner.

I sip my tea, unsure what's going on right now. "Don't you mean... *Mr.* Right?" I whisper.

"Umm...yeah." He takes my tea off me and puts it down on the counter. "Let's get you out of that dress," he whispers.

He lifts me off the counter and leads me into the bedroom. I feel close to him tonight; so close that it almost feels like...

He positions me before the full-length mirror in my bedroom. He stands behind me and then slowly slides the zipper down.

I watch him concentrate on his task, his eyes following the zipper. He slides one spaghetti strap off my shoulder, and then the other.

He bites his bottom lip as he slowly slides my dress down. It catches over my hips, and he uses his hands to work it loose.

This is nothing new. Nathan has seen me undress a million times before.

But this feels... sexual.

I stand before him in a white strapless bra and a G-string, with thigh-high nude stockings.

I watch him in the mirror as his eyes roam up and down my body, drinking me in.

I want to blurt out *What the hell are you doing?* but I don't want to ruin the moment.

Whatever this moment is.

He stands closer and puts his hand on my stomach. We stare at each other in the mirror, and there's an honesty between us.

Maybe it's intimacy or maybe it's just the champagne. At

this point, anything is a possibility because none of this is making sense.

With his eyes locked on mine, he kisses my cheek with an open mouth.

My heart skips a beat.

He runs his fingers up my arms, and goosebumps scatter. "Nathan," I whisper.

"Ssh," he whispers, as if not wanting words to get in the way.

He lets me go and slowly unbuttons his shirt. I can see the ripples of his stomach muscles in the dimly lit room.

I feel arousal slam into my body like a freight train, slow, strong and measured.

Our eyes are locked in the mirror.

I turn toward him, and he picks up my hand and puts it onto his bare chest. It's hot and hard under my touch. He rests his lips on my temple, and I close my eyes.

God, this is wrong.

Unable to stop myself, I slowly slide my hand over his torso, over the ripples, down lower to the small trail of dark hair that disappears into the waistband of his pants.

His dark eyes hold mine.

Tell me to stop.

5

Eliza

WE STARE AT EACH OTHER. My heart is pumping so hard that I can feel my pulse throughout my body. I dust the backs of my fingers through the hair on his lower stomach, and his eyes flicker shut as if he likes it.

I open my mouth to say something.

"Don't," he cuts me off.

Whatever's happening right now, he doesn't want to talk about it.

He trails his finger down my clavicle, between my breasts, and then lower to my stomach. My entire body begins to thrum, as if waking from a two-year long hibernation.

He turns me away from him in a quick movement, and our gaze goes back to our reflection in the mirror. Him, in his white shirt and black dinner suit pants, and me in my white lacy underwear. His hand goes to my stomach, and he pulls me closer.

His open lips dust my neck, and I watch him and the ecstasy on his face. This is too much. I tip my head back to rest on his shoulder. My eyes close in pleasure.

Oh hell, what's happening right now?

With his every kiss on my neck, our breathing becomes heavier, the feeling between us stronger. A river of deep emotion is flowing between us, and it feels sacred and strong.

This doesn't feel sexual. It feels honest. Like we care about each other so much that the worship we have for one another is running over into the physical.

It's magical.

Nathan

My entire body is aroused as my hands trail up and down her body.

The taste of her neck on my tongue is inciting bad thoughts, and I want more.

So much fucking more.

My cock thumps as it becomes painfully hard. I ease my hips back from hers. She can't feel how aroused I am. She can't know how badly I need to fuck her.

"Nathan," she whispers, breaking the spell.

My eyes snap up to hers in the mirror. *What the hell am I doing?*

I step back. "You should take a shower." I run my hand through my hair as I try to calm myself down. "You need to get that make-up off."

Her face falls—*is that disappointment?*

"Yes." She gives her head a subtle shake. "Okay."

She practically runs to the bathroom, and I begin to pace. What the fuck was I doing?

She can't know what's going on with me.

She can never know how I feel.

Do you want to lose her, you fucking idiot?

I sit on the edge of the bed and put my head into my hands.

Shit, that was close.

I sit back to rearrange my cock in my pants. It's painful and restricted.

I need to come or I'm going to... Hell, I can't even think what I'm going to do.

I get a vision of Eliza beneath me, naked, and my entire body tingles.

Fuck.

I unzip my pants with urgency, and I take my cock into my hand. I get a vision of Eliza on her knees in front of me and I begin to pull myself.

Fuck, yeah.

Take it all... take it fucking all.

The grip on my cock is nearly painful. I need it harder, I need her tighter.

I close my eyes and tip my head back. My bicep begins to cramp from the vice-like grip I have on myself.

The shower turns off.

No.

I need it.

I zip my pants up. The bathroom door opens, and I brush past her before she has time to notice the tent in my trousers.

God damn it, woman... I want to fuck your mouth.

I lock the door, turn the water on, and tear my clothes off, desperate for Eliza.

Desperate to ejaculate.

I soap up my hand, get under the water, and I begin to really fuck myself. I need this. I need it hard.

I want it to hurt.

My legs go weak from underneath me, and I put my hand up on the tiles to hold myself steady. I close my eyes and taste Eliza's skin in my mouth. I can almost feel her breath on my chest, and I come hard. My head tips back and I give a low, guttural moan. My heart is racing, gasping for air, and my body shudders as it comes down from the high. I keep stroking to completely empty my body.

Thinking of her when I come is an out of this world experience. I can't imagine what the real thing would feel like. Maybe I wouldn't even survive it.

I stand under the shower, the water running down over my face, and the more I come down from the high, the more guilt fills me.

Eliza trusts me, and I'm jerking off over her like she's a piece of meat in a porno.

What the fuck is wrong with me?

I stand under the water for a long time and slowly wash my hair. I'm dreading facing her.

Eventually, when I can't put it off any longer, I turn off the shower and dry myself. Normally, I would walk out there in a towel and dress in front of her but I can't now. It feels weird.

Every boundary between us has changed, and I have no sphere or reference as to what's right and wrong anymore.

What just happened was wrong... but fuck, it felt so right.

I wrap the towel around my waist and inhale deeply as I stare at my reflection in the mirror.

Cut it out, I warn myself. *She's going to leave if you keep losing your head.*

I close my eyes and shake out my arms as if I'm preparing to go into a fight, because that's how it feels, like I'm constantly fighting myself over her—an internal battle between what I *should* want and what I *do* want.

What I know and what I want to learn.

Everything about this situation is screaming at me to drop it, and every day I decide to.

Yet, every day I fail the task.

I walk out into the darkened bedroom. Eliza is lying on her side with her back to me. I grab my boxer shorts from the drawer and slip them on, and then I get a glass of water, get into bed beside her, and I lie on my back.

I can't touch her because I can't trust myself not to start it up all over again.

We lie in silence for a long time until, eventually, she asks, "Is everything all right?"

I close my eyes, fuck. "Yeah, baby," I whisper.

"Cuddle me."

I roll toward her and take her into my arms. I press my lips into the crook of her neck.

"Do you love me, Nathe?" she whispers. She asks me this all the time. It's an affectionate joke between us.

I screw up my face and pause as my chest constricts. "You know I do." I kiss the back of her head. "Go to sleep."

"Goodnight, Nathe."

I remember how perfect that ten minutes were when she was in my arms, and I smile sadly into the darkness. "Goodnight, Eliza."

———

I stare at the big screen over the bar. It's 10:00 p.m., and after the longest day in history, I just want to go home and sleep.

But home is complicated. Actually, home isn't even my home. It's her home.

I pinch the bridge of my nose and scrunch my eyes shut.

Fucking hell, what a mess.

I sip my scotch and stare up at the television screen.

Here's what I need to do. I need to go back to my house and sleep in my bed. I also need to have sex with someone before I ruin everything.

I sip my drink and stare into space, infuriated at the situation I find myself in.

This isn't how it's supposed to go. Nothing about this is fucking normal.

Am I having a midlife crisis or something?

I think about what the possible outcomes are if I tell Eliza what's going on in my head... and my pants. She could be mortified if I made a move and she wasn't into it. We would become awkward and drift apart. She might just not like me that way, it's probable actually. I mean, in the ten years that we've spent every spare moment together, she has never once hinted at anything like that between us. Neither have I, but things change, apparently. She could be totally disgusted that I've been sleeping with her and seeing her undressed while feeling an attraction to her. What if she feels violated? *Am I* violating her? I don't even know anymore.

This really is a fucked-up situation.

I sip my scotch as the worst-case scenario plays out. What if she does, in fact, feel the same and we sleep together and it feels wrong? What if I don't like it but she does? I would then have to tell her that it was a mistake.

It would hurt her.

My heart drops, I just couldn't hurt her like that. I can't even contemplate that happening, it would kill me.

This is uncharted territory. I have no idea how my body would work with hers. But then... considering the way she makes me feel, I don't think...

Fuck, I just don't know.

I've never been so confused in my entire life.

I puff air into my cheeks as I stare at the screen. I've been here for five hours, going around and round in my head, searching for the right answer, knowing that I should go back to my place, but instead sitting in a bar waiting for Eliza to go sleep before I go home to her.

Home.

My chest tightens. Eliza is my home. I'm confused about everything I thought I ever wanted and if I get this wrong, I lose it all.

I allow myself to imagine what the other side of the coin would look like if, by some miracle, it did work out. I would get to be in love with my best friend. I smile, imagining the life we could have together. We could travel the world, marriage... *children.*

My own family; something I've never even contemplated before.

We could literally have it all.

I tip my head back and drain my glass.

But this could also be a disaster waiting to happen.

Just drop it.

Eliza

I lie on the couch and hold the remote up to turn off the television. I glance at my phone. It's 11:50 p.m. I'm beat. I've been waiting up for Nathan.

He said he was working late but this *is* really late. I hope everything's okay. I keep going over last night and the way we were with each other—the intimacy between us.

Brooke's words from Saturday night keep coming back to me.

Why do you think Nathan has a bachelor pad?

Is he having sex with someone right now?

Uneasiness fills me, and I frown at the notion. I climb from the couch and drag myself into the bathroom. I stare at my reflection as I clean my teeth.

I'm rattled about what happened between us, trying to decipher if this is all in my head. I'm unusually clingy. I feel close to him, and yet, miles away. I hate that he's not here. I can't fall asleep without his hand on my behind.

I shouldn't depend on him so much... or at all actually.

One day he's going to meet someone and never come back and where will that leave you?

The thought of him leaving and never coming back makes me feel sick to my stomach.

Oh God, this situation is worse than I thought. The girls are right; I need to get over myself.

I must be imagining this entire thing, nothing happened between us last night.

It was a figment of my imagination, I'm horny and I'm lonely and perhaps by me making the realisation that I am in a rut and have given up on men, it's making me cling onto him. Of course, that's it. The girls are right, this is all just a mix up of feelings, nothing more and nothing less. The sooner I go on a date with someone the better. I'm way too dependent on Nathan.

Although, I can't even admit this to myself properly but I feel like I might have feelings for him. But that's ridiculous.

It's just because I'm lonely and I want to feel loved.

And I know that Nathan loves me even though it's not the same kind of love.

I'm mixing it up and getting all confused.

It doesn't mean anything.

As soon as I start dating I can stop imagining all this business between him and me. It's all in my head. He would be horrified if he knew what I was thinking.

I turn off the light and climb into bed to lie in the darkness for a while. My mind is spinning at a million miles per hour.

Where *is he* now?

He's never this late. Maybe he isn't coming over tonight.

That's okay—he doesn't have to—he's not my boyfriend or anything.

I toss and turn, and I punch my pillow, annoyed that it bothers me. Half an hour later, I hear the key turn in the door, and relief fills me.

He's here.

Now, I'll finally get some sleep.

I hear his keys go onto the sideboard and then the shower runs. A few moments later, Nathan walks into the bedroom with a white towel around his waist.

"Hi." I smile up at him.

"Hi."

"You're home late."

He sits down beside me on the edge of the bed. "Yeah." He

tucks a piece of my hair behind my ear, and we stare at each other, despite the darkness.

The air between us feels weird again. There's a spark... a crackle. Something's different.

What the fuck is it?

His dark eyes hold mine and he rubs his thumb over my cheekbone as he studies me.

I feel like he wants to say something, but he doesn't.

I put my hand over his against my cheek. "Nathan, what is it?"

"Nothing." He gets up in a rush and snatches his boxer shorts. Then, he storms into the bathroom to get changed.

I lie in the darkness with questions buzzing through my brain. I can't hold my tongue any longer. There shouldn't be any secrets between us. We *are* just friends. Moments later, he comes back into the room and switches his bedside lamp on.

"Why are you so late?" I ask.

"I had something going on." He gets into bed and picks up his book from the nightstand.

"Oh." I look over at him as he turns the page. "Like what?"

He lies on his side toward me and flicks through the pages to get to the place where he left off.

"What did you have going on?" I repeat when he doesn't answer.

"I was working."

"Oh." I roll over toward him and watch him for a moment. "I thought you must have had a date."

His eyes lift over his book to meet mine, and then he raises his eyebrow before his attention goes back to his book.

"Are you seeing anyone?" I ask.

"What?" He frowns as if I'm a major inconvenience.

"Are you seeing anyone?" I repeat. "I mean, I know you haven't had sex for a while, but are you dating?"

"Why do you ask?"

I sit up. "Because you never tell me anything about your personal life."

He turns the page as if annoyed, his eyes don't leave the page. "Stop being nosey."

"Well, are you?" He flicks the page but ignores my question. "I think we need to start being more open about our personal lives, don't you? It's weird that we spend all our time together and talk about everything *except* our relationships."

His eyes meet mine. "It's almost midnight, Eliza, why are we talking about this?"

"We aren't talking." I lie down in a huff. "I'm talking and you're dodging my questions."

He exhales heavily and keeps reading.

"Well, I am." I huff.

"You're what?"

"I'm beginning to date again."

He drops his book. "What?"

"I've decided that I'm ready to date again."

He glares at me. "What brought this on?"

I put my hands above my head. "I don't know. I miss sex, I guess."

He turns the page angrily. "Why don't you go on Tinder and arrange for two guys to double bang you?" he says sarcastically. "Better yet, get one of them to film it and upload it to YouPorn."

"Yeah, I might." I roll my eyes. It's a typical Nathan answer. Smartass. "A threesome has always been on my bucket list, actually. I may as well start ticking things off now that I'm thirty."

"You're thirty-one. And your bucket list must be riveting."

"What's that supposed to mean?" I frown. "Sex isn't on your bucket list?"

"No. If I want sex, I have sex. I most definitely don't have bucket list sex. Jesus."

Fuck he's annoying, I roll over so that my back is to him. "Sorry, I'm not as cool as you and all your groupies, *Dr. Mercer*."

"You want a date, I'll get you a fucking date." He gets up in a rush and storms over to my underwear drawer. He ruffles through it and digs out my vibrator. "Here he is." He eyes it suspiciously as he holds it up. "Although I'm not quite sure what this pissant thing would do."

"Size doesn't count, Nathan." I snap. "Not everyone wants a donkey dick, you know?"

"Does it even touch the sides?"

My mouth falls open in horror and I get up and snatch it from him, throw it back in my drawer, and slam it shut. "I'll have you know, BOB touches all my sides because I happen to have a very tiny vagina." I get into bed in a huff. "Not that it's any of your business."

He gets into bed beside me. I turn my back to him and he picks up his book.

"You're annoying me," I say.

"Well, you're annoying me," he snaps.

I roll my eyes, and after a while, he puts his hand on my hip, our sleeping position. Relaxation instantly begins to roll through me.

"Goodnight, Eliza."

"Goodnight, Nathan."

"Goodnight, Tiny," he says.

I smile against my pillow. He has a name for my vagina now?

"Goodnight," I squeak in a mouse voice.

He chuckles and pats my hip. "Go to sleep."

———

I'm walking down the corridor toward the elevator when I hear someone call from behind me, "Eliza!"

I turn and see the guy from Saturday night. I'm taken aback. *Shit,* what was his name?

"Hi."

"Samuel," he prompts as he falls into step beside me. "Samuel Phillips. We met on Saturday night."

"Yes, I remember." I smile. Oh, he's cute... I don't remember him being this good-looking. "You work here?" I ask.

"Yes, I'm an anaesthetist."

"Oh." I only vaguely remember our conversation from the other night. "Did you tell me that already?" I frown.

"Yes." He gives me a sexy smile. "In great length, actually."

I wince. "Gosh, my apologies. Those cocktails went straight to my head. I'm so embarrassed."

He chuckles. "That's okay."

We arrive at the elevator and I have to get in to go up to level three. "This is me."

He lingers and then bites his bottom lip as if contemplating saying something. "Would you like to go out some time?"

I shrug casually as if super-hot anaesthetists ask me out every day. "Umm sure, why not?"

He smiles and I feel my stomach flutter. "Great."

I hunch my shoulders, I'm being so weird right now but I have no control over myself. "Great." I turn to get into the elevator.

"I need to give you my number."

I give a nervous giggle. "Oh right."

He digs in his pocket and pulls out a little brass case. He takes out a business card and passes it over. "Call me tonight."

I stare at the card in my hand. "Okay." I smile and then turn toward the elevator.

"Don't forget."

"I won't." Oh, he's really cute.

He points at me as he walks backward. "Because I'll come looking for you if you don't call me. I mean it. I'm into you, Eliza. You better call me."

I laugh at his over the top flirtyness. "Yes, okay, I promise." I turn and get into the elevator and he puts his hands into his suit pockets as he watches me.

"Goodbye, Eliza."

"Bye." The doors shut, and I scrunch up my face in excitement.

Oh my God. Eek! This is getting me back into the dating game with a bang.

He is gorgeous.

———

I sip my red wine as I stir the beef Bourguignon I'm making. The potatoes are mashed, and the carrots and string green beans are in the steamer. I rushed home from work because I wanted to get dinner cooked early so that I can call Samuel before Nathan gets home. It would be weird having him listen to the conversation.

I glance at the clock. It's 6:25 p.m. Nathe will be home in about twenty minutes.

Shit, I have to call now or not at all.

I look desperate ringing this early, I hold his card out and stare at it in my hand.

Samuel Phillips

Oh, well, here goes nothing. I drain my glass of red wine and refill it.

What do I say? Nothing...just let him do the talking. Don't appear too eager, I remind myself.

With shaky fingers, I dial his number.

It goes straight to voicemail.

Shit.

"Hi, you've reached Samuel Phillips. I'm either on the phone or unavailable. Please leave a message after the tone, and I'll get back to you as soon as I can. Have a nice day."

"Hi, Samuel... it's Eliza." I begin to pace. "I'll... I'll try again tomorrow." I hang up in a rush before I can make a fool of myself.

Oh, man, that was dreadful. What kind of sexy message was that? I get a vision of him listening to it, unimpressed.

I flop onto the couch and sip my wine.

Loser.

I'm so out of practice when it comes to dating, I have no idea what I'm doing here. I really need to up my game. There should be an up-to-date dating manual you can download on the internet with cool things to say and do.

I hear the key in the door before Nathan comes into view wearing a crisp gray suit and cream shirt, he looks every bit the smooth doctor he is. His sandy hair is longer on top with a bit of a curl, and his big blue eyes smile when he sees me. "There's my girl."

"Hi." I smile as I jump up to greet him. He leans down and kisses me on the cheek. "You didn't go to the gym?" I ask as I straighten his tie.

"No, got held up at work." He walks over to the oven and

peers in through the door. "Not long till we get a home gym. Dinner smells fantastic." He pours himself a glass of wine. "My favorite."

"I thought I was your favorite." I tease.

"Apart from you, of course." He touches his glass against mine. "How was your day?"

I shrug. "Pretty good." I want to blurt out that I got asked on a date but I don't quite know what his reaction will be, so I decide against it. "Dinner is twenty minutes away if you want to take a shower?"

His ass rests on the kitchen counter, and he smiles as he sips his wine. His eyes linger on me.

I do a little jog on the spot. "Seventeen days until we go away. I've just got to get through two weeks at my new job first."

"Can't come soon enough. I need this vacation."

"Me, too." I pull myself up to sit on the counter beside him. "What are we going to do while we're there?"

"Everything."

"Like what?" I smile hopefully. "Tell me everything."

"Sleep in, eat delicious food, lie in the sun, shop... drink cocktails."

I tip my head back in excitement. "I just can't wait."

"Don't forget we've got my parents' party next weekend," he reminds me.

"Oh." I cringe.

"What?"

"I forgot to pick up the cake tin today. I meant to call in on the way home and I completely forgot."

"What do you need a cake tin for?"

"I'm making your dad's birthday cake on Saturday for his party."

"You are not going all the way there to cook all day Saturday. I'll buy a damn cake."

"I am. I offered. My cakes are his favorite, and besides, cooking for people I care about makes me happy."

He rolls his eyes as he drains his glass. "I'm taking a shower." He saunters down the hall.

My phone dances across the counter.

It's Samuel.

I peer down the hall after Nathan. *Shit, hurry up and get in the shower. I don't want you to hear me.* "Hello," I answer.

"Eliza, hi. It's Samuel."

I smile goofily. "Hi." My voice comes out like a high pitch screech, and I push my thumb into my eye socket. I clear my throat, determined to sound better.

I can see down the hall and into my bedroom and I watch as Nathan loosens his tie.

I'll keep an eye on him so I know if he can hear me.

"You called me. I'm impressed," he purrs.

"I said I would."

Nathan slides his jacket over his shoulders and begins to unbutton his shirt, I watch on.

"How was your day?" Samuel asks.

Nathan takes his shirt off, and I watch as every muscle in his back tenses.

"It... was good," I stammer, distracted. My eyes are locked on my best friend. "How was yours?"

"It was great after seeing you," Samuel says.

Nathan drops his pants and carefully hangs them on a hanger. I can see every muscle in his thick thighs. "Same." I frown.

Jeez.

"Where do you want to go on our first date?"

Nathan drops his black boxer briefs and then turns. I get a full frontal view. He's hung and rippled with muscles. His pubic hair is short and well-kept. Fucking hell, my stomach clenches. He walks back up the hall to the bathroom. When he glances up, our eyes lock.

The air leaves my lungs, but he doesn't flinch. It's as if he wants me to look.

He wants me to see why he thinks my vibrator is pathetic...

Holy mother of God. What kind of a dick is that?

6

Eliza

"Are you there, Eliza?" Samuel interrupts my little peep show.

I frown, flustered, and I spin toward the kitchen. "Yes, sorry. I'm easy." I splutter. Oh God, don't say that. "I'm not... easy, easy. I mean I'm easily pleased."

Oh fuck, shut up. You're wrecking it.

I put my hand over my eyes.

"I know what you mean." He laughs. "How about this weekend?"

Um, I don't want a night time thing. It's a bit too... date-ish.

Isn't that the point, you idiot? Oh hell, this is a disaster.

"I can't this weekend, I'm fully booked. I could do lunch, though." I hear Nathan's shower turn on, and I relax a little, knowing that he can't hear me.

"Do you want to have lunch on Thursday?"

"I'm working."

"So am I. We can grab a quick bite in the cafeteria. I mean, I know it's not much of a first date but at least I get to see you."

I smile, he seems eager. "That sounds great."

"I'll call you Thursday morning to arrange a time."

"Okay." I run my finger along the kitchen counter. It feels good to talk to someone.

"You've made my night by calling."

I smile bashfully. "Mine, too." I glance up to see Nathan standing in front of me with a towel around his waist. He raises his eyebrow in question.

"Who's that?" Nathan mouths.

"Okay, I'll talk to you later then. Goodbye." I hang up in a rush. "What are you doing?" I snap.

"Asking you where my shampoo is." He frowns. "What are you doing?"

I turn my back to him and fill my wine, but I'm so flustered it sloshes over the sides of the glass. "Your shampoo is in my gym bag. I ran out... and I was arranging lunch."

"With who?"

I drain my glass as I think of a lie. "Becca."

"Becca who?"

"Becca Bib... Biblicists," I blurt out.

His brow furrows. "Who's Becca Biblicist?"

"A girl from work."

He nods and then saunters back up the hall. He finds his shampoo and closes the bathroom door behind him.

I put my hands over my eyes. *Becca Biblicist.* That's the best fake name I can come up with, seriously? What the fuck is wrong with me?

And why did I lie?

I should have just told him the truth. Ugh, what is wrong with me?

10:00 p.m.

I lie on the couch with my glass of wine in my hand as I go over my options, what I need to do is to just go in the room and tell him I have a date.

It's no big deal. .... why *am* I making this a big deal? Nathan won't care who I date.

Maybe it's me that cares—maybe I'm the one with the issue here.

I tip my head back and drain my glass, knowing this is the exact reason why I need to date other people.

I *am* too dependent on Nathan.

The girls are right, this isn't normal behaviour, why haven't I seen it before now?

Two years with a man in my bed who I'm not having sex with is just plain weird.

I rinse my glass up and brush my teeth, and then I give myself a pep talk in the mirror. I'm just going to go in there and tell him.

Straight and simple; no fucking around.

I walk into the bedroom to see Nathan reading in bed. His hair is messy like he's just been fucked. His arm is above his head, exposing his sculptured biceps. My eyes drop down lower, and I can count the ripples on his stomach. My own stomach flips. He looks like a Greek God or something. Damn it, does he have to be so fucking sexy?

"Will you wear some clothes around here?" I huff as I turn my side of the blankets back.

"What?" He frowns, but his eyes don't leave the page.

"You're half naked all the time." I get into bed, annoyed. It's like he's purposely baiting me. I mean, I am only human; any red-blooded woman would be salivating if she was constantly exposed to this torture. I get a vision of him naked from earlier and his beautiful body.

For fuck's sake.

I roll over so that my back is to him with a huff.

"What's up your ass?" he mutters.

"Nothing."

"My nudity is annoying you?"

"Yes." I splutter. "It is, actually."

"Why?"

"Well, how would you like it if I waved my body around in front of you all the time?"

"You do."

"I do not."

"You're wearing panties and a camisole right now. I see your body wherever I look, so don't play Mother Theresa here, Eliza.
"

I roll my eyes, I'm still lying with my back to him.

"And besides, we've been like this for years. Why is it suddenly bothering you now?" He adds.

"I'm just horny, okay?" I spit before I can put my mouth to brain filter on.

Oh... hell.

"You're horny?"

I scrunch my eyes shut. Did I just say that out loud? "Good night, Nathan."

He rolls me onto my back, and his eyes dance with mischief as he leans over me. "You're horny?"

"No." I try to backtrack. "What I mean is, I'm a single woman, and you shouldn't be naked in front of me all the time."

He gives me a slow, sexy smile. "Why not?"

"Just..." I press my lips together as I try to think of an appropriate thing to say that doesn't make me sound like a pervert. "I'm just saying."

He gets up and goes to my underwear drawer. He grabs my vibrator and tosses it to me. "Go for it."

"What?" I frown.

"Do your best."

I stare at him.

"Don't let me get in the way." He raises an eyebrow. "Fuck yourself. Pretend I'm not here." He picks his book back up and turns the page he was at. "I won't watch... much."

"You're disgusting." I throw the vibrator off the bed and roll over in a huff. I pretend what he just said isn't the hottest thing I've ever heard.

"You did say you want to start being more open about our sex life," he says. "I'm just saying." I can tell by the tone in his voice that he's amused. I hear the page turn, and I know he's gone back to reading.

My mind goes somewhere it shouldn't. I imagine masturbating in front of him. Would he touch himself while he watches?

Would we come together?

My sex clenches as I imagine how hot that would be.

Fuck, where did that come from?

Stop it.

He grabs my hipbone and pulls me back sharply to sit snugly against him. The heat of his touch begins to travel through my system. Like chocolate near a flame, melting as it gets hotter.

Fuck this. I need sex.

Two years is too long, and I need it hard. Really hard. Deep, hard fucking. The kind you are sore from.

I imagine hearing the slapping sound of people hard at it

and, once again, my body tingles. I'm not normally this type of girl but I hope this date works out because god damn it, I need to get laid as soon as possible.

"Goodnight, Eliza."

"Goodnight."

"Goodnight, Tiny." He pats me twice.

"Goodnight," I squeak in a mouse voice.

He chuckles, and I smile against my pillow.

Any night with Nathan is a good night. Horny or not. As soon as I take care of this little libido problem I'm experiencing, everything will go back to feeling normal.

I close my eyes as I try to force myself to fall asleep.

But I can't, because images of Nathan naked are running through my mind...and there's a lot to look at...trust me on this one. Perhaps I'm traumatised from seeing his dick in the hallway tonight, I smile into my pillow as I remember it. What a visual sensation.... he could totally do porn.

I exhale heavily, it's going to be a long night.

———

It's Thursday, and I'm walking into the hospital cafeteria to meet Samuel. I feel awkward and weird. Hell, now I remember why I gave up dating.

Samuel stands and gives me a little wave.

"Hi." I make my way over to the table and he bends and kisses my cheek.

"Fancy seeing you here."

I smile nervously and fall into the seat. "Yes, fancy that."

"What do you want to eat? I'll grab it."

"Oh, that's okay,"

"No, I insist."

"Thanks. I'll have a toasted ham and cheese sandwich with a mineral water, please."

"Okay, back in a minute." He disappears to the counter to order. I watch him for a moment. He really is very good-looking.

I take out my phone and text the girls.

I remember why I don't date.
This shit is nerve wracking.

They won't get my message until they finish work, but whatever. I feel better by sending it.

I stuff my phone back into my bag, knowing I need to get a handle on these nerves.

Samuel comes back and sits at the table. "It will be a few minutes."

"What did you get?" I ask to make conversation.

"Toasted focaccia and coffee." He smiles over at me. "So, where did you say you're going to this weekend?"

"Oh." I frown. "Birthday celebrations."

"Nice." He raises his eyebrow. "Do you need a chaperone?"

"I'm good." I pause as I think of an excuse as to why I couldn't invite him, how about....my best friend is a guard dog who will happily rip your head off. "It's a girls' thing." I shrug. "Tickets were bought a long time ago."

"Ah." He takes my hand over the table. "But seriously, when can I see you again?"

I swallow the lump in my throat as I look at the gorgeous man in front of me. I really should be thrilled that he's so keen. He's called me every night this week. "How about dinner one night sometime next week?" I offer.

"Deal." He smirks.

A deep voice interrupts us. "Hello." I look up to see Nathan standing over the table. His eyes glance down to our entwined hands.

Oh, fuck.

"Nathan." I drop Samuel's hand like a hot potato.

"Please, don't let me interrupt," he says dryly. His eyes flick to Samuel. "I didn't realize you two knew each other."

"Yeah." Samuel's eyes come back to me. "We've just connected... until you interrupted us on Saturday night." He raises an eyebrow.

My eyes widen in horror...what the hell is that supposed to mean?

There was no connecting.... you dweeb, we didn't even kiss.

Nathan's eyes come back to me. "I see."

My heart drops.

"I'll leave you to it then," Nathan says.

"Join us." I pull out the chair as an invitation.

"No. Thank you." His eyes meet mine. "I hope Tiny enjoys her next meal. Send her my love."

I cannot believe he just said that.

"Who's Tiny?" Samuel smiles as he looks between us.

"Eliza has a friend that was a vegetarian." Nathan smiles sweetly. "Recently converted to a carnivore and is apparently starving."

I glare at him.

His eyes flick to Samuel. "Although, I thought she would have preferred a higher quality meat, to be honest."

Samuel's eyes flick between us, confused. "Why, where is she eating?"

"At an all-you-can-eat restaurant," Nathan replies without skipping a beat. "The diseases at those places are next level."

I sit back in my chair, affronted.

Asshole.

"Goodbye, Nathan." I fake a smile.

"Goodbye." He saunters over to the counter and orders his coffee like he's a fucking rock star.

My blood boils.

Samuel's eyes come to me. "How do you know Nathan Mercer?"

"We're friends. There's a group of us that all hang out together on the weekends."

"I see." He smiles. "And this Tiny girl—the meat eater—is in your group, too?"

"Yeah." My furious eyes flick over to Nathan at the counter. "I'll introduce you to her really soon."

―――――

It's Friday night and we are on our way to Brooke's birthday dinner, we are walking down the street toward the restaurant. Nathan has been giving me the silent treatment since he saw me at lunch with Samuel yesterday. He read in bed last night, while I watched television, and he was conveniently asleep when I went to bed. Tonight, he picked me up and hasn't said a word.

"Are you going to talk to me?" I ask.

"I am talking to you." He keeps his gaze straight ahead.

"No, you're not. It was just lunch, Nathan." I sigh. "Stop being a baby. I told you I was ready to date and so I met someone in the cafeteria. I don't understand what your problem is."

He stops on the spot and glares at me. "You're seriously pissing me off."

"Because I dare to go on a date?" I unlink my arm from his. "I told you the other night I wanted to start dating."

"You told me you were horny."

"Same thing."

"They are *not* the same."

"So, what do you do when you're horny?" I bark.

"I fuck someone, Eliza. I most definitely don't have lunch with someone I work with in a professional environment."

We arrive at the restaurant, and he opens the door with attitude. We walk in and see our friends sitting at the back table.

"For your information," I whisper as we weave through the tables. "I don't have sex with strangers. I'm not a fucking sleazebag."

"And I am?" He growls.

"Shut up, Nathan. I don't have to explain my dating life to you. You're not my boyfriend."

"Shut up?" He gasps as he pulls me to a stop. "Shut up?" His eyes look like they are about to pop out of his head. "Don't tell me to fucking shut up, Eliza." He growls. "Do it again and see what happens."

I roll my eyes at his dramatics. "Where am I, Nathan?" I ask him. He glares at me. "I am at dinner with *you*." I prod my finger in his chest, hard. "I will be going home with *you* tonight, and I told Samuel I was busy all weekend because I wanted to see *you* instead. Although, if you keep being a dickhead, I may reconsider." I storm to the table. "Hello." I smile to everyone as I fall into my happy go lucky role.

"Finally." Brooke smiles and stands. I pull her into a hug.

"Happy birthday, baby."

Nathan hugs her, too. "Happy Birthday, Brookey."

"Sorry we're late." I kiss Jolie and the two boys.

Nathan and I fall into our seats opposite each other. He

smiles and greets everyone, and then they all fall into chatter between themselves. Then, his attention comes back to me, and his face drops.

"Stop it." I kick him hard in the shin and he jumps.

He winces in pain.

Oh shit, I didn't mean to kick him so hard, that really connected. "Serves you right." I whisper.

The look on his face is murderous, and I drop my head to try and hide my smile. "That wasn't me," I whisper. "It was Tiny."

He twists his lips, and I giggle.

"Stop it." I mouth as I put my hand out toward him on the table. "We'll talk later. I don't even really like him, Nathan. Can we just enjoy tonight, please?"

He looks at me flatly, and I wiggle my fingers to try and entice him. Eventually, he puts his hand in mine, and I blow him a kiss.

He's just angry that I didn't tell him about my date, and as it turns out, he's right, I should have.

Nathan isn't a controlling person, but he's strong-willed, and so far in life, apart from his parents, I'm the only one who can talk him down from his temper.

I slip off my shoe and rub my foot up his shin. He rolls his lips as he looks over at me.

"You didn't ask me how my last day at the hospital was," I say.

"How was your last day?"

"It was sad. So, can you please not make my day any crappier?"

He nods and gives my hand a squeeze. "Okay."

———

"Okay, good luck, honey." My mom smiles down the phone. "You won't need it though."

"Thanks, Mom."

I brush down my skirt and twirl and look at my behind in the mirror as I speak. "What are you wearing?" Mom asks.

"I'm wearing a gray pencil skirt and a pale pink blouse. My hair is twisted up into a knot. It's gotten so long, I need a trim," I mutter, distracted. "I've got my pearl earrings in that Nathan's parents bought me for Christmas, and I'm wearing sheer stockings and high heeled pumps. I'm hoping I look businesslike."

"Sounds perfect."

"I hope so." I smile. It's Monday morning—my first day at my new job—and I'm as nervous as hell.

"Okay, I'll let you go. Knock them dead, baby."

"Okay, bye. I'll call you tonight."

I glance at my watch. I need to leave soon. My phone rings, and the name Nathan lights up the screen.

"Hi," I answer.

"Hello, Eliza," his deep voice purrs down the phone.

"What do you want?" I smirk.

"I called to wish you good luck, although I know you don't need it."

I smile goofily. "I'm so nervous."

"Don't be. You're going to do great. I'll pick you up from work."

"Really?" I smile.

"Sure, we can celebrate your first day."

"Okay." I put my hand on my chest. "My heart is racing."

"Don't be nervous, and remember: there is a better job waiting for you. You can walk out any time you want."

I roll my eyes. "Yes, Dad."

He chuckles. "See you at five."

"Okay."

He stays on the line, as if not wanting to hang up.

"Nathe?"

"Yeah, baby."

"Thanks for calling." I smile. "It means a lot."

"Yeah, well, you mean a lot."

My heart swells.

"See you tonight, have a good day." He hangs up, and I close my eyes.

Let's do this.

Forty minutes later, I take the elevator to level 7.

"Hello." I smile as I walk into reception.

The young girl's face lights up, and she jumps up from her seat. "Eliza, come through. I'm Lexi."

"Nice to meet you."

"Come with me. Dr. Morgan is in his office." She leads me down the hall and knocks on an office door.

"Come in!" he calls.

Lexi opens the door. "Eliza is here, Dr. Morgan."

He stands from his seat, "Thank you, Lexi."

She nods and leaves me alone with him.

"Lovely to see you again, Eliza," he says. We shake hands, and his eyes linger on my face.

Oh shit, it's there again. I instantly feel his attraction to me, and I have to admit it, he is kind of cute. I was hoping I imagined it last time.

"I'm nervous." I smile as I clutch my bag in my hands.

He gestures toward the door. "You have nothing to worry about." I follow his lead and walk out of the office. "This way." He gestures down the corridor. "You're in very safe hands here."

I wish he hadn't told me he was attracted to me because now everything that comes out of his mouth sounds sexual.

Reason 969 why I need to get laid.

He opens a door. "This is your office."

I look around in awe. The room has dark carpet and a huge chandelier. There's also a large silver, gilded mirror, and a mahogany desk.

"It's beautiful."

"It is. I trust you'll be happy here."

"Thank you. I really appreciate you giving me this opportunity, Dr. Morgan."

"Please, call me Henry."

"Henry."

"Now you have a day to settle in and find your way around." He picks up a piece of paper from the desk and passes it to me. "This has all of your email and server details. I have emailed you our schedule for the week. Take today to familiarise yourself with the girls, your office, and our protocols."

"Okay."

"As of tomorrow, you will be working closely with me. I would like you to work out of my office at the hospital the days that I'm in surgery."

I nod, this all sounds so exciting. "Yes, of course."

"Tomorrow, we will be at the Martyr Private Hospital. We have a rhinoplasty, a breast augmentation, and a labiaplasty."

I frown in question.

"That's a vaginal reconstruction." He smiles at my inexperience.

I widen my eyes, feeling stupid. "I did not know that."

"I wouldn't expect you to." He chuckles. "It's where I reshape the labia and lips of the vagina to make them more visually appealing."

I raise my eyebrows, unsure what to say to that. "Oh, I see. Do you cut and stitch, or laser? How do you even do that?"

"You can do it one of two ways. Either an edge resection or a wedge resection. You see, no two labias have the same thickness, length, or color, and no two vulvas are the same. Most women are prompted to have this surgery by their partner or what they think their prospective partner would want in a woman."

I frown as I imagine getting part of my vagina lips cut off, and how much it would hurt.

He shrugs casually, as if he has this conversation every day. "Men have very different tastes as to what they desire their sexual partner's labia to look like. The one I'm doing tomorrow, for instance. I'm trimming the edges of the labia and filling it with a filler." His eyes hold mine. "She wants it plump and juicy to look at and touch." He pauses. "Hormones sometimes discolor it to a darker shade so we are also going to bleach it down the track so it's a perfect pink."

My face falls. This is a thing?

"It varies," he continues. "Plump, thick labia are to my taste. Personal choice, I guess." His eyes meet mine. "It comes down to how you like it to feel during sex."

"Men can feel the shape of your labia during sex?" I frown. "I had no idea."

He chuckles. "Yes, it's very different from one woman to the next. All a part of the experience, I suppose."

I stare at him, lost for words, and he chuckles.

"Welcome to the world of plastic surgery, Eliza."

I shake my head with an embarrassed smile. "Wow. Okay. Who knew?"

He stands. "Happy you're here, welcome to the team."

"Thanks."

"Oh." His eyes widen. "We have two conferences next month. One in Dallas and one in London. I think the first one is two weeks after you get back from your vacation. The dates are marked in your new calender." He gestures to the calender on the desk.

"And you want me to come?"

"Yes, of course."

"How long will we be away?"

"A week each time."

"Okay." I nod.

"Will that be a problem with your boyfriend?"

"Not at all," I lie.

"Good." His eyes hold mine for a moment longer than they should. "Conferences are a great way to get to know one another properly. You really learn a lot about a person when they depend on you for everything." He gives me a slow sexy smile. "I look forward to it." He turns and walks out of the office, and I sink into the chair. "Eliza?" He pops his head back around the corner.

"Yes?"

"Come and get me any time you need me. I'm at your disposal." He winks.

"Sure." I force a smile. "That's great."

He disappears, and I exhale heavily and look around my office.

Shit...

I really need to get laid before I go on those conferences with him. I could get drunk and ask him for a labia appraisal. This could be a fucking nightmare waiting to happen. I open the calender and flick through to the conference dates that are marked in. I search through the drawer and find a lead pencil, and I scribble the words:

No drinking at conference!

At the end of the day, I walk out into reception. The girls have all left. I take out my phone and text Nathan.

Coming now

A message bounces back.

I'm downstairs.

I smile.

xo

I push the button on the elevator. It arrives, and I step in.

"Hold the door, please," someone calls.

I put my hand in the door to hold it, and Henry rushes in.

"Thanks." He smiles. He's undone his navy tie, and it is hanging loose around his crisp white shirt

"How was your first day?" he asks.

"Great." I smile. "I had a wonderful day."

"Wait till I get you into surgery. I can't wait to fry your brain."

I giggle.

"Penis enlargements are my specialty." He holds his hands apart to signify twelve inches and I laugh out loud just as the door opens.

Henry puts his hand on my waist to lead me out, and I look up into the gaze of Nathan. He's leaning against the wall, his hands in the pockets of his expensive charcoal suit trousers.

He clenches his jaw at Henry.

"Nathan." I smile awkwardly as I walk over to him. "There you are."

He snaps his arm around my waist and bends to kiss me. His lips are a little open, and he sucks with just the right amount of suction. My knees weaken from under me.

Oh, wait, what?

"Hello," Nathan says.

"Good to see you again, Nathan," Henry replies. "She did fantastic." He smiles down at me. "She's like a dream come true."

"Is that so?" Nathan says dryly.

Oh crap.

7

Eliza

HENRY'S GAZE holds Nathan's for a moment longer than he should, and then he smiles.

"Have a good night, you two."

Nathan gives him a smug smile. "We always do." He puts his arm around my shoulders and pulls me to him.

I'm still reeling from his kiss. My lips are tingling. What kind of kiss was that?

Nathan watches Henry walking across the road. "I don't like him."

"You don't even know him."

His attention comes back to me. "Why did you tell him I was your boyfriend?"

"Good idea playing along with that kiss, by the way," I say quickly to try and distract him. "I think it looked realistic."

Nathan takes my hand and begins to power walk up the

street. "Why did you tell him you had a boyfriend?" He demands as he pulls me along. "Did he make a pass at you?"

"N-no," I stammer, nearly running to keep up with him.

"Did he make you feel uncomfortable?"

"No."

"What is it then?" He growls.

"Nathan, I just thought it would make me sound more reliable and grounded, you know?"

He turns toward me and stops. "That's fucking bullshit, Eliza, and you know it."

"You know what?" I huff. "Why the hell did you come and pick me up from work if you just want to be a jealous jerk?" I rip my hand out of his. "Screw you, I'll go celebrate my first day by myself. Go home. You've ruined it now." I storm off. If he wants dramatics, he can damn well have them.

"I'm just saying that I don't like him," he says as he follows me.

"Well, it's lucky he isn't your boss then, isn't it? First, you don't talk to me because of Samuel, and now you want to whine about my boss. Is there anything that doesn't piss you off, Nathan?"

"Nope. You've pretty much got it fucking covered right now, Eliza."

I turn on him like he's the devil himself. "What the hell does that mean?"

"Don't give me that tone." He growls.

"Oh, but you can give me that tone, and that's perfectly fine?" I turn and storm off, once again. "I don't know what's come over you lately; you're acting fucking weird," I bark. "Hot, cold, angry, sulking. Your mood swings are giving me whiplash."

"I just want to protect you," he calls from behind me. "Where are we walking to?"

"To a bar!" I snap. "I told you to go home. I'm not in the mood for a three-hour temper tantrum from a two-year-old."

"You want to go to the bar by yourself so you can pick up a fuck, is that it? Am I in the way, Eliza?"

I roll my eyes. "I'm not even joking now. Go the fuck home."

I see a place that looks nice, and I storm inside and sit down at the bar. Nathan follows and sits down beside me.

"What will it be?" the bartender asks.

"I'll have a margarita, please," I say as I try to calm my anger.

The bartender looks to Nathan, who holds up two fingers. "Make it two."

We sit in silence as I watch the bartender making our drinks.

"Sorry," Nathan finally mutters.

"For what?"

He pauses and I know he's trying to get the wording right in his head. "For being jealous."

I turn to him. "So, you admit it?"

He stares at me.

"Why would you be jealous?"

His eyes hold mine. "Because it's only a matter of time until I lose you."

"Nathe," I say softly and put my hand on his thigh. "You're never going to lose me."

He takes my hand in his and plays with my thumbnail. "Yes, I am, Lize. Let's face it," he whispers.

He's insecure. How didn't I see this before? Empathy fills me, and I smile up at my beautiful friend.

"Why would you think that?" I whisper.

"Here you go. Two margaritas." The bartender puts our drinks on the bar.

"Thank you," we say in unison.

Nathan shrugs and sips his margarita. "You keep telling me you're horny and you need sex, and once you meet someone..."

"You think I'm not going to need you if I meet someone?" I frown.

He stays silent.

"Nathan, I need you." I smile softly. "In fact, I've spent the last ten years trying to find a man who lives up to you."

His eyes hold mine. "What does that mean?"

"I don't even know."

He frowns as if wanting to say something.

"What?" I ask.

"If I wasn't... the way I am." He pauses and looks around the bar as if processing his thoughts. "Would I be the kind of man you would want?"

"You *are* the man I would want, Nathe," I answer honestly. "Fate hasn't been kind to me in this life."

"What do you mean?"

"I have this beautiful, smart and funny man who is so loyal and makes me so happy. But he can never give me..." My voice trails off. I smile sadly. "It doesn't matter. We are not destined to be like that. I really wish that we were."

He stares at me, his jaw clenches, and I know that deep down that he knows I'm right.

The truth sucks. Nathan and I are perfect for each other in every way.

We know that. Everyone knows that.

But I'm the wrong sex for him, and no matter how hard I try, I could never be what he needs.

"You didn't ask me how my first day was," I say.

"How was your first day?" he asks softly.

"It was pretty crappy." I smirk.

A semblance of a smile crosses his face. "Why is that?"

"Tomorrow, someone is getting their labia cut off and injected with fillers so it's plump, and I have to watch."

Nathan scrunches his eyes shut and pinches the bridge of his nose, and I laugh out loud.

"I'm thinking of getting it, too," I add casually.

His eyes snap open. "What the hell is wrong with your vagina?"

"That's for me to know and you to never find out."

He gives me a slow smile and takes my hand in his lap. I know our fight is over.

"I'm getting all the food tonight; every single thing, including all the desserts. There won't be room in our bed for you."

"What's new," He mutters dryly as he opens the menu. "I'm used to it."

———

It's 11:30 p.m., and Nathan and I are walking home arm in arm. We are laughing and joking now, and our earlier fight seems like a lifetime ago. He has me in a headlock, and we are wrestling our way down the street. Those margaritas went down way too easily, and we are way too tipsy for a Monday night.

We make our way back to my apartment, and he takes a shower before I do, too.

We brush our teeth, and I braid my long dark hair. Nathan likes me putting it up or he says he wakes up in the middle of the night in some kind of Rapunzel nightmare.

When he gets into bed, he's wearing his navy blue silk boxer shorts. I take off my robe and am wearing my custom panty and matching camisole set.

I climb in beside him and wince.

"What's wrong?" he asks.

"My back is tight," I stretch it to the left and right to try loosen it. "I tried to get in for a massage tomorrow night but I can't get one till Friday."

"I'll massage it for you."

"What?" I smile.

"Roll onto your stomach. I'll massage it for you." He goes up to lean on his elbow, and then falls back and chuckles. "I'm feeling so fucking drunk."

I giggle. "That makes two of us."

I roll onto my stomach, and he begins to chipper chop me at high speed. "Oww!" I cry. "What the hell is that?"

He sits up, and with two hands, he really chipper chops me with vigour.

"Ah." I laugh. "Stop it, you're making it worse."

He sits over my behind and gently begins to knead my shoulders, and I smile sleepily into the pillow. "Hmm. Now, that feels good," I whisper.

For twenty minutes, Nathan's magical hands roam up and down my back, every now and then, softly dusting the sides of my breasts.

I'm sleepy, relaxed, and I hate to admit it... aroused. I feel like I'm drifting safely, halfway between sober and drunk, Heaven and Hell.

Right and wrong.

As he pushes me into the mattress, I can feel his dick on my behind. Or maybe that's the margaritas and wishful thinking.

I get a vision of him in the nude from the other night and my insides begin to melt.

I let my mind go somewhere that it has never gone before. I let myself imagine what it would be like to have sex with Nathan Mercer.

Would he be rough? Would he be tender? I get a vision of me on top, looking down as I ride him. He would be so deep inside of me. God, he most definitely would touch every single side.

I clench in appreciation, and I feel a rush of moisture to my sex. I begin to feel my pulse there.

"Are you asleep, baby?" he whispers.

I inhale deeply, unable to answer him. It's easier to stay asleep—more restful here—and I don't want him to stop. *Don't stop.*

His hands are magical.

He lies down beside me and pulls my back to his front. His finger trails up and over my thigh and to my hip, slowly moving over my stomach.

His mouth is at my ear, and I can hear his breath quivering. Almost as if he is aroused, too.

What the fuck was in those drinks?

But I'm too relaxed to stop it, too relaxed to think. I just know I want this .... whatever this is....to keep going.

"Are you asleep, baby?" he whispers.

"Hmm." With my eyes closed, I put my hand up over my shoulder, onto his cheek. "Don't stop, Nathe," I whisper.

He inhales sharply as he kisses the side of my face, and I feel his erection up against my behind.

Am I dreaming this? Am I in a hornbag, drunken stupor right now?

What's happening?

I'm too relaxed to care, and I'm completely sure that one of us should be the sober and responsible person right now and stop this idiocy.

His hand goes to my breast and he kneads it hard as he pulls me back against his body.

Fuck.

My sex begins to throb.

"Eliza," he whispers as his lips move to my neck. He kisses me, and I feel his tongue as it swipes over my skin. My sex clenches in appreciation.

His hands are roaming all over me, goosebumps trailing where his fingers go, and our bodies writhing together slowly.

I'm wet—so wet.

I feel like I'm having an out of body experience.

Everything feels magnified. Every breath that he takes, every quiver on his inhale. Every vein I think I can feel in his hard cock.

I just want to roll over, open my legs, and kiss him.

I want him inside of me. I want to feel my Nathan inside me.

Every hard inch.

His phone rings, and we both jump back from each other guiltily.

He answers it. "Nathan Mercer." He drops his head as he listens.

I stare at him as my heart hammers in my chest. With only the moonlight in the room, I can see the tip of his cock as it peeks over the top of his boxer shorts.

He's hard. Rock hard. I didn't imagine it.

His eyes rise to meet mine.

"Yes." He listens. "Give him the other antibiotic and begin fluids." He listens some more. "Call me if there's any change." He hangs up and stares at me for a moment.

Something hangs heavily in the air between us.

I swallow the lump in my throat as I wait for him to say something, and finally, he speaks. "I've got to go."

"Where to?"

His haunted eyes hold mine. "Away from you."

He turns and grabs his clothes in the darkness before he rushes up the hall. A few moments later, I hear the front door click closed.

He's gone.

What the hell just happened?

———

The alarm blares through my room breaking the silence. I frown sleepily and knock it off.

"Ouch." My head feels like it's in a vise. Those margaritas were the devil.

Hazy memories of last night's disaster begin to resurface.

Nathan didn't come back after he cooled down, like I thought he would. He never stays away when we fight.

We crossed a line.

I have no idea why that happened when it's never happened before. We've been drunk a million times together. We've cuddled, spooned, and damn... we see each other half-dressed all the time. I get a vision of him naked, and I remember how I couldn't look away. How he seemed more virile than ever before.

Jeez, my hormones must be crazy at the moment. I need to get laid, stat. This is turning into a nightmare. I reach over and grab my phone from the side table and check it. There are no missed calls.

Nathan's last words come back to me last night.

Away from you.

Does he blame me?

My mind goes back to that moment in bed, and what I said. *Don't stop.*

I wince in regret. Why did I say that? He knows I'm struggling with my libido right now, my hormones are running out of control and taking over. Did I force myself on him? I sit up, filled with disgust.

I need to fix this between us. I need to fix this now.

I dial his number.

Ring, ring, ring, ring, ring, ring. No answer; it goes to voicemail.

I frown, and look at my clock. It's now 6:00 am. Nathan will be in his car on the way to the hospital.

He's not answering my call. *He does blame me.*

I begin to get annoyed. Is he for real? It wasn't just me in this bed. He was hard and good to go, too. I hang up angrily and storm to the shower.

Damn him, I don't want to feel like shit. Why couldn't he just answer his phone?

I storm into the bathroom and turn on the hot water.

Damn fucking libido. That bitch is going to Hell and she is dragging me down with her.

———

I pace back and forth in the hospital courtyard. It's my lunch break and I need to talk to someone about this. I dial my sister April's number. She's my best friend, and I've been waiting for her to wake up. She's six years younger than me and has just moved to London. She got a scholarship for a law degree at some fancy university over there. I miss her desperately.

"Did you wet the bed?" she grumbles. "Its fucking early, Lize."

"Oh my God, April, it's a fucking disaster."

"What is?"

"Nathan and I made out," I whisper as I look around guiltily. "Well, we didn't make out—there was no kissing—but we felt each other up, and he was kissing my neck."

"Good."

My eyes bulge from their sockets. "What do you mean, good?"

"About time."

"Are you fucking insane?" I whisper angrily. "This is a disaster and now he's angry at me."

"Why?"

"Because he thinks I don't care about our friendship."

"Oh God." She sighs. "Was he hard?"

"Yes." I feel naughty even discussing this. "Very hard."

"Did you like it?"

"Will you stop it?"

"No, this was always going to happen. He adores you, I could see that from the day I first met him and saw you together."

"Have you forgotten one very important detail?" I whisper. "He likes men."

"And you, apparently." I can tell she's smiling.

"This isn't funny."

"It kind of is." She laughs. "Stop being frigid and just have sex with him to find out if he's as hot as I imagine he is. I want all the details."

"Oh my God!" I snap. "You are no help."

She laughs again.

"How are you anyway?" I ask. "Settling in any better?"

"Ugh, I don't know if I've done the right thing, Lize. I feel like a fish out of water over here."

"Oh no, why?"

"I don't know." She sighs. "Everyone in the dorms is just so young and into partying, you know? I knew I'd be a little older than everyone, and it's one of the reasons I came to London. It was the only place I could get a full scholarship that included all my accommodation. But seriously, the drugs, the orgies, the fake giggles... it's just not my style."

"They'll settle down. Surely they can't keep this up. What is it, like, week eight?"

"It's getting worse, not better."

"Why don't you move into your own place?"

"Have you seen the price of rent for apartments in London? It's ludicrous. Even the dumps are way out of my price point."

I exhale heavily. "Hang in there, babe. Try and find a better paying job."

"I am."

I smile. "I'm so proud of you."

"Thanks, Lize. Some days I think I must be crazy."

April broke up with her fiancé when she caught him cheating with a girl he worked with. He broke her heart. She packed her clothes and left everything in their house which they had bought together. She's now following her dream to become a lawyer, and she's starting over from scratch with nothing to her name.

She's the bravest, badass bitch I know.

"How's the coffee house going?" I ask.

"Good. I love it there, and the girls I work with are so nice. We're going out on the weekend."

"See? You'll settle in, I know you will, and I'm going to come and see you as soon as I can."

"Great, now go talk to Nathan. I'm sure he's as stressed as you are."

"Yeah, I guess." I sigh.

"Call me tonight."

"Okay, love you."

"Bye, love you, too."

————

I'm sitting in the office at the Martyr Hospital, trying to concentrate on the task at hand.

But I can't. I'm freaking out about Nathan and what I've done.

I should have listened to the warning signals my body was giving me. We have been acting different toward each other lately. If I'd just listened to my gut and taken a step back from him, this wouldn't have happened.

I hear a familiar voice out in the hall near recovery.

I jump up and step out into the corridor, where Nathan is talking to a nurse about a patient.

His eyes come to me.

"Dr. Mercer," I say. "Sorry to interrupt."

"Yes," he says as if I'm an annoyance.

"Can I see you in my office for a moment when you're finished here, please?"

"I have to get going. I have an appointment."

"It will take one minute," I reply sharply.

He clenches his jaw, unimpressed by my tone. "Fine."

I march back into my office. He can be such an asshole when he wants to be. Moments later, he walks into my office and puts his hands into his suit pockets. "What do you want, Eliza?"

"What do you mean, what do I want?" I whisper angrily.

"Exactly what I said."

"Are we going to talk about last night?" I ask.

"Nothing to talk about," He snaps.

"Are you kidding me? If there was nothing to talk about, why did you leave last night?"

"Because I wanted to." He sneers.

I narrow my eyes. Nathan is never like this with me. This is the behaviour he saves for everyone else. "What is your problem?"

"*You* are my fucking problem."

"Me?" I point to my chest. "What did I do?"

"Oh, please." He scoffs with an eye roll. "You know exactly what you fucking did."

My fury begins to boil. "And what is that?"

"Waving your half-naked ass all over my dick, and..." He clenches his jaw as if to stop himself spitting out poison.

"You were massaging me." My eyes bulge. "It was your hands on me. Are you kidding?"

"Do I look like I'm fucking kidding? What is this? A big joke to you?"

I frown. He's really rattled by this. "Nathan, calm down. So, we got a little tipsy and crossed the line. It was just an accident."

"That won't happen again." He growls.

"You're overreacting."

His eyes nearly bulge from their sockets. "And you are underreacting. It's blatantly obvious that you don't give a flying fuck about our friendship." He heads for the door.

What the hell?

"We'll talk about it tonight." I try to calm him—he's about to have a heart attack or something.

"There is no tonight, Eliza."

"Why not?"

He glares at me. "I need some space."

My heart drops. "From me?"

"Yes. From you."

We stare at each other for a moment. Something *has* shifted between us.

He rushes out the door. I stare at it for a moment, shocked.

I pinch the bridge of my nose. For fuck's sake... what a disaster.

Nathan

"Nathan, this way, please." Elliot smiles as he calls me from his waiting room. I follow him into his office and take a seat.

"How are you?" He smiles.

"Terrible." I've been rattled since seeing Eliza at the hospital this afternoon.

The look on her face.

He sits down. "Tell me, what's been happening? I take it there have been developments with Eliza?"

I drag my hand down my face. "It's gotten worse. Everything is worse. I can't even look at her now."

He frowns. "Why is that?"

"Last night." I screw up my face at the memories. "We fought, and then we went out to dinner and had cocktails." I pinch the bridge of my nose.

"What did you fight about?"

"My jealousy."

"We'll come back to that. Go on."

"We got into bed and... she just felt so good, you know? I couldn't help myself. For two hours before that, I'd been ...." I swallow the lump of shame in my throat. "Picturing her in every sexual position known to man." I pause for a moment. "Picturing her head between my legs... her mouth full of... me."

"I see."

"When I got into bed, something snapped."

He narrows his eyes. "How did this start?"

"Her back was sore, so I offered her a massage. I shouldn't have. I knew before I started that it was a bad idea. I knew it was wrong."

"It's not wrong to offer a massage to a friend, Nathan."

"It is when the sole purpose of it is to feel their body."

"You wanted to feel Eliza?"

I nod and close my eyes in regret. "More than anything."

"What happened?"

"I massaged her and then..." I think back to how she felt beneath my hands, and I feel my arousal creeping in again.

Fuck. Stop it.

"Go on, Nathan."

"We laid on our sides, and my hands were all over her body."

"What did she do?"

"She told me not to stop."

He frowns. "So, your fears may be unwarranted?"

My eyes flick to him. "My fears?"

"That she wouldn't want to be sexual with you?"

"I know that I can get her to want me... sexually," I stammer. "At least once. That's not my concern."

"What's your concern?"

"That the sex won't be what I think it will be."

He nods. "You're worried you won't like heterosexual intercourse."

"What happens then? What do I tell her? Sorry, I tried you out but we don't fit?"

"And you think that will be what ends your friendship?"

"One hundred percent. Or maybe I won't please her." I shrug. "I have no idea how to please a woman. I could be a huge disappointment to her."

"This is true. You could."

I run my hands through my hair in despair. The thought sickens me. "I hate this," I whisper angrily. "I hate feeling like this."

"Yes, let's talk about that. How are you feeling?"

"Like I'm about to explode. I've never wanted anyone that I can't have before."

"And being bisexual is confusing?"

I screw up my face in disgust. "I'm not bisexual."

"What do you think a bisexual person is, Nathan?"

"Somebody who has sex with anything."

"That's not true. A bisexual person is someone who is aroused by members of both sex."

"I'm not bisexual."

"Have you considered the possibility of being pansexual?"

"What's that?" I ask.

"A pansexual person doesn't see a body when they are attracted to someone. It's the personality and heart they desire, regardless of their sex."

I shrug as I contemplate that theory, that could be it. "Okay."

He pauses as if getting the wording right in his head. "Tell me... what's the worst possible scenario that could happen with Eliza?"

"That we have sex, and one of us likes it and the other one doesn't."

"You're afraid that you aren't going to like it?"

I nod. "Or that I won't know what to do with her body and therefore be a disappointment."

"Nathan, have you ever thought about the possibility of having sex with a female other than Eliza to see if you do like it?" My eyes search his. "Perhaps you could explore this side of your sexuality away from your relationship with Eliza."

I drop my head. Why haven't I thought of this before? "Why? Why am I feeling like this now, after all this time?"

"How old are you?"

"Thirty-four."

"Many people reach a deeper level of themselves around your age. They're searching for their truth. An awakening, if you will."

"You think being straight is my truth?" I whisper, horrified.

"I think that perhaps you are curious, which is completely normal." He pauses. "And I think that you are going to have sex with a woman at some stage in your life— curiosity like this doesn't just disappear. Now, whether that is with your Eliza or a stranger will be up to you."

I listen intently.

"You need to calculate the risk, Nathan, and only you can do that. Do you want to explore your sexuality without the chance of hurting Eliza? Or do you want to risk it? The choice is yours."

I think for a moment.

"Is there another woman who interests you? One where the gamble isn't so high?"

I swallow the lump in my throat. "There are a lot of

options, I guess. I don't have a problem getting female attention. Women throw themselves at me all the time."

"Anyone in particular that takes your interest?'

I think for a moment. "There is... one woman."

"Who is she?"

"Her name is Stephanie. We go to the gym together. We have coffee sometimes."

"And you're attracted to her?"

"I wouldn't say attracted." I scowl. "It's not like my attraction to Eliza. She is gorgeous, though."

"But you feel something there? Is she attracted to you?"

"Yes, she wants me. She makes her intentions clear quite often."

He raises his eyebrow. "Perhaps you should investigate this further. Calculate the risks with each woman."

"There's no contest. I'm not risking Eliza... under any circumstance."

"But you *are* curious about the female body and how it would work with yours?"

My brow furrows as I contemplate his question. "Yes. I am."

"Can you imagine yourself naked with Stephanie like you do with Eliza?"

"No," I answer without hesitation.

"Do you think that's something that you want to investigate?"

I twist my lips as I think. "Perhaps."

"Can I make a personal suggestion, Nathan? Off the record."

"Of course."

"If it were me, and I was searching for answers, I would perhaps explore the possibility of having casual sex with another female before I made any decision that may risk a lifelong friendship. This is your sexual awakening, nobody else's. Don't tie your decision to one person. This isn't about Eliza; this is about you. You would be doing yourself a disservice to rush into anything. And may I add, you haven't been sexually active with anyone for a long time."

"Meaning?"

"Perhaps your body is giving you distorted signals. You love Eliza, so it's presenting as arousal but perhaps your body is just craving physical touch again."

"That makes sense," I nod as I contemplate his advice. "Thank you."

"What are you going to do?"

I sit up with renewed purpose. "I don't know, but you're right about one thing: I do need to know if I'm sexually compatible with a woman." I hold my hand out to shake his. "Thank you." I give him a lopsided smile. "You've actually helped me today."

"I didn't help you at the last visit?"

"No." I smirk. "You pissed me off."

He chuckles and dips his head playfully. "Then my mission was accomplished."

———

I bounce the tennis ball against the wall and it falls back into my hands.

I do it again.

And again.

I'm lying on my bed with my feet on the pillows. For two hours, I've been bouncing this ball while staring at the wall.

My mind isn't here, though. It's with my Eliza, across town. I keep seeing her face when I told her I needed space.

It hurt her.

What a joke! I don't want space. I want just the opposite. I want to be curled up in her bed, with her head on my chest and her heart beating against mine.

My heart hurts not being with her tonight.

But I have to do this. I wasn't lying.

I *do* need space.

I have to get my head around this and navigate my next move. Elliot's advice keeps going around and around in my head on repeat. Was he right?

Can I imagine myself touching another woman like I want to touch Eliza?

I scroll through my phone until I get to the name Stephanie. My thumb hovers over her name.

What would I even say to her?

Hi, I don't really want anything to do with you but you're smoking hot and I know you could turn me on and get the job done. Do you mind if I use your body to find out if I like sex with a woman?

I close my eyes in disgust and throw my phone onto the floor.

Fuck this.

I stare at the wall for a while longer. I wonder what my girl is doing now. This is our second night apart in two years.

I blow out a deep breath and throw the tennis ball at the wall. It bounces and flies back into my hands.

I do it again.

It's going to be a long night.

8

Eliza

IT'S JUST GONE 5:00 p.m., and I pack up my desk. My phone beeps with a text.

It's from Samuel.

Hope you're feeling better

God, I'm such a bitch.

I've been so upset about Nathan and my fight on Tuesday that I didn't have the energy to go out with Samuel. I lied and told him I was sick. Guilt fills me.

I'm a bad person.

I text back.

You're so thoughtful.
Thank you, I am. I'll call you later.

I put my phone into my bag. I'm supposed to be going to Vermont for the weekend for Nathan's father's birthday tomorrow night, and I haven't even heard from him.

I shake my head in disgust. What is going on? Maybe I should just call him.

He's obviously having some kind of meltdown.

No, be strong. He said he needed space. Give it to him.

I hear a knock at the door, and I look up to see Henry there. "Eliza."

"Oh, hi, Henry." I smile.

"I just wanted to say how happy I am that you joined us. The girls all love you and are telling me how lovely you are. It's all working out wonderfully."

"Really? Thank you."

Turns out I was wrong about Henry. He's not sleazy, he's just weirdly honest, and he's like that with everyone he speaks to. So far, this week he has told our receptionist that he dislikes her perfume, and then another that her skirt is too short. The girls were having a laugh in the lunchroom about when they first met him and how wrong their first impressions of him were. I didn't tell them what he said to me, of course, but hearing their stories most definitely put me at ease with him.

"You heading off?" I ask.

"Yes. Going to the gym before I need to give myself liposuction."

I giggle. "Okay, have fun."

He smiles, and with a wave, he takes off down the hallway, and I continue packing up my desk. Everything is falling into place except with Nathan. That feels like it's falling apart.

At least I'm going out to dinner with the girls tonight. I would love to talk to them about it and get their thoughts, but I can't. They are both friends with Nathan and me, and if I tell them that we had a moment in bed, it will become a thing. And I don't want anyone to know, and I can't trust them not to tell the boys...because then it will be a big thing and it will snowball out of control.

Ugh, what a mess.

I pick up my bag and make my way to the elevator. I'm eating all the food tonight.

The diet is officially over.

"So, anyway," Jolie says as she waves her wineglass in the air. "I have a confession."

"What?" Brooke asks.

We are at our favorite Thai restaurant.

"I may have..." She pauses as she looks between us. "I may have called Santiago today."

"The porno guy?" Brooke frowns.

I screw up my face. "What?"

"I can't stop fucking thinking about him." Jolie grins. "He's so damn hot, and did you see the way he fucks?"

Brooke's eyes widen. "You can't be serious!"

"I am." Jolie sips her wine as if totally convinced. "I need it. I've dreamt of having sex with him every night this week. He's had me in every position possible. I'm desperate to go to sleep at night."

"You're going to end up being just another pussy on his phone, being shown to other women when he picks them up to fuck them," I warn her.

"I don't care. In fact, I think that's half the attraction. That was the hottest thing I've ever seen. You have to admit it."

I stare at her, horrified. "Have you lost your fucking mind?"

"He most definitely has diseases." Brooke huffs into her wine glass. "All of them."

"He had a rubber on in the videos."

Brooke and I look at each other and burst out laughing. "How close were you watching? Were you studying it?" I ask.

"Very fucking close." She mutters dryly as she sips her wine. "He's calling me tonight."

"Oh God." I wince.

"You're going to meet him?" Brooke gasps.

"No. I'm going to get him to dirty talk me for a while. I need some phone love."

"Don't meet up with him yet," I warn her. "Find out if he's a serial killer first."

"I don't care." She tuts. "It would be worth it. If he fucks like that, he can do what he wants to me."

We all giggle.

"What a way to go."

An hour later, I get into the elevator in my building and my phone vibrates in my handbag. I dig it out. The name Phyllis lights up the screen.

Shit. Nathan's mother. I'm supposed to be making the fucking birthday cake. I haven't spoken to Nathan at all. What am I going to tell her?

I steel myself to answer happily.

"Hi, Phyllis."

"Hello, darling."

"How are you?" I smile. I really don't have to pretend to be nice. I adore this woman.

"I'm so looking forward to seeing you both this weekend."

"Did you speak to Nathe?"

"No, he's not answering his phone. He must be working."

I roll my eyes, knowing he's not working. He's just not answering her. I speak to his mother more than he does.

"Yes, he must be," I lie.

Jerk.

"Listen, darling, I was wondering... do you think I should get some extra catering in for Saturday night?"

"Why?"

"Because all these people who weren't originally coming have all messaged me and are now coming after all."

"Oh. Have you added to the menu since we worked everything out?"

"No, and now there are close to sixty people coming. I'm freaking out that I don't have enough food. Do you think that would be enough?"

"I'll have to look at our list but don't worry, we can make extra if we need to."

Nathan's mother doesn't have a daughter. I'm it.

"I don't want you cooking all day on Saturday," she says.

"I really don't mind. You know I love cooking." And besides, it will also mean less time I have to spend with him.

"Oh, darling, thank heavens I have you. Jessica offered to help but we both know what her cooking is like. I'll leave her to drink wine with us while we cook."

"She's good at that." I giggle. Jessica is Nathan's brother's girlfriend. She's hilarious, and it's true, a terrible cook who burns everything she touches. But she definitely entertains us in the kitchen. "I'll look at the list and call you back, okay?"

"Okay, speak soon."

I hang up and text Nathan.

What time is our flight tomorrow?

He texts back.

You don't need to come.

My head nearly bursts with frustration.

**I'm not coming to see you, you conceited jerk.
What time is the flight?**

No answer. I walk up the corridor and wait... and wait...
I open the door as I stare at my phone. *Text back, asshole.*

I'll pick you up at 5:00 p.m. from work.

I text back.

Don't be late.

An answer immediately bounces back.

Don't push me.

I narrow my eyes, and text back.

Don't you push me!

———

5:00 p.m. on the dot, my phone beeps with a text.

I'm downstairs.

I exhale heavily. Just reading his name on a text infuriates me. This weekend should be interesting. *No fighting*, I remind myself.

I look around, have I forgotten anything?

I grab my small suitcase and jacket, and I make my way downstairs.

Nathan's black Tesla is parked in a loading zone. He sees me approaching, gets out of the car, and he takes my bag from me.

"Hi," he says in a clipped tone as he puts it in the trunk.

"Hi." Without making eye contact, I get in the car and slam the door.

Moments later, he pulls out into traffic. His jaw ticks as he looks in the rearview mirror. He's clenching his teeth, and I know he's still pissed. This is all apparently my fault.

Well, screw him.

He's acting like a complete baby.

So what? We got drunk and had a momentary brain snap. So what? He had an erection. I've felt that damn thing in my back every morning for two years, he's kidding himself if he thinks this is something new for me. He's acting like he's been violated or something. He was there and in the moment, too, but of course, he's blaming me.

Ugh.... boils my blood just thinking about it.

I cross my arms and look out of the window. Well, if he doesn't want to talk, neither do I.

Twenty silent minutes later, we arrive at the airport, and Nathan pulls into the long-term parking lot. He scans his card, and the boom gate rises to let us in. My eyes flick over to him.

He parks, gets out of the car and goes to the trunk. He puts my suitcase down.

"I'm surprised Samuel didn't drive you here," he says dryly.

I roll my eyes. "Here we go."

"I'll give you here we fucking go."

I snatch my suitcase off him and march off toward the check-in lounge. I can hear his suitcase wheeling along behind me.

"Don't walk off on me."

"I'll do whatever I want." I huff.

"Don't push me."

"Nathan," I warn. "Cut it out, stop acting like a baby."

I march on, and he hurries to catch up with me. We get to the road and he grabs my hand. I don't pull away because I know he'll go thermonuclear. My road crossing skills aren't worth the meltdown.

"How am I a baby?"

"Look at you!" I snap. "We got drunk, Nathan. We had a temporary brain snap. It was nothing."

He smiles sarcastically. "I see how this is." He drops my hand and marches off in front. I roll my eyes, fuck's sake. What is his problem? We never fight like this for an extended time.

I follow him into the building and over to the check-in. The line is huge, and we wait in the roped-off section. I take out my phone and scroll through Instagram. My phone pings as a message comes through from Samuel.

I glance up to see that Nathan is reading over my shoulder, and I snatch my phone away. "Do you mind?"

"Not at all." He glares at me.

I widen my eyes. "Will you stop?"

"He's an idiot."

"And I will find that out in my own time." I shake my head in frustration. The truth is that I already know I don't like Samuel, but still. "I don't tell you who to date."

He looks at me, deadpan.

"Not that I would even know who you date," I mutter under my breath. "Mr. Secretive." I mouth.

He rolls his eyes and we step forward in the line. We stay silent for another ten minutes until we are called up to the desk. Nathan hands over our passports.

"Hello, how are you this evening?" the ticket lady asks.

"Fine, thanks." Nathan's tone is clipped and his face emotionless.

"Do you have any checked luggage?" She smiles.

"No, just carry on." He looks around impatiently.

She eyes Nathan. I can tell she's thinking what a handsome bastard he is. For once, I can actually agree with someone. His bastardness really is eclipsing his handsomeness today.

She prints our tickets, and he tucks them into the inside pocket of his suit jacket. "Thank you, have a good night." He marches off.

I give her an embarrassed smile. "He's not my boyfriend," I whisper.

She widens her eyes in a thank god symbol. "Have a good weekend."

"I'll try."

Nathan stops still at the gate, and I walk past him. "Why are you so rude?"

"I waited for you, what are you talking about?"

I keep walking past him. "I meant to her, you jerk."

We go straight to our usual bar. We fly a lot between my parents and his parents and all his work conferences. We know the drill.

We both take a seat at the bar. "What will it be?" the bartender asks.

"I'll have a Blue Label scotch and a margarita, please!" Nathan orders.

"Sure thing." The bartender gets to making our drinks and we both stay silent.

"What did he want?" Nathan eventually asks.

"Who?" I frown.

"Don't act dumb, Eliza, it's pissing me off."

"Will you stop it?" I whisper angrily. "Samuel told me to have a good weekend, that's all. I don't even like him, Nathan, so stop carrying on about it."

"You don't like him?"

"We ate lunch together, and to be honest, there was no chemistry. I don't know him well enough to decide yet."

"He's a dick."

I let out a heavy sigh, honestly this man is impossible.

Nathan is the most complicated person I know, and when someone is aggressive toward him, his natural instinct is to fire it straight back. He's like a mirror projecting your reflection, and I know the only way to ease his temper is to ease my tone.

"Then, stop it." I put my hand on his on the bar to try and calm him. "We are going away for the weekend, why are we fighting all the time lately? Why are you being such a jerk?"

He looks down at our hands.

"Nathe, I've missed you this week, and I don't want to spend the weekend fighting about crap."

He turns his hand over and takes mine in his. "Me neither." He sighs sadly, and he picks up my hand and kisses my fingertips.

I smile. There he is. My sweet man is back.

"Why are you so angry with me?" I whisper.

"I'm not angry with you." His eyes search mine. "I'm angry with myself."

"Why?"

"Here you go." The bartender puts our drinks in front of us.

"Thank you," we both reply.

"I took advantage of you when you were drunk," Nathan says quietly.

"What?" I frown. "No, you didn't."

"I did, Eliza. By letting me into your bed, you trust me with your body and I betrayed that trust."

I smile up at my beautiful best friend, always so gallant in looking after me. "Nathe..." I lean up and kiss his cheek. I've missed the feel of his stubble against my skin. "We are a team, you and I. I know you would never take advantage of me. I was there, remember? I was tipsy, too. We just got a little carried away and lost in the moment. That's all."

I stare up at him and brush the hair back from his forehead. His big blue eyes search mine before they drop to the floor. "I can't fuck this up between us, Lize. Our friendship means everything to me."

"You won't, it was one time. It's okay, I promise you that I don't think anything of it. It's okay."

He puts his arms around me and pulls me to him. I smile as he holds me, but after a while, an uneasiness fills me.

There's an edge to his grip, and it feels like fear.

"Baby, what's going on?" I whisper.

"Everything," he whispers as he pulls away and his eyes search mine. "Everything's changing."

He's anxious about me starting to date again, or maybe it's just Samuel. I put my hand on his thigh to reassure him. "Nathe, we will never change."

"Promise me." He cups my face in his hand and dusts his thumb over my bottom lip as he stares at me. "Promise me that whatever happens in our life, we will always be close."

I smile softly up at my beautiful man. "I promise."

My face is cupped in his hand, his eyes hold mine, and then they slowly drift down to my lips.

My heart stops.

Is he going to kiss me?

We stare at each other in the airport bar, surrounded by people, and I have no idea what's going on here.

Time stands still, and I lean closer.

"Do you want another one?" the bartender interrupts. We jump back from each other. My heart is racing, and I frown, totally dishevelled. I pick up my glass and drain it. "Yes, please."

Nathan picks up his drink and drains his scotch. We sit in silence for a while as we stare straight ahead. I'm rattled.

He's rattled.

I think we just had a moment.

Maybe, I imagined it.

We couldn't have had a moment—that's impossible.

I'm not the right sex for Nathan.

I go over the last few days in my head and if Nathan wasn't the way he is, I would swear something is happening between us. The jealousy, the touching, the longing stares and the fights.

The bartender puts my drink in front of me, and I pick it up and take a huge gulp.

I look over at Nathan and fake a smile. Sadness creeps into my heart.

The sooner I start dating someone else, the better. I think I'm falling for my best friend.

And this can only end badly. A sense of dread fills me because I know that we could never be like that. No matter how much we care for each other, it just can't be.

My best friend's love is completely unobtainable.

Nathan stares down at his fingers on the bar, his face solemn, and I think he knows it, too.

———

The car pulls up out the front of the grand house. We are in Vermont at Nathan's parents' farm. We flew into New York and got onto a connecting flight. Now, it's the middle of the night.

Nathan and I have been quiet, both lost in our own thoughts.

On the plane, I rested on his shoulder while he read his book but my eyes weren't closed and I could see that he didn't turn the page for the entire six hours.

What was he thinking about?

Maybe that's why he was so upset that we crossed the line. Maybe he could sense something that I haven't up until today.

Nathan gets our things out of the trunk of the rental car, and the front door of the house opens. His mom and dad come out to greet us.

"Eliza." Phyllis smiles as she wraps me in her arms. "Oh, it's so good to have you both home."

"My turn, woman." Neil laughs as he swats her away. Nathan's father wraps me in his arms. "How's my favorite girl?"

I giggle as he squeezes the life out of me.

"I'm right here, you know?" Nathan says dryly, holding out his hands.

"Oh, darling, so you are." Phyllis laughs. "Come here."

He hugs her with a big smile, and then he shakes his dad's hand.

"Come in, come in." Neil ushers us inside.

"Why are you two up so late?" Nathan asks.

"We were in bed but set the alarm," Phyllis says.

Nathan rolls his eyes. "We can let ourselves in, Mom."

"I know, darling. I just wanted to make sure you got in safe. I'll let you get to bed now; you must be both exhausted."

"We are, thank you." He kisses his mom and shakes his dad's hand again. "Good to be home. We'll see you in the morning."

"Bright and early for a walk, Lize?" his dad asks me.

"You got it. I brought my runners."

I follow Nathan up the stairs and into our room. It's gorgeous here—a huge property. It's a beautiful house with rolling green hills all around. We always stay in the same room in the guest wing. It's separate from the rest of the house. It has its own bathroom and a huge king bed with all the trimmings.

Nathan puts the suitcases down and rubs his hands over his thighs. His eyes rise to mine. He seems nervous.

"I'm going to go downstairs and make a cup of tea," I say. "Do you want anything?"

"No, thank you. I'll take a shower, I'm beat."

I go downstairs and make my tea. The rest of the family have gone to bed so I sit at the kitchen island counter for a while. I'm grappling with everything. My head is spinning.

Confusion.

Why am I feeling like this about him?

Why now, after all this time, does it feel different between us?

Did we have a moment at the airport?

I drop my head into my hands. I'm just so confused.

Fifteen minutes later, I go back up to bed to find the room in darkness, lit only by the lamps. Nathan is shirtless in bed. I can see every muscle in his torso and shoulders.

His big blue eyes meet mine across the room, and my stomach flutters.

What the fuck is going on?

"I'm going to take a shower." I fake a smile.

With a racing heart, I put my hair up in a top bun and get under the water. I have it so hot that it tingles my skin.

I don't know what's wrong with me.

I shower and brush my teeth, and I put on the pretty pink nightdress that Nathan's parents bought me for Christmas before I walk out.

Nathan's eyes lift from his book, and he watches me get into bed.

I wonder has he turned the page yet?

I get in and pull the blankets up. Nathan rolls onto his side toward me and leans up onto his elbow.

We stare at each other, and something hangs in the air between us.

Longing...

I'm longing for him to touch me again, and I want to stand up and take off my nightdress.

I want him to see me. I want him to want me.

Where the fuck is this coming from?

Nathan's dark eyes drink me in. His stare is hungry, wanting, and eventually he whispers, "Have you ever wanted something so badly that you can taste it?"

Goosebumps scatter up the back of my neck.

"Like you might just fucking die, if you don't get it," he breathes.

My heart begins to race.

What's he talking about?

I stay silent.

He cups my face in his hand and stares down at me. His thumb dusts over my bottom lip for the second time tonight, and my heart feels like it stops.

"Say something," he whispers.

My eyes search his, but I have no words. I have to be reading this wrong.

He doesn't like women.

"What do you want me to say?" I whisper.

He stares at me for a moment, and then his brow furrows. Without another word, he flops back onto his pillow and exhales heavily. "Don't worry about it."

We stay silent for a few minutes until, eventually, he rolls over and turns his back to me.

I watch him, unsure what to say. You could cut the air between us with a knife. It's thick with tension, filled with angst.

"Goodnight, Eliza." He sighs.

I close my eyes in regret. I don't know what he wanted me to say, but I obviously didn't get it right.

"Goodnight, Nathan."

9

Eliza

THERE'S a knock at the door.

I frown as I try to focus my eyes. "Hello?" I call.

The door opens, and Neil comes into view. "Ready for our walk, Eliza?"

I smile. "Sure am." It's our little ritual when I'm here. Neil gives me the walking tour around the property and shows me all the baby animals that have been born since I was here last. I glance over and notice Nathan isn't in bed with me.

"Give me a minute to get dressed, I'll be right down." I smile.

"Sure thing. I'll put the coffee on." He disappears down the stairs, and I get up and peer into the bathroom. "Nathe?"

He's not here. I open the door and look down the hallway, left and right. It's still nearly dark. Where would he go?

I walk down the hallway and notice a bedroom door is closed. I slowly open the door and peek in.

Nathan is asleep in the bed.

My heart drops. He didn't want to sleep with me.

I quietly close the door and tiptoe back down the hall to sit on the edge of my bed in the semi-dark room. I drop my head in sadness.

He didn't want to sleep with me.

Nathan

My mother's laugh rings out through the house, and I stop on the spot and listen for a moment. She loves Eliza. Both her and Dad beam with happiness when she is home.

Home. What a joke. This isn't her home, this is my home, and she's not my girlfriend. I need to stop this fucking nonsense before I drive her away forever.

I walk to the doorway of the kitchen and lean on the doorjamb as I watch them.

Eliza is wearing an apron that my mother bought her for her birthday one year. She's chopping up vegetables and smiling as she talks.

"Yes, you wouldn't believe the things that people get fixed. The other day, someone had their labia cut off. Well, trimmed, actually."

"Oh God, like with scissors?" Jessica, my brother's girlfriend, winces.

"I think so." Eliza shrugs.

"Are you serious? Can you imagine how much that would frigging hurt?" Jessica is sitting at the stool icing cupcakes while my mom is mixing something in a bowl. They listen as Eliza relays the ins and outs of her new job.

"And what's your new boss like?" Mom asks her.

"He's really nice." Eliza smiles. "Although, I got the wrong idea about him in the interview."

"Why?" Jessica asks.

Eliza stops chopping. "He's just really forward, and I kind of got the feeling that he liked me."

What?

She goes back to chopping and shrugs. "But now I realize that he's just super upfront and doesn't mince his words. He has no mouth to brain filter at all, so if he thinks something, he just blurts it out."

"What did he say that made you think that he liked you?" Mom asks.

"He told me that he didn't think he could hire me because he found me attractive."

What the fuck?

I step back from the door so I can listen, unnoticed. Who says that in an interview? I get a vision of strangling Henry fucking Morgan.

How dare he?

"What?" Mom splutters with a giggle. "That's so inappropriate."

Eliza laughs. "I know, right? I was so shocked at the time, but I know now that it was just a misunderstanding."

Fury begins to pump through my veins.

"But I told him that Nathan was my boyfriend so he knows I'm not interested," Eliza adds.

Mom laughs. "Oh, wouldn't that be something? You and Nathan together. All of my prayers would be answered."

Jessica laughs. "I'll say, although being married to a plastic surgeon would have its perks, too. You could design your own body. What would you get done if you could have anything? Like, anything in the world. I think I'd have a nose job."

"Oh, I'd get a boob lift, for sure," Mom replies. "I've always wanted one."

Their line of conversation moves onto plastic surgery and its horror stories, and I walk out into the back yard.

Henry Morgan likes her.

What the fuck? *He likes her.*

I knew it. I just want to punch something, hard.

"What's wrong with you?" my brother Alex asks. "Looks like you want to kill someone."

"It's tempting."

"Who's tempting?" He laughs.

"You boys going to go into town and pick up that alcohol order for me?" Dad calls. "Can you swing by the rental place and pick up that extra canopy? I'm going to tack it on the side here. Rain is predicted for later tonight. It won't take us long to get it up, and it's better to be safe than sorry."

"Yeah," I call. "Okay, text me the address."

Half an hour later, I'm sitting at the bar with Alex.

"What is it?" he asks.

"What's what?" I sip my beer.

"What's wrong with you?"

I shrug. He knows whenever something is wrong with me, usually before I do. He's the only person I talk to, and he knows me better than anyone.

I can't hide from him.

"Shit's been going down."

"What shit? "

I shrug, I don't want to say it out loud.

"Shit with Eliza?"

My eyes shoot to his. "What makes you say that?"

"You like her, don't you?"

"She's my friend."

"Friends don't watch their friends like you watch her."

I frown. "How do I watch her?"

"I was watching you at breakfast—could almost read your mind. You want her, don't you?"

I clench my jaw, angered that I didn't hide it better. "I don't know what the fuck is going on with me lately." I sigh sadly.

"Why, what's happened?"

"I don't know, man." I rub my forehead in frustration. "I've started having these... thoughts... about her."

"Sexual?"

I nod.

"For how long?"

I exhale heavily. "A while ago things changed between us. But just lately I've got a raging boner every time I'm with her. It's like I'm barely hanging on to control."

"What did she say about it?"

"She doesn't know. Fuck!" I widen my eyes. "Are you stupid?"

"What changed between you?"

I frown at him, not understanding the question.

"You said that a while ago that things changed between you, so what changed?"

I blow air into my cheeks. "A couple of months ago, I stopped having sex with other people."

"Why?"

I shrug. "Didn't feel right."

He listens intently.

"But I didn't realize at the time that it involved Eliza.

Elliot thinks that I stopped having sex with people because I felt like I was betraying Eliza."

"Who's Elliot?"

"My therapist."

His eyes widen. "You're seeing a therapist?"

"I'm telling you, Alex, I'm fucked in the head over this. It's messing with me, big time."

"Well, what does the therapist say?"

"He thinks..." I pause as I try to articulate Elliot's words, "that perhaps I was unconsciously trying to protect myself from getting hurt again, and it's only recently that my body has caught up with my heart."

He listens intently as he watches me. "Is that what you think?"

I shrug and take a gulp of my beer.

"You do love Eliza." He offers an explanation.

"I do," I reply without hesitation. "No doubt about that. I have always loved her."

"So, what's the problem? If you love her and you're physically attracted to her, what's the problem?"

"Eliza is home to me, Alex. If I fuck this up..."

"Nathe." He sighs. "I know that Eliza is the only thing that kept you sane while you were going through your breakup with Robert, but...."

"She was." After I broke up with Robert, I went through a particularly wild time in my life. I was single and young with a broken heart. I'd never been sexually active and free before. It was all so new. I would party hard, and my friend dates with Eliza were the only thing that kept me on the straight and narrow. I toed the line because of her. I take a big gulp of my beer. "Another two, please," I ask the waiter.

"She probably doesn't feel the same, and... what if I don't like it?" I stare straight ahead.

"Like what?"

"The sex. How the fuck do you suddenly start liking women at the age of thirty-four?"

He shakes his head and laughs quietly, like I'm an idiot.

"What's that laugh for?"

"You want to hear what I think? I think that you just happened to fall in love with a guy first. And I think that it perhaps molded you into thinking that only men could give you the type of sex you want."

"What?" I scowl.

He holds his hand up. "Listen to me for a minute. You have said to me on many occasions that you like rough sex, have you not?"

"Yes."

"Tell me, Nathe, do you think that a woman could handle how rough you are in bed?"

"No. I don't." I shake my head. "No way."

"Do you think that when you broke up with Robert, you gravitated toward men because they were familiar to you and you didn't have to think? You could just fuck and forget about the world. Is it possible that you associate the type of sex you like... to the sex of the person?"

"What?"

"I believe that you think only men can take it how you want to give it."

I stare at him, a clusterfuck of confusion tearing through my mind.

"Nathe, women like it rough. I can't fuck Jessica any harder than I do."

"What are you saying?"

"I think that if you slept with a woman... you maybe wouldn't..." His voice trails off.

My eyes hold his, waiting.

"Okay, let's go through this." He begins to count on his fingers. "You don't have any gay friends, other than ex-boyfriends. Your male friends are all heterosexual. You hate gay bars. You hate anything camp. You have never picked up someone in a bar in front of anyone you know. You have never ever battled with your sexuality like most do. You have never battled with coming out because a title has never bothered you." He holds up his counted fingers. "That's eight. Ten. Don't you think that if you were truly a gay man that you would want the world to see who you really are?"

I sit back in my seat, affronted.

"You would be out and proud if that's who you really were. You're not ashamed of being gay."

"What are you saying?"

"I'm saying that maybe you just happened to fall in love with a guy first and that it doesn't have to define who you will love in the future."

My eyes drop to the counter in front of me. "I wouldn't change meeting Robert."

"I know."

We sit in silence for a while, and my head is spinning about his revelations.

"Tell me this, Nathe. If you could go out tonight and pick up anyone in the world, male or female, and have sex with them, who would it be?"

Eliza.

I can't bring myself to say it out loud. I exhale heavily and put my head into my hands.

"I feel like the walls are closing in. I've never been so

confused in my life." I sigh. "I'm watching things I shouldn't be watching. Thinking things I shouldn't be thinking." I shake my head in disgust. "I don't know what the fuck is going on with me, and you know what I noticed this week?"

"What?"

"Maria, my receptionist, has great legs."

He frowns.

"She's worked for me for four years, and just this week, I noticed she has great legs."

"Why?"

"You tell me." I gasp. "I'm like a fucking pubescent teen again. I'm confused and angry... anxious." I shake my head in frustration. "I'm having wet dreams and jerking off in Eliza's bathroom, for Christ's sake. I don't know what the fuck is going on with me or how to deal with it. It's like I've been rewired or something."

His eyes light up. "Yes. Maybe that's just what's happened? Maybe by not having sex with anyone, you've wiped the slate clean. You've been guided for so long by what's familiar, that maybe now, it's time for a change."

"But what if this has nothing at all to do with Eliza?" I ask.

"It might not." He shrugs. "All these new feelings you're having may be misplaced toward her. Maybe you're clinging to her because she wants to date again and you don't want to lose her."

"That's the worst thing I could ever do," I whisper.

"And the most selfish."

"Fuck." I pinch the bridge of my nose. "This is a nightmare. So much to... and all I want to do is... "

"You can't touch her. You can't fucking touch her until you get your shit sorted."

"I know."

"I mean it, Nathe. If you sleep with Eliza before you work out what's going on with you, you will fuck up everything."

"Do you think I don't fucking know this?"

We fall silent, once again, as we both stare at the bar.

This situation is impossible.

"That's if she'll have you. Assuming that she would even like you. I mean, I wouldn't if I were her."

I drop my head and chuckle. "Me neither."

Eliza

The music is pumping and the night has been a great success.

Everyone is dancing. I laugh as I watch Nathan swing his grandmother around by the hand. These old tunes that Nathan downloaded are a hit.

"Eliza?" Phyllis calls me over to the music stand.

"What's wrong?"

"Neil's phone is almost dead. Do we have any more back up music?"

"I'll run upstairs and get my phone," I tell her.

"You have the right music on it?" She frowns.

"No, but this is Nathan's playlist, and I'm pretty sure he downloaded it onto my phone today. Back in a sec."

I run inside and take the stairs two at a time. I go to the desk in our room. My phone is plugged into Nathan's computer, and I open it to make sure everything is finished.

I can hear the party going on downstairs. They are all laughing and clapping. The song *Bus Stop* is now playing. I smile as I imagine them all lining up and doing the dance.

Nathan's phone is sitting beside the computer, and I pick it up.

There are three missed calls from someone called Stephanie.

Hmm, that's weird.... Who's Stephanie?

I sit down at the desk, open the computer, and see if the download is complete.

Where do I look? My eyes scan the screen, and I click on the history.

Pornhub

"Pornhub. Jesus." I click out of it and smile with a roll of my eyes. Where do I see if the download is complete?

I glance back to the history. I never pegged Nathan as someone who would watch Pornhub. Curious, I click back on it.

It's a girl giving a guy head. She's naked, and he's watching her in the mirror behind her. He's really fucking her mouth as he pulls her by the hair.

Huh?

I scroll through the history to see there's a heap of porn on here.

"What?

I frown. "Nathan watches straight porn. *A lot* of straight porn."

I look at what he's been watching. They are all girls with long hair and great bodies.

It's hardcore stuff in every single one, and the girl is always getting absolutely hammered by a guy with a huge dick.

I hover over the history and scroll down to see the category.

Gay To Straight

My mouth falls open. "What the fuck?"

"What are you doing?" Nathan's voice snaps from behind me.

I spin toward him guiltily. "Just getting the music."

"Why are you on my history?" He takes the computer off me and slams it shut.

"You watch straight porn?"

"So?"

"Why?" I frown.

"What do you mean, why?"

"Why would you want to watch someone fuck a girl?"

He glares at me, and I can see the muscles ticking in his jaw.

"Nathan?"

He drops his head and stares at the floor.

"Answer me."

"I'm curious."

"Why?"

"Just drop it, Eliza."

"No. Explain this to me."

"This isn't how I wanted to tell you." He reaches for me, and I step back away from him as uneasiness fills me.

"Tell me what?"

"I've met someone."

What?

"Her name is Stephanie."

I stare at him, confused. I must have heard him wrong. "What did you say?"

"Can we talk about this later?"

"No."

"Now is not the time."

My eyes nearly bulge from their sockets. "Now is the time," I reply. "What do you mean you've met someone? A woman? You've met a fucking woman?"

He swallows the lump in his throat but doesn't answer me.

"Where? Where did you meet?"

He runs his hand through his hair in a fluster.

"Who is it?"

He stays silent, infuriating me further. "Start fucking talking, Nathan." I whisper angrily.

"Calm down."

"I will *not* calm down!" I snap. "Is this some sort of sick joke?"

He turns his back to me before he goes to the window and looks down at the party below.

Uneasiness fills me. "Nathan?"

Is this why he's been acting so weird lately?

I feel a lump forming in my throat.

"You said our relationship would never change," he replies quietly.

"And you told me you like men," I spit. My nostrils flare as I try to hold in tears. My gaze drops to the floor, he's been hiding this from me.

A woman.

"How long have you been lying to me?" I whisper.

He spins toward me, angered. "You think I want to lie to you? You think I want to go through this fucking shit?" He throws his phone and it hits the wall with force. I jump, startled. "I don't even know who I am anymore."

His silhouette blurs from my tears.

His eyes hold mine, and then, without another word, he picks up his computer and his phone from the floor and storms from the room.

I stare at a spot on the carpet for a long time, unsure what to think, unsure what to do. Did that really just happen?

Ten years.

I go to the window and look down at the party. Everyone is dancing and having the best time. I see Nathan take his computer and hook it to the speakers.

Who is she?

Betrayal washes over me like a wave in the ocean and I pinch the bridge of my nose as I try to calm myself down. And here I was thinking... feeling.

My stomach rolls at the thought of him with a woman. *Another woman.*

He was mortified for touching me the other night because he saw it as cheating on her. He doesn't want to sleep beside me anymore... because of her.

God, I'm a disaster.

And here I was thinking that there was something developing between us.

It has nothing to do with me.

My tears break the dam, and I drop to sit on the bed.

This hurts.

I always knew that one day I would lose him to someone else, but I was mollified by knowing that it would never be completely because I would always be the only woman in his life.

I think back and see the haunted look on his face, and his words come back to me.

I don't even know who I am any more.

Sadness fills me. That makes two of us.

Half an hour and a good cry later, I wash my face and reapply my makeup.

I'm here for Neil's birthday, and I need to get over myself.

I have no right to feel hurt. Nathan isn't my boyfriend—we're just friends.

I'm going to put a smile on my face, and I'm going to go

downstairs. I'm going to be the friend that Nathan needs. I can't stop seeing the pain on his face when he told me he doesn't know who he is.

I know who he is. He's a beautiful man that I care about, and I want to wrap him in my love and support him through whatever he's going through.

I practice my broad smile in the mirror.

"Nathan, let's dance," I say.

My smile slips because behind it I can see the hurt in my eyes, even if no one else will. There's no denying it to myself. I'm cut to the bone. A tiny part of my heart wishes it were me that Nathan had feelings for. Maybe that tiny part of my heart loves him, and maybe that tiny part of me will always feel like this.

I smile sadly. Nathan calls my vagina Tiny. Oh, the irony.

"Eliza?" I hear a voice call.

I quickly wipe my eyes and pat my cheeks. "In here!" I call happily from the bathroom.

Alex, Nathan's only brother, comes into view and smiles. "There you are. I was looking for you."

I put my lipstick back into my beauty case and zip it up. "I'm coming now."

His eyes linger on mine, and I know that he knows. Alex is the only person that Nathan talks to about his sexuality.

"You okay?" he asks softly.

I nod, but suddenly, I feel all weak again, and my tears simmer dangerously close to the surface. "Yep."

Don't be nice to me or I'll crack.

He sits on the side of the bathtub. "You want to talk about it?"

I shake my head. "Nope." I do, but I know that I can't, because I will cry and make this selfishly about me.

Why am I feeling like this?

Alex stands and takes me in his arms. The kindness of that act makes the stupid tears well again.

"I have to ask you something," he says. He pulls back to look at me. "Do you have feelings for Nathan?"

"I love Nathan, you know that." I sigh as I pull out of his arms.

"So, what do you make of all this?"

I exhale heavily. "I don't know. I guess I'm just rattled because of the way I found out. He didn't even tell me, Alex."

"He doesn't have feelings for her, he's just attracted to her. That's all. It doesn't mean anything."

"Same thing." I shrug.

"No, it's not—not for a guy. They are a mile apart."

"Did Nathan send you up here to check on me?"

He puts his hands into his jacket pockets, not wanting to answer me.

"That means yes." I roll my eyes. "And of course. I don't have feelings like that for Nathan. We're friends, Alex, that's all."

"So why are you upset?"

"Because he's been lying to me for ten years," I whisper in an outrage. "Never once in ten years has he mentioned a woman to me."

"Has he mentioned a man to you?"

"No, but..." I throw my hands up in frustration.

"Nathan is different from most people, Eliza. He doesn't talk about his feelings openly, not even to the people he sleeps with."

"Well, he tells you everything." I huff.

"You know why he tells me everything?"

"Why?"

"Because I walked in on him and Robert in a compromising position when they were sixteen."

I frown. "How old were you?"

"Eighteen. I talked to Nathan about it because he had no choice. I had seen it with my own eyes, so he eventually opened up and told me everything. It changed for us on that day. We grew closer. I understood where he was coming from and I became his only confidant."

"And what's he telling you now, Alex?"

"He's petrified that if he tells you the truth, he's going to lose you."

"So, he lied?"

His eyes hold mine. "He's just testing the waters with her, Lize. She means nothing. Trust me on this."

Are you for real?

Nathan's going to use a girl to test his waters, and Alex expects me to rejoice in this?

Anger bursts through me for him lying to me while lying beside me every night. For him using someone, for him sending his brother to talk to me instead of doing it himself, and for me acting like an immature idiot. The list is endless, and I can feel nastiness building on my tongue.

"I'm not discussing this with you, Alex." I storm from the bathroom and into the bedroom.

"Then discuss it with him!" he calls from behind me as he follows me out.

I turn like the devil. "The only word I am capable of saying to your brother at the moment is *liar*."

His face falls. "Don't be angry."

"I'm not!" I snap. "I'm going downstairs. You coming or not?"

His eyes hold mine and I know he's disappointed at how our talk has gone. How did he think this was going to go?

"I'll see you down there," he eventually replies.

"Fine." I turn and storm out.

It's official.

Mercer men are pissing me off.

––––––––

The plane bounces on its landing, and I grip my armrests. It's been a long trip home.

Actually, it's been a long twenty-four hours. Nathan and I have spoken about ten words to each other. He slept in the spare room again last night, and I guess if I was searching for an answer, he gave it to me then and there.

Things have changed between us; it's clear now.

Crystal clear.

We leave the plane, and I follow him through the airport in silence. When we get to the street, he takes my hand and my heart nearly breaks.

It won't be my hand he's reaching for soon.

It's the weirdest thing. Stephanie is probably a lovely girl and could make Nathan happy, but all I can feel for her at the moment is resentment. And rather than say something snarky and showing Nathan my horrible jealous true colors, I remain silent. If I don't say anything, I can't ruin it any more.

It's already pretty bad, I need to salvage it as soon as I get control of myself.

We arrive at his car. He puts our bags in the trunk and we drive out into the traffic.

There's a tension between us, and I'm trying to be a good friend, I really am. But it feels like I don't even know him anymore.

My mind keeps going over the last twenty-four hours, Pornhub...the kinds of sex he was watching. The moment I thought we had at the airport on Friday.

The lies.

Twenty silent minutes later, we arrive at my apartment. Nathan parks the car, he gets out, opens the trunk, and he takes his suitcase out, too.

"What are you doing?" I ask.

His face falls. "Can I stay?"

My eyes hold his. "Why, Nathe? So we can have more awkward silence?"

"What do you want me to say, Eliza? Tell me what can make this better so I can fix it."

"Nothing." I force a smile. "There is nothing wrong with you, Nathe. It's me. The problem is me."

"Why?"

"I just need some time to get my head around this."

"Around what?"

"Around you being with a woman."

He frowns, as if confused.

"It's just something that was never on my radar. I feel like —" I cut myself off.

"Like what?"

"Like there is this whole other part of you that I don't know."

"There is." His eyes hold mine. "I'm a very sexual person, Eliza."

I get a vision of him kissing a girl, and my stomach twists. I nod, unable to push anything intelligent through my lips. "Do you think about her when you're in bed with me?" I whisper.

His face falls. "No, I do not." He reaches down and tucks a piece of my hair behind my ear before he cups my face in his hand, and it's there between us again.

This feeling of want...

Belonging.

An emotion that has no place in this current climate.

"Can I please come up?" he whispers as his eyes search mine. "Let me make it up to you."

"Nathe," I sigh. "I've been a really shitty friend this weekend. You have nothing to make up to me. I should be making it up to you." I turn away from him. "I'll see you tomorrow night, okay?"

Then I remember my date with Samuel and I spin back to him. "Oh, I can't tomorrow night. I have something on."

"What do you have on?"

"I'm going out with Samuel."

"You told me you didn't like him."

I open my mouth to say that I was going tomorrow to tell him I don't want to see him anymore, but I stop myself.

I don't need to elaborate any more. Nathan cares for someone else now. "I don't know. Maybe he isn't so bad."

His jaw ticks.

"What's that look for?"

He shakes his head and steps back from me. "See you later."

"Nathan."

He ignores me and walks around to get back into his car.

"What's your problem? I'm just seeing if I like him, okay?"

He opens the door and holds onto it. "I don't like him, Eliza. I don't want you going out with him. Find someone else."

I put my hands on my hips, annoyed. "You don't get to pick who I date, Nathan."

"Oh, but it's all right for you to not speak to me all weekend when I tell you who I'm dating?"

My mouth falls open in surprise. "You lied to me."

"I have never fucking lied to you, Eliza. Not once." He bangs on the roof of his car.

"You didn't tell me!" I fire back as I feel adrenaline surge through my bloodstream.

Damn it, I *am* angry. I feel so betrayed.

"Because I wanted to tell you when I knew for certain what was going on."

"Well, it hurt."

He shakes his head.

"What's that look for?"

"You have no idea what hurts." He sneers.

"Oh, and you do?"

"Yeah, I fucking do."

I roll my eyes. "Oh, please, what Nathan? You tell me," I fire back. This is all about him, my anger begins to escalate. "You tell me what hurts!"

"It's wanting what you can't fucking have!" he cries. He glares at me and gets in the car before he speeds off down the street. I hear his tires screeching in the distance.

I stare down the street and feel my heart beating hard in my chest.

What the hell is going on with him?

10

Eliza

I WALK INSIDE with a heavy heart, and I get into the elevator.

Damn it, what the hell is wrong with me? The one time... the only fucking time, that Nathan needed me to be there for him, and I couldn't do it. I was so self-absorbed, so green with envy over her.

Ugh, I can't even say her name without twitching. *Stephanie.*

I close my eyes in regret. Why didn't I handle this better? So, he likes another girl. So he told me about it. Would I rather he lied?

And here I was thinking that me and him were perhaps... having moments.

I close my eyes and bump the back of my head onto the elevator wall.

You idiot.

God, Eliza, this takes the cake for the most selfish dick move of all time.

Your best friend opens up and tells you he's confused about his sexuality, and you get angry with him.

I'm a selfish fucking cow.

The doors of the elevator open, and I stare out into the corridor for a moment.

I can't go inside feeling like this. I hit the ground button, hard. I'm going over there. Nathan needs me, and God damn it, I'm going to show up.

This is not about me, this is about him. Why would I act like this?

Jealousy. God damn it, why am I so selfish?

Twenty minutes later, I get out of my cab outside Nathan's apartment.

I dial his number as I peer up to the lights on the tenth floor.

"What's wrong?" he answers.

"I'm downstairs."

"What, why?"

"Are you letting me in or not?" I ask in frustration.

"I'll call the doorman." The phone goes dead.

I pace as I wait out on the sidewalk. Nathan's building's security is tight, and this is the first time I've come here without him. He's always at my house. I've never needed a key to his. Jolie's words come back to me.

It's his booty-call place.

My stomach rolls at the thought. God, I really need to get a handle on myself here. What in the hell is all this ownership about? Moments later, the doorman opens the door to the building.

"Eliza?"

"Yes."

"Come in." He gestures to the lift with his hand and then swipes his security pass and presses the button to level ten.

"Thank you." I smile, and he gives me a kind nod.

I ride to level ten with nerves dancing in my stomach. After being shocked into silence all weekend, I've suddenly so much I want to say. Not that any of it makes sense...

The elevator opens to the private landing. The apartments in this building take up an entire floor. The door opens, and there he stands, wearing gray sweatpants and a T-shirt.

"Hi."

I force a smile. "Hi."

His hair is wet, and he's freshly showered. "What are you doing here?"

"I came to apologize."

"For what?"

"Being a crappy friend."

His eyes hold mine.

"It was just such a shock, you know? I didn't mean to get angry."

He gestures to the door and I walk past him into his apartment to look around at the swanky surroundings. Why he stays at my little dumpy apartment every night, I'll never know.

The floor is polished slate with oversized rugs over it, and the walls are all distressed brick with huge colorful abstract art hanging from them. It's set out like a trendy warehouse apartment. It's state of the art and it looks more like a funky bar than a home.

Nathan walks in and through to the kitchen. I tentatively follow him, unsure what to say. The kitchen is black, stainless steel with copper appliances. He goes to the tall wine fridge that goes nearly to the ceiling and has a glass door.He takes out a bottle of red wine and holds it up in question.

"Please." I nod and watch on as he pours two glasses.

He sits down on the other side of the island counter and takes his wine to his lips as his eyes hold mine.

"Can we talk about it?" I ask.

He shrugs, uninterested.

"We don't have to talk if you don't want to. That's okay, too," I offer. "I can just be here, you know, in case you need me." I hold my hand out over the counter and he stares down at it.

"You know that I need you, Eliza." He sighs sadly. "That was never in question."

"I'm here, baby. I'm not going anywhere, I promise."

I don't know what he has going on inside of that beautiful mind of his, but I want to be here for him. I love Nathan. I need to swallow my hurt and help him work this out.

He eventually takes my hand and squeezes it in his. He takes a sip of his red wine, and then swirls it around in his mouth as he watches me. The act is almost sensual.

And it's there again; this feeling that bounces between us. Only now I know for certain that it's all in my head, and yet I still feel it.

I get a lump in my throat and I want to howl to the moon.

"You tired?" he asks.

I nod. "It's been a long day."

"You should take a shower."

"I will."

We stare at each other. His eyes are dark, and I feel like he wants to say something, but then he doesn't. What is he thinking?

It's like I'm dealing with a completely different man—one I don't know.

I pick up my wine glass and walk into Nathan's bedroom, and then through to the bathroom, which is mostly made from beautiful, natural green stone. There's a huge pendant light that hangs over the big, black bathtub that sits in the center of the room.

We really should stay here more often. It's beautiful.

Oh, but that's right.... I won't even be here soon.

Stephanie will.

Stop it.

Dejected, I take a sip of my wine and put it down onto the counter. I turn the hot water on in the shower. I take my T-shirt off over my head.

"Can I get you anything?" he asks.

I turn to see Nathan leaning on the doorframe as he watches me. We stare at each other, and God, he's not the only one confused here. I have so many feelings running through my body. Empathy, jealousy and now when I look at him... ownership. Nathan is mine, and I can't imagine another woman laying a hand on him. I just can't stand it.

I close my eyes in regret before I open them again. *Cut it out.*

"No." I smile. "Thanks."

"You hungry?"

"Not really, are you?"

"No, I'm good."

"Let's just go to bed, hey? It's been a big day." I don't even know what to say to him so I'll just avoid the entire topic. Bed is the easiest option here.

"Okay."

We stare at each other for a moment. It's as if he's waiting for something, but god knows what it is.

"Are you all right?" I ask.

He nods, but he looks so sad.

Empathy fills me, and I smile softly and hold my arms out for him. "Nathe, come here, baby."

He hugs me. We squeeze each other tightly and stay in each other's arms for a long time. I can feel his torment.

"Can I do anything to help?" I whisper.

"Just be here." He kisses my temple.

"Okay." I hold him tighter. "I can do that."

"I'll let you shower." He leaves the room and, oh man, I feel like a bitch. I shower as quickly as I can and then throw my pajamas on before I walk out to find Nathan already in bed. He's lying on his side with his back to me.

"You're not reading tonight?" I ask.

"I'm tired."

"Okay." I switch off the lamp and climb in behind him. I'm unsure if I should touch him or not.

"Cuddle my back," he murmurs.

I smile and snuggle up to his back. I kiss it. "Good night, Nathe."

"Night, babe."

———

"Okay, we have a serious fucking issue on our hands right now." Jolie sighs.

"What is it now?" Brooke rolls her eyes.

We are at a café just around the corner from work. Jolie called an emergency lunch meeting and they came and met me.

"I can't stop thinking about him. I literally can't stop thinking about him."

"Oh, this is bad." I sigh.

Brooke frowns as she looks between us. "Who are we talking about?"

"Santiago." I huff.

"Oh God." Brooke winces. "Why? I'm trying my hardest to forget that shit." She fake shivers. "I'm scarred for life."

Jolie's eyes come to me in question.

"I get it, Jo. He was hot. And those movies... they were hot too," I say to comfort her. "I totally get it."

"I've called him, and we are going out," Jolie announces.

"What?" Brooke gasps.

"Why?" I ask. "What could you possibly achieve from that?"

"I want to be fucked like that," she blurts out.

The people on the table next to us look over, and I giggle. "Will you keep it down?" I whisper.

"It's all I think about, it's all I dream about. I need this fuck."

"Are you kidding me?" Brooke whispers. "He's going to film you having sex and show it to other women."

"I don't care."

"Oh God." Brooke and I roll our eyes.

"We are going out."

I shake my head, unable to believe this situation. "What's that code for?" I ask.

"Let's make a porno," Brooke mutters dryly.

I get the giggles. It feels good to be with the girls. Everything is so normal.

I desperately want to talk to them about Nathan, but he is their friend too, so I can't. It isn't my story to tell. This is his. If he wants anyone to know, it has to come from him.

I would dearly love to dissect my feelings with them on the whole thing though. I feel like I'm battling with this just as much as he is. I'm jealous and hurt, and to be honest, I just want Nathan for myself. I don't know why, but for some stupid reason I always assumed that if Nathan were straight, it would be me he would want.

Guess not.

Ugh.... I hate feeling like this. I'm annoyed that I do.

He was gone when I woke up this morning. He left a note saying he had something on and won't be over tonight. That, in itself, is weird, he normally won't stay away from me.

He's going to see her.

So, what if he is?

"How's your guy going?" Brooke asks, interrupting my thoughts.

"Who?"

"The guy." She widens her eyes.

"Oh, Samuel," I say with a curl of my lip. "He's okay, I guess."

"Not feeling it?" Jo asks.

"Nope." I sigh as I pick up my coffee. "Not in the least. I have to go out with him tonight."

"Just don't go." Brooke frowns.

"He's so keen and calling me all the time. I kind of feel like I have to explain why I don't want to see him, you know?"

"Ugh." They both wince.

"This is why it's easier not to date."

"Well, I don't know about what you boring bitches are doing tonight, but I'm sexting Santiago."

"Great," Brooke mutters dryly. "I look forward to seeing you on Missing Persons as a murder victim."

I chuckle.

"But, what a way to go." Jolie smiles darkly. "Fucked to death."

"At least the police will have footage as evidence, I guess." I smile.

Jolie gets out her phone to message Santiago, and she does a little dance in her seat. "This is so fucking exciting. Okay, what will I say?"

———————

I pace back and forth in my living room as I talk to April on the phone.

"He said that?" she asks. "He actually said that he likes another woman?"

"Are you listening to me at all? Her name is Stephanie."

"Well, fuck me. I did not expect that."

"You think I did?"

"How do you feel about that?"

"Pissed off. I always thought that if Nathan wanted a woman, it would be me."

"Same." She sighs. "I actually don't know if I believe it."

"Oh, come on April." I throw my hand up in the air. "Why would he lie about that?"

"I don't know. Why do men do anything they do?"

"Right?" I agree.

"Anyway, poof to him. If Nathan wants Sonya then he can have her."

"It's Stephanie."

"Whatever her fucking name is." She huffs. "We don't like her, regardless."

I love April. She always knows just what to say. "I guess I'm just feeling territorial."

"I would be, too. I'd be fuming mad."

"Hey." I frown as I remember what I wanted to ask her. "Are you okay for money? Do you want me to transfer you some? Because I can. I've been saving really hard."

"Don't you dare."

"April, I don't want you struggling over there alone."

"I'm not struggling. I'm budgeting hard."

"Isn't that the same shit?"

She laughs. "Probably."

"Why don't you call Roy and demand for all your money that the bastard took? You own half that fucking house, you know. It was your money used for the deposit."

"I don't want his slutty money. I want nothing to do with him ever again."

I exhale heavily. "Why are you so stubborn?"

"Because I'm not giving him the satisfaction of asking that prick for anything, least of all money." Just the mention of Roy's name sends her raging mad.

"Okay, okay. Well, you can ask me for money."

"You're going to need your money too, soon, now that you don't have Nathan to spoil you."

"God, don't remind me." I hang on the line. "Do you think they've slept together?"

"I don't know. Did you ask him?"

"No."

"Would he tell you if they had?"

"I don't know."

"See, that's weird, don't you think? If he didn't have feelings for you, wouldn't he just tell you? Why would he hide other people?"

"The girls think he's kept his apartment for booty-calls."

"For sure."

I frown. "You think?"

"Eliza, have you seen how gorgeous that man is?"

"Yes. I saw him naked just the other day."

"Oh my God... and?"

I exhale heavily, that's private between him and I, the term *packing heat* runs naked through my mind. "No comment."

She laughs. "That means its too good to elaborate on."

I chuckle. "I'm going."

"Come on, more info." She teases.

"Goodbye."

"Have fun on your date."

"We both know I won't."

"Maybe you need a hot one night stand. Fuck Nathan out of your system, so to speak."

I giggle. "Maybe. Bye." I hang up before she can try and talk me into having sex with Samuel. That is not happening.

It's Monday night, and the buzzer sounds at my door. I close my eyes. Here goes nothing.

I'm going to try and let Samuel down gently. I'm just not feeling it.

"Coming down," I say into the intercom.

"Okay."

I take the elevator, and with my heart beating hard in my chest, I walk out of my building. Samuel is waiting near the doors, and he smiles when he sees me.

"You look beautiful."

"Thanks." Oh crap, please don't be nice.

He takes my hand. "Let's go."

Nathan

I sit at my desk and stare at my computer. I don't know if I've ever felt like this before. I'm so wound up about everything, my head feels like it's about to explode.

A voice comes through the intercom. "Dr. Mercer, have you finished dictating for me?"

"No, Maria. I haven't."

"If you want me to finish the reports today, sir, I really need to get on it. I'm running out of time and feeling pressured."

"I am well aware, Maria," I bark. "Stop micromanaging me." I push the button with force. Fuck...they piss me off out there.

Knock, knock, sounds at the door. I roll my eyes. "Yes!" I call.

The door opens, and Maria stands before me with her calender in her hand. She smiles. "Can we go through your schedule, Doctor?"

"Not now, Maria."

"But—"

"Not. Now," I cut her off. I go back to my computer, and from the corner of my eye, I notice she hasn't left. I glance up to see her standing there watching me. "What is it?" I snap.

"Is everything all right, sir?" she asks timidly.

"Of course, it is." I bang the buttons on my keyboard. I feel her still standing there, and I look up once more. "For God's sake, what, Maria?" I snap.

"You've just been very..."

"What?"

"Very testy, and I know how much pressure you are under and I wonder... "

I glare at her and raise my eyebrow as I wait for her elaboration.

"I wonder if maybe you shouldn't go this week."

"Go where?"

"That there, that proves my point, Dr. Mercer. You never

forget anything. You're booked out for the week to attend a conference here in San Fran. But I don't think you should go. Take the rest of the week off instead. You're not speaking. There is nothing imperative you can't miss."

What the hell? I had something on this week and had no idea. What the fuck is happening to me?

"I'm fine, Maria." I sigh.

"No. I'm sorry, sir, this time I'm making an executive decision. I'm cancelling for you. Take the six days off and unwind. You don't get the opportunity to do this, ever. Do it while you can."

Six whole days.

I put my head into my hand. "God, I could do with some time off," I murmur.

"I know you could."

My eyes rise to meet hers. "Thank you, Maria."

She smiles. "There's a motive to my madness, you know? Maybe you won't be such an ogre on your return."

I chuckle. "I doubt that."

"Me, too." She laughs. "But miracles do happen. We all live in hope."

She turns to leave.

"Maria?" I call.

"Yes." She turns back.

"Thank you for putting up with me. You're a saint. I hope you know how appreciated you are."

She smiles broadly and then winks. "Enjoy your time off, Nathan."

I nod. "I will." She leaves and I turn back to my computer.

Six days to sort my life out.

———

"Nathan Mercer!" Elliot calls me into his room.

"Hello." I nod as I walk past him and fall into his leather chair.

This is my third visit in ten days.

Elliot smiles warmly. He's a calming force. I feel better just by being here, knowing that I have someone to talk to about this.

"How are you, Nathan?"

"I'm okay."

"Really? Are you?"

I nod.

He sits back and crosses his legs as he assesses me. "If that were so, why did you need an emergency appointment today?"

I exhale heavily, my cover well and truly blown. "Eliza went on a date last night."

"I see. And how did that make you feel?"

"Like I wanted to kill him."

"What happened?"

"I followed them."

He frowns.

"I watched him pick her up, and then..." I pause.

"And then?"

"I left, and I went and saw Stephanie." I swallow the lump in my throat.

"How did that go?"

"I don't know. I drove to her house and sat out the front in the car. Eliza was all I could think about, so I didn't go in. I left and went back to wait out the front of Eliza's apartment so I knew she got home safe."

He frowns. "What happened?"

I stare into space as I get a vision of her with him in the

car. "He tried to kiss her and she turned her head. She didn't want to kiss him."

"That's good then?"

My eyes meet his. "I don't know, is it?"

"Did they see you?"

"No. I was standing in the alleyway across the road."

He stays silent.

"She knows," I say. "That I'm curious. She found the porn I've been watching."

"What was her reaction?"

"She was angry that I've been lying to her."

"Did you tell her why?"

I shake my head. "No."

"Why not?"

"Because if she doesn't feel the same... I'll lose her." I run my hands through my hair in despair. "I'm not risking it."

"Nathan, you do realize that if you do nothing, you will lose Eliza, anyway, don't you?"

My eyes meet his. "What do you mean?"

"It's inevitable. She will meet someone, and he will be in her bed every night and he will become her confidant. She will learn to depend on him and him alone."

I frown.

"You told me that you don't want to ruin the friendship between the two of you."

"I don't," I reply.

"How long do you think Eliza will want to be best friends with someone and share a bed with him when he is keeping secrets from her? You are already putting a wedge between yourself and her by being dishonest. Whether you realize it or not, Nathan, you are already actively pushing Eliza away."

I've never thought of it like that before.

"So, what you need to decide is whether you can live with yourself in years to come, watching her being happy with someone else, having someone else's children, and knowing that you wanted her and yet you never let her know."

"You don't understand." I drop my head. "It's not that black and white."

"Isn't it?"

"No."

"You said she is angry with you for lying."

"She is."

"So be honest. Tell her the truth."

I pinch the bridge of my nose as I imagine how that conversation would go.

What if she doesn't want me?

"You can't cover a lie with a lie, Nathan."

"I know."

We sit in silence for a while as I try to process my thoughts.

"What are you going to do?"

"There's no way to know what to do unless I know for certain. I can't risk opening up to Eliza and then having sex and not enjoying the physical act of it."

Although I can't imagine that happening with her... but it might. I have no idea what to do with a female body, and I have to face the reality of that.

My eyes meet Elliot's, and for the first time in weeks, I know what I have to do. "I'm going to find out for sure."

———

I drive up the highway with the headlights leading the way through the darkness.

Never once do they second guess their direction. You turn them on, they do their job.

Where are my headlights?

I've been driving around for hours now, too anxious to go home to Eliza.

Too wound up to go back to my place alone.

If there was just some way of... I don't know, seeing a woman without any interaction. Somewhere I could watch and just work out the logistics of my body and what it wants.

I know who my heart wants, but physically, I'm confused.

A thought comes to me. I frown and pull over the car as I go over the possibility in my mind.

Yes, why didn't I think of that before?

I turn the car and do a U-turn.

I know where I need to go.

I take out the gold card from my wallet and stare at it.

CLUB.. EXOTIC

I've had this for what seems like forever, and I've never once even considered it. It's a gold membership visitor's pass. I was given it by my friend, Cameron Stanton, years ago. He always frequents here on his trips into town. At least he used to.

Every member gets to sponsor a guest, and at the time, he gave this card to me. I paid it no attention but now I have to wonder why. Did he know this day was coming?

It's 11:00 p.m., and I walk up to the entrance. There are no signs, no advertizing—just a black door with four big security men guarding it.

This club is exclusive. It's $150,000 a year for the membership, and from what I understand, anything goes.

Which suits me to a tee, because it just so happens that I'm in the mood for anything.

The badder, the better.

I hand the card over and they scan it before they open the door with a nod.

"Thank you." I walk through and come to a gold reception desk, where three beautiful women stand before me. They're wearing short, tight chocolate leather dresses with cream thigh-high boots. Their cream, lace bras are peeking out from their low-cut dresses. Their breasts are voluptuous and tempting.

My hungry eyes don't have to behave here, and I drink them in.

I can do whatever the fuck I want.

Adrenaline rushes through my bloodstream, and for the first time in a long time, I feel wild and alive.

Free.

"Hello, sir." The girl with the long, blonde hair smiles. "How lovely for you to join us this evening." She scans the card through and takes my hand. "My name is Bunny. This way."

She leads me into the club, which is sultry and sexy. There's an overall feeling of luxurious fantasy, and a low tantric beat thumps through the sound system. The place is dark with moody lighting.

The hairs on the back of my neck stand to attention.

I've never been anywhere like this before.

My eyes scan the room. It's huge, on three levels, and exotically furnished. There's a runway with a stage on the bottom floor. A woman with long gold hair is writhing naked on a black leather chair on the stage, and my eyes narrow in on her. Her legs are wide apart.

She has a vibrator. It's big... and hard.

I watch it slide into her body, and then back out.

I watch her do it again.

She puts it in her mouth and sucks it off. My dick clenches in appreciation.

Fuck, yeah.

"Do you want a private booth, sir?"

"Yes."

She leads me into a boxed off area of the club. There's a large, leather couch, and a table in front of it. I have full view of the stage.

She sits me down in the chair, and then without warning, she straddles me. Her legs wrap around my body. Her sex, plush up against my cock. She puts her lips to my ear and whispers, "What do you want to drink, sir?"

"Scotch," I whisper back. My hands slide up her thighs, and I lick up her neck—the temptation too great.

"Do you want a little pick me up?" she breathes against my neck.

I grab her face and turn her ear to my mouth. "I do."

She smiles darkly, and then rotates her hips over my cock. She puts a cigar in my mouth and lights it.

I inhale deeply as we stare at each other. She stands, and I watch her walk off through the crowd as I blow out a stream of smoke.

Fucking hot.

I rearrange my cock in my pants. It's near painful.

My phone dances across the table in front of me. I glance at the caller. Alex.

Shit, he's called me three times already tonight. I'll answer it quickly so he leaves me alone.

"Hello."

"Hi, where are you?"

I glance at my surroundings and smirk. I wish he was here with me. "In a bar," I lie.

"You all right?"

"Sure am."

Two women walk into my cubicle and I frown. One has long dark hair, and one has long red hair. They are in G-strings only—topless and stunning.

What are they doing?

"Did you talk to Eliza?" Alex asks.

The girl with the long dark hair lies down on her back on the table in front of me.

"No," I answer, distracted by what's going on around me.

The blonde gets something out of her little gold clutch purse, and they fuss around a bit.

"I was thinking that maybe you should just tell her," Alex continues.

"Yeah, maybe," I murmur. "Listen, I've got to go. I'll call you tomorrow."

I look down to see four lines of coke on the brunette's stomach.

"Okay," Alex says, "Speak tomorrow."

My eyes are locked on the brunette in front of me, and she smiles up at me. "You ready to go, bad boy?" she whispers.

I smirk.

"Hey, Nathan," Alex says.

"Yeah?"

"Don't do anything stupid, hey?"

I bend and slowly lick her lower stomach, and her eyes flutter closed.

"Don't worry," I whisper. "I won't."

———

I knock on the door. I'm on a fact-finding mission.

Mercer Research.

Stephanie opens it up, and her eyes widen. "Hey, you."

Urgency takes over.

I can't hold it together for one minute longer. I step forward and take her into my arms, and I kiss her. My tongue sweeps through her open mouth, and she smiles against my lips.

"Now, that's a greeting."

I kick the door closed behind us.

I don't want to talk.

I don't want to feel.

I just want to find out what's possible.

For Eliza.

We stumble forward with her hands in my hair. The kiss is wild and unbridled.

My hands are on her ass, and my hard cock is up against her stomach.

I fall onto the couch and pull her over me. She straddles my body, and I grind her over my cock as our tongues thrash between us.

She falls to the floor between my knees, and I smile darkly as I unzip my pants. I grab my cock at the base and hold it up for her.

"Suck me."

11

Nathan

I STAND under the strong stream of water in my shower, and I let the hot water pour over my head. I stare at the floor beneath me.

I feel like shit.

I drag my hand down over my face in disgust. What the hell happened last night?

One minute, I was driving around, thinking, and the next moment, I'm having a brain snap in a strip club. I get a vision of the brunette lying back on my table—the blow lined up ready for me.

I pinch the bridge of my nose. Jesus.

I haven't done shit like that in years. I thought it was well behind me.

There was a time in my life, when I first moved here, that I was broken-hearted over Robert, and nightlife like that was the only thing that kept me sane.

I lived a double life.

I would hang with Eliza through the day and take her out for dinner at night. We would care about each other and laugh. It was wholesome and pure, and then, after I dropped her home and said goodbye, I would go to my other life—the seedy one with clubs, sex, and drugs. The one where I used a fake name, didn't care about anyone, and did whatever the fuck I wanted to do.

I tip my head back and let the water hit my face, full force, hoping it will wash this feeling of shame away.

I remember standing at the front door and Stephanie opening it. I get a vision of taking her in my arms and kissing her. I close my eyes in disgust.

Fuck. What was I thinking?

Eliza.

What I should have done was go home to her. But she doesn't feel that way about me.

I put my head in my hands. I'm sick of this. I'm sick of feeling so torn.

My heart is still racing. I can feel it in my chest. I put my fingers on my neck and take my pulse. 200 over 120.

Fuck.

Hurry up and wear off. I want to go to sleep and forget last night ever happened.

I've hit a new low.

Eliza

My fingers hover over Nathan's name on my phone. Should I call him?

It's just so weird that I haven't heard from him at all today. I haven't seen or heard from him since Sunday night, and it's now Tuesday night. This is unheard of.

Stop worrying, he's fine.

He's probably with her.

He texts me three times a day, normally. Something's changed. Maybe I broke something between us at a time when he needed me. I made it all about myself.

Stuff it, I'm calling him. I dial his number, and it rings.

"Hello, you've reached Nathan Mercer. Leave a message."

"Hi Nathe, just checking in." I pause as I try to think of the right thing to say. "Are you coming over tonight?" I begin to pace. "I mean, it's okay if you have something going on, but... call me. I'm missing you."

I hang up and throw my phone onto the couch.

Damn it, why didn't he answer? Now I have to wait, and I'm not good at waiting.

———

It's Wednesday lunchtime, and I'm sitting in the café, scrolling though Instagram until I get to my messages from Nathan. He was last active on Sunday.

He hasn't been on Instagram since Sunday. What's going on?

I'm beginning to get worried, so I call him. It goes straight to voicemail.

"Nathan, call me," I demand. "I'm getting worried."

By 5:00 p.m. on Wednesday, I can't stand it anymore. I dial Nathan's office.

"Hello, Dr. Mercer's office," Maria answers.

"Hi, Maria." I smile.

"Hello, Eliza."

"Is Nathan free?" I ask.

"Umm." She pauses. "I thought you would know. He's taken the week off."

I frown. What? "Oh… I'm away," I lie. "I haven't had any service to speak to him."

"Yes, I sent him home on Monday. He's so stressed at the moment. I cancelled his conference."

"I know, I'm a little worried about him. Have you spoken to him this week?"

"No, and he's not answering his phone. It's switched off. We've been trying all day."

Fuck…something's wrong.

He would never switch his phone off in case a patient needed him. "Okay, thanks."

"Ask him to call us when you find him."

"Okay." I hang up in a rush and dial his number again. It goes straight to voicemail.

Fuck!

I text him.

Nathan, I'm worried. Where are you?
Check in with me or I'm calling the police
to come and break into your apartment.

A text bounces back.

I'm fine.

What?

I screw up my face in surprise. I dial his number again.

"Yes!" he snaps, exasperated.

"Why aren't you answering your phone?" I bark.

"I'm trying to relax."

"So, you let me worry about you because you can't be bothered to answer your damn phone?" I shake my head in disgust. "I'm coming over."

"No!"

"Why not?"

"I don't want to see you."

My heart drops. "What?"

"I just... I just need some time, Lize."

"For what?"

"To work myself out."

"Nathe, is this about me being angry with you? I'm sorry okay?"

"This has nothing to do with that."

I stare at the wall. "Are you okay?"

He stays silent.

"Can I come over?"

"Lize..."

"Talk to me."

"I'm fine." He sighs sadly. "I promise, I'm fine."

My eyes well with tears. He's not; I can hear it in his voice.

"Can we do something later in the week?" I ask.

"If you want."

"And we go away on Saturday." I smile hopefully.

He stays silent.

"You still want to go, don't you?"

"Of course, I do."

"What's going on?"

"Nothing, I'm fine. I'll call you tomorrow."

"Promise me."

"I promise."

We both hang on the line, waiting for the other to speak.

"I love you," I whisper.

"Do you?"

"I do."

He inhales deeply. "I'll call you tomorrow, babe."

"Okay, night."

"Night."

———

It's just gone 6:00 p.m. when I get off the bus on the corner of my block. It's raining, and I have no idea what I'm having for dinner. I didn't get any meat out of the freezer this morning. My routine is well and truly fucked up. I can't be bothered to stop and get takeout. I guess I'll have toast or something. I make my way to my building and notice someone standing to the side in the shadows, under the awning, out of the rain.

It's Nathan.

"Hi." I stop. "What are you doing? Why didn't you go inside?"

His hands are in his pockets as he stares at me.

"What's wrong?" I step toward him.

He stares at me for a long time. "Do you feel it?"

"Feel what?"

He gestures to the air between us. "This."

I frown up at him.

"I can't fight it any longer. I tried, Eliza, but I just can't."

Ever so slowly, he takes my face in his hand, and he bends to slowly kiss me. His tongue gently sweeps through my open lips, and I feel it to my toes.

"Nathan," I breathe.

He cuts me off with another open-mouthed kiss, and my eyes close instinctively.

What am I doing? I pull out of his kiss. "N-nathan." I splutter.

His face falls.

"Let's go upstairs," I suggest softly. I take his hand and we walk into my building, and into the elevator. My heart is racing. What the hell just happened?

He watches me intently, as if he's scared I'm about to run. We make it to my floor and head down the corridor to my apartment.

I open the door, and he takes me in his arms again. His lips softly take mine, and oh...

"I'm sorry. I'm so sorry," he whispers. "I fucked up," he murmurs against my lips.

Wait.... I'm kissing Nathan.... what the hell? I pull out of his grip. "What are you doing?"

"Kissing you."

"Why?"

"Because I want you." He presses his lips together and takes my hands in his.

I stare up at him in shock.

"I don't want to be friends anymore. I have feelings for you, and I have had for months."

"*What*?"

"I want to be lovers. I want you to know the other side of me. I can't take it anymore. I know I've been acting weird but it's because my feelings have changed."

"How can you possibly like me?" I whisper.

He stares at me, as if he's searching for the right thing to say.

"You... you told me yourself," I splutter. "You told me on the first day we met that I was the wrong sex for you." I begin to feel confused and hurt and I step back from him. I need some distance between us.

"I didn't plan on this, Eliza."

"You told me you liked Stephanie just this weekend." I throw up my hands in disgust. "So, what? You like us both now? So, you're like a straight player now? Should I take a fucking ticket and get in line?"

"I don't want her. I want you."

"Then why did you tell me you liked her?"

"Because I was going to try and go out with her to see if I could make my body work with a woman's."

I stare at him, my mind a clusterfuck of confusion. *His body, work with a woman.*

"What does that mean?" I frown.

"I wanted to see what would happen with a woman."

"And?"

He clenches his lips together as if not wanting to elaborate.

"Nathan?" My blood begins to boil.

"I saw her," he says quickly. "But she has nothing to do with us." He reaches for me, and I pull away.

He went to her?

He likes me but he went to her?

That green-eyed monster appears again. "And did your body *work* with hers, Nathan?"

"That's the only fucking thing you heard in that sentence?"

"Did you have sex with Stephanie or not?"

"I'm not discussing Stephanie with you."

"So, you did?" I shriek.

He glares at me.

Something inside of me snaps. "You're an asshole," I whisper angrily. "You say you've had feelings for me for months, yet you go and sleep with another woman before you tell me?" My eyes well with tears. "How could you?"

Blind betrayal is all I see.

"I didn't have sex with her."

"But you touched her?"

"See, you do have feelings for me, too?" He says hopefully. "You wouldn't care if you didn't." He smiles. "This is good. This is progress."

"Did you touch her?" I sneer. "And so, help me god, don't you dare lie to me."

"No."

"Did she touch you?"

"Eliza!" he snaps. "Just drop the fucking Stephanie thing, okay? It means nothing."

"Did. She. Touch. You. Or. Not?"

He puts his hands on his hips and drops his head.

Anger boils, and the need for more information takes me over. "What, did she kiss you?"

He rolls his eyes. "This is supposed to be a special conversation between us. Momentous, even. You are completely wrecking it."

"Did she give you a hand job?"

He glares at me.

"Did she suck you off?"

"Enough!" he barks, betraying his guilt.

Horror dawns, and I step back and stare at him...what the hell? "Let me get this straight," I say softly. "What you're telling me is that you have feelings for me?"

"Yes." He smiles hopefully. "I do."

"And how long have you felt like this?"

"A long time. It feels like forever." He takes my hands in his.

"You're everything to me, and I want to make a go of it. Tell me you feel the same."

"Did you blow in her mouth?" I ask flatly.

"Eliza, for fuck's sake. Drop it. This is about you and me."

That means yes.

My anger explodes. "So, you went to another woman when you claim to care for me, and you ejaculated down her throat?" I cry. "How did it feel? Did you blow hard? How was her face, Nathan, when she was drinking you down? Were you thinking about me then, huh?" I scream as I completely lose control.

He glares at me.

I picture her on her knees in front of him and him looking down at her. Disgust fills me.

"You know what? Just get out."

I go to the window and turn my back on him. Hurt runs through my veins.

"If this is your other side, Nathan, then I don't want to know him."

Silence hangs between us.

"I said, get out," I repeat.

"Eliza."

I turn on him. "If you cared for me like you say you do, you would never want to touch someone else," I cry. "And you most definitely wouldn't want your dick in someone else's mouth."

"Eliza." He pauses as he tries to articulate himself properly. "I had to find out."

I throw up my hands. "And now you know."

I storm into the kitchen. I need to get away from him. What a self-absorbed asshole.

If he had feelings for me, he wouldn't have gone to her. What am I? A new challenge in his midlife crisis?

He follows me. "Eliza," he says quietly. "I know you don't

understand my reasoning but I did it to protect our friendship. I wanted to be sure."

He gave his first female sexual experience to another woman.

I stare at a spot on the carpet. I'm so disappointed, I can't even look at him. My broken heartbeat pounds in my ears.

"Can we talk about this?" he asks.

"Just go, Nathe," I whisper.

He eventually goes to the door and hesitates.

I close my eyes.

"Eliza," he says.

I turn toward him.

"If you didn't like me that way, too, it wouldn't bother you that I was with her."

We stare at each other for an extended time.

He drops his head and walks out, closing the door behind him.

My eyes well with tears.

Asshole.

———

I watch the clock tick over to 3:13 a.m.

It's dark and still, yet inside my head it's so noisy that I can't sleep. That, and the small fact that my sleeping partner isn't here.

I hate that I can't sleep without him.

My mind goes over tonight and everything that came to light. So much to process. Nathan says he has feelings for me.... I smile softly, imagine that.

But he went to Stephanie for physical confirmation, so he can't care about me too much. His mind definitely wasn't on me when his dick was in her mouth. The fact that he came only adds salt to my wounds.

He liked it with her. My mind runs off on a tangent, wondering what her physical attributes are—height, shape, the color of her hair.

His first female sexual encounter was given to a stranger.

I wanted it.

My heart hurts that he gave it to her, I can never get that back.

If he cared, he would have saved it for me.

I picture the way he was looking down at me while he was kissing me.

But Nathan likes men. He's always liked men. There has never been any doubt, whatsoever.

Even if he does have feelings for me, I couldn't physically hold him for forever.

He would always need something that, no matter how much I wanted to, I just couldn't deliver: a male body.

It hurts to come to this realization.

Because I do love Nathan, and now that this has all come to light, it's put doubt into my mind about how I feel about him. It's made me realize that maybe I always have had feelings for him, too. Maybe he's the reason I have never found Mr. Right. I've compared every man I've dated to him, and nobody has ever stacked up.

He's always come first.

I exhale heavily and toss and turn, trying desperately to go to sleep.

I can't believe this, my most trusted friend on Earth goes to another woman right before he tells me he has feelings for me. How dare he put me in this position.

Selfish, that's what it is. Nathan and I are too close to fuck around. It can't be like that between us, and the way he was talking makes me think that he perhaps wants to try a relationship.

There are so many things wrong with that idea that I don't know where to start.

There's no denying that Nathan and I care about each other, and maybe in some ways, even love each other already. Could we work it out?

Imagine if we could. He would be the most perfect man for me. I smile as I imagine how happy we could be. I think, on some level, I may have always loved and craved a future with him.

But what if it turned bad and I lost him forever?

I can't risk it. I can't give my heart to a man who will break it one day, and even though he would never willingly do it, I know that he will. Nathan oozes sexual chemistry. Everyone wants to either sleep with him or be him.

I could never hold him physically.... He would, one day, eventually stray. And not because he would want to but because he would need to.

You can't help who you are.

Sadness sweeps over me. If Nathan and I did ever fall in love and we broke up and never saw each other again, I wouldn't survive it.

He is in every corner of my heart, and I can't ever risk losing him.

I get a lump in my throat just imagining that heartbreak.

But he wants to try.

No.

Nathan Mercer has the ability to break my heart beyond belief. And I know that he can't see it now, and would never intentionally hurt me, but he did already.

I get a vision of him with Stephanie. What face did he pull when he came in her mouth? Did she drink him down? A part of him is still inside of her now. Can she still taste him on her tongue?

My eyes well with tears.

His words from earlier come back to me. *If you didn't like me that way, too, Eliza, it wouldn't bother you.*

I roll over and punch my pillow in frustration.

This has to stop, now.

———

It's just past 8:00 a.m. when my phone rings. The name Nathan lights up the screen.

I feel like I've been in a fight with Mike Tyson. I'm exhausted.

"Hello," I answer.

"Hi." His voice is deep and husky

My eyes well with tears at the familiar sound of his voice. "Nathe." I sigh. "We need to talk."

"I know. Can we have dinner tonight?"

"Yeah, sounds good."

"I'll pick you up at seven."

"Okay."

We both hang on the phone, not wanting to say goodbye, and I close my eyes in pain.

This is the beginning of the end; I know it.

I miss him already.

"Bye, Eliza. Have a nice day," he says softly before the line goes dead.

———

The key turns in the door at 7:00 p.m., and I inhale deeply to try and calm my nerves. Nathan's beautiful face comes into view and he smiles. "Hi."

"Hi." Seeing him in the flesh is a huge relief.

I miss him.

His eyes drop down my black dress. "You look beautiful."

"Thanks." I twist my fingers nervously in front of me.

We stare at each other for a moment before he pulls me into a hug and we hold each other. I feel so fragile that I may burst into tears at any moment.

"It's going to be okay," he whispers against my temple, he must be able to sense how I'm feeling. "No matter what happens, it's going to be okay."

I pull back to look at him. "Is it?"

He forces a smile. "I promise." He grabs my hand and pulls me toward the door. "The cab is waiting."

"We're taking a cab?"

"I need alcohol for this conversation."

I smile softly. "Me, too."

Our favorite Italian restaurant is dark and romantic, with candles adorning all the tables.

The waiter fills our glasses and leaves us alone. It feels weird to be intense and nervous. This is one of our favorite places, and we have so many happy memories here.

Nathan's eyes are locked on me, it's as if he's expecting me to run at any moment.

"So?" I say.

"So?" He sips his drink, and I know he's as nervous as me.

"We need to talk."

"I know." He tips his head back and drains his glass before he refills it. "Top off?"

I smirk as my eyes flick to my full glass. "No. I'm good."

I watch him for a moment, and I know I have to put him out of his misery. I reach over and take his hand in mine. "Talk to me, Nathe."

He rubs his thumb back and forth over my fingers as his eyes search mine. "Where do I start?"

"At the beginning."

He picks up his glass, drains it again, and then refills it. It sloshes over the side of the glass.

"Nathan." I squeeze his hand in mine. "It's okay."

"So." He exhales heavily. "When you broke up with Callum, I... I was glad. Ecstatic ,even. I told myself that it was because he wasn't good enough for you. But the truth was, I was jealous of him. I was jealous that he got to be with you every day and I didn't." His eyes search mine. "I slept at your house those first few nights and..."

"And what?"

"I liked it. I felt at home. I wanted to be with you all the time. Over the last two years, we've become closer and closer, and then about four months ago, I stopped having sex with other people."

I frown, this is not what I was expecting him to say. "Why?"

"I didn't realize it at the time. I didn't want to. The thought of leaving your side to go and have sex with someone else felt wrong." His eyes drop to the table. "It felt like I was cheating on you. "

I take his hand over the table again as I listen.

"But I didn't put the puzzle pieces together. I didn't understand it, and to be honest, I didn't put any thought into why I was acting that way."

His eyes meet mine for reassurance, and I give him a soft smile. "Go on."

"Three weeks ago I went shopping with you, and you put on that little gold bikini."

What in the world?

"And I got hard." He picks up his drink and takes a huge gulp. "You can imagine my horror, seeing as it's never happened to me before in my life. It confused me—horrified me. I felt sick to the stomach. It was like I was being seedy. You were my best friend, and there I was, perving on you."

"Oh, Nathe."

"I started lying beside you every night in the dark, imagining the two of us naked together, filled with guilt but unable to stop my thoughts. After you would fall asleep, I would go in the bathroom and jerk off so that I could fall asleep, too."

"I don't know what to say."

"I began watching straight porn." He picks up his wine with a shaky hand and sips it. "She always had to have long, dark hair like you." His eyes meet mine for reassurance, and I force a smile, hoping he can feel my love across the table.

"Nathan," I whisper. "There's no shame in liking women."

"Gender has nothing to do with this. I can't explain it." He thinks for a moment. "But when I look at you, I don't see a female or a male."

I frown. "What do you see?"

"I see happiness."

My eyes fill with tears.

"Nathe, I'm not a man. I don't have the body parts you need. I could never make you happy."

"What?" He frowns as if confused. His eyes widen suddenly. "Eliza, I don't get fucked. I fuck."

"You've never...?"

"No." He scowls. "God, no, I have never." He takes my hands

over the table. "Eliza, you have everything that I would ever need. Physically, I mean."

I smile softly, somehow weirdly relieved.

"Why am I doing all the talking?" he asks.

I spin my wine glass by the stem as I stare at it. "I don't know what to say. This has all come out of nowhere, and I'm shocked, to be honest."

"You never felt anything for me?"

My eyes meet his, and I know I have to be honest. "I love you." I shrug bashfully. "I have always loved you. I just never let myself think this way about you because it would lead to heartache, and it has already. Look at last night."

He frowns. "What about last night?"

"Why did you go to Stephanie?"

"Elliot said not to tie my sexuality to one person."

"Who's Elliot?"

"My therapist."

"You have a therapist?" I frown in surprise.

"I had to talk to someone about this. I've been going insane."

"Well, what did he say?" I ask, excited by the prospect of a professional opinion.

"He thinks that I haven't let myself fall in love with anyone since Robert, and that perhaps I've loved you for a long time, and that my body has only just caught up with my heart."

I stare at my beautiful friend across the table....so confused.

"He said something the other day, which made me realize what I had to do. All along, I hadn't considered telling you any of this because I was afraid that, if you didn't feel the same, I would lose you, and it would be the end of our friendship. It would become weird between us." He picks up my hand and kisses my fingertips. "But the reality is, it's already become strained between us because I haven't been honest and I'm going to lose you anyway."

"Why would you say that?"

"Because as soon as you meet someone and get married, I'll lose you to him."

"We will always be friends."

"Not the same way." He sighs. "Your focus will be on him and your children, as it should be."

I take a big gulp of my wine.

"So, I had to make a decision on how I'm going to lose you. Either tell you how I feel and risk rejection, or watch you marry someone else and always regret not being honest with you."

God, this is all so deep, I put my head into my hand. "Nathan."

"What do you think?"

"I don't know."

His face falls. "You don't feel the same?"

"I don't know." I see the sad look on his face, and I can't stand it. "I mean, I do, I love you. That isn't the question here."

His lips curl in hope.

"But I don't know if we can make this work." I shake my head. "There are so many questions and... I'm hurt that you went to her. Your first sexual experience with a woman, and you gave it to her, not me. I wanted it, Nathan. How could you go to her?"

He stares at me for a moment, and then as if having an epiphany, he gives me a slow smile.

"Why are you smiling about that?"

"Don't you see, the fact that it bothers you means there is hope for us."

"I need to know what happened between the two of you. It's eating me up."

"I don't want to talk about it."

"There's no point continuing then." I push my chair out. "I'll go."

"Sit down." He inhales deeply and takes another big gulp of his wine.

"Start talking, Nathan. What happened with her?"

"I was driving around, trying to think. I went to a strip club. I thought it might give me some clarity, you know?"

I frown.

"I did some blow."

"You did cocaine?" I whisper angrily. "Nathan, you're a fucking surgeon, are you stupid?"

"Yes." He nods. "Obviously, I am. I was just so fucked up in the head. I have no excuse, it was appalling. Next thing I knew, I was at Stephanie's."

I sit back in my seat, furious.

His eyes hold mine, and I know he's doing an internal risk assessment as to what he's about to say.

"Go on," I urge. "I need to know what happened."

He hangs his head. "I was off my head, not thinking straight. She opened the door and... we kissed."

My stomach twists.

He frowns. "Next thing I know she's on her knees."

I close my eyes in horror. I don't know if I actually want to hear this.

"I was going to stop." He takes my hand over the table.

"But you didn't?"

He hangs his head. "No."

I watch him, filled with contempt. "What happened then?"

"I ..."

"You came," I snap.

"I freaked out and I left in a rush."

I frown. "What did you say to her?"

"Nothing. I ran."

"So, you let a woman suck your dick, you blew in her mouth, and then ran out without saying anything?" I gasp.

He puts his head in hands and chuckles, as if embarrassed. "Oh my God, I'll never get over the horror."

I put my hand over my mouth, shocked to the core. "She must hate you."

"Undoubtedly." He pinches the bridge of his nose.

"Have you spoken to her since?"

"No. I texted her the next morning and apologized. I hope to never see her again in my life. I'm mortified." He takes my hand over the table. "I saved myself, Eliza. I only want you."

"A head job is not saving yourself, Nathan."

"That's all that happened; I swear."

"That's a fucking lot Nathan," I whisper angrily.

He takes my hand over the table. "Please, just give me a chance."

I exhale heavily. "I need to think about this."

"Take all the time you want. I'm not going anywhere. I'll wait for as long as it takes."

I press my lips together as I try to think of the right thing to say.

"What if we try and it doesn't work out? Where will our friendship be then?" I ask.

"I will always be your best friend, Eliza, and we need to promise each other this won't affect our friendship at all and separate everything. I'm not taking this lightly. I know the risks, but I think we're too close for that to come between us."

"But does that ever really work?"

"We go away this weekend. Majorca, remember?"

I shake my head in disgust. "If anything were to happen

with us, it would have to be like we'd just met. I don't know you romantically. I need some time to think this over."

He smiles. "Okay."

"I mean it. I don't know what's going to happen. I can't give you any guarantees."

"Okay." He holds his glass up. "A toast."

I put my glass to his.

"To starting again."

I clink my glass with his.

His eyes glimmer with something I haven't seen before. A naughtiness. "Can I stay over tonight?"

"No." I smirk. "You cannot."

———

I stand in the café and look at the menu board.

It's Friday, and after the longest week in history, I start my vacation today after work.

I haven't seen or heard from Nathan since our dinner date. I know I asked for space but I thought he would have at least called me or something.

"What's good here?" a familiar, deep voice asks. I glance over to see Nathan standing beside me, also staring up at the board, totally entranced by the selection. "It's my first day here." he says.

My eyes flicker to him in question.

"I want a do over," he says. "I want to go back to the day that we met. I want to start again. Give me the chance to be the man you want me to be."

I smile softly. I can't believe he's doing this. My eyes drop to the floor, and I know that it's now or never.

Do I want to see where this goes or not? I force a smile, I

know that it's something I can't walk away from without at least exploring our options. Nathan's made it quite clear that he's struggling with our platonic friendship, and if my jealousy over that other woman is anything to go by. So am I.

I exhale heavily. Here goes nothing. I may live to regret this.

"It's your first day?" I ask. "Mine, too."

A smile crosses his face when he realizes I'm playing along. "Really? Where did you move from?"

"Florida. And you?"

"Vermont, although I studied in New York."

"Do you know anyone here?" I ask as we shuffle forward in the line.

His eyes hold mine. "Nobody that matters."

I smile softly.

He holds out his hand to shake mine. "I'm Nathan."

"Hi, Nathan, I'm Eliza. I think I'm going to have the turkey on rye," I say.

He nods as he peruses the choices.

"Next," the lady calls. Nathan steps forward. "Can I please have two lasagnes and salads?"

I drop my head to hide my smile, and my heart swells. He remembered what we ate that first day.

"Drinks?" the woman mutters, uninterested.

"No, Nathan, I'll get mine."

"You can buy my lunch tomorrow. Then I can have something to look forward to."

I smile up at the beautiful man beside me. He remembers everything from our first meeting. He pays the lady, and we walk over to a table to sit down.

"Do you want to go out with me tonight?" he asks as he puts salt and pepper on his lasagne.

"Like, as friends?"

"No." He shakes his head. "Like a date."

My eyes hold his, and I know that this is it: the defining moment where I find out what I'm made of. "I'm willing to try."

"That's all I'm asking for." He smiles softly.

"Where do you want to go?" I ask.

He picks up my hand and kisses the back of it. "Anywhere with you."

12

Eliza

I KNOCK on the door and stick my head around. "I'm out of here."

Henry looks up and smiles. "Have a great vacation."

I hunch my shoulders in excitement. "That's the plan."

"Where are you going again?"

"Majorca. We leave in the morning."

"You going with your boyfriend?" He frowns.

"Ah, yes." That sounds weird. Is Nathan my boyfriend now? I raise my eyebrows in surprise, the concept mind blowing. "Yes, with Nathan."

"Okay." His eyes hold mine. "Have a great time. I must say, I'm very jealous."

I chuckle, and with one last wave, I rush out of the door. I power walk to the elevator as I make an internal list of what I need, I have so much to do before Nathan gets to my house tonight and I haven't even started packing yet. I need to get to my laser appointment, and then I want to buy that other swim-suit in red. I also want to pick up some new date dresses and lingerie.

Nerves dance in my stomach. Lingerie... for Nathan. I exit the building and step into the street. The sun is just going down, and I walk up the street toward my beauty therapist.

I don't know what's going to happen between the two of us, but I do know that I'm going to give it my best shot.

I'm bringing out the big guns. I want him to see me in a new light and to be new and exciting for him. I want to do things he hasn't seen me do and wear things he hasn't seen me wear before.

All the things I save for the men I'm dating.

In our friendship Nathan is bossy, but in a relationship, I don't want to be mousy and submissive. I want him to know how much I love being in control and intimate, too. I love sex as much as anyone—more than anyone, probably.

I exhale heavily as I power down the busy sidewalk.... The thought of having sex with him is terrifying, nerves dance in my stomach at just the thought of it. I imagine us fumbling around in bed, and how I'm probably going to have to take the reins the first few times until he gets the hang of it.

He doesn't know about vaginas.

"Oh God." I wince. I feel my skin heat with perspiration as I imagine that moment.

It will be momentous, that's for sure. I just hope it's for the right reasons.

Nathan said that he didn't know how his body would work with a woman but it worked with hers, and it has me secretly freaking out.

What if his body doesn't work with mine? What if we get to that crucial moment and he can't get it up?

I will die—literally die. Like dead in the fucking ground.

Suddenly, I am banged hard in the shoulder by a passing man. "Ouch!" he cries. "Watch where you're going."

"Sorry," I call as I turn toward him. "I was distracted."

I begin to rush again. I wasn't lying. I am distracted by all things Nathan Mercer.

I'm nervous and anxious and excited and nervous, triple nervous actually.

Somehow, I don't think this vacation is going to be as relaxing as I once thought it was.

I'm well aware that this could be a complete fucking disaster.

I stare at my open suitcase on my bed, and I run through what I will need: underwear, dresses, swimsuit, shoes, hat, sweater, jeans... umm, what else?

Lingerie.

My stomach rolls. Lingerie is code for sex.

Fuck, I really can't imagine having sex with him. We are so familiar with each other, it seems foreign. I get a vision of his beautiful body, and my insides clench. I've looked at Nathan's body so many times over the years and wondered what it could do. I guess I'm about to find out.

Of course, that's if it works with mine.... gah, why do I keep worrying about that?

I begin to fold my clothes at double pace to try and take my mind off of worrying.

Deep down, I know why I'm nervous. It's because this means something. I really want it to work between us. The more I've thought about it, the more it makes sense, and the more excited I become.

I love Nathan. He knows me better than anyone else and he still wants me. He's the perfect male. Handsome, smart, with a beautiful body, but it's his heart I adore. He cares for me like nobody else.

I glance at the clock and see it's 9:00 p.m. He worked late and then went home to pack his suitcase. He's going to be here soon. I better take a shower.

Half an hour later, I'm showered and wearing my standard pajamas of a white camisole with spaghetti straps. But tonight, I decide to wear my pink silk boxer shorts. It seems weird wearing just panties around him now. *He's seen it before.*

Stop it.

I hear the key in the door, and my stomach drops. I close my eyes...

Here we go.

He comes into view and gives me a slow, sexy smile. "Hi, there."

My heart somersaults in my chest, and I twist my fingers nervously in front of me. "Hi."

He wheels his suitcase in and puts it up against the wall. He opens it and pulls out a plastic bag, and then his attention comes to me. "I bought you something."

"You did?"

He produces a bottle of champagne and a box of my favorite chocolates. "I thought that, since it's our first date, we should probably celebrate." He shrugs as if nervous too.

My heart swells. "It's our first date?"

His eyes hold mine. "It is." He bends, and his lips take mine to softly kiss me, and my knees nearly buckle from beneath me.

His lips are big, wet, and... *oh hell.*

I begin to throb between my legs.

"Do you want some champagne?" he murmurs against my lips.

"Yes, please." I whisper. I run my fingers through my hair, embarrassed by my body's physical reaction to him. I'm like putty in his hands.

Good God, woman, play it fucking cool, can you?

He takes my hand and leads me into the kitchen. He sits me up on the counter, then he turns and pours our drinks and passes one to me as he stands between my parted legs.

This is nothing new. We always stand like this. But tonight it seems so sexual.

Maybe I've been missing cues all along? Or maybe his kiss just has me feeling drunk already?

He clinks his glass with mine and takes a sip. His hand slides up my thigh as his dark eyes hold mine. "What do you want to do tonight?"

The air leaves my lungs at the feel of his big hand seductively on my thigh.

What's the correct protocol in this situation? If we have sex on the first date, does that make me easy? Or does ten years together count as a million dates? Oh, I don't know, this whole situation is fucked up. I tip my head back, drain my glass, and I hold it out for a top off.

He smiles softly as he watches me. "You okay?"

I nod. "Yes. Probably a bit nervous." I admit with a shrug.

"Eliza, it's me," he whispers. His lips drop to my neck, and he kisses me with an open mouth. Goosebumps scatter across my arms. His mouth hovers over my ear. "You know I'll look after you, baby," he whispers. His hand trails up underneath my shirt and cups my breast. His thumb dusts back and forth over my erect nipple as he softly kisses up and down my neck.

Jesus... let's get straight to it then. I want to snatch the wine from the counter and start drinking from the bottle.

His hands explore my breasts, his lips dust up and down my neck, and his thick thighs are cradled between my legs. It's sensory overload, and my eyes close from the pleasure.

"I have a problem," he whispers, despite his obvious arousal.

"What's that?" I breathe.

"All the way over here in the car, I told myself not to rush you." His lips take mine aggressively, losing control, and he sucks on my mouth with just the right amount of pressure. "That I should take it slow, not push for anything." His tongue curls around mine with the perfect come-out-and-play dance.

Our breathing becomes laboured, and my sex clenches in appreciation as my hands move to the back of his head.

"But it's really hard not to rush when I have no control over myself." He pants. "I've been waiting so long to touch you." He grabs my face and kisses me hard.

Good fucking God.

The way he kisses...

He pulls out of our kiss and steps back from me as he realises in two minutes he has his hand up my shirt and his hard dick in my crotch. "I'm sorry." He pants, his chest rising and falling as he fights for control.

We stare at each other, and he picks up my glass and passes it back to me. His brow furrows as if searching for the right thing to say.

He's nervous.

This is his first time, and he needs to get it over with so he can relax.

The pressure he must feel would be enormous.

"Nathe," I whisper as I put my glass down and reach up to push my fingers through his hair.

"Yeah, baby."

"I don't want to..." I cut myself off. I don't even know what I want to say.

His eyes hold mine. "Okay."

"But... maybe we could just..."

Fuck. Because, I really want to fuck..... *No, behave....no fucking, you sex maniac.*

He leans down and kisses me. His lips curl with a smile as his hands jerk my body toward his hips. "Play it by ear?"

"Yes," I whisper, overwhelmed with desire.

His teeth take my bottom lip and stretch it out, as if his sanity just broke. He bites my neck again, and I begin to see stars. Okay, one thing is very clear: he knows how to turn me on. Goosebumps, tingles, butterflies. Check, check, double check.

I'm about two minutes away from coming from his lips alone.

"I... I need to finish packing," I pant. I need ten minutes to pull myself together and stop acting like a horny schoolgirl.

Nathan gives me a slow, sexy smile as he tucks a piece of my hair behind my ear. "Okay, you finish packing, and I'll take a shower."

Nathan... naked in the shower. "Okay, sounds good," I squeak, my voice is high and sounds like a mouse. Oh hell.... shut up, now. I jump down from the counter, and with one more kiss, I make my way into the bedroom and stare at my open suitcase.

My lips are tingling from his touch, and I close my eyes, overwhelmed by the sensations that are running though my body. It's been a long time—two years—and now it's going to happen with my best friend? No wonder I'm in a fluster. This is a lot to digest.

So unexpected and yet, it feels so natural.

I hear the shower turn on, and I go to the mirror to stare at my reflection. My hair is a mess and my face is flushed. But other than that, I'm surprised I look the same when everything feels so different.

"Just finish packing, will you?" I whisper to myself. "Have your meltdown later."

I get back to my jobs and tick things off my list. An hour later, I walk out into the living room to find Nathan lying on the couch, watching television. He has my big, fluffy blanket over him. He smiles over at me and flicks the blanket back as an invitation to lie in front of him.

Oh hell.... here we go.

I force a smile and climb in under his blanket. I face the television, and he wraps his arms around me from behind, dropping a kiss to my temple.

"What are we watching?" I whisper.

"The game."

We lie for a while, and his hand slowly floats up and down my body. Goosebumps follow his fingers. He begins to kiss my neck, and my eyes close from the pleasure. His fingers roam up underneath my tank top and over my breasts, and I can feel his erection growing behind me as it presses into my behind. He rolls me onto my back, and instinctively, my legs open. His fingers drift over my panties, lowering down to my sex as his eyes hold mine.

Back and forth, back and forth, and I can feel myself getting wet as his kiss turns passionate. Our tongues thrash against each other's.

We kiss and, as if he's unable to help it, his hand goes down the front of my panties.

Oh God, this is it.

With his eyes locked on mine, his fingers slide through my wet, swollen sex, and his body clenches in appreciation.

"Fuck." He moans in an unrecognisable voice.

I can feel his cock as it becomes nearly painful hard against my hip. He slides his thick fingers through my sex once more, and his mouth hangs open, as if he's unable to control himself.

"Can I see?" he breathes. "I have to see."

We pant as we stare at each other, and I nod, understanding where he's coming from.

This is so new to him. He needs to see it with his eyes.

He sits up to lift my tank top over my head before he sits between my legs. He slowly slides my panties off over my hips and inhales heavily as his eyes roam over my sex in awe.

I close my eyes.

This is too much. The intimacy is just too much.

He lifts one of my legs and puts it up on the back of the couch, and then with his eyes locked on my sex, he slowly slides his fingers through my swollen lips.

"So wet," he breathes.

I nod, unable to form a coherent sentence.

He slides them through again and then parts my lips. His eyes drink in every inch of me.

"Pink," he murmurs to himself.

He pushes a finger inside me. His face scrunches up as he experiences the feeling for the very first time.

I put my hand on his forearm to bring him back to the here and now, and his eyes rise to meet mine. I smile softly, hoping he can feel my love.

He pulls his finger out and then slides it in again deeper. I moan as I arch my back in appreciation. "That's it," I pant.

His eyes widen, and as if spurred on by my arousal, he pushes in another finger as his eyes darken.

Oh....so good.

I'm writhing beneath him, wanting everything that he can give me and then without warning, he drops his head and kisses my inner thigh.

My breath catches as I wait.

He drops lower and lower, and then kisses me on the sex with an open mouth. His eyes close in reverence, and his tongue peeks out as he softly licks me there.

I can't breathe.

He licks me again, this time with more purpose. Looking down at him between my legs is too much, and I shudder.

No... don't you dare come!

He really goes to town. His tongue swirls deeper and deeper and I scrunch the couch between my fingers as I moan out loud. He's all in. His whiskers begin to burn my sex. He's like a man starved, and he really begins to eat me as if he's been waiting all his life to do this.

No... no... no.

My back buckles off the sofa, and I cry out as I come in a rush.

"Fuuuuuck." He lets out a guttural groan as he slides his fingers back in deeper and begins to work me. Without warning, he rises above me and pulls his dick out over the top of his boxer shorts, and with a jerk of his hand, he comes all over my stomach.

We pant, both gasping for air as we stare at each other. Goosebumps scatter over my skin.

We're shocked to our core. That lasted all of two minutes.

Our bodies don't just work together, they start fires.

He leans down and kisses me as he rubs the semen into my skin. The emotion between us is at an all-time high, and I cling to him, so overwhelmed by the situation that I feel close to tears.

He takes my face in his hands as he kisses me, and I know he feels it, too.

Something wonderful just happened between us.

It's raw and real, and most of all, honest.

"Nathe," I whisper as I cling to him.

He smiles against my lips. "I know, baby. I know."

Nathan

My heart pounds hard in my chest as I try to float back to Earth. Eliza is tightly snug up against me in my arms, and the euphoria I feel is indescribable.

She's beautiful, more than beautiful. I knew I would like her body because it was hers, but I didn't just like it... I fucking loved it.

I want to do it again, only harder.

Much harder.

My hand, wet with my semen, glides up and over Eliza's breasts as I rub my body against hers, as if, somehow, it will preserve this feeling between us—a closeness I only dreamed of.

My lips take hers, our tongues starting to slowly appreciate each other, and once again, I feel a pulse in my dick.

Don't push your luck. She wants to take it slow.

Our kiss turns passionate. Unable to help it, I roll her onto her back again, my knee spreading her legs.

I want in. I want it fucking all.

No.

I stop myself and pull back from her. If I push her too hard now, I will pay for it later. She needs to want this, not be swept away in the moment by arousal.

My hand drops to between her legs. I run my fingers through her hot, dripping wet flesh as she opens her legs in invitation. My eyes roll back in my head, and my balls clench up into my stomach.

I need to fuck her.

Oh God, I need to fuck.

I sit up in a rush. It's either that or I'm going to have her legs up around her ears in about five minutes flat. I imagine myself plunging into her, balls deep, and pre-ejaculate beads on the end of my cock. *For fuck's sake, get a hold of yourself, man.*

"Shower, baby," I whisper.

Her face falls as if disappointed. She wants more. "What are you doing?" she whispers.

I cup her face and lean in to softly kiss her. "Giving you time."

"I don't need time."

My tongue sweeps against hers, and I smile against her lips. "Tomorrow, we go away. We have all the time in the world, Lize. I don't want to rush this. It's too important."

She smiles as I pull her head to mine. Our foreheads touch.

Oh ......my heart.

Nothing has never felt so right.

"So, you don't want me to suck your cock tonight?" She smirks.

I smirk back, surprised she just said that. That is not a sentence I thought I would ever hear Eliza say.

"That's not fair."

With dark eyes, she runs her index finger through my semen on her stomach, and she slowly puts it into her mouth, moaning softly. "You taste good."

The air leaves my lungs.

She grabs my cock and slowly strokes it. "You got any more for me?"

Get fucked... *she's dirty.*

This just gets better and better by the minute.

I spread my legs for her, and she slowly strokes me as she leans over and kisses me, her tongue inciting anything but time.

Urgency is all I feel.

Her strokes become harder, and our open mouths hang over each other's, as if we're too aroused to even kiss. The sofa begins to rock and my balls clench.

Fuck, ...fuck, ... Fuck.

"Get on me," I growl. "Get the fuck on me, now."

She smiles and climbs over to straddle me. "We're not going to fuck."

I grab her hipbones as I struggle for control. "What?" I push out.

"I'm going to slide over you until we both come." She rubs herself over my cock with her wet flesh. She's hot and slippery, and I begin to see stars.

I moan softly. Dear God, this woman is a temptress.

She slides over me again, and I look up at her beautiful face and large breasts as they bounce.

She's fucking perfect.

I break out into a sweat as I repeat the mantra in my head, *Don't come, don't come. Don't fucking come.*

She tips her head back as she rides out her own pleasure, and something inside of me snaps.

Control.

I grab the base of my cock and hold it up. "Fucking get on it."

She smiles darkly, and in one quick movement, she's on her knees. My cock is in her mouth and she sucks hard.

I convulse as I come in a rush into her mouth. She smiles around me as she drinks it down, her hand still stroking my shaft to empty me out.

Oh. Dear. *Fucking God.*

I tip her off me and flip her onto her back. I place her feet onto my shoulders and open her up with my tongue. My eyes close as something dark takes me over—something primal that wants to claim her as mine. The feeling of her open thighs in my hands, her feet on my shoulders, and the taste of her arousal on my tongue is pure pleasure that makes my eyes roll back in my head.

I bite her clitoris, and she jumps with a yell and then shudders as she comes in a rush. Her hands tenderly come to my hair, and she pushes it back from my eyes.

I lap her up in a half-dazed state. I'm overwhelmed with emotions; filled with awe.

Eliza, *my Eliza,* is hot as fuck.

We finally come back to Earth, and she drags me up to kiss me. We lie in each other's arms.

I adore this woman. I just want to blurt out how I feel about her...but I can't.

I have to hold myself back for a while until I know for certain that she feels the same.

She tenderly kisses my chest, and I smile as I hold her tightly.

Please feel the same.

Eliza

The alarm rings out, and I stretch with a smile.

Did I dream last night? Because, holy shit, it was one hell of a dream.

I feel fingers swipe through my sex, and I look up to see Nathan lying on his side, facing me. He leans down and kisses me with a prolonged suck on my mouth.

"Good morning," he says with a lazy smile.

"Morning." My legs instinctually part for him. "What are you doing?" I smile.

"Playing with my favorite new toy." His tongue runs over his bottom lip as he slides two fingers deep inside me. I moan softly as my back arches from the bed.

He seems different today—more like the Nathan I know. "So, I'm your toy now?" I ask.

He nods slowly, his eyes alight with mischief. "Fuck toy."

I giggle, shocked. "Fuck toy?"

He bends and takes my nipple into his mouth. "Uh-huh."

"But you didn't fuck me."

He bites my nipple hard, and I wince as I buck him off. "Ouch."

He rolls on top of me and holds my hands above my head. "Rest assured, my Eliza, when I do fuck you—and I will—it will be an all-day affair." He grinds his hips against mine.

Arousal heats my blood as we stare at each other ...all day. *Jeez.*

Can he really fuck all day? Wouldn't surprise me. If dicks did sport, I'm positive his would be an elite athlete.

He puts his mouth to my ear and whispers. "So, here's what

we're going to do today, my beautiful girl. We're going to get up and we're going to go catch our flight, and while you sleep on the plane..."

I smile. "Yes?"

"I'm going to pretend to read my book while I think of all the ways I'm going to fuck you in Majorca."

My eyes widen as I listen. "I thought you wanted to wait."

His cock slides through the open lips of my sex, and I shiver. "I just didn't want to break you before we got there." His tongue slowly slides over his big lips. "You won't be able to walk for a week when I'm done with you, Eliza."

We stare at each other. His eyes are dark, and nerves sweep through me. The thing is, he's serious. He says it casually, as if it was a joke, but I know that it's a warning to prepare myself for him.

Nathan Mercer is as intense in the bedroom as he is in life.

And that's hardcore.

I only hope I can handle him. I know I desperately want to.

I feel his hard length up against my stomach and butterflies dance in my stomach.

Not walking may be in my very near future.

I smile to myself, lucky I'm not getting off a deckchair on the beach for the entire trip then, isn't it?

Oh God, I'm so excited.....bring it on.

An hour later, we're wheeling our suitcases across the parking lot at the airport when Nathan takes my hand to cross the road. He watches the oncoming traffic and pulls me along when the time is right.

I frown as we walk along, this is so familiar and nothing new, Nathan has grabbed my hand crossing every street for ten years and yet, today, it feels substantial—so much more than the simple gesture it is.

Our car trip was made in relative silence, and I know it's just because the goalposts between us have been moved. He's normally lecturing me on something or I am rambling on about a random subject. Everything seems so different now.

But maybe I'm imagining the differences because I feel so different inside.

It's like he's woken someone up inside of me that I didn't know existed, and I'm dying to let her out.

We arrive at the check-in counter. "Hello," Nathan says to the ticket lady.

She's blonde and beautiful, and her eyes drink him in as she looks him up and down. "Hi." She smiles. "How can I help you?"

"I would like to check us in, please." He says in his deep velvety voice.

"Sure." She tucks a piece of her hair behind her ear as her eyes linger on his face. It's obvious she's quite taken with him. I stare at her, deadpan. I'm used to women flirting with Nathan. I make fun of him for it. But now it's different.

This time, it's pissing me off.

"You're going to Majorca." She smiles as she types our details into the computer. "It's beautiful there, have you been before?"

"No." He puts his arm around me and pulls me close, as if sensing my annoyance, "We haven't."

Her eyes flicker to me as if only now remembering I'm here. I force a smile.

"I've been a few times," she says as she types. "It really is something special. The beaches are to die for."

"I'm excited to get there." Nathan's eyes glance over to me, and I force another smile. Towering over everyone, he's wearing a white linen shirt that hangs over his broad shoulders, along with fitted blue denim jeans that are tight in all the right places. His sandy hair is messed up to perfection. He casually puts down his *Louis Vuitton* suitcase on the conveyor belt. Everything Nathan owns is top of the line; he doesn't do cheap.

The machine flashes up the weight. "It's light," she purrs.

"I won't be needing many clothes."

Her eyes rise to meet his and she smiles sexily.

"It's hot there," he reminds her.

She remembers I'm here again and turns back to her computer. "Of course."

Damn it, why does he have to be so charismatic? Nathan Mercer has two modes: bossy and cranky mode, which is super-hot, or swoony and smooth, which is double fucking hot.

No wonder she's perving at him. He's damn delicious.

This is just great. I'm starting a relationship with the world's most gorgeous man. I mean, I already knew women flocked over him, but this is just another reminder, I guess.

I'm going to have to get used to it. I know it shouldn't bother me but it kind of does. A little annoying voice whispers a warning in the back of my mind. He's never been with another woman. When he gets so much attention from them, will he ever get curious?

Stop it.

She hands over our tickets. "Here you are, two business class tickets to Majorca. Your flight boards twenty-five minutes before departing at 11.00am." Her eyes hold his. "Have a great time."

"Thank you." He smiles.

"Bye," I say.

"Goodbye," she replies as she looks down at her computer.

I stare at her, deadpan. Where's my eye contact, witch?

Nathan takes my hand and leads me toward the door. "You won't be wearing many clothes?" I scoff. "Are you serious?"

"What?" He frowns.

"Could you be any flirtier?"

He stares at me as if shocked and then breaks into a swoony smile. "Eliza Bennet, are you jealous?"

"No," I snap.

He chuckles as we walk through the door into the check-in area.

"I don't get jealous," I snap.

He turns to me and picks up my hand to kiss it. "Okay." His eyes hold mine as a trace of a smile crosses his face.

"Don't tell anyone that you won't be needing clothes again." I smirk, amused that my annoyance has been exposed.

He chuckles, leans in, and kisses my cheek. "Yes, dear."

"And don't patronize me."

"Yes, sweetheart." He turns and pulls me along.

"You're doing it now. Saying yes, dear, and yes, sweetheart, is patronizing, Nathan."

"Eliza, shut up," he says, putting me firmly back in my place. "Is that better?"

I giggle, there he is, the cranky man who doesn't listen to me ramble. "Yes, it is, actually."

"Okay, noted."

"What's noted?"

"Eliza, shut up is now code for yes, dear."

I giggle as we walk along. This is kind of fun, getting to know each other in a new light. We have so much to learn.

We walk down through security, and then out into the airport lounge. We stand and look around, a little at a loss on what to do. We've got three hours to kill.

"We should celebrate," he offers.

"The bar?" I ask, surprised. It's 8:00 a.m.

He takes my hand and pulls me toward our favorite bar. "It's five o'clock somewhere."

I stare out of the window of the plane with a goofy smile on my face. Nathan is reading his book with his hand on my thigh. Everything just seems so natural between us.

This is happening. This is really happening. Nathan and I are actually doing this.

He looks over and notices my stupid face. "What?"

I lean in and whisper, "Can you believe this?"

"What?"

"This." I gesture to his hand on my thigh. "You know, you and me... naked and shit."

Surprised, he tips back his head and laughs out loud. "You have such a way with words."

"Well, what would you call it?"

He narrows his eyes, and his teeth catch his bottom lip. "I would like to think that this is the beginning of something wonderful."

I smile up at him. "But we are going to be naked."

He smiles and pulls my face to his so he can kiss me tenderly. "That we are."

13

Eliza

THE CAR CRAWLS TO A STOP, and I stare out the window. My eyes flicker to Nathan. "This is where we're staying?"

He kisses me quickly as he opens the car door. "Only the best for my girl."

Holy crap. This isn't just the best; it's incredible.

It's an old traditional mansion, built with huge sandstone brickwork. It looks like it may have been a castle at one point back in time. It's on a huge patch of land, with beautiful, manicured gardens at street level. There's a grand, circular driveway, as well as a large, black and white striped awning hanging over the entry. The back of the building looks like it's a few stories high, hanging on the top of the cliff, overlooking the ocean. Nathan takes my hand to help me out of the car. I'm hit with the heat of the air and the smell of the ocean. I smile broadly as the breeze whips over my face.

"Nathe." I sigh.

He gives me a playful wink, clearly happy with his choice.

"Good morning, sir." The bellman smiles and nods. "Checking in today?"

"Yes, thank you."

"Are you Mr. and Mrs. Mercer?"

"We are."

"I am Pablo," he introduces himself with a nod. "Welcome to Refugio." He gestures to the grand front doors. "Please, come this way."

Nathan takes my hand, and when Pablo turns his back, I do a little happy dance jig on the spot. "I'm so excited," I whisper.

"Really?" Nathan smirks, delighted in my reaction. "Couldn't tell."

We walk in through the foyer, and my mouth falls open, "Oh, Nathe." I gasp as I look at the detailed ornate ceilings. My eyes float around the luxurious space. This is next level beautiful. Everything is over the top luxury.

Nathan's eyes drift to the magic above us. "Wow."

I giggle and just want to jump around. I'm so excited. I kiss his shoulder. "Thank you, I love this place."

"Hello," Nathan says to the receptionist. "We are checking in today for fourteen nights, booking in the name of Mercer."

Fourteen nights.

God, this is the world's best birthday present.

"Yes, sir." She smiles as she types our details in the computer. "Ah, yes, you are in the penthouse."

My eyes widen.

"That's right," Nathan replies calmly.

The penthouse.

She smiles, and Nathan hands over his credit card. She processes our details in the computer.

How much did this place cost?

She walks out from behind her desk. "This way," she says.

I hunch my shoulders in excitement, you can always tell which hotels are top notch because they take you to your room and show you how everything works. Attention to detail is everything, and there are so many beautiful details here.

Nathan takes my hand, and we follow the nice receptionist into the elevator.

I just want to be over the top excited, I hate having to be cool as a cucumber while people are around. She puts our key into the slot inside the elevator and a picture comes up on the little screen.

Penthouse

I bite my lip to hide my smile, and Nathan squeezes my hand. I squeeze it back.

Moments later, the doors open into a private foyer, and the receptionist takes our key and opens the large double doors, holding them open for us.

Holy crap.

The place is huge, with white décor and light timber furnishings. The furnishings are in aqua. The entire back wall is glass, overlooking a huge deck with a private pool and deckchairs. There's a big outdoor day bed that has a white net hanging off a four-poster frame, as well as a bar and two hammocks. The timber woodwork is pale and weathered, as if it's been washed up onto the beach.

"Oh, wow," I whisper.

She opens the sliding door. "You have a private pool, and a server who is on call twenty-four hours a day. He will make your drinks. Whatever you want is at your fingertips."

Unable to help it, I walk out onto the deck. The one

hundred and eighty degree view over the Mediterranean Sea is breathtaking. I smile goofily as I stare out at the ocean.

I've died and gone to Heaven... with a god. *How ironic.*

The receptionist goes through the details of the Penthouse with Nathan, but I can't make myself leave the deck. I already know that this is my happy place. I'm in love.

Nathan eventually walks out and smiles as he takes me in his arms.

"This is beautiful. You spoil me too much."

His lips take mine. "No such thing."

I feel so warm and relaxed after finally arriving. I put my head onto his chest, and he holds me. Now that we're here, I'm suddenly dead tired.

"Come on, we need to sleep," Nathan says. "It's four in the morning at home."

"No wonder I'm tired." I smile sleepily. "What time is it here?"

"9:00 a.m."

"We'll have a few hours' sleep and then get up and have a swim. Tonight, we'll go out for dinner."

"Okay." I kiss his big, perfect lips. "I'm going to take a shower." I look around. "Oh, our bags aren't here yet."

"That's okay, I'll get them." He pulls me in for another kiss, and his lips linger over mine with a promise of what's to come.

I squeeze him tightly, and he grabs my behind playfully, "Go."

I make my way inside and find our bedroom.

"Holy shit," I whisper to myself.

The room is navy blue with white linen furnishings. It's the most beautiful room I have ever been in. The headboard is high-backed and velvet—the same beautiful color as the walls. I open the double doors and gasp.

The bathroom is decorated in navy with the suite made from white marble. It looks like something out of a magazine. There is even a bench seat in the double-headed shower. The circular bath is sunk into the floor, and the entire upper walls are mirrored. A huge chandelier hangs over the center over the bath. I smile as I look down into the bathtub. I'm going to have sex in there. I look at the shower...and in there, too.

In fact, I'm going to have sex on every damn surface in this place.

I turn the shower on and smile to myself. "Can things get any better?"

I wake to the soft sound of Nathan breathing, and I frown in confusion.

What happened?

I remember showering and sitting on the bed, and then I must have fallen asleep. I glance at the clock and see that it's 7:00 p.m. local time.

I'm going to get up and get ready for our date, I quietly slide out of bed and tip toe out of the room. My suitcase is still out here from when the porters dropped it off. I'll shower in the other bathroom and get ready out here so Nathe can sleep a little more. He must be exhausted. He didn't sleep on the plane at all.

I glance out to the balcony, and my breath catches. The sun is just going down and a beautiful red glow hangs over the water. White candles are lit and scattered everywhere, and they flicker with the breeze. The staff must do this in their turn down service. I smile with a shake of my head. This place is next level.

I slowly unzip my suitcase. Now, what am I going to wear? It's my first official date with Nathan, and I need to be utterly irresistible.

I turn and look at my behind in the mirror. I love this dress. It's a smoky gray and fitted with a plunging V that dips between my breasts. It fits my figure perfectly and is super sexy without looking like I try too hard. My long, dark hair is down and styled, and my makeup is minimal. I rearrange my breasts into my dress. I'm wearing some new lacy underwear. This bra feels off. I twist it to try and get my boobs into place. Damn it, why is pretty underwear always uncomfortable?

There's a very valid reason why married women don't wear this stuff every day.

I turn to the side and look at myself. My boobs do look good, though; even I have to admit that. I smile and take out my lip gloss. I begin to apply it when I feel two hands come around me from behind, followed by a kiss on my temple.

"Hi." I smile.

"Hey," he whispers. His voice is groggy and still half asleep. He shifts my hair around to one side and gently kisses my neck. "I slept in."

"You did. Get ready. We have a very important night ahead." I kiss his lips, and they linger over his. "Our first official date."

His eyes glow with tenderness. "So it is." He takes my hand and holds it up as he steps back to look me up and down. "You look beautiful."

"Thank you."

"Give me a minute, I won't be long." He goes out to the kitchen, and I hear him fuss around and a cork pop. Moments later, he comes back in with a glass of champagne. "Have some bubbles while I get ready." He kisses me softly.

"Thank you." I watch him disappear into the other room, and I walk out onto the balcony and stand at the rail. It's dark now, and the candles flicker around me. The ocean is loud, and in the distance, I hear music playing—maybe a saxophone or something. I sip my champagne and shake my head in disbelief. This is all so surreal. I feel like I'm on the precipice of something teetering between my old and my new life. I smile as Nathan's words come back to me... *the beginning of something wonderful*. I already know that it's going to be wonderful.

Nathan is special, our relationship is special, and last night eased all my nerves.

I can't wait to take this next step with him.

I feel soft lips on my shoulder. "There you are."

I turn toward him and my breath catches. He's the epitome of masculinity. He's wearing a black linen shirt and tight black jeans. His hair is messed to perfection, and his only accessory is his chunky silver *Rolex* watch. He clinks his glass with mine, and his dark eyes hold mine.

"Are you ready?" He lifts his glass to his lips. The double meaning and the weight of his words doesn't go unnoticed.

I smile softly as butterflies dance in my stomach. "Am I ever."

———

"This way, please," the waitress says as she leads us through the restaurant.

We follow, and she takes us through to an outdoor courtyard where colorful fairy lights are strung through the trees and fire lanterns are lit around the perimeter.

There is a man in the corner playing a guitar and singing.

She gestures to the table, and Nathan pulls out my chair. "Thank you."

"Can I get you any drinks?"

Nathan gestures for me to go first. Always such good manners. I open the menu as I try to look what to get. "I'll have a..."

"What's a good choice?" Nathan asks as he scans the menu.

"Sangria?" she offers. "It's our most popular cocktail."

"Oh, sounds good." I smile. "I'll have a glass of that."

"Make that two," Nathan agrees.

"We serve it in a jug."

"Sure, sounds great." Nathan hands her his drinks menu, and I do the same.

"I'll be back to take your orders soon." She leaves us alone.

I look around in awe. "Look at this place, Nathe." It's alive with chatter and the guitar music creates a wonderful atmosphere. The waitress arrives back at the table with a huge jug of sangria and two glasses not long after.

Wow, that was quick. They must have this stuff on speed dial.

"Here you are." She places them on the table, and I giggle at the size of the glasses. They look like jugs, too. She pours us two, and with another smile, she leaves us alone.

Nathan takes a sip of his drink and raises his eyebrows at the red drink in his glass. "Hmm, not bad."

I take a tentative sip. I hope I like it. There must be ten liters here. I'm happily surprised. It's fruity and delicious. Ten liters may not be enough.

Nathan chuckles and we clink glasses.

"I love this place," I whisper as I look around.

"Nice, huh?" Nathan opens his menu and looks through the choices. "What are you having?"

"Hmm." I go through the choices, too. "I think for entrée, I'm going with the pasteles de cangrejo."

"What's that?"

"Grilled crab cakes with mustard sauce."

"Hmm, sounds good." He twists his lips as he looks through the choices. "For the main, I'm going to have the Arrachera steak."

"Hmm, yum." I smile goofily. "I'm having so much fun in Majorca already and all I've done is sleep and order dinner."

He chuckles. "Good news."

I take a drink of my sangria. "This is so good—too good, probably, although most definitely adding to my fun. For a main course, I'm going to have the pollo al ajillo chicken."

The waitress comes back over and we order our meals. She leaves us alone again.

Nathan refills our glasses.

"Not too many," I say. I can feel my head getting woozy already. "This is potent."

We fall silent and stare at each other across the table. I don't know what he's feeling, but I'm feeling a little starstruck.

"So..." He smiles as he takes a sip of his drink.

There's an undercurrent of excitement buzzing in the air between us.

"So?" I beam.

"What do you normally talk about on your dates?"

I shrug. "I usually ask about forty questions so I can do an internal risk assessment."

"Ah, the dreaded forty questions." He raises an eyebrow.

"Why, what do you talk about on your first dates?"

"Well, this is my first one."

I frown. "What do you mean?"

"This is my first ever first date."

"How is that possible?"

"Well, I was too young when I met Robert, and since then..." His voice trails off, and he shrugs.

"You've never taken someone on a first date?" I stare at him in horror. "Like... ever?"

"Nope." He catches his bottom lip in his teeth, as if slightly embarrassed. "Another of my firsts given to the lovely Eliza Bennet."

"Well." I smile proudly, happy with that answer just quietly. "I'll have to make it memorable."

"You already have." His eyes hold mine.

I smile softly. *Oh, this man...*

"So?" He rolls his hand out. "Fire away."

"What?"

"Ask me your date questions. I want to see if I qualify."

"Okay." I take a sip of my drink as I narrow my eyes while I think of one. "What makes you happy?"

"Seeing my family happy." He pauses. "And seeing you happy."

I swoon and take his hand over the table. "I *am* happy."

He dusts his thumb over the back of my knuckles. "I know."

Our eyes lock, and electricity passes between us. If he keeps this up, we won't make the main course. I'll jump him across the table.

"What's your biggest achievement?" I ask.

"Developing the bionic heart. No brainer."

"I'm so proud of you for that."

He smiles, and I know he's proud of himself, too.

"Biggest regret in life?" I ask.

"Hmm." He frowns, falling deep into thought. "Like, ever?"

"Yes." I smile as I sip my drink, I like this game.

"Probably waiting ten years to fall for you."

I giggle. "Apart from that."

"Umm." His brow furrows. "Leaving Robert."

What?

My alcohol high instantly dissipates. "Why is that?"

"Well," He pauses as he gets the wording right in his head. "At the time, I demanded that Robert follow me to San Francisco. I had it in my head that if he loved me, he would follow me anywhere."

"And he didn't?" I have always known this story but haven't paid it much attention before, now I need all the details.

"No." He sips his drink. "At the time, I saw it that he wasn't committed to me so I broke up with him."

"But now?"

"Well, now I realize that he wasn't ready to make that commitment to anyone. I asked him to leave all of his family and friends to be with me. He was too young." He shrugs, as if ashamed. "I should have given him time and space. He would have come eventually. Things that are meant to be will always return."

I stare at him as fear rolls through me like a tsunami.

"Nathan." I frown. "Are you still in love with Robert?"

"No." He shakes his head as if the thought is preposterous. "God, no, but as I've gotten older, and since being with you, I now know that I was very selfish back then. I put my needs before his, and that wasn't fair." He thinks on it for a moment. "It's not something I'm proud of, that's for sure."

I stare at him, my mind a jumble.

"So, yeah." He shrugs. "Breaking someone's heart out of selfishness is my biggest regret."

"Wow." I sip my drink. "Well, I guess that settles it."

"Settles what?"

"You just completely flunked the questions. Biggest regret in your life is leaving your ex. Red flag, Nathan," I reply flatly. "Motherfucking red flag. I'm drinking this entire jug of sangria and eating my meal, and then I'm pretending to go to the bathroom and never coming back," I reply as I try to act serious. "It was nice knowing you."

He throws his head back and laughs. It's deep, rich, and does things to my insides. "I'm talking about my behaviour. Not losing Robert... that came out wrong. I'm disappointed in myself, not with the outcome." He reaches over and takes my hand. "Do I get to ask any questions?"

"Fire away. I'm completely at ease with my questions now that I know how badly you fucked up yours."

He chuckles. "And so you should be." He stares at me for a moment as he thinks and finally he responds. "Where do you see yourself in five years?"

"That's it? That's your million-dollar question?" I laugh. "You're ridiculous, Mercer."

"What? It's a good question." He laughs back. Boy, these Sangrias are going straight to our head. "I'm serious. " He splutters. "Answer it."

"Well." I smile goofily. "I would like to be happily married, with one child and another on the way."

He stares at me and blinks slowly, as if he's processing my words.

A weird thought comes over me. We've never actually discussed this before. "Do you want children, Nathan?"

"Umm." He pauses. "I've never really thought about it." His brow furrows, as if contemplating it and then he gives me a soft smile with a shrug. "I guess with you by my side..., anything is possible."

My heart swells.

"Is that your attempt for brownie points after your abysmal last answer?" I ask.

"One hundred percent."

We burst out laughing, and he holds up the jug of sangria. "Another?"

"Yes, please."

Five hours later, the moon is dancing over the water as we walk hand in hand along the boardwalk on the beach. We're on our way back to our hotel. We've had a great time, eaten wonderful food, and had lots of laughs. Gone is the awkwardness of last night where we felt we just needed to get through it. Tonight is different. It's as if we are unable to waste a single moment of our time together. Every conversation, every topic, every laugh seems special.

"I had a wonderful first date," I tell him.

Nathan stops and takes me into his arms. He bends and kisses me softly. "Me, too."

We stand cheek to cheek as the ocean breeze washes over us. He kisses me again and then takes my face in his hands. "You ready to go home?"

I stare up at him. "I am."

His lips take mine again and I melt into his arms. *This feels so right.*

He takes my hand and begins to walk with a sudden urgency toward the hotel.

"What's the rush?" I ask.

"I'm being a gentleman," he replies, distracted as he pulls me along.

"Huh?" I frown. "Gentlemen rush?"

"They do." He continues to walk. "They make sure they get their dates home safe and sound."

"And what do gentlemen do with their dates when they get them home?"

He turns and takes me in his arms aggressively, nearly knocking me off my feet. "Bad things." He bites my neck, and I laugh out loud in surprise.

Well, I guess I did ask for a bad man to teach me bad things.

I never guessed it would be my Nathan.

He pulls me along so hard that my arm nearly comes out the socket. Ten minutes later, we are in our apartment, and Nathan is dragging me into the bedroom.

He's been patient and gentle with me up until this point, but I get the feeling that his control has slipped. He's on autopilot now.

He turns me away from him and slowly slides down the zipper on my dress. My heart beats hard.

He kisses my neck as he slides my dress down over my hips. His lips linger over mine, and then as if remembering what he was doing, he spins me back toward him and holds me still. I'm in a black, lacy bra and matching G-string.

Nathan hasn't seen me in anything like this before—not in this context, anyway. His eyes drop down my body, and when they rise to my face, his eyes are blazing with desire.

I stand still, unable to move. The heat of his gaze is burning my skin as his eyes roam all over me.

He's *so* hot like this.

He sits on the bed and lifts one of my legs onto the bed beside him. He pulls my panties to the side and kisses me there.

"Do you have any idea how badly I want you, Eliza?" he whispers.

Hearing him say my name, watching him kiss me there... it all makes goosebumps scatter up my spine.

He reaches up and takes off my bra, and his eyes darken as he sees my hardened nipples. He cups my breast in his hand as his lips take mine.

His tongue slides effortlessly through my mouth as if he's done this a million times before—as if he was meant to do it all along.

He takes my face in his hands and kisses me hard. My knees nearly buckle from underneath me. The emotion in his kiss tears my heart wide open. I whimper softly, overwhelmed by the tenderness between us.

He stands and slides my panties down my legs, and then twirls them on his finger as he circles me—his eyes drinking me in.

I stand still, waiting his next command. I've never seen him like this. I always knew that my Nathan was bossy, but his sexual dominance is next level.

He scrunches my panties in his fist and lifts them to inhale deeply, and my eyes widen. "You smell good."

Oh, hell....

He drops to his knees in front of me and nuzzles into my sex to inhale deeper. "Open," he moans as he lifts my leg onto the bed. He pulls my sex apart with his fingers and licks me soft at first, and then harder and harder with his thick tongue. My head falls back in pleasure.

I need him naked.

I reach down and pull his shirt over his shoulders, and I catch my breath as I look down at him between my legs.

Naked from the waist up, I see the muscles in his shoulders flex as he works me. His stomach muscles catch the light as he clenches against his hand. His eyes are closed as he licks up what my body is giving him.

Lord almighty. What a sight to behold.

His eyes rise to mine, and he slides a finger in deep. I bite my bottom lip as I clench around him, and he hisses in approval.

He adds another finger, and I want to show him what I can do. I clench harder, and his jaw ticks, fighting for control. "Fuck me, Eliza."

"That's the plan." I smile darkly.

He snaps and in one quick movement he's on his feet and throws me back onto the bed, he spreads my legs wide and tears his jeans down, his eyes are fixed on my sex as he slowly strokes himself. Preejaculate drips from his end and my stomach clenches in appreciation.

I stare up at the beautiful specimen of man before me. Those broad shoulders and that rippled abdomen with a scattering of dark hair that runs in a trail from his navel down to his well-kept pubic hair. His thick cock hangs heavily between his legs, and his quads are full and strong. There's only one word that comes to mind:

Virile.

He bends to lick me again, and I can't wait any longer, I just want him inside of me. "Now." I reach for him. "Nathan, get up here."

His eyes close as he licks me, over and over—the pleasure so strong. He's a master at this. I can't stand it anymore. I reach for him.

"Now, Nathan. Please."

I writhe beneath him, begging for him to fill me.

He crawls up my body and nestles in between my open legs. His cock slides through my wet flesh.

Electricity crackles in the air. I can feel it. This is something special.

"Fuck me," I mouth.

Fire dances in his eyes. He reaches down and grabs the base of his cock.

He's so different to anyone I've slept with before. His sexual power is so all consuming that it takes over. I can hardly breathe.

His dick slowly slides through my open sex, up and down, and we fall serious as we stare at each other and I run my fingers through his stubble. Ten long years, and it all comes down to this. The moment in time where we connect on a deeper level—his body inside of mine.

He repeats the movement, and my hips rise from the bed to meet him, my body chasing a deeper connection. I need this. *Hurry.*

He nudges forward, and the tip goes in. Ohh... a little burn.

Nathan's dark eyes hold mine, watching for my reaction, and then he stops still.

"What is it?" I ask.

'I don't want to hurt you."

"You won't, baby." I smile as I kiss him. "I need you."

"You'll tell me to stop if I hurt you?"

"I promise."

He pushes forward, and I'm driven into the mattress. Ah, okay, that burns.

"Big?" I wince.

"Small," he whispers back.

Holding himself off me by resting on his elbows, he pushes forward and a searing burning sensation tears through my body as he slides in deep. My legs lift around his waist to try and ease the pressure. *Fuckkkkk.*

My man is big.

Ouch.

Thump, thump, thump, goes my heart. My senses are in overload and we stare at each other. He gives me a slow, sexy smile, and he circles his pelvis to try and stretch me out. He circles the other direction, and I frown as I get used to the sensation.

"Is that okay?" he asks before he takes my lips with his. He circles again in the other direction, and a wave of pleasure begins to heat my blood.

Unable to form a sentence, I nod as I slide my hands up his arms and over his broad shoulders.

He slowly slides out and then pushes himself back in. He repeats the delicious circular movement, and I feel a rush of moisture as my body relaxes around him. "That's it, baby," he breathes.

"Oh..." I whimper.

He kisses me again... passionately, perfectly, and my hands go to the back of his head as I pull him to me.

"Feels good," I murmur against his lips. "So good."

I glide my hands over his back and behind. I can feel the muscles contract as his body works mine.

I want more. I need more. I lift my legs. "Harder."

He clenches his jaw and pulls back. His moves slowly get harder. I smile up at him in awe. Oh God, this is good.

He pulls his hips back and then he hits me hard. The air is knocked out of my lungs, and I wince.

"Oww," I whimper.

"Sorry." He frowns, as if he's struggling to control himself. He slows the pace. "How's that?" He pants, sweat beginning to bead on his brow.

I smile and reach to kiss his big beautiful lips. I couldn't adore this man more than I do now. He's so worried he's hurting me.

My back arches off the bed. My body is now wet, supple... open for him.

We keep going and the bed begins to rock hard.

"That's it," I pant. "Oh, that's good, Nathe. Give it to me... *harder.*"

His eyes darken as if he's been waiting for those words. He lifts himself up on straightened arms, and he spreads his knees wide. He slams in hard, and the air leaves my body.

Holy. Fucking. Shit.

The bed begins to hit the wall with force from his deep, punishing pumps, and I can do nothing but hang on as I see stars. The entire fucking universe of beautiful stars.

I can feel my orgasm building, and my body begins to quiver. Oh no, not yet.

Please, not yet.

Nathan's eyes roll back in his head as he loses control.

"Eliza," he moans. "You need to fucking come." He lifts my leg up to his shoulder, and he turns and tenderly kisses my foot.

We stare at each other in a moment of perfect tenderness.

Clarity.

It's too much. The emotions between us are too strong, and I can't hold it. My body convulses hard, and I shudder deep in my core.

He completely loses control and really lets me have it, and he tips his head back and moans as he comes hard.

His face contorts. He's so beautiful when he orgasms.

Breathtaking. My heart soars as emotion fills my every cell.

We hold each other close, our hearts beating hard and fast, kissing for a long time, like there's nowhere else to be and nothing else to do. Out of all the places I could be on Earth tonight, I want to be here doing this with him.

Nathan studies me as he holds my face. "You're perfect," he whispers.

"No. You're perfect." I smile softly.

He kisses me again and again, and then he flexes his dick that still lies deep inside of me.

"I love you, Eliza," he whispers. "So much."

I get a lump in my throat. He really does. I can feel his love for me.

"I love you, Nathe." I smile.

I put my head on his chest and he holds me close. I smile sleepily. There's no going back now.

We're really doing this.

14

Eliza

I ROLL OVER AND WINCE. "Oh God," I whisper as I put the heel of my hands into my eye sockets. "My head is pounding."

"Like my dick," Nathan says dryly.

I look over at him in question. "Your dick is pounding?"

"Uh-huh." He gives me the side-eye. "Some crazy bitch, tiny kitty, drunk on sangria, thought she might like to squeeze the fuck out of him."

I laugh out loud. "Tiny kitty?"

He chuckles, rolls over me, and holds my hands above my head. "There's only one way to fix Tiny." His lips drop to my neck and he nips me.

"And how is that?" I giggle as I try to escape his teeth.

"Train her up." He bites me hard, and I laugh out loud as I struggle to break free.

He puts his leg between mine and spreads my legs apart before he rolls between them.

"And you thought you were going to lie around and do nothing on this vacation, didn't you?"

I giggle. "I did, actually. Why? What did you have planned?"

"The only thing you're going to be doing..." He slides deep into my body as his teeth bite my neck again and I smile up at the ceiling. "Is me."

———

It's our third night, and Nathan holds up my hand and twirls me around. I come back and hit his body with a thud, and I laugh out loud. We've been dancing in this bar for hours. We wandered in here on our way home from the beach. We had dinner, and now with our beach towels and sunscreen in a bag on the floor, we are having the time of our lives.

Nathan swings me around, and his deep, carefree laugh permeates my bones. This vacation is the stuff dreams are made of.

We've eaten at beautiful restaurants and swam in the Mediterranean Sea.

We've made love under the stars, and fucked until we couldn't breathe.

Nathan is swoony, attentive, dry, sarcastic, funny, spontaneous... and I'm in love. Utterly, completely, and irrevocably in love.

Nathan Mercer is everything I never knew I needed. How was I so blind not to feel it before?

———

We sit at the small table outside the restaurant. The cobblestone streets house medieval looking buildings. It's late afternoon, and day five on our vacation. We've arrived in the town of Alcúdia.

"Can you believe we're actually here, Nathan? This place is magical."

He sits back and sips his wine. "It is."

I take out my brochure and begin to read it out loud. "The historic center of Alcúdia is enclosed by Mallorca's only entirely preserved walls, erected in the 14th century by King Jaumex II to protect Alcudia's inhabitants." I smile and raise my eyebrows. "It wasn't, however, enough to keep out the marauding pirate who attacked the city again and again in the 16th century, causing many of the population to flee. Today, it's hard to believe that this bustling town was once at risk of being deserted completely. Thankfully, in 1779, the construction of the harbour saved Alcúdia from decline." My eyes widen. "Marauding Pirates. Can you imagine what this town was like back then?"

Nathan smiles as he listens. He has this whimsical look on his face as he holds his wine glass, his leg crossed at the ankle.

I put my brochure down. "What's that look?"

"I love listening to you read to me."

"You love me reading brochures to you?" I smirk.

"Yes." He smiles softly as he lifts his glass to his lips. "Perhaps one day you will read me a story about us."

I smile as the air swirls between us. "Well...." I pause as I try to think of a story. "There were once two beautiful birds named Nathan and Eliza. And they were the best of friends. They loved and looked after each other for the longest time."

He watches me.

"And one day they decided to be brave and fall in love."

He smiles softly. "And what happened to the beautiful birds?"

"They flew off into the sunset and lived happily ever after."

He takes my hand over the table and kisses my fingertips. "I like that story."

"Me, too," I whisper. "Me, too."

———

I lie on the deckchair and smile up at the sun.

I'm wearing my gold bikini—the one that started everything. I've worn it every day, and Nathan has taken it off every night.

It's day seven of our holiday. We've swam, eaten, sight seen, and made love under the stars. Majorca is so beautiful.

It's now 7:00 p.m, and the sun is just starting to set over the ocean. We are on the beach drinking margaritas. Nathan is on his phone, and I'm lying in a lazy state of heaven.

"Hey," he says as he reads. "Your apartment settles tomorrow."

"Your apartment," I remind him.

"*Our* apartment." He sips his drink as he watches me. "So, I've been thinking."

"Did it hurt?" I ask as I tilt my face to the sun and close my eyes.

"What if I...?"

I open one eye to look at him. "What if you what?"

"What if I moved in with you... permanently?"

I sit up, suddenly interested in this conversation. "You mean, like a boyfriend in a real relationship?"

"Yes." A trace of a smile crosses his face, and then he chuckles. "Real relationship." He mouths as he repeats the words.

I bite my bottom lip to hide my smile. "Nathan Mercer, are you asking me if I'll be your girlfriend?"

"No." He sips his drink casually. "You're already my girlfriend. I'm merely stating the facts. When I told you I loved you and you said it back, so then...." He shrugs, as if I should already know what he's talking about.

"You didn't ask me yet." I smirk.

He puts his drink on the table in between our deckchairs, and he turns his attention to me. "Eliza, do you want to be my girlfriend?"

"I'll think about it," I reply casually as I lie back down.

"Right, that's it." He jumps up and he sweeps me up into his arms like a bride. "You asked for it." He strides toward the water.

"Asked for what?" I laugh. "Put me down, people are watching."

"They're going to see a lot more in a minute."

"Like what?" I laugh.

"I'm going to hold you under water until you agree."

I burst out laughing as I feel the water meet my stomach as he walks further into the Mediterranean Sea.

We fall into the ocean, laughing, and he takes me into his arms. My legs instinctively wrap around his waist. Skin to skin, we fall silent. He wraps my ponytail around his hand and pulls my head back so that my eyes meet his. "Be my girlfriend."

"What do I get for it?"

"Me."

The most wonderful reward of all time.

My heart swells, and I smile and kiss him softly. "It's a good thing I love you."

"It's the best thing."

His lips take mine.

And just like that, I have a boyfriend who lives with me.
Look at me being all grown up.

————

It's day eight of our holiday and I close my eyes as the masseuse's hands roam up and down my back. Nathan has gone off on his own, and I have spent the afternoon at the spa. I've had a manicure and pedicure, and now she's just finishing a two hour massage. I really am living this up.

When I finish here, I'm going to go and buy a new date dress. Nathan is taking me to some fancy restaurant for dinner and dancing tonight. I want something really special.

"There you go." The masseuse smiles.

"That was wonderful," I say. "Thank you so much." I dress and pay before I make my way out into the street. My phone rings, the name Brooke lighting up the screen. My stomach flips with nerves. I haven't spoken to anyone since Nathan and I got together.

"Hello."

"Oh my god, it's a disaster!" Brooke cries.

"What is?" I frown as I walk along.

"Jolie has drunk too much kombucca and gone totally fucking insane."

I stop walking. "What, why?"

"She's been fucking Santiago and letting him film her."

"*Noo!*" I gasp.

"She thinks she likes it; says it's turning her on to know he's watching it back when he's alone."

My eyes widen. "Are you serious?"

"Yes. She doesn't even know this guy, and now she doesn't

care if he shows anyone. Oh, and get this. She thinks they have something special—that he could be the one."

"She has lost her mind. This is disturbing."

"You need to talk to her."

"I'm on the other side of the world."

"Call her right now and tell her how stupid and irresponsible she's being."

"She's a big girl."

"... who is making a huge mistake she's going to regret when she's uploaded onto a porn site for millions of men to jerk off to. She's going to become a public come-bucket."

I wince at the horrendous analogy. "She hasn't thought this through at all. I mean, okay I get it if she wants to sleep with him. But to let him film it when she knows he openly shows everyone. I mean... what the hell?" I whisper.

"My point exactly. You need to talk to her."

"Why do I have to do it?"

"Because she's not listening to me. She thinks I'm a prude and don't get it. We had a huge fight about it, but as her friends, it's our responsibility to look out for her... even if she doesn't want us to."

I roll my eyes. "Okay, yes, you're right. I'll call her."

"Call me back and tell me what she says."

I hang up and dial Jolie's number.

"Hello," she answers abruptly. "If you've called to tell me that Santiago is a bad idea, I don't want to talk to you."

I cringe, jeez, she really is set on this. "No," I snap. "I called to say hello, bitch."

"Oh. Sorry. I thought Brooke had been in your ear. Hello. "

I roll my eyes feeling guilty, Brooke has so been in my ear.

"How's the vacation?"

A big smile crosses my face. "Amazing. " I don't know

whether to tell her about Nathan and I. No, I'll wait to tell them in person. "Majorca is beautiful. You need to come here; it really is incredible."

"I'll add it to my bucket list."

"So, what's this about Brooke and Santiago?" I ask as I sit down on a bench.

"I've started seeing him and, oh my God, Eliza, he's amazing."

"The porno guy?" I frown.

"Yes, but, you know what? I appreciate his honesty."

I need to try and be understanding here. "Well... I guess."

"There's just this sense of honesty between us, and we really connect on a deeper level."

I pinch the bridge of my nose. Brooke is completely right: Jolie's lost her fucking marbles here. "Okay, so have you been sleeping with him?"

"Yes. Holy fucking shit, he's so hot I can't stand it."

"Right."

"And the orgasms."

"Is he filming you?"

"Yes, but he's not going to show anyone."

"Jo," I sigh.

"Don't ruin this for me."

"I'm just saying. It's a bit of a red flag, you know? And, as my friend, I just need to point out the potential dangers here. I'm just trying to be a good friend."

She exhales heavily. "I know."

"Look," I try to think of a solution, "why don't you just film yourselves having sex on your phone or camera? That way, you have possession of the film."

"Hmm... maybe."

"I'm just saying, you don't know him, and you don't know

what he's going to do with that footage. Do you really want your future kids seeing mommy getting banged on porn sites in years to come?"

She stays silent, and I know my words are resonating with her.

"Look, I'm all for you and him having a great time. Have fun. Fuck his brains out. But just guard yourself. Guys who pick up girls in bars by showing them footage of themselves fucking other women... they aren't really husband material."

"That's his past, Lize."

"I know, baby, and it may be all behind him, but as your friend, I have to have this conversation with you."

"I guess." She sighs.

"Look, I've got a video camera you can borrow. You've got a key to my place. Go over and get it. It's in the top shelf of my linen closet. That way, you own the footage and not him. The risks are lessened. It's the perfect solution."

"Really?"

I smile. Nathan is going to freak and throw the camera in the garbage as soon as she returns it, but whatever. "Sure."

"Thanks, Lize."

"Love you."

"Love you, too."

"You're wearing condoms, right?"

"Goodbye, Eliza." The phone goes dead, and I giggle. That may have been pushing it.

I arrive back at our apartment just after 5:00 p.m. and find Nathan sitting out on the balcony. There's music playing, and he's overlooking the ocean with a Corona beer in his hand. He turns and flashes me a slow, sexy smile. The way he looks at me now is so different to how he used to look at me. I can feel his adoration from across the room.

"Hello." He stands and walks to me.

"Hi." I kiss him, and he slides his hand down my behind to squeeze it.

"How was the massage?" he asks.

"Heavenly." I take his beer from him and take a sip. "How was your afternoon?"

"Good." He smiles. "I got you a present."

"You did?"

He lifts his shirt to reveal a tattoo of three birds with long wings flying across the side of his ribcage, toward the front of his body. There's one bird at the back and two at the front. It's red and swollen but its beauty can't be hidden.

My eyes widen and rise to his.

He points to the two birds at the front. "Those are the two birds in that story of yours."

I smile goofily. "You and me?"

He kisses me softly. "Uh-huh, that's us flying into the sunset."

My mouth falls open. "Nathe," I whisper in awe. I point to the other swallow at the back. "Who's this?"

"The life I left behind."

My eyes rise to his, what does that mean? I stare at him for a moment as I process that statement. Does it bother him?

"Is that okay... that you left that life behind?"

"It's like it never happened," he whispers as he tucks a piece of my hair behind my ear.

My heart freefalls. "I love you, Nathe," I whisper. "So much."

He kisses me softly and hugs me tight. "I love you, too, baby."

We stand in each other's arms for a long time. I feel so close to him... like he's a part of me—two souls connected together by their hearts.

"How haven't I seen what's between us before now?" I ask. "How did we live without this?"

"I don't know." He chuckles and pulls me closer. "I think we always knew on some level, but we were just too dumb to read the signs."

His lips take mine, and his kiss is slow, tender, and erotic. His tongue slides through my open lips, and I smile against them as an idea comes to my head. "What happens if we smudge the tattoo?"

"I don't know but I'm happy to try." He raises an eyebrow mischievously.

I giggle, and in one sharp movement, he picks me up and throws me over his shoulder. He stomps into the bedroom and I put my hands down to his lower back as I laugh.

He throws me onto the bed, and I laugh out loud as I bounce. He lifts his shirt over his head, and my breath catches. His skin is olive and tanned from the sun. His muscles ripple his torso, and with the addition of the new art...

I don't know if I've ever seen anything more.... "You're so beautiful," I whisper up at him in awe.

He drops his pants. His thick cock hangs heavily between his legs, and my breath catches. No matter how many times I watch Nathan undress, I will never take it for granted.

The fact that he is undressing for me is just beyond words.

He takes his dick in his hand and slowly strokes it as his dark eyes hold mine.

My back arches off the bed, and my legs instinctively open. Nathan bends and lifts my dress over my head, and his eyes drop to my gold bikini bottoms.

"Do you know how many times I imagined you laid out on

the bed for me like this?" He slips two fingers under the side of my panties and runs them through my sex. He then puts them in his mouth. His cheeks hollow as he sucks his fingers hard.

My heart beats faster. Nathan's naughty side is the ultimate aphrodisiac.

"You taste fucking good, Eliza."

With my eyes locked on his, I spread my legs wider so that they rest on the mattress.

He smiles darkly and, taking my cue, he slides my bikini bottoms off and tosses them to the side. His large hands hold my thighs apart, and he dips his head. His thick tongue slides through my sex, and his eyes close in pleasure.

"You have no fucking idea how much I love doing this," he murmurs into my sex.

My back arches from the bed. "I'm pretty sure I do." I smile as I run my fingers through his hair.

Nathan's new addiction is going down on me. I wake, and he's there. I fall asleep, and he's there. I don't know how many times he's made me come on his tongue, but holy fucking shit... he's not the only one addicted.

He flicks his tongue as he slides three thick fingers deep into my sex, and my legs lift to hang in the air as I let out a guttural moan.

He pumps me hard with his hand, and the bed hits the wall.

Here we go again.

Fuck, yes...

———

We exit the plane in single file, and a sense of sadness rolls over me. No more Majorca. Our heavenly vacation has come to an end. But I have arrived home with a boyfriend who I am madly in love with. We have an exciting future together.

We make it through customs and get our luggage before we make our way to the parking lot.

"That flight is a killer." I sigh.

"Sure is."

We get to the car and Nathan puts his arm around me and pulls me in for a kiss. I look over and see Brooke's friend from work walking toward us. I step back from Nathan immediately. Shit, I haven't told the girls, and I don't want anyone to know just yet.

"What are you doing?" He frowns.

"Amanda is just there." I gesture to her with my chin. Amanda is the world's biggest gossiper. We may as well put it on the front page of the New York Times if she finds out.

"So?" He frowns.

"Just—"

"Eliza, Nathan, hi," Amanda cuts me off as she approaches us.

"Hi." I smile. Shit, fuck off, busy body. I want to tell the girls myself. I don't want them hearing this from her before I get a chance to tell them in person. "We just got home from Majorca."

Maybe she won't ask questions.

Nathan steps forward and puts his arm around me and pulls me toward him. "Hi, Amanda." He smiles.

Shit.

"Hi, Nathan." Amanda frowns as she looks between us. "Are you two together now?"

"No," I snap before Nathan has a chance to reply. "Still best friends just going on vacation and stuff together." I fake a laugh. Oh, hell, lying is uncomfortable. "Nothing new here."

Nathan frowns over at me anyway. I splutter. Oh hell, this is the worst timing, bitch.

"Good." Amanda smiles as she looks between us as if sensing something is very off here.

Nathan's gaze drops to the ground, and his jaw ticks. He's angry... *fuck*.

"We're in a really big rush. Bye, Amanda," I say as I walk around to get in the car. "Nice to see you."

Amanda smiles as she waves. Her calculating eyes are still assessing us, and she finally walks off.

Buzz off, mole.

Nathan glares at me across the roof of the car.

"I just told her that because I don't want anyone to know we're together yet," I whisper.

"Are you ashamed of me?"

15

Eliza

"WHAT? NO." I scoff. "I just... we haven't told our friends yet, or our families. I want them to find out from us, not via the seedy grapevine."

He narrows his eyes, unimpressed with my answer. He throws the suitcases into the trunk and we get into the car. He pulls out, and we drive through the parking lot with his jaw ticking in anger.

My eyes flick between him and the road. "Nathan, you can't seriously be angry about that."

He stares at the road as he grips the steering wheel with both hands.

"I just want to tell our friends first."

"And when will that be, Eliza?" He snaps. "I would have thought you would have called them from Majorca to do it, seeing how you all know when each other fucking fart."

I roll my eyes. "You're being dramatic."

"Dramatic? Did you speak to April or your friends while we were in Majorca, Eliza?"

"I did but I want to tell them in person."

His eyes flick between me and the road. "Are you sure that's the reason?"

"Of course, it's the reason," I fire back, but it's not. Not even close. The truth is that I'm not sure how they are going to take it, and I don't want them to rain on my parade. I know April will be all for it, but last time we spoke about Nathan and me, I was telling her all about Stephanie. I didn't want it to seem like Nathan railroaded me into going on vacation.

"I'll tell them tomorrow." I cross my arms in a huff. "You sure do know how to ruin my post-holiday glow."

He screws up his face in disgust. "Oh, it's all about you, isn't it?"

"What's that supposed to mean?"

He wobbles his head around, all righteous like. "And I quote, *I don't want anyone to know we're together.*" He hits the steering wheel. "You want to talk about ruining someone's post-holiday glow, let's fucking talk about that sentence, shall we?"

I roll my eyes. "You took it out of context, Nathan, and you know you did. I simply want to tell our friends and family first out of respect for them. Stop carrying on about this. You're beginning to piss me off."

His eyes bulge from the sockets as they flick between the road and me. "Well, I'm already pissed off, Eliza. Don't fucking talk to me."

"Good!" I fire back. "I won't. Don't talk to me."

"Don't worry, I'm not."

I cross my arms, and he takes a corner fast.

"Slow down!" I snap as I hold on. "You're driving like a maniac."

"Don't tell me how to fucking drive." He growls.

"Well, I can't tell the girls about us tomorrow if I'm dead, now, can I?"

He screws up his face, and I can see he's muttering something to himself.

"What?" I say.

He stays silent as he glares at the road.

"Go on, say it."

"I'm just wondering if you think our relationship is all about you."

"What?" I screw my face up, fuck he's still on that, what's he going on about now?

"I've already told Alex that we're together. I called him, all excited from our vacation. I have nothing to be ashamed of. You spoke to your friends and purposely didn't tell them."

I roll my eyes and I snuggle back into the seat. "Shut up, you're supposed to not be talking to me. Do it."

"Watch it," he warns.

"You're just looking for a fight and you're not getting one. I told you the reason, now drop it. I've just been in transit for fifteen hours, Nathan, and the last thing I want to deal with is your dramatics."

He narrows his eyes as he watches the road.

I bite my lip to stifle my smile. There he is... my cranky Nathan. I wondered how long he would take to show up.

Goodbye, holiday love bubble. Welcome back to reality, Eliza.

———

I wake to the sound of the shower on, and I stretch out wide. Oh man... the gym.

I glance at the clock and see it's 5:30 a.m.

I don't want to go back to routine.

Nathan didn't talk to me at all last night, and we slept with our backs to each other.

Two weeks joined at the hip have taken their toll.

I smile sleepily at the ceiling. Reality bites.

I hear the shower turn off, and moments later, he walks in with a towel around his waist. When he gets his suit from the wardrobe, his eyes glance to me.

"Hi." I smile.

"Good morning, Eliza," he says coolly.

"Still hate me?" I ask playfully.

"I do, actually." He unzips his suit bag and takes the suit out before he walks out into the living area.

Great, he's going to make me grovel. I lie for a moment, listening to him move around as he dresses, and then I hear the coffee machine switch on. That's it. I'm up. I walk out into the living room naked to see Dr. Mercer in all his glory, wearing perfect-fit navy suit, a crisp white shirt, and a striped tie, as well as his usual expensive shoes and designer chunky watch. His hair has a bit of a curl to it and is messed to perfection. He smells delicious. The aftershave Nathan wears to work must hypnotise all his female patients. Who am I kidding? It would hypnotise everyone who came into contact with him.

I slide my hands around under his suit as I cuddle up to him. "Nathe, I'm sorry about last night."

He stares down at me but doesn't put his arms around me.

"I didn't mean for that to sound the way it did. It came out wrong." I go up onto my tippy toes and kiss his big, beautiful lips. "I love you."

"I didn't like it."

I kiss him again as I run my fingers through his stubble and stare into his big blue eyes. "I'm sorry. I realize how it must have sounded. I'm going to tell everyone about us today. I can't wait to see them."

He gives me a lopsided smile, and his hands slide around to my behind and he bends and kisses me, our lips linger over each other's. "Okay."

I straighten his tie and dust off his shoulders. "I'm going to make it up to you tonight."

"How are you going to do that?"

I put my lips to his ear. "I'm going to suck your dick so fucking good," I breathe.

He smirks as his eyes darken. His hand slides up my body and cups my breast. He tweaks my nipple hard, and he grabs my face and turns it to the side. Then he bites my ear. Goose-bumps scatter up my arms. "I look forward to it."

He kisses me aggressively. His tongue is full of power, and want, and oh... let's go back to bed.

"Goodbye, Eliza." He picks up his briefcase, and without another word, he walks out. The door clicks shut behind him. I stand and stare at the back of it for a moment with a goofy smile on my face.

I love that man.

———

I walk into the hospital at 7:00 a.m.. Henry is in surgery today so I work out of his office here at the private hospital. I take the lift up to my level and make my way down to the office. Henry is sitting at his desk with his laptop open.

"Hey, there she is." He smiles happily. "Thank fuck you're back."

"Hi." I laugh at his excited reaction.

"How was the trip?"

"Oh, so good. Majorca is beautiful. You should go one day."

He turns back to his laptop and types something. "I think it's more of a romantic getaway, isn't it?"

"No, singles, too." I frown. Hang on, the girls mentioned he has a girlfriend, "Aren't you with your girlfriend anymore?"

"No." He twists his lips, as if frustrated. "While you were on the other side of the world being a love bird, I was back here breaking up with my girlfriend of four years. It's been a rough two weeks."

"Oh, no." I slump into the seat beside him. "What happened?"

"Well." He shrugs. "She was pressuring me to get married and I figured that if getting married to someone feels so wrong, maybe she isn't the right one."

"That sucks. I'm sorry."

He smiles sadly. "That's okay. Shit happens, right?"

"It does." I look through the surgery sheet for the day.

"Well, at least you get to break someone's nose today." I smile.

He chuckles. "This is true, I do. It's going to feel good to smash that fucker."

I laugh. "Do you want a coffee from the cafeteria?"

"Only if you're getting yourself one. But go to the café downstairs, though. The one on this level is shit."

"I know, I remember from last time. Why didn't you warn me? Back in a minute."

I make my way down to level one and through to the cafeteria. I order our coffees and stand and wait. I glance up and see Nathan with his four interns walking down the corridor. He's talking as they all listen and hang on his every word. I smile as I watch him. He's explaining something in great depth, using animated hand gestures as he talks. He directs them into a room and they all file in. He catches sight of someone in the hall and then stops.

I watch on as a woman approaches him. He says something to her, and they both laugh. Oh, I've met her before. She's a doctor. Pretty, too. She's at some of the balls we go to. I forget her name, though. They continue to laugh and talk for a few minutes. Nathan says something, and she rubs his upper arm. Her body languages seems flirty.

I watch on for a moment, my eyes fixed on them, and then he says something and she laughs out loud. He steps into the elevator, he says something else, and she laughs out loud again. What's so funny, bitch?

I begin to hear my jealous heartbeat in my ears.

I'm snapped out of my daydream by the words, "Coffee for Eliza."

I get my coffee and turn to look up the hall. The same flirty woman is now talking to another doctor, and she's laughing with him, too. That must be just her personality. I shrug my shoulders and make my way back upstairs.

This jealousy thing is new. Now that I know he's attracted to women, the goalposts have been moved again. Every relationship with his friends is new, and it makes me wary of everyone now. I know I need to cut this jealousy out; nothing good could ever come from it. I make my way back upstairs to find that Henry is still working on his computer.

"We only have three surgeries this morning and then we will call it a day. Early mark."

I say as I sit down at my desk. "I have to start packing. I'm moving this week."

"Where to?"

"The other side of town. Nathan just bought a new place."

"Nice."

"Not the moving part." I sigh. "I'm dreading it."

"True. Do you want to go grab some Italian for lunch? I'm craving carbs."

"I can't, I'm meeting my friends for lunch." I open my computer. "And besides, I'm all carbed out. Operation slim-down starts today or else I'm not going to fit in this chair for much longer."

He chuckles. "Okay, I'll eat enough for the two of us."

I smile broadly. "Deal."

———

I sit in the café waiting for Brooke and Jolie. I'm nervous to tell them everything that's been going on. I've missed them, and I can only hope that they are as excited as I am. I spoke to April today, and she's ecstatic. I'm not telling mom and dad until I see them in person.

Brooke and Jolie walk in, and I can hear Jolie laughing.

"Hello." They both kiss me and fall into their seats. "How was Majorca?" Brooke smiles.

"Look at your tan," Jolie gushes. "You look so refreshed."

"It was fantastic and I am so refreshed."

The waitress comes over. "Can I take your order?" I quickly scan the choices.

"I'll have a Greek salad with poached chicken, and a mineral water, please," I say.

"Oh, me, too," Jolie says.

"Me, three," Brooke pipes in. "But can I have a Diet Coke instead?"

"Sure thing." The waitress leaves us alone.

We chat for a few minutes about Majorca and what's been going on back here.

I turn to my friends; how do I word this.... I'll start with deflection, "Um, how is Santiago?"

"Don't encourage her." Brooke scoffs.

Jolie rolls her eyes. "You get yourself some sex that is this good and then you can compare, okay?"

"Is it really good?" I smirk.

"I'm not even fucking joking, Eliza." She grabs my hand across the table. "My legs are jelly for half an hour after sex because the orgasms are so good. I can't even get up to go to the toilet."

"Does he film you while you go to the toilet?" Brooke asks, deadpan.

"No, but he did ask me to pee on him the other night."

"Oh God," Brooke cries. "What the fuck?"

I burst out laughing. "Are you serious?"

The waitress puts our drinks onto the table. "Thank you," we all reply.

"You know, like squirting." Jolie shrugs.

Brooke's eyes widen as she leans closer. "What do you mean, like squirting?"

"Don't tell me you don't know what squirting is?" Jolie whispers. "Who are you? Motherfucking Theresa?" She turns her attention to me. "You know squirting, don't you?"

"Yes." I frown. "Everyone knows what squirting is, but I do think that actual real squirting is different to porn squirting."

Jolie points her fork at me. "Right, so do I. There lies the question."

Brooke frowns as she looks between us. "What are you talking about?"

Our salads are put on the table in front of us. "Thanks."

I continue explaining, "So, some women, when they orgasm, squirt their come out of their pussy."

Brooke screws up her face in disgust. "What... like a clamshell?"

Jolie and I laugh. "Yes, exactly."

"But in porn," I explain, "women piss while they are taking it up the ass, or they piss while they are getting fucked."

"Why on earth would someone want to piss while they fuck?" Brooke whispers, mortified. "That's just fucking wrong, and who's cleaning the goddamn sheets?"

"It's supposed to be a turn on." Jolie shrugs. "God, Brooke, you really need to gct out more."

Brooke widens her eyes. "Obviously."

"Anyway," Jolie says. "He wants me to squirt on him."

"Are you going to?" I wince.

"Yeah." She shrugs. "Why not?" She takes a forkful of her salad. "And he asked me last night if I wanted his friend to join us in bed."

Brooke and I stare at her, dumbfounded.

"Who are you?" Brooke holds her temples. "I can't deal with this guy. He's stressing me out."

"You know what?" Jolie scoffs as she chews a huge mouthful of food. "He's fucking hot, that's who he is. I'm in the prime of my life, and I'm having fun while I can. Fuck it."

"And fuck all his friends," Brooke mutters dryly. "If you film that, I swear to God, I'm getting you sectioned in a fucking straight jacket."

I get the giggles. This really is hilarious.

Jolie picks up her drink and frowns as she stares into it. "Oh no, a little bug just flew into my drink."

"Scoop it out," I say.

"Well, I can't drink it now, it's ruined."

Brooke looks at her. Deadpan. "I know for a fact that you've had worse things in your mouth."

Jolie rolls her eyes, and I giggle.

"So, tell us about your trip?" Brooke says to change the subject.

I swallow my food whole and it scrapes all the way down my throat. "Well." I hit my chest to try and make the food go down. "Something happened... something wonderful."

They continue to eat.

"Nathan and I..." My voice trails off.

They both look up from their plates, waiting for my reply.

"We... we... fell in love."

Brooke's fork hits the plate with a clang. "What?"

I swallow the lump in my throat. "We've been having these feelings."

"Since when?" Jolie screws up her face.

"Before we went away, Nathan told me that he had feelings for me, and it kind of went from there and just happened."

They look at each other, and then look back to me, horrified.

"Eliza, he's gay," Jolie says.

"N-no," I stammer. "He's just been with men before. It doesn't mean he's completely gay."

"Eliza, honey." Brooke takes my hand over the table. "Don't mistake one night of sex with love."

"It's not just sex. We're in love. I thought you'd be happy for us."

"Eliza, men don't just turn straight one day. It doesn't happen," Jolie says softly.

"Well, it did." I shake my head, disappointed in their reaction, but on some level, I knew it was coming.

"It didn't," Brooke says. "Babe, he's been having sex with

men for twenty years. He's probably going to go back to wanting men. I know he loves you as a friend, Eliza. He's mistaking the two. You can't be so gullible as to think that you could actually hold onto him. You don't have the equipment he needs. No man ever turns gay to straight and stays that way forever."

I stare at her in disappointment as she holds my hand.

"Babe, he's probably curious and he cares about you. He sleeps with you every night, and it's confusing his emotions."

My face falls.

Brooke squeezes my hand. "Whatever you do, you can't fall in love with him. This is a heartbreak waiting to happen."

My eyes well with tears, I hate that they are saying out loud my greatest fear. "Don't say that," I whisper. "It's too late, I already am in love."

They sit silent as they watch me angrily wipe away my tears.

"You know, I thought my two best friends would be happy for me to finally fall in love."

"We are," they say.

"But you just can't fall in love with Nathan."

"Why not?"

"Nathan is perfect," Brooke says softly. "Honey, if there were any chance that this could work, I would be dancing in the streets because Nathan is the perfect man. But this is going to end badly... *for you*. Not him, but for you."

I stare at her as I process her words.

"He won't even be able to help it, Lize," Jolie says. "He's going to be out one night or at a conference, and he'll have a few drinks, and some guy is going to pique his interest. You can't pretend to be someone you're not forever. Primal instincts don't work that way." She takes my other hand in hers. "I'm sorry, baby, but this is a tragedy waiting to happen."

I snatch my hands out of theirs. "You're wrong. We are moving in with each other permanently this week."

"Oh God," Jolie whispers as she puts her head into her hands. "Have you lost your fucking mind?"

I can't take this. I need to get away from their hurtful words. I screw up my napkin and throw it onto the table. "You know what, I'm not listening to this. I'm happy for the first time in years. I'm fucking happy." I get up. "And if my friends can't support me..."

"Sit down!" Brooke snaps as she grabs my arm. "You're not going anywhere."

I sit back down.

"It's our duty of care to you as our friend to warn you of potential dangers," Brooke says.

"Yes, like you told me Santiago is a bad idea," Jolie says.

"That *is* a bad idea." I pick up my fork again.

"Lize." Brooke sighs sadly. "Yours is much worse."

"Nathan is your whole world. He has been for years," Jolie says. "How do you think you're going to cope if he leaves you for a man?"

I get a lump in my throat, almost feeling the betrayal wash over me. "I wouldn't," I whisper.

Jolie and Brooke stare at me, as if unsure what to say next.

"Anyway," Brooke says to change the subject. "Back to squirting. What do I put into Google?"

"Go to Pornhub and type squirting into the search bar," Jolie says. "I can't believe you don't know this shit." She rolls her eyes. "You are one frigid, old mole."

The girls continue talk and chatter but I can't concentrate. My mind is fixed on one sentence only:

How do you think you're going to cope if he leaves you for a man?"

———

It's just after 4:00 p.m. when I arrive home. I'm feeling super flat after having lunch with the girls.

I know they are only trying to look out for me, and I know that most people are going to react the same way and I need to get over it, but I guess it feeds my deepest fear with Nathan. No matter how much we love each other, I will never be everything that he needs. And no matter how hard I try...

I open the door, dejected, and I look around my apartment. We're supposed to be moving into the new apartment this week.

Supposed to be. What the fuck does that mean?

I *am* moving in with Nathan, and you know what? He's right. I am an asshole.

I didn't want anyone to see us last night because I was afraid of the reaction.

Afraid of judgment, and it happened today with my closest friends.

And Nathan had every right to be disappointed in me. Damn it, I'm disappointed in myself.

I storm through my apartment.

I'm going to snap out of this sad mood and start packing. I'm moving in with a wonderful man who loves me, and I don't give a damn what anyone else says. This is our love story. The world and their opinions can go fuck themselves.

I throw my bag down, get changed into some comfy clothes, and I begin to go through the kitchen. I throw things into boxes like a woman on a mission. With every item I pack, a little of my doubt disappears. I work and work, and I'm sitting on the floor going through my Tupperware cupboard when the door buzzes.

I climb up and go to the security buzzer. "Hello?"

"I have a delivery for Eliza Bennet."

"Oh, okay, I'll be right down."

I make my way into the foyer and see a man standing with the biggest bunch of deep red roses I've ever seen. "Eliza Bennet?"

"Yes?" I beam in excitement.

He hands me a screen. "Sign here, please."

"Thank you." He passes me the roses, and I dance back to the elevator.

I ride to my floor with a huge goofy grin on my face, and I run down the hall to my apartment. I open the door and tear open the small white envelope.

Truly. Madly. Deeply.

xox

I hold the card to my chest and swoon. "Oh, I love you too."

I stare at the beautiful roses and inhale their perfume. I count them. There are forty-eight in total. I don't even have enough vases for all of them. I smile as my heart sings.

He gets it.

He's the only one who gets what's between us, and damn it, I'm all in.

I lie in the deep bath and relax into the steamy room.

After my confidence crisis today, I'm feeling much better. I have a couple of glasses of red wine under my belt, and I've cooked dinner. Now, I'm soaking in the tub as I wait for my man.

I hear the door and then his keys clang as they hit the side table. He appears at the door. His eyes roam over my naked body, and he gives me a slow, sexy smile as he leans against the doorframe. "Hey, there."

I sink down in the bath as I smile under the water, my eyes above it. "Hi."

He undoes his tie with a jerk, his dark eyes holding mine. "Do you have any idea how hot you are?"

I open my legs as an invitation. "Get in here with me, Mercer."

He walks in and bends down to take my nipple in his teeth. "I would but this bath is too fucking small." He kisses me. "I can't wait for this new apartment. Get out here with me."

He takes my hand and I stand. His eyes drop down my body, and he bites his bottom lip, as if excited. He wraps me in a towel and begins to dry me.

"Thank you for my roses."

His hand goes to between my legs, and he parts me with his fingers. "You're most welcome."

We fall silent as he strokes me there, enticing bad things. "I got you another present, too."

"You did?"

He finishes drying me and takes my hand. He leads me into the living room, where a black box with red ribbon sits on the table. He picks it up and passes it to me.

"What is it?" I smile.

"Something for you... that's also something for me." His hand cups my breast and his thumb dusts over my hardened nipple. "Something for us."

I frown, untie the ribbon and slide the lid off the box, and my eyes widen.

There sits two silver butt plugs in a black, velvet-fitted tray.

They look designer or something—expensive and heavy. One is medium and one is large.

My eyes rise to his as I swallow my fear.

"I've never..."

"I know." He leans down and kisses me, his mouth sucking on mine. My legs instinctively part. "That's what these are for... to get you ready."

"Ready?" I whisper.

"Training."

"Oh..."

He licks up my neck. "I need you there, Eliza. Fuck. I've never needed anything so bad. It's all I can think about."

What... *this* is all he's thinking about?

My eyes close. I can't think when his tongue is on me. "Okay..." I catch sight of us in the mirror—me naked and him towering over me in his custom blue suit.

He kisses me hard. "Come." He takes my hand and pulls me into the bedroom. My heart begins to race with fear.

Nathan's big. Huge! I'm a wimp. These things don't meld well together. This could be a fucking disaster.

He lies me down on the bed and spreads my legs out wide until they are touching the mattress. He takes the box from me. He carefully inspects the two butt plugs.

"I think we'll start with the medium one." He takes the smaller one out of the box and holds it up for me to see. It's big and silver and looks like it has no right to be doing the rude things he wants it to.

"So?" He trails it up between my breasts slowly. "Here's how this is going to go. I'm going to put this in."

My scared eyes hold his.

"And then I'm going to make you come so fucking hard that your body will nearly snap it in two."

Fuck. I have no words for this situation.

"After a while of doing this, your body is going to recognize that something going in here,"—he rubs his finger over my back entrance and gently eases the very tip of his finger in—"is pleasure."

I stare at him, fully dressed in his business suit and having this conversation, as cool as a cucumber.

He kisses me as my senses begin screaming.

Why does he want to do this?

Aren't I enough?

"How does that sound?" he breathes against my lips.

I nod, nervously. "Good."

He puts his finger under my chin and brings my face up to his. He wants more than that.

I want to please him. I desperately want to be everything that he physically needs. "A little scary," I whisper.

A trace of a smile crosses his face. "I'll never hurt you."

Not physically you won't, but are you going to rip my heart out!

"I know," I lie.

He puts the butt plug into his mouth, and my insides clench as I watch him suck on it. He slides it in and out a few times, and then he puts it in my mouth. "Suck," he commands.

I close my eyes when I feel the hard-heavy metal in my mouth, and I suck it. I twirl my tongue around the tip, opening my mouth so that he can see. He loves it when I do this to his dick.

He inhales sharply as he watches, his hungry eyes fixed on my tongue.

"I'm going to have a quick shower. Keep warming this up in your mouth for when I get back."

He bends and kisses my forehead, and then he stands and

goes to the bathroom. I hear the shower turn on and the deaf-ening sound of the pounding of my heart echoes in my ears.

Why does he want to do this? Does he miss anal?

I suck on the large, hard, metal thing in my mouth... warming it up for my ass.

God.

I know I said I wanted a big, bad man to teach me bad things, so perhaps he's doing just that. But after the conversa-tion with the girls today, this all seems a bit too real.

On one hand, the thought of something new excites me. On the other hand, it reminds me of his past life. I know that it shouldn't but it does and I don't like it.

Stop it.

I hear the shower turn off.

Here we go. I open my eyes.

He reappears out of the bathroom with a white towel around his waist, his eyes darken when he sees me with the butt plug still in my mouth, he leans on the doorframe and watches me for a moment. "Fuck, Eliza, you look hot."

I smile nervously around the butt plug as my eyes hold his. My heart is about to go into cardiac arrest.

This feels like a monumental moment in our relationship. I want to enjoy it. I want to be everything for him.

I want to be everything he needs.

He saunters over and spreads my legs wide. When he drops his head, he licks me with his thick tongue.

"Give me some cream, baby," he whispers into me. Goose-bumps scatter my body every time Nathan says that. It does things to me...rude things.

My body rushes with pleasure and obeys his command.

He moans against me... *Jesus.*

He lifts my legs back so that my knees are up against my

chest, and his tongue moves to my back entrance. Deep, penetrating licks of his strong tongue consume me, and I begin to screw up the bedsheets. His eyes are closed in pleasure, he's totally lost in the moment.

Oh, fuck, I did not think I would be doing this tonight, that's for sure.

I feel the burn of his stubble on my cheeks—feel my sex weeping in pleasure. I almost feel guilty for enjoying this.

This should feel wrong but it feels intimate and special.

I whimper and my back arches off the bed. He reaches up and takes the butt plug from my mouth. With his eyes locked on mine, he trails it down my body.

He slides it into my sex and then leans down. With his hand flattened on my stomach, he flutters his tongue over my clitoris.

I begin to build deep inside, and my back arches again. My fingers twist in his hair.

How does he know how to do this so well?

With his tongue still fluttering over my clitoris, he moves the plug to my back entrance and slowly slides it in.

He bites my clitoris to take away the sting, and I moan. "Oh, God."

He leans up to watch me as he slowly slides it in and out.

"You like that?" he whispers. "Tell me how it feels."

I writhe beneath him, and he jerks the plug in harder.

I whimper out loud. "Ahh!"

"That's it, baby, ride it. Imagine it's my cock deep inside of you."

Oh God, I want him there.

My body begins to dance on her own, moving to a rhythm with the butt plug.

This doesn't feel wrong. This feels good.

Too good.

"I want the bigger one," I whisper.

His eyes flicker with arousal. "And you shall have it."

He gets the larger one and puts it in my mouth as he works my behind. I reach down and pull his towel off. His large cock springs free, and my sex contracts at the sight of him.

Fuck, he's beautiful.

He gives me more sexual satisfaction than any other man I've been with in the past. His intensity and experience are out of this world. Or maybe it's the higher level of intimacy we share. Whatever it is, he drives me wild.

His tongue flutters over my clitoris again, and I shudder.

"Don't come."

"Well, you'd better stop doing that," I warn him.

"Don't fucking come, Eliza. I mean it." He takes the butt plug from my mouth and swaps it with the other one. He slowly pushes it into my ass. My body resists it, and he has to break through the barrier.

"Oww." It burns.

He takes it slow for a while, and then my body accepts all of it.

He smiles into me as his tongue lashes my sex. He's lost control now and is all in. His face glistens with my arousal as his thrusts on my behind get stronger.

"I'm going to come," I whimper, reaching for him. "Nathan."

He stands and rolls me over onto my knees.

"Fuck." He moans as he watches me. He rubs his hand across my cheeks. "You look so fucking hot with this in your ass."

I sway my behind from side to side to try and get some traction. Oh, I need this orgasm. I need it bad.

He leans over me and licks my back as he plays with the

butt plug. My eyes roll back, and he slowly sinks his cock into my sex.

He pushes in slowly, and then slams in hard. His movements push the plug in deeper, and a jolt of pleasure flies through me.

My mouth hangs open. I have no control over myself. This is so dirty.

He grabs my shoulders and slams in hard. The air is knocked from my lungs, and I cry out again and again... the ecstacy shooting through me in technicolour waves.

He spreads my legs so wide that I can hardly hold myself up, and then he lets me have it.

The bed begins to hit the wall with force. I scream out as a freight train of an orgasm rips through me.

"Yes...yes." He pumps harder. He begins to chant as he fucks me, lost in his own ecstasy, and then he tips his head back and holds himself deep. He comes in a rush deep inside me, and I feel his hot seed as his cock jerks. He takes the butt plug out and smears the semen over my back entrance, and then he pushes just the very tip of his dick into my behind before he pulls it out and empties himself.

He repeats the delicious movement as he smears himself everywhere, again and again.

I close my eyes in pleasure, don't tell me how.... but this feels so intimate.

Like he's branding me with his love.

Truly, madly, deeply.

Unable to hold myself up, I fall to the mattress, and he soon falls beside me. He smiles against my lips as we kiss.

It's official. I've crossed to the dark side... and it's fucking good.

16

Nathan

MY INTERCOM BEEPS on my desk.

"Yes?"

"Alex on line two, Dr. Mercer."

"Thank you." I pick up the phone. "Hello."

"Hey, man."

I smile broadly. "What do you want?"

"Guess where I am?"

I swing on my chair. "I don't care."

"San Fran."

"You are? What for?"

"I had a meeting that was supposed to be in Boston and it got changed to here late last night."

"How long are you here for?"

"I catch the red-eye out tonight. Do you want to catch up for a drink after work?"

"Yeah." I smile. "Sounds good. What time's your meeting?"

"I should be finished by three."

"I'll reschedule my last few appointments. Call me when you're finished for the day."

"You got it, bye."

I hit the intercom. "Maria."

"Yes, Doctor."

"What are my last few appointments this afternoon?"

"It's an easy afternoon. You have Mr. Griffin in at three to go through his results, and then you have a consult with Mrs. Anderson in at four."

"Can you call them and try to reschedule until tomorrow, please?"

"Of course."

"How did you get on with the removal service?" I ask.

"They just got back to me. They can do a load tomorrow at six in the evening if you want."

I think for a moment. "Can you book that in, please? It won't be the full apartment, but book them again for Saturday morning to do the remainder of the furniture, if that's okay. Tell them that some of it may be going into storage."

Merging two apartments full of furniture into one is going to be a nightmare.

"Of course, Doctor."

I hang up and dial Eliza's number.

She answers on the first ring. "Hi."

Her sexy voice brings a smile to my face, and I swivel on my chair. "Hello."

"What are you doing?" I can tell she's smiling.

"Not you, unfortunately."

She laughs. "Haven't you had enough, Dr. Mercer?"

"Of you? Impossible."

God, I really should temper it down a bit. I'm fucking this poor woman to death.

"I booked the removal truck for tomorrow night."

"What?" She gasps. "Nathan, I'm not ready. I have a million things to sort, and what about—"

"Calm down," I cut her off. "They're just going to take the bed, the kitchen stuff, your clothes, and a television."

"Oh."

"We will move the rest of our things over the next few weeks. Some of it will have to go into storage. At least this way, we can stay at the new place."

"You sound eager."

"I am."

"All you care about is that bath, isn't it?"

I chuckle. "It is, actually."

"Okay then. We have so much to do tonight."

I cringe. "Yeah, about that. Alex just called. He's in town for tonight only."

"Perfect timing, Nathan. Why would you book a removal truck for tomorrow when you have to go out tonight?"

"You're coming, too. It's just dinner. Won't be a late night, and we have to eat."

"No, that's okay. You catch up with your brother. I have too much to do. Send him my love."

"Are you sure?"

"Yeah, of course. Listen, I've got to go."

"Okay." I hang on the line, waiting to hear my favorite three words.

"I love you."

I smile. There it is. "I love you, too. Bye, sweetheart."

———

It's 3:30 p.m. when I walk into the lingerie store. It's high end, with black carpets and navy walls, huge chandeliers, and silver gilded mirrors everywhere.

The sales assistant sees me, and her eyes light up. "Can I help you, sir?"

"Just looking, thank you."

"Okay, call me if I can be of any assistance."

"Thank you." I put my hands into my suit pants pockets and look around. There are so many options. I have a new addiction to anything soft and feminine.

Like my girl.

I take a cream, silk nightdress with thin spaghetti straps, and a floor-length matching gown. I also pick up a pale pink, short nightdress with lace around the plunging neckline. It has a split up one leg.

I hold it out, and I get a vision of Eliza wearing it. My dick throbs. Yes, that's a definite. I throw it over my arm.

I continue looking. I pick up a white, silk corset that laces up with ribbon, and matching panties.

Fuck, she'll look hot in this.

I can hardly wait to put it on her so I can take it off. Actually, I'm leaving this one on.

I'll fuck her in it. I smile to myself as I imagine her laid out on the kitchen table, ready for me to eat.

God, I need to snap out of this. I am like a horny teenager. I can't get enough. No amount of fucking can take away my hunger. The more we do it, the more I want it. I am totally addicted to Eliza's lush body. She's got me well and truly by the balls. I've never been like this before. I'm constantly walking around with a semi. Who knew my dick could be so hungry?

I put the things on the counter, and the sales assistant starts to go through them, one by one.

"Will that be all, sir?"

I glance around. "Have you got any of those...?" I click my fingers as I search for the word. "It's like a lace thing that goes to stockings?"

"Suspender belt?"

"Yes." I smirk, feeling stupid. "That's it, I'll take the matching one for the corset and the stockings, too, please."

"Yes, sir." She smiles as she begins to wrap them. "There's nothing sexier than a man buying for his woman."

I smile and drop my head. *You haven't seen her.*

There is nothing on this Earth that could eclipse Eliza, least of all lingerie.

———

I walk into the bar just after 4:00 p.m., and I see Alex waving from the back corner. He stands and pulls me in for a hug when I get to him. "Hey." He laughs, and we shake hands.

We fall into the seats, and a beer is already waiting for me on the table.

"You look great, man." He smiles. "All tanned and shit."

"Thanks." I take a sip of my beer. It's icy cold and crisp. "It was a great vacation."

"Yeah, you recommend Majorca?"

"God, yeah."

He smirks as he watches me.

"What?"

"So...?"

"So, what?" I ask, knowing exactly what he means.

"Eliza?" He widens his eyes. "How is she?"

I shake my head, excited to be able to express myself to someone. I can be open with my brother. He knows the real me.

"Alex... fucking hell, she's incredible."

He laughs and holds his hand up to high five me. "I knew it. I knew it all along. And?"

"The sex is just..." I press my fingers to my temples and mimic an explosion. "No words."

"I told you. Pussy love is the best love."

"No shit." I clink my beer with his, and we both chuckle.

"How are you getting along?"

"Great, haven't missed a beat." I shrug. "It's so familiar. You know, like I was always meant to be with her."

He smiles. "You seem happy."

"I am." I smile. "For the first time in my life I feel... finished."

"What do you mean?"

"You know when you're with someone and there's always something wrong simmering in the back of your mind about them?"

"Like what?"

"Eliza is the first person I've been with who has ticked every single want and need of mine."

He smiles. "That's great man, I'm so happy for you. You two are fucking great together."

"With everyone else I've been with, there has been something holding me back from moving forward, you know?" I sip my beer. "Like I couldn't possibly fall for them, but I don't have it with her. I have to constantly remind myself to slow down." I smile wistfully. "It took all of my strength not to drag her into a church and make her marry me in Majorca."

His eyes widen. "Fuck!" He shakes his head in disbelief. "Are you serious? You really are all in?"

"Totally fucking all in." I chuckle. "It just feels so right, you know?"

He shrugs as he sips his beer. "Wish I did."

I frown. "What does that mean? Everything all right?"

"I don't know." He drags his hand down his face. "I'm having a fucking midlife crisis or something."

"Why?"

"Jessica. I'm just… it's not the same as it used to be."

"Why not?"

"We've started fighting all the time, and she's on my case about every fucking thing, pressuring me to get engaged."

"You don't want to get married?"

"I do… just not sure if it's to her. You know when you're with someone and on paper everything is perfect… but something is missing, and for the life of you, you can't put your finger on what that is?"

"Yeah." I watch him. I know this feeling. It's all I've ever known before now. "I do."

"Maybe I'm just freaking out about marriage. People say nerves play tricks on you. These doubts about her seem to have come from nowhere. I woke up one day and, like, bam!"

"I have heard that." We fall silent for a moment. "Can you imagine Mom and Dad if you broke up with Jessica?"

He pinches the bridge of his nose. "Don't even fucking go there. I'd never hear the end of it."

I chuckle as I imagine my mom crying, and dad lecturing him about ruining his life. "Hey, do me a favor: don't tell Mom and Dad about Lize and me. I want to tell them in person. I'm going to take her home in a few weeks."

"Sure thing." He smiles. "They are going to lose their shit."

I laugh. My parents have wanted Eliza and me together for ten years.

"It's good to see you." He smiles.

"You, too."

He glances down at my shopping bag. "What did you buy?"

"Oh." I smirk, embarrassed. "Lingerie."

He bursts out laughing. "What the hell have you been doing all this time?"

I laugh, too. "No fucking idea."

———

It's just after 9:00 p.m. when I put the key into the door of Eliza's apartment. I'm later than I thought. I find her sitting on the kitchen floor with a glass of wine.

"Hi," I say.

She smiles up at me. "There's my man." She holds her arms up for me, and I bend down to kiss her lips.

"Sorry I'm late."

"That's okay, I've got it under control."

I pull her up to her feet. "I bought you a present." I hold up the black bag.

"Is this one going to fuck my ass?"

I chuckle and take her in my arms. "No, but I might." My lips drop to her neck, and she laughs as she opens the box.

"Oh." Her eyes widen in approval. "What is this?" She holds up the short, pink, lace and silk nightdress. "I love it."

"Me, too." I raise my eyebrow.

"I'm going to put it on right now." She runs off to the bathroom, and I pour myself a glass of wine and take a seat on the sofa. I kick off my shoes. It's good to be home.

Eliza appears, and my mouth drops open in awe. It hugs her body, and her voluptuous breasts are on display. I can see every one of her killer curves. "Now we're talking," I whisper.

"You like this?" She holds her hand up and twirls.

"I like this."

She walks toward me and drops to the floor between my legs. She unzips my zipper. "You like this?" she whispers darkly as she opens my pants with a sharp snap and pushes me back in my seat.

My eyes hold hers and I spread my legs in an invitation. "I like this, too."

She takes out my cock and licks up the length of it. My stomach clenches as I watch her hungry tongue explore me.

"What about this?" She takes the tip and puts it into her mouth. Her tongue swirls around the tip, and I close my eyes as arousal heats my blood.

"Yes," I grind out. "What's not to like?"

She takes me slowly into her mouth, and I look back at her and brush the hair back from her face. Fuck, she's beautiful. She always is, but especially with a mouthful. She moans around me, and I begin to see stars. She strokes me with one hand as she really begins to fuck me with her mouth. I grip her hair hard and watch her head bobbing up and down.

Waves of pleasure shoot through my balls, and my legs open farther. I need it deeper. I want inside her.

Now.

I drag her off the floor and pull her over me and in one hard pump I'm halfway in. She whimpers and, with my hands on her hipbones, I move her from side to side to loosen her up for me. She rises onto her knees a little higher, and I circle my thumb over her clitoris to open her up. Unable to help it, I slide my fingers lower and wipe them through her dripping wet lips, and I hiss out loud.

My cock begins to thump.

The air crackles between us. I've never had sex like I do with her—intimate and raw. *She's on fucking fire.*

She slides down and takes the full length of my cock, and we both stare at each other as we hold off moving, teetering on the edge of our orgasms. It's deep like this, making both of us come almost instantaneously.

It just feels too good.

"Legs up, baby," I mouth.

Like the good girl that she is, she brings her legs up into a squatting position and rests her hands on my shoulders. The room begins to spin.

I tip my head back, and she licks up my neck and runs her teeth along my jaw. "Fuck me," she breathes into my ear.

My jaw clenches. *Careful*, I remind myself as my hands tighten on her ass. My eyes drop to her bouncing breasts. I'll never get sick of this view.

The ultimate aphrodisiac.

Something snaps when I'm inside of her; I lose all control, blinded by the ultimate target—the need to fuck and come hard.

Slowly, I lift her up, and she smiles in anticipation. Then, I slam her down onto me.

She cries out, and I'm lost to the sensation.

Lost to her.

I lift her and slam again and again, and her beautiful, hot cunt ripples around me.

Her lips take mine and, oh... fuck, *I love this woman.*

She clenches down, and we both moan as an orgasm runs between us. Our lips fall tender, and she holds my face in her hands.

"I love you," she whispers.

I smile up at her in awe and kiss her chest. I hold her body to mine, my head against her breasts.

I'm home.

Eliza

Nathan pulls the car into the underground parking lot.

"This is it?" I frown as I dip my head to look up at the swanky building. It looks like a trendy warehouse with big archway windows. The bricks are dark and distressed, and the doorman stands by the grand entranceway, wearing a black suit. "How many apartments are in here?" I ask.

"Eight."

"What's in the rest of the building?" I frown as he scans his key and the garage door goes up. We drive down two levels.

"Nothing, it's all apartments."

"What the hell?" My eyes flicker to Nathan. "This is all apartments? How much did this cost you?"

"Enough." He parks the car and gets out. He opens my door and he takes my hand before he leads me to the elevator. Moments later, the elevator doors open up to a private landing.

"Who else is on this floor?" I ask.

"Nobody." He puts the key into the door.

"It's the entire floor?" I gasp.

He opens the door, and my mouth falls open. "Nathan," I whisper.

It's beautiful. It has an industrial, trendy kind of vibe. My eyes are wide as I look around at the splendor.

"This is the kitchen." Nathan smiles proudly as he plays tour guide. "I knew you would love this room."

"Holy shit." It's huge—the size of my old living room—and has every swanky appliance known to man.

"Living area." He shows me through to find a gigantic living area and dining room.

"This is the gym." He smiles. "My office, your office."

I shake my head in disbelief. "This place is too fancy for us, Nathe."

"Too fancy for me, probably, but just right for you." He takes my hands in his. "Do you like it?"

"I love it." My eyes dart around, too excited to look at just one thing.

"Our bedroom is down here." He leads me down the grand hallway and into a huge master bedroom. My eyes widen. "This is bigger than my entire apartment."

"Wouldn't be hard," he mutters dryly as he looks around.

The bathroom has an oversized circular bathtub sunken into the floor. "It's like a movie." I step into the bathtub and lie down. I smile up at him. "How do I look?"

"Hot." He sits down on the side of the bath. He has a very smug look on his face. "I think we'll be very happy here."

I reach up and run my fingers through his stubble. "But you do know that I don't need a fancy apartment to be happy, don't you?" I kiss his big, beautiful lips. "I could live anywhere as long as I have you."

He pulls my face to his and deepens the kiss. "And you do, my love. And you do."

———

It's Friday, and I'm walking down the sidewalk to meet my two bitch-ball friends. I'm annoyed with them. They've called me every day, asking to go to lunch. I've been using the move as an excuse—said I was too busy. But the truth is, I don't want to hear their judgemental crap.

They rattled me the other day, and at a time when Nathan and I should be blissfully in love, they put this annoying little voice in my head that won't go away. It's like a poison—a bad spell that's seeping into my bones.

How will you cope when he leaves you for a man?

I wouldn't. I wouldn't cope if Nathan left me for any reason... but to lose him to a man?

I've heard of it happening before; careless whispers: *her husband left her for a man*, and you don't really think about the consequences of it or how badly it would scar you as a woman. But I've only ever heard of straight men leaving their wife for a man. Never the other way around.

But Nathan is different....so different, to anyone I know actually.

It's the weirdest thing because the reality is, I can't even imagine that Nathan has ever slept with a man. Especially not now that we have the most incredible sex ever. He's so in tune with me and is absolutely besotted with my body.

To think that he has... no. I can't. I won't.

I get a vision of him with a man, and I close my eyes in pain. My stomach rolls. I hate this visual. I had it yesterday, too.

Is sex with them better than what he has with me?

Couldn't be.

I keep reminding myself that that's his past, and he can't change it even if he wanted to. Whatever he has done over time to get to where and who he is now, I should be grateful for it.

But what if he needs it in the future?

Stop it.

I hate this feeling, damn them for ruining this for us, it's like I'm waiting for the shoe to drop. For him to come out to me one morning and say that he changed his mind and it was all a big mistake.

I know that maybe it's just fear that something is going to go wrong because I'm so blissfully happy and maybe if he didn't have this past, I would be fixating on something else, scaring myself to oblivion.

Because that's what I am.

I'm scared—petrified that I'm going to lose him, and even more terrified that I won't deal with it if I do. Last night, I laid in bed and watched him sleep for two hours. My mind was going over and over every little detail about the things I remember about his past. Dates he's been on, men he's been with... and then there's Stephanie.

She's a whole other problem. Thankfully, Nathan has been too busy to go to the gym since we've been home, and quite frankly, I don't want him to go back. Well, he won't have to soon because our new place has a gym... thank God. I don't want him to ever see her again. She would be after him, I know she would, especially now that she knows how beautiful he is and that he's packing heat.

Damn him and his big, magical dick.

I know we weren't together when he was with her, but he had feelings for me....so in my mind, he cheated. I know he didn't really, but it kind of feels like he did.

Maybe he was curious about women in general. He said that she was a means to an end.

My stomach rolls. Fuck, he could leave me for a million reasons. I don't know why I'm fixated on the male thing. Nathan is attractive to everyone who meets him.

Memories of my first boyfriend, Thomas, come flooding back. There are a lot of similarities between him and Nathan. Well, there isn't at all, actually, but the way I loved so whole-heartedly is similar. I was seventeen, and so in love, but he broke my heart when he left me for another girl. I got over it quickly, and I bounced back well. Looking back, it was only puppy love, but maybe that's where all this fear is coming from. Perhaps knowing Nathan so well and knowing how much I stand to lose if we don't work out is just making me batshit crazy.

Ugh, I hate feeling insecure.... maybe, I need to see Nathan's therapist too?

I open the door of the restaurant in a rush.

I just want to stop all these negative thoughts and go back to our Majorca love bubble. Where nobody else existed except him and I.

I see the girls near the window, and I give them a small wave. "Hi." I kiss them both and fall into my seat. I put my hand up. "Before you say anything, I don't want to hear it." I push my chair in. "I'm not discussing Nathan with you. You've made me all insecure, and I've been going out of my mind."

Brooke's face falls. "Oh, baby, I'm sorry."

"Yeah," Jo says. "We were assholes the other day, sorry. We were just worried."

"I know." I sigh. "I get it." I pick up Jolie's wine and take a sip. "Trust me, I'm worried, too."

"You are?" Jo frowns.

"I'm not stupid, girls. I know the chances of this turning bad are high."

"Not necessarily. We don't know that, it's Nathan after all, he adores you. Nobody could love you more than he already does."

"That's the worst part about it." I sigh. "I know that he loves me....and even if he wanted to leave me. He wouldn't."

Jolie frowns. "What are you saying?"

"I don't know." I snatch up my menu, feeling over emotional. I shake my head in disgust with my train of thought. "I don't even know what I'm talking about." I look through my menu, change of subject. "What are we eating?"

———

It's Sunday afternoon, and I'm pottering around, unpacking. The new apartment looks amazing, and we have worked all weekend to pull it together.

The furniture is in place. We ended up bringing my couch, although it is way too small for this space. It will have to do until we get a new one. We left most of Nathan's furniture in his apartment, bringing only his personal belongings and clothes.

Nathan has stopped unpacking to watch the game, and I'm sorting the linen closet. I'm almost done. I have to go back to my apartment through the week and pack the rest of the things up to go into storage. Either that or sell them. Nathan says to throw it all into storage and we will sort it out later. We are too busy at the moment.

I tend to agree—we are too busy—and there's the small issue of me going away on a conference with Henry next week. Worst timing ever.

I haven't told Nathan yet. I've been skirting around it because I know he's going to hit the roof.

"Come and sit with me, babe!" he calls.

"I just want to get this finished!" I call back.

"I'll help you tomorrow night. You haven't stopped all day."

"I know, but I have a busy week next week, remember?" I close my eyes. *Now. Tell him now.*

"Why, what's going on?"

"We have that charity ball next weekend, and then I have my work conference in Dallas. I leave Sunday afternoon, remember?"

I open my eyes and continue to fold the towels. I see movement out of the corner of my eye.

"What did you say?" Nathan comes into the laundry room.

"I have a work conference next week."

"With who?"

"Henry."

He glares at me. "No."

"Nathan."

"I said fucking no. You're not going anywhere with him."

17

Eliza

I ROLL MY EYES. "Nathan, I have to go; it's a condition of the job."

"You're not going."

"I agreed to this conference at my interview and I can't get out of it. I'm not discussing this with you."

"Was that before or after he told you he was attracted to you?"

I open my mouth to say something smart back, but no words come out.

How does he know that?

"I misunderstood him." I fire back as I march up the hallway, and he storms after me.

"Well, Eliza?" he calls. "Which was it? Before or after he literally told you he wants to fuck you?"

"He did not say that." I snap as I walk into the bathroom, and I turn the shower on with force. "You're making shit up now. He does not want to fuck me. This is all in your head." I take my clothes off and get under the hot water. "Get out, I want to shower in peace."

"I'm not making shit up, and you know it." He growls. "Over my dead fucking body will you be going to a conference alone with that fucker."

I shake my head in disgust. "Tempting."

"Tempting? What's fucking tempting?"

"Knocking you out with a shovel. It's a work conference, Nathan, in a professional environment. I don't go to your work things."

"What?" He yells in an outrage. "I don't go to any conferences without you, and you know it."

God, he doesn't really. That was a bad example.

I put my head under the water, hoping it will block him out. I wash my hair as he paces back and forth in the bathroom, livid.

"I know how this goes. He takes you to dinner, gets you drunk, and the next thing you know, you wake up naked in his bed, full of remorse."

I roll my eyes. "You make it sound like I don't get hit on, ever. I get hit on every day by men, you know, Nathan? I can look after myself, and quite frankly, I'm fucking annoyed that you would even say that, let alone think it."

"I'm not saying it about you," he splutters, "I'm saying it about him."

I turn my back to him, my anger rising by the second. "Well, don't. I'm offended at the mention of it. This is my job, Nathan. Get out."

"Resign. Come and work for me. It's only a matter of time before you do, anyway."

"No." Here we go again. "I'm not working for you, I told you that. Besides, I like my job."

He narrows his eyes. "You do, do you?"

My rubber band snaps, and I step out of the shower. Water sloshes everywhere. "Listen, asshole, around the time I had this interview and accepted this job and the conditions that I had to go to this conference, you were snorting cocaine from strippers' stomachs and getting a head job by a girl called Stephanie."

His face falls.

"So, don't you dare,"—I poke him hard in the chest—"have the audacity to slut-shame me for going on a work conference. If you want to fight, Nathan, let's fucking go! Because I sure as shit have more to be pissed about than you do."

He puts his hands on his hips and glares at me, knowing full well that he doesn't have a leg to stand on.

"Do not bring this up again," I warn him. "I'm going to my work conference, and you are going to support me like a loving partner. Grow the fuck up."

He storms from the bathroom.

My heart races as the adrenaline pumps through my body, and I get back under the water. Eventually, I calm down and smile proudly. I won that fight, fair and square.

Take that.

Nathan turns the page of his book, and I glance over at him as he sits on the lounge chair. He's in his navy-blue, silk boxer shorts, and he has been reading for hours. "Are you not talking to me?" I ask.

"I'm talking to you." He says as his eyes stay glued to his book.

"Doesn't feel like it."

"What do you want me to say?"

"I don't know. Come over here and kiss me, perhaps?"

He turns the page again. "I'm not in the mood for kissing."

I roll my eyes, there's no way he read that page that quick, he's sitting there sulking, that's what he's doing. "Okay, suit yourself." I get up and walk into the bedroom to clean my teeth.

"What are you doing?" he calls.

"Going to bed."

"You don't say goodnight now?"

"I'm not in the mood to say goodnight!" I call, I smile to myself. If he wants childish, I'll give him childish.

"Very funny."

"I thought so."

I brush my teeth, braid my hair, and I climb into bed. I'm not grovelling to him when he's being an unreasonable dick. No way in hell.

I lie in bed for a while and eventually I hear the television turn off. He fusses around for a bit and brushes his teeth, and then he gets into bed. He turns his side lamp on.

"What are you doing?" I frown.

"I'm reading."

"Why did you bother coming to bed if you want to read? Why didn't you just stay out there and read?" I huff with my back to him.

"Because I wanted to be close to you, but of course, you are completely wrecking it, so stop talking."

I smile against my pillow. "What does it feel like to be the world's biggest baby?"

"I'm not a baby." He snaps.

I roll over and look up at him. "I beg to differ."

"I just know what these medical conferences are like, Eliza. They're a free-for-all fuck fest."

"Nathan, it's me," I say softly. "I don't care who Henry sleeps with on his conference but it won't be me because I'm in love with you."

His eyes hold mine.

I rub my hand up his thigh. "You know I'm not like that. I've never cheated on anyone in my entire life."

He exhales heavily. "I just...." His voice trails off.

"You just what?"

"I just know how beautiful you are." He brushes the hair back from my forehead. "Any man would give his left nut to sleep with you."

I smile softly.

"It's true, Eliza."

"Would you give your left nut to sleep with me?"

"Both nuts." He turns the page of his book again. "I'm pretty sure you carry them around in your purse now, anyway." He shakes his head. "I'm fucking doomed."

I giggle and reach over to take his book off him and throw it onto the floor.

I sit up and pull my silk nightdress over my shoulders. Nathan's eyes drop to my bare breasts. He runs his tongue over his bottom lip, distracted.

I'm not playing fair. I win all the fights when I get my boobs out. He's got no defense.

He's besotted with them now.

"So, here's the thing," I whisper as I bend and kiss his lower stomach. I trail my tongue over his hipbone and see his cock twitch in his boxer shorts. "You have me, naked and at your disposal."

He smirks as he watches me.

"Are we really going to spend the week fighting about stupid Henry Morgan?"

I slide his boxers down and kiss his penis. He flexes it in approval and it bounces up.

"Or are we going to spend the week having fun?" I take his tip in my mouth and swirl my tongue around it as my eyes hold his. "Spend the week having fun."

His hand cups my face, and he tenderly dusts his thumb over my bottom lip. I turn my head and take his thumb in my mouth. I give it a slow, seductive suck. He watches on as his eyes darken. He sits up suddenly, takes my nipple into his mouth and sucks it hard. Pleasure shoots through me in waves, and he flips me onto my back and lifts my legs over his shoulders, causing me to laugh out loud.

Yessss.

"I'll take option two." He growls.

———

It's Wednesday at work, and I'm scrolling through my emails as I tidy up my junk folder. I notice that I have an email from the employment agency from when I was looking for my job. It's a notification of a new role for a paediatric nurse—exactly what I love doing.

I read through the job description and feel a little sad, to be honest. I don't know if I'm really cut out to work in plastics. I mean it's a nice job here that I've got, but it's an office job. I miss nursing. It just seems so superficial compared to the meaningful work that I'm used to. I miss that buzz of helping people and making a difference. If I'm going to work in an office, maybe I should just accept Nathan's offer and go and work for him.

But then he wins. I can't give in to him after our first fight and let him think he can tell me what to do. I need to set a precedent for how he treats me. I'm not putting up with him thinking he's the boss of me. If I give in now, I'll pay for it for forever.

I need to stick with this, and if I do want to leave in a few months, I will, but on my terms and when the time is right.

But these positions don't come up for months after they are advertised, anyway. By then, if I'm successful, I will have a good idea of what I want to do.

I mean, even if I got it, I don't have to take it. I can always decline the offer, I think for a moment. Yeah, sounds like a plan. I click on the apply button for the job. The agency has all my details. If it's meant to be, it's meant to be.

———

I sip my wine as I dance through the kitchen. It's Thursday night. I walk back out into the living room and stare at our new rug with the hugest goofiest smile plastered on my face.

I can't stop looking at it. I move a chair so I can see it a little more, and then I move it back. I stand and look at it from one angle, and then go to the other side of the room to look at it some more. I take another photo of it and stare at it on my phone. I've been doing this for an hour. I just love it. It really sets the mood and changes the entire feel of the place.

It's massive with beautiful hues of green and pink. It cost a bomb and got delivered today and I am loving myself absolutely sick.

I adore this apartment already. It's beautiful and feels so special.

Our first real home.

Picking furniture and art for it together with Nathan to

make it ours is my new obsession. I've been stalking Pinterest all week.

I text Nathan again.

Hurry up

A text bounces back.

Jesus, woman. I'm on my way.
Surely a rug can't be this exciting?

I've texted him three times since it arrived already. I text back.

You're wrong.
This is the rug of my life.
HTF UP!

I continue to cook dinner, and twenty minutes later, I hear the key in the door before Nathan comes into view.

I skip across the kitchen to get to him and throw myself into his arms. "Oh my God, wait till you see it," I gush.

He chuckles as he holds me in his arms. "For God's sake, show me."

I lead him out and hold my hands up toward the monumental rug of my life. "Tada." I smile.

"Ah." He nods as he looks at it, hands on hips. "Looks good."

"I know." I beam. "Isn't it amazing? I think the green arm chair is now a definite yes, and we'll get the ottoman, too, and put it over here by the window for you to read in. What do you think?"

He smiles as his eyes linger on me.

"What?" I shrug, slightly embarrassed by my over the top excitement.

"Nothing," he takes me into his arms and kisses me tenderly. "I missed you today."

I smile up at him as I run my fingers through his dark stubble. "I'm so happy, Nathe."

"I know, baby. Me, too." He kisses me again and we stand in each other's arms for an extended time, holding each other, unable to part. The days are long without him. "I can't wait to get this rug dirty tonight," he mutters against my hair.

My eyes widen in horror and I pull out of his arms. "We are not having sex on this rug.... *like ever.*"

His eyes dance with delight, and he unzips his trousers as if I just issued him with the ultimate dare.

"Nathan, no," I warn as I step back from him. "Getting semen on this rug is a huge trigger for me."

"Not getting semen on this rug is a trigger for me." He pulls his dick out and crash-tackles me onto the couch. I laugh out loud and try to escape his clutches.

Life is good. *Really good.*

———

"The car will be here in ten, babe!" Nathan calls from the kitchen. I hear the pop of a champagne cork.

"Okay, nearly ready!" I call back as I put my earrings on. It's Saturday night, and Nathan and I have a charity ball to attend. We seem to go to so many lately.

They are fun, but I would really rather stay home tonight. I take one last look at myself in the mirror. I'm wearing a white, fitted, strapless dress. My long, dark hair is down and bouncy, and I have a fancy rhinestone clip pushing it back on one side. I fluff it up at the bottom. I wish I could do my hair this good. I spent the afternoon in the salon. I'm wearing silver stilettos and holding a matching clutch. Underneath, I have on Nathan's corset and suspender belt that he bought me. It will be a nice surprise for him later.

An idea comes to mind and I smile. I should give him a little taste now. Actually, yes. I've got ten minutes.

I quickly wriggle out of my dress and have a quick look in the mirror to look at the white corset and matching panties with a suspender belt, and the thigh-high, sheer white stockings. I pick up my clutch and smile broadly as I walk out into the kitchen in the sex kitten get up. "Ready," I reply casually.

He holds his champagne glass mid-air and blinks. "Yes, you are." He purrs as he puts his drink down so fast that it sloshes over the sides. "Ready to be fucked." His hands go to my behind, and he bends his knees to put his dick right between my legs as he sucks on my neck. "Hmm, for once I got the shopping right," he whispers against my skin as he sits me up onto the kitchen counter and pulls my panties to the side. "This is going to get you into trouble."

I smile as I watch him drop between my legs as he spreads them wide. He closes his eyes as his thick tongue sweeps through my sex. I inhale deeply as I watch on. God. What a visual.

Nathan on his knees in a black dinner suit, licking me up like I'm his last supper.

His dark eyes hold mine, and he turns his head and kisses my inner thigh. He slides three thick fingers deep into my sex, and my back arches. He begins to move them quick and rough over my g-spot as his lips take mine.

He works me hard, and I moan in pleasure.

The man has the ability to make me come in approximately sixty seconds.

"Wait," I moan against his lips. "When we get home, baby," I breathe against his lips. "Good things come to those who wait."

"And good men come in your mouth." He bites my bottom lip and stretches it out, his dark eyes hold mine and the air crackles between us. He has that look in his eyes and I know I'm going to get it hard tonight. Excitement flutters in my stomach. I love that look.

The door buzzer sounds, and he licks his lips as he looks at me. "Saved by the bell." He bends and licks me once more, as if unable to help it, and then he pulls my panties back and lifts me off the counter.

"Put your dress on."

He turns me toward the bedroom and smacks my behind hard. I yelp.

"And stop making me hard before I go out."

"Yes, dear." I smile as I walk into the bedroom. I put my dress on and catch sight of myself in the mirror. My face is flushed and aroused. I smile broadly.

Nathan Mercer, you are a bad man.

———

We walk into the ballroom half an hour later. It's beautiful and grand. Although I can't really appreciate the splendor because I'm too aroused.

Nathan had his hand up my dress the entire car ride here. He wouldn't let me come. He'd get me to the edge and pull back, again and again.

Payback, he called it. I call it torture. That will teach me to prick tease. It was an epic fail because I just prick teased myself.

It's me who's about to come with the change of the wind...not him.

How am I going to get through the night without humping him on the dancefloor?

I feel a dull ache in my vagina as he leads me to our table.

"Hello." We arrive and take our seats. "I'm Nathan and this is Eliza, my girlfriend." He introduces us and we smile and shake hands with our table buddies. Nathan's hand goes to mine in my lap, and he takes it in his.

Eliza, my girlfriend.

That's the first time he's ever said that out loud. It sounds good. I like it. Love it, actually.

"Do you want a drink, darling?" he asks.

"Yes, please. Bubbles."

"Okay." He smiles mischievously and puts his mouth to my ear. "Would you like to go to the bathroom with me?"

"Don't tempt me," I whisper back. "I'm not even joking, Nathan, I'm aching."

"Good." He chuckles and kisses me quickly. "Back in a minute. Ache away."

I watch him disappear to the bar. He's so handsome in his black dinner suit. People greet him, and he shakes hands with people he sees along the way.

I smile proudly. He's so well respected in the industry. Another older couple come to find their place at our table.

"Oh, Eliza." The lady smiles. "Hello, again, my dear."

"Nadia." I smile as I kiss her cheek. "How are you?"

Nadia's husband Peter is an oncologist in the children's floor where I used to work. I know them well.

"Hello, Eliza." Peter kisses my cheek. "We miss you on the children's floor."

My heart drops. "I miss it, too. You never know what the future may hold." I wink.

I glance over to the bar and see Nathan talking to that pretty woman I saw him talking to in the hospital last week. She's laughing, all animated, and he smiles back at her. My eyes roam up and down her body. She's beautiful with a figure to die for. Dark hair and olive skin. She says something as she rubs his upper arm, and the hairs on the back of my neck rise. *Don't touch him.*

I sip my glass of water as I watch the two of them. He seems very comfortable with her. When did I become such a green-eyed monster?

"Tell me about your new job?" Peter interrupts my thoughts.

"It's great," I lie. "I'm working for a plastic surgeon as the office manager. Just needed a break from nursing for a little while; I'll be back soon. I'm missing it too much."

"Good to hear. A change is as good as a holiday, or so I hear."

Nathan falls back into the seat beside me. "Peter, Nadia." He smiles as he kisses her cheek and shakes his hand. "How are you both?"

They fall into conversation as Nathan's hand slides under the table to hold mine on my lap. I sip my champagne and smile as my world returns to normal again.

Dr. Dreamy is here, and I am his faithful patient.

Nathan smiles as he holds me on the dancefloor. We've had a wonderful night, with great company.

"Can we go home now?" he murmurs into my ear.

"I thought you'd never ask." I kiss him softly. "I'm going to the bathroom before we go."

"Okay, I'll meet you back at the table." He kisses my cheek, and I weave my way through the tables, out into the lobby. There's a bathroom attendant, and she opens the heavy door for me.

Wow, it's all marble in here with large palms in matching plant pots.

I go to the bathroom and come out and wash my hands. I reapply my lipstick, and the attractive, dark-haired woman in the red dress comes out of one of the cubicles—the one who was talking to Nathan.

"Hello." She smiles when she sees me. She washes and dries her hands. She definitely is friendly enough.

"Hi." I smile.

"It's a beautiful turn out, isn't it?"

"It is."

"I love your dress. It's Eliza, isn't it?"

"Yes, thanks." I smile as I roll my lipstick together on my lips. "I'm sorry, I'm terribly rude. I know we've met before, but I can't recall your name."

"Oh." She holds her hand out to shake mine. "I'm Stephanie."

I stare at her as my brain misfires.

What?

But he knows that Stephanie from the gym, not work.

"You go to the gym with Nathan?" I ask as a test.

"Yes." She smiles warmly. "We work together, too. I'm a cardiovascular surgeon. We operate at the same hospitals."

"Ah." I fake a smile. "How wonderful."

I stare at her beautiful face as the sky turns red. I begin to hear my furious heartbeat in my ears.

This is Stephanie?

A woman that he is friends with. A woman he works with. A

beautiful woman that he trusts and knows well is who he went to... over me.

I get an image of the two of them together, kissing—her on her knees, drinking him down.

"Goodbye," I force out.

"Lovely to see you."

I fake a smile and storm back to the table. Nathan catches my eye, and I glare at him as I fall into my seat.

His brow furrows and he puts his hand on my thigh. "Everything all right, sweetheart?"

I flick his hand away. "Don't touch me," I whisper angrily.

"What?" He frowns.

"I just met Stephanie."

His eyes widen.

I push my chair out. "I'm leaving."

18

Eliza

"Goodbye." I smile at the people around our table. "Lovely to meet you all."

"Goodbye," the table sings.

I fake a smile and storm toward the entrance.

I can't believe this, *I am fucking livid.*

Nathan quickly shakes hands with his associates around the table—his manners not letting him leave without doing so first. I march out to the undercover entrance, and I walk straight up to a taxi and get into the back seat.

"Eliza!" Nathan calls as he runs after me. "Wait."

"Smith Street," I say to the driver as I slam the door behind me.

Nathan runs up and opens the back door and dives in beside me. "What are you doing?" he hisses.

I cross my arms and glare out of the window. I am not having this argument in front of a cab driver.

Nathan puts his hand on my lap and I flick it off. "Don't you fucking dare touch me," I growl.

He clenches his jaw and sits silently. I already know that he's preparing his speech. The car pulls up out the front of our apartment. "Thank you," I say as I open the door and get out. I march into the building as Nathan pays our fare. He shuffles through his wallet and throws cash at him, not waiting for the change.

I force a smile at the doorman as he opens the door for me, and I march past and hit the elevator button with force.

Nathan rushes in.

"Good evening, Mr. Mercer. Nice night." The doorman smiles.

"Is it?" Nathan mutters as he dives into the elevator beside me.

I clutch my purse and glare straight ahead.

Nathan stands tentatively beside me, as if I'm a wild animal he doesn't know how to control.

I cannot believe.... I cannot *fucking believe* that he would have the audacity to stand and talk to her in front of me, knowing full well that I had no idea who she was. What were they talking about? How hard he came down her throat?

Fuck, I'm so furious, I'm about to explode.

Nathan opens the door and I march in, heading straight to the fridge. I pour myself a drink and I stand at the sink and drain it as he watches on in silence.

"Eliza."

"Don't!" I growl. "Don't you fucking dare tell me one more lie."

He stays silent, as if unsure what to say.

I pour myself another glass of wine and take a huge gulp as a million hurtful things run through my mind. I'm so angry, I can hear my heartbeat in my ears, like a speaker echoing my pulse throughout.

"I didn't lie to you."

"Excuse me if I don't believe anything that comes out of your mouth." I sneer.

He puts his hands into the pockets of his suit, his jaw clenches. "So, I know her..."

"Oh, I can see that."

"You know...." He holds his hands up in surrender. "It was just one night. And it meant nothing, I fucking swear to you, Eliza. It meant nothing."

"She's your friend." I get a lump in my throat. I feel so betrayed. My eyes well with tears.

His face falls. "Baby, don't cry." He pauses as he tries to get the wording right in his head. "I was as high as a kite. What would have happened if I'd have gone to you, off my face, and put that shit on you?"

"So, instead, you put it on her?" I bark.

He swallows the lump in his throat as his eyes hold mine.

"You told me that you had feelings for me but you went to her to see if your body worked with a female's."

"Yes." He nods. "That's right, I did."

"That's bullshit, and you know it. You already knew that your body worked with mine. You were hard the night before. Do not fucking dare insult my intelligence one more fucking time, Nathan," I scream as I lose all control. "You went to her because you wanted her."

"Calm down."

"I will not calm down." I throw my glass at him, and he ducks. It hits the fridge behind him and smashes on the floor.

"*Just* a girl from the gym. *Just* a girl I'll never see again." I shake my head in disgust. "You flirt with her all day at work,

Nathan. I've seen it with my own fucking eyes." My eyes nearly pop from their sockets. A thought comes to me. "Have you talked about that night with her?"

He clenches his jaw, and I know that he has.

"So, you can talk to her about it but you can't talk to me," I whisper through the hurt.

"Eliza...." he whispers.

"You stood there tonight and talked and laughed with her for ten minutes, with me not far away, watching on, knowing full well that I had no idea who she was. If that's not betrayal, Nathan, I don't know what is."

He drops his head and closes his eyes.

I watch him as angry tears roll well in my eyes. "Tell me what happened," I demand.

"You tell me what happened that night. I want a full description of every single fucking touch. You knocked on the door, and then what..."

"It doesn't matter what happened!" he snaps. "It doesn't mean anything."

"You're wrong," I whisper. "It does to me."

"I didn't want you to feel insecure," he says calmly.

"You would rather I feel stupid?" I cry.

"No." He gasps. "I didn't want you to think about it again. I told you that it happened. I was honest, and it doesn't affect us. It changes nothing."

"It doesn't affect *you*, Nathan." My eyes hold his. "It changes everything for me."

"Why?"

"Because *my* Nathan..." I point to my chest with force. "My *best friend*, Nathan, would never deceive me. He would talk to me and tell me all about it. He would point the girl out to me and discuss it openly. He would have nothing to hide." I shake my head. "I don't even know who you are as a lover."

His face falls.

"What else haven't you told me?"

"Nothing."

I stare at him, his silhouette blurred through tears. "I wish I believed you."

He reaches for me. "Baby, don't." He pulls me into his arms and holds me tight against my will. I struggle to pull out of his arms.

"You being with her doesn't make me feel insecure, Nathan. Lying to me about the reason you did it, does."

He stares at me, clearly lost for words.

I walk past him and go into the bathroom where I lock the door. The lump in my throat hurts as I try to hold it together. I just want to howl to the moon.

I tear my dress off, and through tears, I wrangle myself out of this dumb corset. And to think I've been hanging off his every word tonight, and all the while, he was probably making eye contact across the room with her. *Their dirty little secret.*

I feel so stupid.

I was so swept away with his admission of love in the beginning. I knew that he went to her, and I knew I didn't like it back then, but to know it was with a friend of his—someone he talks to regularly, and a colleague he respects. Someone he sees every day at work. *Another female friend.*

He would care about her, just like he does me......Oh, *this hurts.*

I get under the hot water and let myself go, I screw up my face in pain as the tears roll down my face.

Betrayal tastes bitter...especially when you don't expect it.

That was the last thing I expected to come out of tonight.... but I guess, at least now I know.

I get out of the shower an hour later. I sit on the floor and cry like a baby for way too long. I'm being over dramatic, I know, but I can't seem to stop myself. I wrap my hair in a towel and put my nightdress on. I brush my teeth and make my way into the bedroom.

Nathan's bedside lamp is on, and he lies on his back in the semi darkness, wide awake and waiting for me. His fingers are linked on his chest.

I get into bed and turn my back on him.

He snuggles up close to me and takes me in his arms. "I love you," he whispers against my temple. "You know that, don't you?"

I don't answer him as I stare at a wall. I don't have any fight left in me. I'm too tired. I don't want to think about this shit any more.

And with Nathan clinging to me for dear life, I close my eyes and let myself drift off into sleep as the sad realization sets in: the man I love isn't who I thought he was.

He thinks like a man.

———

I wake to the gentle dusting of kisses over my shoulder. My heavy eyelids flutter as they battle waking up.

"Hi." Nathan says softly. He kisses my shoulder again.

"Hi." I sigh, disappointed that I didn't have a bad dream last night. It was real. I roll over to face him.

An over dramatic reaction, but a real one, just the same.

We stare at each other. I drag my eyes down to the sheets, I'm still annoyed with him.

"I'm sorry, Eliza.

"For what?"

"I should have told you that I knew her."

"You should have. Do you have any idea how stupid I felt when she introduced herself to me?"

He presses his lips together but stays silent. I run my fingers through the hairs on his chest as I think.

"What do you want to know?" he asks. My eyes hold his. "Ask me anything about that night, and I'll answer you honestly and truthfully. I promise."

I focus on the hair on his chest as I run the backs of my fingers back and forth.

"Lize," he says softly as he puts his finger under my chin, bringing my face to his. "You wanted to talk about this last night, so let's talk about it."

I press my lips together, unsure what to say without sounding whiny. I hate jealous insecure girls, and here I am being a queen one.

"Talk to me..."

"I feel betrayed," I whisper.

"Why?"

"Because you say you cared for me and you went to another female friend for sexual favors. How can I not be upset? It feels like you cheated on me."

He exhales heavily as if frustrated.

"Imagine if the role was reversed, Nathan. You are going ballistic about me going on a work conference with Henry. Imagine if I told you that I have feelings for you but I went to Henry for sexual satisfaction."

His eyes become murderous. "Don't even fucking say that."

I shrug. "That's how it feels."

"You and I weren't together at that stage."

"So why did you tell me that you didn't know her?"

"I told you I knew her."

"Not as well as you do."

"Because she's irrelevant to our story."

"Not to me."

He stays silent as his eyes hold mine.

"Tell me what happened that night with her."

"I don't want that shit in your head, babe." He sighs sadly as he pushes the hair back from my face. "Why would you want to know that?"

"It's eating me alive, Nathan. I need to know."

"Promise me that we aren't going to fight about this. I mean it, Lize. If we talk about this, you can't hold it against me. It's not fair."

"Don't talk to me about fair, Nathan, because you have no fucking idea of the meaning of the word."

"*Promise me.*"

"Fine."

"Kiss me."

"Just spit it out." I snap in frustration.

He exhales heavily as if he's walking to the execution chair. "I know Stephanie quite well." He pauses. "We worked together on a few cases, and when she was having trouble with her husband—"

"She's married?" I gasp.

"Ex-husband," he corrects himself. "She talked to me about a few warning signs she had about him cheating on her with a man. He'd started hanging out with someone and going on trips away with him. He was wanting things they've never done before in the bedroom, and so on. She knew that I was... "— he pauses—, "the way I am."

"Gay."

"I'm not gay, Eliza," he corrects me.

"Why do you hate that title so much?"

"I don't identify with it."

"So, what.... you're bisexual?" I frown as I try to understand. "Explain this to me, Nathan, I don't understand."

He shrugs. "Elliot thinks I'm pansexual. Although, I feel totally fucking straight when I'm with you."

"What does pansexual mean?"

"It just means that I fall in love with a soul rather than a body type."

"Oh..." I've never heard of that before.

"Anyway, we talked over lunch one day in the cafeteria about her husband, and I told her I thought he was probably having sex with men."

"What made you say that?" I ask.

"He wanted her to wear a strap-on and fuck him."

My eyes widen.

"Yeah." He shrugs. "In your words: red flag."

"Right." I listen intently.

"I didn't see her for ages. She worked out of a different hospital, and months later I saw her again alone at the cafeteria. She told me that her husband had just left her for this friend. She was distraught, and we just started talking casually. Not super close or anything, but we had this open line of communication between us, you know? We had talked about subjects that you don't talk about with the average person."

"You crossed the line?" I ask.

"Perhaps, but not in a sexual way. Kind of in a therapist-like way, if that makes sense." He shrugs. "This sounds ridiculous when I say it out loud." He pauses and exhales heavily as he prepares himself for the next part of the story. "When my feelings for you started changing, I was terrified that I was going to lose you. I needed someone I could talk to about it from a female's perspective."

I clench my teeth as I watch him.

"I talked to Stephanie."

Jeez, *I fucking hate this story.*

"You have to understand, my biggest fear about opening up to you was that I was going to profess my love and then we had sex and I didn't like it. I didn't know if I would like a vagina, Eliza. I had no idea how I was going to perform or if I could even get it up."

I close my eyes in regret. "You talked to her about this?"

"Yeah, I did." I know he's uncomfortable with this conversation.

"She had said to me on more than one occasion that, if I wanted to test the waters, she would be my guinea pig."

"Of course, she did." Now I've really heard it all. "Wow."

"The thing is, I didn't care if I fucked it up with her because my feelings for her are platonic." He kisses me. "But I was in love with you, and I know you don't understand this, but I couldn't risk hurting you by sleeping with you and not liking it. At the time, a female body was so foreign to me. I had no idea what was going to happen."

"Is it still foreign to you?" I whisper.

"Now I can't imagine anything else. It's like you woke me up inside." His eyes search mine. "I can't imagine not having sex with you. It's the most natural love I've ever felt."

I smile softly as he kisses me again, and he brushes the hair back from my face.

How is he talking himself out of this? I sigh, frustrated with my forgiving, wimpy ass.

"So... when you found the porn on my computer. I had been watching it non-stop, and watching tutorials on giving women orgasms. "

I frown. "What?"

"I was terrified that I was going to be a dud in bed for you."

"Nathan." My mouth falls open in shock. "Are you serious?"

"Deadly. I had told Stephanie on the Friday before we went to my parents that I was going to tell you everything, and she was calling me to see how it went. But you found the porn on my computer before I spoke to you, and I panicked and I lied. I told you that I liked another woman."

"Stephanie," I reply flatly. "You told me you liked Stephanie."

"And you were jealous." He smiles as he pokes me in the ribs.

I twist my lips. "Maybe a little."

"Anyway, the next week I was well on my way to insanity. I was watching porn all night, every night at my house, unable to touch you. We were fighting, and I was watching these tutorials on the female body that had me so fucking horny."

I stare at him, deadpan. Do I really want to hear this? "Careful," I warn.

He bites his bottom lip to hide his smile. "In a moment of weakness, I decided I was going to a strip club to jerk off to a woman. To test the waters, so to speak."

I inhale deeply with a roll of my eyes.

"They offered me a pick-me-up."

"Cocaine?"

"I snorted so much of that fucking shit it was a joke." He pauses. "I was seriously good to go. Like, nearly out of control. I knew I couldn't go home to you like that, and I didn't want to be with a prostitute."

"You called Stephanie."

"Yes."

"What did you say?"

"It doesn't matter what I said."

"I need to know."

He stares at me as if doing an internal risk assessment on how much to actually tell me.

"All of it," I snap. "I want to hear it all."

"No."

"I mean, if you want me to forget this, Nathan, so we can move on, you need to just spit it out."

"I said something along the lines of that I had a hard cock that needed to be taken care of," he blurts out in a rush.

I clench my jaw as my anger rises. "Classy."

He raises his eyebrows. "You asked."

"What then?"

"I got a cab to her house and I stumbled through the door. We kissed once and fell onto the couch, and she dropped to her knees." He says it in a rush as if hoping I won't hear what he's saying.

I stare at him as I imagine the scenario he's explaining.

"Halfway through it, I wanted to stop."

"But you didn't."

"No, I..." His voice trails off, not wanting to elaborate. It obviously felt too good and his body wouldn't let him stop. *Fucking asshole.*

"What then?"

He exhales heavily. "I came, she swallowed, and then I zipped my jeans up and wanted to get the hell out of there." He throws his hands up in disgust. "There were no feelings, no sweet tender moments. It was a clinical procedure."

I clench my jaw as I feel the adrenaline pump through my veins. "What did she say?"

"She wanted sex. When I declined, she got angry."

I narrow my eyes as I see the movie playing out in my head.

"We had a fight and I took off."

"She wanted sex?"

"Yes."

"What did you fight about?"

"Just what I said. She started abusing me because I didn't want to fuck her. It was appalling, Eliza. I'm mortified I even went there. What was I thinking? I walked about five kilometers down the road until finally a cab pulled up."

"Then what?"

"I texted her to apologize the next day when I woke up."

"Have you messaged or called each other since?"

"No, and you can check my phone. I swear to you that since that day it has been completely platonic. I told her that I'm with you, and she hasn't brought it up. When I talk to her now, it's like it never happened. Sometimes I wonder if it actually did."

"Nathan." I exhale heavily. "You really piss me off, you know that?"

"I do."

"And I'd really like to punch you in the face for being such a fucking douchebag."

"I know."

"And if I see you laughing and talking to her again, I'm going to go postal."

"Deal." He smiles as he watches me as if sensing that he somehow talked himself out of this mess.

I get out of bed.

"Where are you going?" he asks.

"I need to sulk on this for at least two more hours," I mutter dryly. "You're not out of the dog house yet. Don't dare come near me."

"Okay." He smiles as he leans up onto his elbow. "Then can you come back to bed so we can make up?"

I smirk, annoyed that he's almost talked me around so quickly. "I'll think about it."

I walk into the bathroom. "I would suggest that you start watching those tutorials right now!" I call. "You better be fucking good in bed today. I want at least ten orgasms to make up for you being such an asshole."

I hear him chuckle. "Okay, I'm on it boss. I'll give you fifteen."

———

Nathan drives past the drop off bay at the airport. "What are you doing?" I ask.

"Parking the car."

"You don't need to come in."

His eyes flicker to me in annoyance. "I'm coming in, Eliza."

I roll my eyes.

"I'm just seeing my girlfriend off. There's nothing wrong with that, is there?" He grips the steering wheel with two hands. "It's what a caring supporting boyfriend would do."

Oh great, this won't be awkward at all. I'm meeting Henry in the check-in area.

I can almost feel the tension already. I begin to perspire.

After spending the afternoon in bed, Nathan has well and truly delivered on his promise, and with jelly legs, I'm leaving for my conference. It's a miracle I can even walk. The man is an animal, and I hate to say it, but make-up sex is highly, *highly* recommended.

He parks the car and gets my bag out of the trunk. He sat on the bed and watched me pack like a hawk-eye. He knows every damn thing there is in my case.

He takes my hand in his. "What check-in?"

"American Airlines."

"Okay." He glances at his watch. "We have time for a drink."

"Um." I frown. "I'm meeting Henry in the foyer."

"Oh, really," he says, deadpan. "So, you'll be having a drink with him before the flight, will you?"

"Yes. And don't start." I widen my eyes to remind him of his manners.

He marches toward the terminal, dragging me along by the hand, and I know he is holding in his tantrum with all of his strength.

"You call me every night," he says.

"Yes."

"And mornings."

"All right."

"And don't accept drinks from anyone. They could drug you."

I roll my eyes. "It's a medical conference, Nathan, not Ibiza or a strip club. I wonder if there are any men I can snort cocaine off, though."

He fakes a smile as he drags me along. "Hilarious, you should do stand-up." He mutters dryly.

"I'll consider it."

"Where are you staying? I want the name of your hotel and your room number."

345

"Will you stop?"

"No, I will fucking not. I don't like this. I don't want you to go. I don't trust that fucker as far as I can throw him."

I smirk because I knew he couldn't help himself. "Well, that's too bad, Nathan, because I have to."

"I don't want you to go with us fighting. The timing is all wrong. Call and tell him you're sick."

The truth is that I'm kind of looking forward to going away now. I need a week away by myself.

"We're not fighting anymore," I say.

He clenches his jaw as he narrows his eyes and we arrive at the terminal check-in.

Henry sees me, and he smiles and waves. He looks Nathan up and down, and Nathan does the same to him as they size each other up.

"Hello." I smile.

"Hello, Eliza," Henry says chirpily. His eyes flicker to Nathan, and he nods.

Nathan glares at him and pushes his hands into his pockets. "Hi," he mumbles.

I look between them.

Oh jeez.....

Awkward.

"You ready to go?" Henry asks. "I've been looking forward to this conference."

Nathan's jaw ticks as he fights to control his temper.

"Me, too." I laugh, trying to compensate for my rude pig of a boyfriend. Ooh God, please earth swallow me up now.

"Okay, got to go." I turn to Nathan. "I'll see you on Friday?"

His mouth twists as he glares at me.

"Don't worry, Mercer, I'll look after her." Henry gives Nathan a cocky wink.

The blood drains from my face. Oh no.

Nathan steps forward and stands an inch from Henry's face. "You touch one hair on her fucking head, Morgan, and see what happens to you."

19

Eliza

"Nathan!" I snap.

Henry smiles broadly as Nathan glares at him, as if he's excited by the challenge, "Down boy." He chuckles and bends to pick up his bag, totally unfazed by Nathan's threat. "See you at the gate, Lize." He turns and walks off, and I close my eyes in disgust. How embarrassing.

I turn to Nathan. "I cannot fucking believe you just did that," I whisper angrily.

"He baited me." He glares after Henry.

"No, he did not." I snatch my bag from him, but he hangs onto the handle, not letting it go. "He said he was looking forward to the conference, nothing more, nothing less."

He rolls his eyes.

"You know what? I'm actually looking forward to a break away from you."

"What's that supposed to fucking mean?"

"It means the whole world doesn't revolve around you. I'm on a work conference, Nathan. Grow the fuck up." I move to snatch my bag, but he still holds the handle, not letting me go.

"How do I think the whole world revolves around me?"

I shake my head in disgust. "Why don't you go and ask fucking Stephanie the answer to that question? Isn't she the Google you go to when you need to know something? I'm sure she will be happy to unzip your pants and oblige you with an answer."

He narrows his eyes. "How long are you going to throw that in my face, Eliza?" He growls.

"As long as I fucking want." I snatch the bag from him and storm off, adrenaline pumping through my veins. I have never been so embarrassed in my life. What must Henry think? Oh hell, the horror. My boyfriend gets in his face and warns him not to touch me on a work conference.... I cringe just thinking of it.

I get to the check-in gate, and Henry smiles as he waits for me. I smile, embarrassed as I approach him.

"I'm so sorry," I splutter.

"That's fine." He smiles kindly. "If I had a girlfriend as hot as you, I'd be a pit bull too. Think nothing of it. It's already forgotten."

"Thanks."

"Trouble in paradise?" He smirks.

I exhale heavily. "You could say that."

"Next!" the girl on the desk calls.

Henry steps forward and hands over his ID. I glance back to see Nathan standing at the door watching us. His face is murderous. I turn back to the front and ignore him. I'm so mad at him, it isn't funny.

Once cleared, we walk through the gates, and I don't look back to Nathan. I don't want to give him the satisfaction.

I wasn't lying—I want to get away from him. He's messing with my head.

————

The trip to Dallas was made in relative silence. Henry read and I watched a movie.

I'm still embarrassed by Nathan's little caveman act, and my cheeks heat every time I think of it.

The car pulls up at our hotel, and Henry gets out with the driver. They retrieve our bags from the trunk. I get out of the car and look up at the signage.

The Ritz Carlton.

Well, at least that's something. A week of luxury.

We check in and are given our keys. Thankfully, we are on different floors. We make our way to the elevator.

"Do you want to grab something to eat?" Henry asks.

I pause as I consider it. "I'm tired. I think I'm just going to grab some room service and have a hot bath."

"Okay." He smiles. "Call me if you need anything. I'll be in the bar, drinking my tax deduction." He winks.

I laugh. "Okay." We ride up in the elevator.

"We have to be in the conference room at 9:00 a.m.," he says.

"Do you want to meet for breakfast?"

"Yeah, sure. Call me when you're ready."

Another man gets into the elevator. Henry knows him.

"Hey." They both laugh when they see each other. "I was

wondering if you were going to be here," says Henry to the other man.

They chatter as we ride up. I watch the dial over the door. "Okay, this is me." The elevator arrives on my floor and the doors open. "Have a good night." I smile.

"Bye." Henry smiles casually.

"Goodbye," the other man says.

I walk down the hall and shake my head. I wasn't lying to Nathan; Henry doesn't have the slightest bit of attraction to me. I don't feel threatened or weird around him at all now.

I arrive at my room and let myself in. I'm pleasantly surprised. The room is big and nice. It has an oversized bath, and a view of the city. I go to the window and smile as I look at all the twinkling lights below.

I peruse through the room service menu and call reception.

"Hello, can I order some room service, please?"

"Sure, what would you like?"

I scan the choices. Give me all the calories. "I'll have the prawn and chilli fettuccine, a bottle of white wine and the chocolate fudge cake."

"Okay, it won't be long."

"Thank you."

I unzip my suitcase and take my toiletries bag out. I put it in the bathroom and put my laptop on the charger for tomorrow.

I look in the fridge for something to drink while I wait for my wine. There's a selection of mini bottles of spirits. I go through them and decide on a scotch and Coke. "This will do, I guess."

I pour myself a drink and look out over the beautiful view.

I smile and sit back in the silent room, and for the first time in a long time, I feel myself beginning to relax.

It's been a hectic month. There's been a new job, finding

out about Nathan, going away, getting my brains fucked out, falling in love... moving. Hell, moving house was huge, and I haven't stopped working like a dog for two weeks. Every second of every day, I've been busy. No wonder I'm stressed out.

I get up and find my phone in my handbag.

10 missed calls: Nathan

I roll my eyes and switch the phone off. I'm not in the mood for him tonight.

I drink my scotch and stare out of the window, and I don't want to think about a thing.

I can't, there is too much to think about.

I just need to relax.

I lie in the darkness and watch the movie on television. I had a two-hour hot bath while I talked to April on the phone. Well, I didn't really talk. I vented and she listened, and then I drank a bottle of wine. Now I'm in a state of bliss—a carbohydrate coma.

The phone in my room rings and I jump, not expecting it. I reach over the bed to answer it. "Hello."

"Hi," Nathan's deep voice says.

I roll my eyes and lie back down. "Hi."

"Not turning your phone on?"

"I've nothing to say."

Silence hangs between us.

"You know, when he winked at me—."

"I don't want to hear it," I cut him off.

"Look, I feel shitty enough about it, okay?"

I shake my head in disgust. It's always all about him. "Okay," I reply flatly.

"I apologize; I should have kept quiet."

"Yeah, you should have."

We fall silent.

"That's it?" he asks.

"What do you want me to say, Nathan?"

He exhales heavily, and we fall silent again.

"Is your room nice?" he asks to try and make conversation.

I roll my eyes. "Yep."

"You're not going to talk to me?"

"I told you, I have nothing to say."

"This is about the Stephanie thing, isn't it?"

I shrug, is it...I don't even know. "Maybe."

"But we talked about it and you said you understood."

"I didn't say I understood. I acknowledged what happened. I also acknowledged that she's your friend and you've been spending time with her since it happened."

"Stop it."

"Those are the facts, Nathan, are they not? Do you or do you not spend time with her?"

"At work, Eliza. I can't help seeing her there."

"At a ball, two meters from me, while you laugh at your secret jokes with her is not fucking work, Nathan. Stop insulting my intelligence."

"But we spent all afternoon in bed. How can you still be going on about this?"

"I'm not going on about it."

"You are."

We fall silent again. He's right, I know I need to let this go. But for some reason, I can't control it.

"I don't like you there without me, feeling like this."

"You think I want to feel like this?" I snap. "You think I like feeling betrayed?"

"Lize." He sighs sadly. "I didn't betray you, babe, and I know how this sounds. I would be angry, too, if I were you. But I swear to God, there is nothing between Stephanie and me. I'm in love with you, and this all happened before we started. It's purely platonic between her and me. I would never betray you."

I hate sounding insecure and whiny, and I know I do. My eyes well with tears. What's wrong with me? This isn't who I am.

"I'll call you tomorrow." I sigh sadly.

"I love you."

I frown through my tears. "Goodnight, Nathe."

He stays on the line, unable to hang up.

"I love you," he whispers again.

"I love you, too." I sigh sadly. Before he can reply, I hang up the phone.

I exhale heavily and switch the television off. I can't even stay mad at him.

Sleep, I need some sleep.

———

I walk into the breakfast restaurant, feeling a lot better with some sleep under my belt.

A new day and all that. "Morning." I smile at Henry as I take a seat beside him.

"Hello," He says as he butters his toast. "I should have gone to bed when you did last night," He mutters dryly. "I'm suffering this morning."

I giggle. "Sucked in. I feel great."

He rolls his eyes.

"So, what's today's agenda?" I ask.

"God, do we have to go?" He sighs.

I giggle and pour myself a coffee from the pot. I look around the restaurant and notice a heap of men in business suits. Many have women with them that are in work clothes, too. "Are these people all from the plastic's industry?"

He sips his coffee as he looks around the restaurant. "Pretty much."

"Do you know everyone?" I ask as I serve myself breakfast from the platters.

"Yes, but if I don't know them personally, I know who they are."

"You come to conferences often?"

"There's so many new developments in the industry that we have to constantly attend to be able to keep up."

"Like products and things?"

"Yeah, and techniques. Take this afternoon, for example. It's a surgical tutorial on a new method of lower rhytidectomy."

"Neck lift?" I frown.

"Yeah. When someone is using a new method in surgery and getting good results, they are asked to give a class at one of these things. I imagine Nathan is always teaching at these. He's very respected in his field."

"He is," I agree.

Nathan didn't call me this morning like I thought he would, but he had his rounds so...

"Anyway, you have the afternoon off," Henry says.

"I do?"

He smiles. "You do. Get a massage or whatever it is that women do in their spare time. But we have a dinner on tonight."

"Where's that?"

"It's in the restaurant here—nothing fancy. Just drinks and dinner for opening night."

"Okay."

"There's a black-tie ball on Friday night for closing of the conference, but I said we wouldn't be attending. We both want to get home as soon as possible. These things are long enough, I'm happy when they're over."

I smile. "Okay, great. Sounds good."

———

I take a look at myself in the mirror, I'm wearing black pants and a cream silk shirt. I didn't feel right putting on a dress to go for drinks tonight. My hair is down and full, and my makeup is natural.

I had a wonderful afternoon. I had a massage and went shopping. It felt good to just be me for a while, with nothing to do. I put my phone into my bag and roll my eyes. Nathan still hasn't called and I know he is waiting for me to call him.

I'll get it over with. I dial his number, and he answers on the first ring.

"Hi, there," he purrs, and I can tell that he's smiling.

"Hi." I smile at the sound of his deep voice.

"How was your day?"

"Good, I only had to be there in the morning. I had the afternoon off, so I had a massage and went shopping."

"Ah, working hard, I see," he teases.

"Yes."

"What's on tonight?" he asks.

See.... this is normal.....this is a normal conversation, why can't he be so chill all the time?

"A welcome dinner."

"Where is it?"

"Just here at the hotel."

"Okay."

I smile. It makes me miss him when he's like this. "I'll call you when I get home."

"Okay, babe. Love you."

"Love you, too."

I hang up feeling happier, and I make my way down to the bar. It's packed with people from the conference. Henry waves when he sees me. He's standing with a group of people near the bar. I smile as I approach them.

"Hello, Eliza," Henry says in a husky voice. Boy, is he tipsy already? How long have they been here? He turns to the men he is standing with. "This is my wonderful office manager, Eliza."

"Hello, Eliza." They all smile. Henry goes around and introduces me to everyone, and I shake all of their hands. They are all around Henry's age or a little older. They are also heavy in conversation. Henry gets to the last man in the group. He's very good-looking with dark hair. He's tall and well built.

"And this is Zavier," Henry introduces.

"Hello, Eliza." He smiles as he shakes my hand. "Lovely to meet you."

"Hi." I smile. Zavier has a really lovely feel about him. I instantly feel at ease.

"Zavier is from San Fran, too," Henry says.

"Oh, you are?" I smile.

Zavier holds his drink up. "Best city in the world." He laughs.

"Actually, you might know Eliza's boyfriend," Henry says.

"Who's that?" Zavier smiles.

"Nathan Mercer."

Zavier's brow furrows and his eyes come to me. "Nathan...
Mercer?"

"Yes." I smile.

"The heart surgeon?"

"Yes." I chuckle. "That's him."

Everyone continues on their conversation, and Zavier raises
his eyebrows, as if surprised.

"Do you know Nathan?" I ask.

"Um." He pauses. "Yes, he... dated someone I know for a
while."

"Oh." My eyes hold his. The only people who know who
Nathan has dated in the past are the people he dated.

"How long have you been together?" Zavier asks.

"It's only new; just recent." I sip my drink.

He smiles as if relieved, and my stomach sinks.

Nathan has dated Zavier. I can feel it in my gut. "When did
your friend date him?" I ask.

"Last year."

"For long?" I ask.

"Couple of months."

"Oh." I force a smile feeling suddenly weirded out. Zavier is
a beautiful looking man, and although I already knew it, the
concrete evidence is hard to swallow. Nathan Mercer can literally have anyone he wants. Male or female. The thought is
unsettling.

"He's an excellent doctor." Zavier smiles as if to change the
subject.

"He is."

He rocks on his toes awkwardly.

I point to the bar. "I'm going to get a drink."

"Okay." He smiles. "Have fun."

———

It's late, near 2:00 a.m., and its been a great night. I should have gone back to my room hours ago but I've been having too much fun. I think I've met everyone in the world and these margaritas have gone down way too easily. I sit at the end of the bar, watching Henry laughing out loud as he dances on the dance-floor. He's rap dancing... at least that's what I think he's trying to pull off. He's dry, crass, and yet everyone seems to adore him.

He's actually hilarious and nothing at all like what my first impression of him was.

I glance over and see Zavier watching me from his place in a group of men. I offer him a small wave, and he waves back before he comes over.

"You lonely over here?" he asks.

"A little."

"Want some company?"

"Sure."

He pulls up a stool and sits down beside me. "Is this your first plastics conference?"

"Yeah." I smile. "Are they all this wild?"

He chuckles. "They get wilder every night. Wait till the end of the week."

I giggle, and we fall silent.

"It was you, wasn't it?" I say. His eyes meet mine. "The friend who dated Nathan. I mean, it was you."

He presses his lips together and nods. "So, you know?"

"Yeah, I know." I smile. "We're very serious. I know everything there is to know."

He nods.

"You seemed surprised that I was dating him."

He raises his eyebrows. "To be honest, I am."

"That he's with a woman?"

"Yeah." He shrugs. "I just would have never thought..." His voice trails off. "You think you know someone, hey?" His eyes smile. "But I can totally see why." He offers a playful chaser to the hit I just received.

"Forgive me if I'm intruding, but why did you break up?" I ask.

"Ah." He smiles wistfully. "How long have you got? He's a very mercurial man."

"I know." I smile as I sip my margarita. I should feel uncomfortable talking to Zavier, but I don't. Not in the least. "Very much so."

He stares into space. "I always felt like there was something off." He frowns as if thinking back. "Like my gut was telling me to run."

My stomach drops as I watch him. *That sounds familiar.*

"Why, did you catch him cheating or something, or...?"

"No. Nothing like that." He shrugs. "When we were together, it was magical."

Nerves flutter as I watch the beautiful man in front of me. I get a vision of him and Nathe together.

"It was never a problem when we were together. It was when he left," he says.

"What do you mean?"

"Well, it started out great. We met, and it was all fireworks. We went away, like, four weekends in a row."

"When was this?" I frown.

He frowns as he thinks back. "Last August, I think."

I was in Paris with the girls for a month.

"But then something happened, and just out of nowhere, he would never stay over anymore."

I swallow the lump in my throat. That's because he was in *my* bed.

"It dragged on for a few months. I would get to see him for a few hours here and there. Nothing substantial."

Zavier was Nathan's booty-call.

"Anyway, the long and the short of it was that I fell in love with him and he didn't fall in love with me."

"Did you ask him why?"

He shrugs. "Said something about how he never got over his first love."

My heart drops. "Ah." I smile sadly as I desperately try to hide my emotions.

"But then he met you." He smiles happily. "So he obviously did in the end. Tell me everything."

"Well..." I pause, still rattled by his last statement. "We just moved in together."

"You did?" he says excitedly. "This is great."

He seems genuinely pleased for me, and I don't feel threatened by him.

"He's a really great man." Zavier smiles as he sips his drink.

"He is." I think for a moment. "So... you and him are still friends?"

"No." He shakes his head. "He cut all ties the moment I told him that I loved him."

"Oh." I put my hand on his thigh. "I'm sorry. That's shitty."

"Yeah, well, what are you going to do?" He shrugs. "Shit happens." He smiles. "How did you two meet?"

"We were best friends for ten years."

He frowns as he listens.

"And then one day, he professed his love for me."

His eyes hold mine. "I see." He thinks on that for a moment.

"That makes a lot of sense now." His brow furrows and he looks at the ground as if putting a missing piece in a puzzle.

"Eliza!" Henry calls from across the bar. "You're up." He points to the bar, and I laugh.

"Excuse me," I say to Zavier. "I have to get my drunk and disorderly boss another drink."

He chuckles as his eyes linger on Henry dancing around a pole. "Oh, I feel sorry for you having to sit next to him tomorrow in the conference. He's a mess."

"I know." I stand.

"It was nice meeting you, Eliza." Zavier leans up and kisses me on the cheek. "I wish you and Nathan all the happiness in the world. Take care of each other."

"Thanks." I smile. "It means a lot."

I make my way up to my room at 3:00 a.m.

I couldn't wait for Henry any longer. The man is a party animal. My mind is heavily on my conversation with Zavier earlier.

It was the weirdest thing; I didn't feel threatened by Zavier at all and I found him fascinating to talk to. As if I could finally put a piece of the Nathan puzzle together.

One thing keeps playing over and over in my mind, though.

That makes a lot of sense now.

What did he mean by that? Is it the fact that Nathan and I were friends? Or does he think that Nathan loved me all along? Hmm, I wish I asked him what he meant at the time. It's going to eat away at me.

I get into my room and take my phone out of my bag.

17 missed calls: Nathan.

I smile and immediately dial his number.

"Where have you been?" he snaps.

I smile. "Drinking," I slur. Boy I feel tipsy.

"With who?"

"Everybody."

"Where are you now?"

I smile at his bossiness. "At home. I mean I'm in my room... alone."

"Ah." I hear him relax. "I was worried about you."

"Don't be." I sit on the edge of my bed. This alcohol fog has me missing him and feeling over affectionate. "Do you know I love you?" I whisper.

"I do. Do you know that I love you?"

"Sometimes." I smile as I lie back on the bed.

"All the time." I can tell he's relieved that we aren't fighting anymore. "Put me on speaker and take your makeup off."

I close my eyes. "Stop nagging me."

"Eliza."

"Yes." I frown, sit up, and I drag myself into the bathroom. I put the phone on speaker and take my makeup off. I also brush my teeth while he listens on.

"Now get into bed, babe," he says.

"Hmm." I roll my eyes and follow his instructions.

"Keep the phone in bed with you so you can call me if you need anything."

"Nathe..." I smile as I close my eyes.

"Yeah, baby?"

"I love you."

"Good, now go to sleep."

"Night, night," I whisper into the darkness.

"Goodnight, sweetheart."

_____

It's Friday—the last day of the conference. It's been great. I haven't had to come to all the lectures, and I've had plenty of time to do my own thing. Henry has been the perfect companion, although a bit of a drunk. But all in all, it's been enjoyable.

We are at lunch, and I'm standing at the bar to order a lemonade.

"Hi, there," Zavier says from behind me.

"Hi." I smile. I've chatted to Zavier briefly for most of the week. He's lovely. There's a burning question about our conversation we had on the first day, and I know I'm never going to see him again to ask later. We order our drinks and wait.

"Can I ask you something?" I say.

"Sure." He gestures to a seat at the bar, and we both sit down.

"You said something to me the other night and it stayed with me. I wondered if I could ask you what you meant by it?"

"I hope I didn't offend you." He frowns.

"No, not at all."

"What did I say?"

"I told you that Nathan and I had been friends for years, and you said that it all made sense now."

His tongue slides over his bottom lip as he watches me.

"What did you mean?"

"Oh, Eliza." He frowns. "Pay me no attention. I was out of line for saying that."

"No." I put my hand on his leg. "I'm never going to see you again, Zavier, and I won't tell Nathan that we even met, but I would really like to know what makes sense to you. Because so much doesn't make sense to me. It would be nice to get your perspective on this."

"I wouldn't want to upset you."

I fake a smile. "You wouldn't." My eyes search his. "Please tell me what you meant."

"I think..." He pauses. I smile and take his hand in mine. "I think that perhaps Nathan wants children."

I blink. *What?*

"He's at an age where he has to..."

"Settle with a woman," I whisper as I finish his sentence.

"I'm not saying that's what he's done, and he's probably madly in love with you."

I fake a smile as I process his words. "Tell me something, Zavier." I pause as he watches me. "If you wanted children, what would you do?"

He inhales sharply but doesn't answer me.

"Please?" I prompt.

His eyes hold mine and he squeezes my hand in his. "I would fall in love with somebody I trusted for a period of time to make that happen."

"Is this a common thing?" I ask. "Like, in the gay world. Is this a thing?"

He shrugs. "It can. They fall in love with a woman for a period of time, five or ten years, have their family, and then... Well, then they return to their old life. I'm not saying that's what has happened between you two, but he probably wouldn't be aware of it even if it has."

"What do you mean?"

"It's intrinsic to want to procreate. It's primal, buried deep within our DNA. Especially for a man as dominant as Nathan. His body would be seeking out a female and he wouldn't even know why."

I stare at him as I begin to hear my heartbeat in my ears.

"Are you attracted to women?" I ask.

"Yes," he says softly. "And to be honest, I'll probably love a woman one day."

"So that you can have a family?"

"Yes." He nods. "Children are the greatest gift, and it is something that I will explore when the time is right. You never know, she may be my soulmate. That would be wonderful." He smiles. "I believe that you and Nathan will work out. You're so lovely and beautiful. I see exactly what he sees in you."

I smile sadly. "Thanks for being so honest. I appreciate it."

His eyes hold mine. "I hope I didn't upset you."

"Not at all," I lie. "You just opened my eyes."

20

Eliza

THE DRONE of the plane hums through the cabin. I stare out of the window, miles away.

I learned a lot today about life... about myself.

Zavier's words run through my mind. *His body would be seeking out a female and he wouldn't even know why.*

The thought is depressing, but if I'm being completely honest with myself, it does make a lot of sense.

I think back to when this all began and how shocked Nathan was that he was physically attracted to me. It hit him like a ton of bricks.

Nobody was expecting it. Least of all me.

I mean, there's no denying that he loves me. I know that, and physically, we are so good together... but is his body just longing for a uterus to impregnate?

Someone it can trust to bear his fruit?

Is that why he suddenly wanted me physically?

I close my eyes and put my head back onto the seat as I go over the facts of what I do know.

He never got over his first love.

I think about that for a while and what he has told me over the years about Robert and their time together. It's no secret that Robert has been the biggest influence in Nathan's life. His words from our first night in Majorca come back to me.

My biggest regret is leaving Robert.

Ten years later, and the biggest regret in Nathan's life is leaving Robert.

Wow.

Not wishing that he professed his love to me earlier. Not going to Stephanie and giving her what should have been mine. Nothing about us or me at all.

His biggest regret was leaving Robert. *His first love.*

Why didn't that bother me at the time that he said it? Thinking back, it should have. It was so off. Am I really so blinded by Nathan's sunshine that I just swoon on his every word, regardless of the content?

I mean, I shouldn't be surprised. He never really broke ties with Robert. I know they speak regularly, and when Robert comes to town, they always catch up.

Do they still sleep together?

I think about his tattoo and the three swallows. He said they were of him and me, and the life he left behind. It's weird. Why would he get a swallow for the life he left behind if it wasn't symbolic? I think on it as I go over every possible explanation.

Is the third bird Robert? Is that who Nathan left behind?

Zavier said that Nathan told him he never got over his first love.

Hell...

I close my eyes because, now that I think about it, Nathan really might still love him.

And regardless of the uterus issues, and Stephanie, or the possibility that Nathan may be yearning for a man one day in the future. The worst problem of all would be him still loving Robert. That is a hill too steep to climb. We can't get over that, no matter how hard we try.

Fuck, this is a mess. How do I find myself so deeply in love with a man who has so many unanswered questions hanging over his head? Actually, that's unfair. Nathan doesn't have any unanswered questions hanging over him.

They are all mine.

"You okay?" Henry asks softly. "You're very quiet?"

"Yeah." I smile over at him, grateful for his simplistic, sweet personality. "Just tired."

He puts his back against the seat. "Me, too."

Nathan

I pace back and forth. It's been the longest week of my life. I can't tolerate being without Eliza. Having to give her distance this week has nearly killed me.

I glance up at the arrivals screen as it flashes:

Landed.

She's here.

I wait and wait, and I wait until, finally, I see Henry walking out with Eliza behind him. She looks up and sees me. She gives me a soft smile, and my heart swells.

Fuck. *I love this woman.*

I want to run to her and take her in my arms... but I

won't. I'll stand here and act cool, as if my entire world hasn't nearly ended this week without her.

Henry waves and nods, and I wave back, embarrassed by my behaviour before they left.

Eliza comes over to me, and I take her in my arms and kiss her softly. "Here she is."

"Hi." She smiles as she runs her fingers through my stubble.

"Feels like a long time since I've seen you," I murmur as I hold her tight.

"I'm home now, baby." She smiles and kisses me. "Come on." She takes my hand in hers. "Let's go home."

We walk to the car hand in hand, and she chats away, telling me about her week. I watch her in a detached daze.

How have I come to depend on her so much? I can't even sleep without her in bed with me. I've tossed and turned every night, watching the clock until the sun came up.

We arrive at the car and, unable to wait any longer, I take her face in my hands and kiss her deeply. My tongue pushes through her soft open lips. Her hands rest on my hips, and my cock begins to swell with every sweep of our tongues.

"What's for dinner?" she asks, pulling away.

"I don't know what you're eating," I say as I open her door, "but I'm eating you."

Once in the car, we drive in silence, and I hold her hand in my lap.

She's quiet.

"Are you tired, babe?" I ask.

"A little." She kisses my fingertips. "What's been happening here?"

"Nothing. I had surgery on Wednesday, and clinic all week. The apartment is lonely without you."

She presses my hand to her cheek as she watches me. But it's a weird kind of look, as if she's assessing me. Maybe she can sense my fragility. Perhaps it's just in my imagination.

"I missed you," she whispers.

Relief floods me. "I missed you, too... more than you know."

We arrive home, and I put my hands over her eyes as we walk through the front door.

"I have a surprise for you."

"What is it?"

I walk her into the living room and stand her in front of the wall and I take my hands away from her eyes. Her mouth falls open as she stares at the huge painting hanging on the wall.

While she was away, I had a photo of us on our first night in Majorca commissioned to be painted in a semi-abstract way. It was copied from a photo of her and me facing each other. We are holding hands and staring at each other dreamily on a bridge in front of the ocean. We look so deliriously happy. It was the night we went home and made love for the first time. I'd asked a stranger to take a photo of us, and this one was taken when we weren't looking. Eliza loved the photo so much that she made it the background of her cell. I loved it so much that I made it the focus of our apartment.

Eliza stands still and stares at the huge painting on the wall.

"Do you like it?" I ask.

She nods, her eyes welling with tears. "It's perfect."

"What's wrong?" I frown.

"Nothing. These are happy tears." She takes me into her arms. "I love it. Thank you."

We kiss as she holds me tight. She screws up her face against my chest, as if pained.

"Baby, what's wrong?" I whisper, something is off with her.

"Nothing." She smiles sadly and takes my hand in hers. "Come on, shower time."

We walk into the bathroom and she lifts my shirt over my head as we kiss. I unfasten her dress and throw it aside. We stand in our underwear for a long time, kissing, drinking each other in. For the first time all week, I feel like I can breathe again.

"God, I missed you," I murmur against her lips.

Her face creases and tears form again. An uneasy feeling washes over me. Something's wrong, she's never teary.

"What is it?" I frown.

"I'm just glad to be home. I'm over-emotional— hormones, probably." She pulls me into the shower.

I pin her to the wall of the shower as my arousal escalates. We kiss like it's our last kiss, and I lift her and she wraps her legs around me. Her soft, lush body pressed up against mine is the ultimate aphrodisiac. This is when we are at our best, when there is nothing between us. I grab the base of my cock and slide her down onto it. She moans, deep and loud as we stare into each other's eyes.

I've missed her.

My need for friction takes over and I slowly begin to move her up and down on my body, her beautiful cunt rippling around me.

Milking me, making me hers.

She tips her head back and moans as she comes hard. I feel the vise-like grip on my cock, and I put my hands on the back of her shoulders for leverage and let her have it. The sound of our skin slapping in the water echoes throughout the bathroom.

Fuck, I love that sound.

I give her all the emotion I've suffered this week without her. I give her all of myself. Every inch.

I hold myself deep, and then I come, hard, deep inside her body. Her face creases as if she's overcome with emotion before she drops her head to my chest. She clings to me and I hold her up, my heart racing. She's panting, and I frown as I hold her. *What's going on here?*

She's different.

———

It's late, and we're in bed, on our sides, staring at each other.

We've made love for hours. We crossed over to a new level of intimacy.

It was soft and tender, intense and passionate, as if tonight is all we have.

Eliza is teary every time she comes, and I don't know if it's because the love we're making is so special or if it's something else, but she won't tell me why. She keeps telling me that she's just hormonal. I hope to God that that's the truth.

Is she feeling guilty about something?

I want to push her for an answer but she seems so delicate and close to the edge.

The edge of what, I just don't know.

She sits up and runs her fingers over my tattoo of the three swallows.

She kisses the first two—her and me—and then she runs her finger over the back one as she stares at it.

"Who is this bird?" she asks. I frown as our eyes lock. "Who is this bird at the back?" She traces it with her finger.

"It's..." I pause as I search for the right description. "It's... symbolic."

"Of who?"

"I told you. Of the life I left behind."

Her eyes hold mine before they go back to the swallow. She's deep in thought, miles away.

"Are you going to tell me what's wrong?" I ask.

"Nothing," she lies and climbs back up into my arms. I hold her tightly, and our lips meet, our bodies a naked tangle. The sex we had is still smeared on our skin. "How long have you wanted children?" she asks.

I frown, where is this coming from? "What?"

"You said that you were open to anything."

"I am and I know that you want them, so I've actually started to look forward to it one day." I smile softly as imagine Eliza with a baby—my baby. "Why do you ask?"

"I wondered how long you wanted them, that's all."

"I hadn't ever put any thought into it before." I rub my whiskers back and forth across her cheek. "But the world is full of possibilities with you by my side."

I feel her smile against my chest.

I kiss her forehead and hold her tightly in my arms.

"You know you will always be my best friend," she murmurs sadly.

I frown, that sounded......off. "What does that mean?" I ask.

"Nothing. I just wanted you to know that." She kisses my chest. "I love you. I really do love you, Nathan. More than anything."

"I love you, too."

"Goodnight, Nathe," she whispers as her eyes flutter closed.

"Night."

An uneasy feeling washes over me. It's like she's reassuring me of our friendship.

Why?

Why would she say that unless she was pre-empting an end to our relationship?

What the fuck is going on?

Eliza

I wake to the sound of the shower, and I drag my hand down my face. It feels late. The sun is up.

"What time is it?" I reach over and grab the phone from the side table. "Oh, it's Nathan's phone, not mine." I swipe it on, put in his code, and look at the time. It's 7:00 a.m.

Huh, Nathan has usually left over an hour ago.

His phone flashes silently with a notification.

Missed call: Robert.

Hmm, I click out of it in disgust. What, does he call him when he gets to work every morning?

I frown at the thought and click through to his call register.

Mom outgoing
    Eliza outgoing
    Eliza incoming
    Robert outgoing
    Robert outgoing
    Eliza outgoing

Eliza incoming
Robert incoming
Alex outgoing
Eliza incoming
Robert outgoing
Dad incoming
Office incoming
Robert outgoing

"What?" I sit up, and, suddenly interested in the call history. I look at the times and dates of when he spoke to Robert. I scroll down and go back over a long period of time.

Sometimes Robert calls him, other times Nathan calls Robert.

They speak nearly every day, I look through the call times. Sometimes for five minutes, sometimes up to nearly an hour.

On the second day that I was away, they spoke four times. *What the fuck?*

I hear the shower turn off. I turn the phone off and put it on the side table, and I pretend to be asleep.

Nathan comes out and gets his clothes out of the walk-in closet. He takes them out into the living room to dress to be less noisy.

I stare at the ceiling. Wow.

There are so many things that are fucked up about this relationship, I don't even know where to start. I have every right to feel insecure. This isn't in my fucking head.

Anger begins to bubble deep in my stomach. So, he can get crazy jealous whenever he wants, but it's okay for him to speak to his ex every day? They're friends, I remind myself.

Ugh...whatever. I don't want him to know I snooped in his phone so I can't even say anything.

I get up and shower as I mouth angry, fighting words to the shampoo bottles.

I can't say them to him, so I'll let them have it.

Don't be the insecure girlfriend.

That isn't who I am, and I'm not lowering myself. When the time is right, I'll address the Robert issue. Until then, I'll carry on as if normal.

Calm, calm. Keep fucking calm.

After many deep breathes and a huge pep talk to myself, I get out of the shower and dress for work. I put on a fitted black dress and high-heeled pumps with sheer stockings. I make an extra effort and put my long dark hair into a high ponytail. I apply a full face of makeup to make myself feel confident.

I look at my lipstick selections all lined up in my makeup drawer.

Red. It's a red lipstick day. I put it on as if it's war paint and I'm preparing to battle. Don't mess with me today, anyone, or you will go down, and it *will* fucking hurt.

I walk out into the kitchen to find Nathan dressed in a dark charcoal suit. He has a light blue shirt on and a navy tie. His hair is longer on top with that just-fucked messy perfection. He looks fucking edible. Ugh, it's so annoying.

"Morning." I fake a smile as I kiss his cheek.

His eyes drop down to my toes and then back up to my face. His eyebrow rises as if angered. "Red lipstick for work?"

"Yeah," I reply casually as I pour myself a coffee from the coffee machine. "Why haven't you left yet?"

"I wanted to talk to you. I'll drive you to work."

I turn toward him with my coffee in my hand. "What about?"

"Last night.'"

My eyes hold his. "What about it?"

"You were acting weird."

"Was I?" I sip my coffee as I act casual. "Maybe I'm a little over-emotional."

"Why?"

"You asked me this already last night, Nathan. Why are we talking about it again?"

He steps toward me, and his eyes hold mine. "I wanted to have the conversation again when we were dressed. What happened at that conference, Eliza?"

"What?" I frown.

"Do you feel guilty about something? Is that why you got teary every time we had sex?"

I stare at him as my brain misfires. What the fuck?

I point to my chest in disbelief. "You think *I* feel guilty about something?"

"You sure are acting like it."

"Ha." I scoff as my temper begins to soar. "Of course, in Nathan's kingdom this has to be something that *I've* done wrong."

"What the fuck does that mean?" He growls.

"It means that people in glass houses shouldn't throw stones."

"What?" He explodes. "I'll throw a fucking rock if I want to. Why do you look like that to go to work?"

"Like what?"

"Like you're good to fucking go."

I lift my chin as I glare at him. I don't think I've ever been so furious in my entire life.

I was emotional last night because I am petrified that I'm going to lose him, and here he is accusing me of being a floozy.

"You are un-fucking-believable!" I snap. "Don't bother driving me to work."

"Is the lipstick for him?" He growls.

"What?" I scream. "Are you fucking kidding me?" The pressure explodes. "I'm not even seeing him today. I'm at the hospital. And for your information, the lipstick is for me, to make myself feel better so I can act like I haven't got a care in the world." I storm into the office and collect my laptop from the charger.

I grab my things and head out the door. Nathan follows me. I hit the elevator button with force, and he stands beside me. "I'll drive you."

"Don't bother."

"Stop it."

"Fuck." I close my eyes. "Seriously... Nathan, leave me alone. I'm not even joking."

The elevator doors open in the lobby and he pushes the button for the basement. "Shut up."

The doors open, and I march out to the car. You know, his little jealous alpha thing was cute when we were friends, but this bullshit he's carrying on with now is infuriating. I have a reason to be jealous, and I'm holding my tongue. Yet he can do and say whatever the fuck he wants.

Like hell.

He opens my car door and I get in. He slams the door hard and goes around to his side. Moments later, he drives off with a rev.

I sit and glare out the window.

"What the fuck is wrong with you?" he asks.

"Nothing." I cross my arms.

The phone rings in his Bluetooth. and the name Robert comes up on the screen.

He immediately hits decline.

My eyes flicker to him. "Why didn't you take that?"

"I'll call him later."

"Oh, you will, will you?" I sneer sarcastically.

His eyes flick between me and the road. "What does that fucking mean?"

"When are you going to cut the umbilical cord, Nathan?"

He narrows his eyes, and it's clear he has no idea what I'm talking about.

"Would you like it if I spoke to my ex all the time?" I ask.

"What?" He screws up his face as if I'm crazy. "We're friends."

"Okay, fine. I'm going to call Samuel today and..." I hunch my shoulders casually. "Might have a drink with him, since we are"—I hold my fingers up in quotation marks—"friends."

"What the hell is wrong with you?" He punches the steering wheel.

I close my eyes. God, how did this fight escalate to this?

I sit and stare out the window. We drive into the hospital parking lot, and he pulls over into the parking bay.

I look over to him, and we glare at each other.

"Is that it?" he asks.

"Yep."

He gives a subtle shake his head.

"Is that it from you?" I ask.

"I'll pick you up."

"Don't bother." I get out and slam the door. He winds the window down.

"Eliza?" he says.

I lean down and look through the window. "Yes."

"Have a nice day." His face softens.

Wow. Dr. Jekyll and Mr. Hyde.

"I will. Oh, and Nathan? On one of your ten conversations with your ex-boyfriend today, send him my love." I fake a sweet smile.

He narrows his eyes, and I turn and march into the hospital.

I walk through the doors on a mission.

Fuck. I'm a bitch. I'm a total fucking bitch, but I don't give a damn. He deserved it.

Is that lipstick for him?

Of all the fucking nerve. I need coffee. I walk down to the cafeteria. My face is flushed, and I can feel the adrenaline still surging through my veins.

Nobody can piss me off like Nathan Mercer can.

"Eliza!" a woman's voice calls.

I turn to see Stephanie in her white coat with her stethoscope around her neck.

"Hi." She smiles.

"Oh, hello." I'm taken aback. I didn't expect to see her.

"Have you got a minute?"

"I haven't actually, I'm in a rush," I lie. I'm an hour early. I was so pissed off, I didn't even look at the clock. "What do you want?"

Her face falls. She looks around as if uncomfortable. "I was just hoping we could talk."

"About what?" I ask flatly.

"Um." She fakes a smile, and it's obvious she's uncomfortable. "I was just... I was hoping we could be friends. Nathan mentioned that..."

He's talked to her about me? My temper explodes like a firecracker, and the sky turns red.

"You're not the kind of friend I would want, Stephanie."

Her face falls. "Why not?"

I pinch the bridge of my nose with a chuckle. This woman is fucking stupid.

"I would expect a friend of mine to direct me back to the person I had feelings for. Not ask him to..." I pause and search for the right word. "Practice his skills on me."

"That's not fair."

"Isn't it?"

"Don't be a fool." Her eyes hold mine. "Do you know what I would do to have a man like Nathan Mercer in love with me?'

"I do." My furious eyes hold hers. "Fall to your knees and suck his dick." I turn and march off.

I storm into my office and throw my bag on the desk. I text the girls.

We are going out tonight.
Stretch up.

21

Eliza

IT'S 2:00 p.m. when an email pings in my inbox from Nathan Mercer. I roll my eyes and open it.

Good afternoon, Miss Bennet,

I hope you are having a nice day.
    This is a welfare check to see if my girlfriend is feeling any more stable this afternoon.

xoxoxo

I smirk. Asshole. I have calmed down considerably, but whatever. I reply:

Dear Dr. Mercer,

Your girlfriend is still feeling unhinged.
It is best to avoid her for your own health and safety.

xoxoxox

I smirk as I wait for his reply.

Miss Bennet,

Does she need me to come over and fuck the crazy out of her?
I'm happy to put her health and safety above mine.

xoxoxo

I smile. *Don't be cute, asshole.*
I reply:

Dear Dr. Mercer,

Undoubtedly. However, it will have to wait until this evening.
Miss Bennet will get fired for having sexual relations at work.

xoxox

I tap my pen as I wait for his reply. I look around guiltily.

Miss Bennet,

Is that supposed to be a deterrent?

It's an incentive to fuck you twice on the reception desk.

xoxoxo

I giggle. How can he calm me down with a few flirty emails? Oh well, I'm sick to death of fighting. All relationships have their problems, I guess. I just have to work out the best way to navigate through ours. I reply:

Dear Dr. Mercer.

I shall take you up on your offer.
    I am going out to dinner with my friends tonight.
    You can pick me up afterwards, if you wish, for my therapy session.

xoxoxox

I hit send and smile as I wait.

My phone instantly rings, the name Nathan lights up the screen. "Hello."

"You're going out tonight?" he snaps.

"Just for dinner."

"I don't want you to. I haven't seen you all week."

"You don't have a choice."

"Who are you going out with?"

"Jolie and Brooke. It's just dinner, Nathan. I haven't seen my friends in ages, and I live with you. You get to see me all the time."

He exhales heavily, unimpressed.

"Unless you want to start another fight over nothing," I snap. "I'm only too happy to go there."

"Don't be late," he warns.

"Will you pick me up?" I ask.

"Fine." He stays silent as he hangs on the line. "And?" he asks.

"And what?"

"Is that it?"

He's waiting for me to tell him that I love him. Well, too bad. I'm not. "Is that it from you?"

"Yes, it is," He snaps and I know he's holding his temper.

"I'll text you where we are tonight. Goodbye." I hang up in a rush.

I can just imagine his fuming face right now.

Oh well…. he can get over it.

———

I see Jo and Brooke at the back of the restaurant, sitting in a booth. I make my way over to them.

"Hi." I fall into my seat.

"Hey." Jolie laughs, and Brooke gets up and kisses me.

I glance down to see a near-empty bottle of wine, and I frown. "How long have you two been here?"

"A while," Jolie replies dryly. "I've got issues."

I chuckle as I fill my glass with the remainder of the bottle. "Join the club."

Brooke rolls her eyes. "I don't have issues."

"Yes, you do," Jolie mutters dryly. "You're fucking boring, that's a big issue. It's worse than ours."

I giggle as I sip my wine. "What's the issue, Jo?"

"Well, you know how I'm seeing Santiago?"

"Yeah. Did you wee on him yet?"

"No, but he wants me to go to Spain with him on a holiday."

I frown. "Right."

"But Brooke thinks he's going to sell me on the black market or some shit."

My eyes flicker to Brooke. "What? Why?"

"He wants her to have a threesome."

My eyes go back to Jolie. "Didn't you do that already? You were talking about that last week."

"No." Brooke smiles sweetly. "He's saving her for his buddy back home. Isn't he so thoughtful?"

I open my mouth to say something but nothing comes out.

Yuck.

"So, this fool," Brooke sneers, "is actually considering going to another country with a man she hardly knows so that he can share her with his friends. Where she doesn't speak the language, and has no idea who he is or what the laws of possession are."

"You don't know him!" Jolie cries.

"I don't think I want to," I reply. "Jo, you can't be seriously considering this."

"Why not?"

"It's fucking dangerous. I'm with Brooke; you have no idea what he's into. He could be a sex trafficker and his job is to come to the states to bring pretty girls back home."

"He's not, and you two have read too many dark romance books. That shit doesn't happen for real."

"You don't know that." Brooke scoffs. "Seriously, you are killing me. You can't be this stupid?"

"Well, I want to go." Jolie huffs. "I've always wanted to travel, and it's only one week. He's going to take me to San Sebastian."

"To probably kill you," Brooke mutters under her breath. "He might make snuff movies or some shit."

Jolie rolls her eyes, and I chuckle. "Jeez, your story makes mine sound tame."

"Why?" Jolie sighs uninterested. "What's happening with you?"

It feels good to be with my friends. I've been building up all this stress and I'm bursting to vent about it.

"I'm going to tell you bitches everything, and I want your support and understanding because my head is about to explode."

"Fire away," Jolie does a little wave to the server. "It will take my mind off of sex trafficking."

I giggle. "Well, to start with, there is a chick at Nathan's work who sucked his dick," I blurt out in a rush.

"What?" they both gasp and sit forward in their seats.

"She wants him and she's beautiful. She's also a doctor."

"What the hell?" Brooke whispers. "Everyone fucking wants him."

"Oh, you don't know the half of it. While on my conference last week, guess who I met."

"Who?" They both frown.

"A guy who used to go out with Nathan."

Brooke's eyes widen. "Oh, hell."

Jolie cringes. "Is it weird meeting guys he's been with?"

"It's weird meeting anyone your partner's been with." I huff. "And now I find out that Robert is calling him all the time."

"Who's Robert?" Brooke frowns.

"His ex," Jolie and I both say in tandem. Jolie has met

Robert a few times. She doesn't know him well but she knows who he is.

"God." Brooke sighs. "So, who's the girl? I thought he's never been with a woman before you?"

"Well," I whisper. "Where do I start?"

The waitress arrives with our new bottle of wine. Jolie takes the bottle from her and refills our glasses. "At the very beginning."

Nathan

I walk into the cocktail bar just around 11:00 p.m.

Eliza hasn't called me so I'm assuming she wants me to just show up.

I see the girls sitting at a high table. Eliza waves in an unexaggerated way, and I smile. She's well on her way to being drunk. As I get closer, I can see that they all are.

"Hey, there." Eliza smiles as she slides her hands around my waist, under my jacket. I lean and kiss her lips, and then look up to the girls. It looks like I'm forgiven. "Hi."

The girls both smile. "Hi, Nathe."

Brooke puts her hands over her eyes. "You two are actually together. I mean, I knew it, but I haven't seen it with my own eyes until now."

Eliza smiles as she leans into me, and I hold her tight. She's so cuddly and affectionate when she drinks.

"I'm finishing my drink, and then we'll go home." She smiles up at me.

"Okay."

"I'm going to go to the bathroom," she says.

"I'm coming," Brooke says. She jumps from her stool, and

they toddle off arm in arm, leaving me to sit down. I pick up Eliza's margarita and take a sip.

Jolie's eyes hold mine as if she has something on her mind.

I raise my eyebrow at Jolie. "What's that look for?"

"How's this going to go, Nathan?" she slurs. She's a lot drunker than she looks.

"How's what going to go?"

"Eliza's heart."

I bite my lip as I try to hold my tongue. Jolie winds me up on the best of days. "You don't need to worry about Eliza's heart, Jolie."

"Don't I?"

I glare at her. My fury begins to boil.

"Your ex-boyfriend told her at her conference that you're just looking for a uterus. Is that true?"

"What the hell does that mean?" I snap.

"What are you planning? Give her five years and three kids, and then go back to your ex, while your best friend raises your kids alone?"

"What the fuck?" I growl as my temper breaks.

"Nathan," Eliza whispers from behind me as she arrives back at the table.

I stand in a rush, and Eliza grabs my arm.

"Nathan, calm down. What... what did you say to him?" Eliza stammers to Jolie.

"How dare you even suggest such a thing!" I yell.

Brooke looks between us. "What did you say, Jo?"

"I asked him if he's in love with Eliza or if he's just looking for an incubator to make his babies." She huffs.

Eliza's face falls. "Jolie." She gasps.

"You make me sick. You're a fucking hypocrite, just like the rest of them." I sneer at Jolie. "I thought we were friends?"

"How am I a hypocrite?" She gasps, as if offended.

"Oh, I'm your friend, Nathan. You have my full support. I love all people, Gay Pride, I go to Mardi Gras and celebrate. Let's change our Facebook banner to prove we love gay people. Much like the rest of society, you play the game of acceptance, don't you? *Love is love,* they all say... until it's fucking not!" I cry. "A man who's been with men in the past, who then falls in love with a woman must have an agenda, mustn't he?" I yell. "There's no way that I could just be in love with Eliza, is there?" I lose all control. "Love isn't fucking love, is it?" I cry. "Love is judgement."

"I didn't mean—"

"Yes, you did. So, don't you sit there with your pathetic hypocrisy and pretend to be accepting." I slam my drink down on the table. "This. *This,* exactly right here, is why people like me don't feel accepted in society. Because back-stabbing assholes like you play the acceptance game until it's on someone you know and care about. Then it's wrong, and you suddenly can't get your head around it."

"Nathan." Eliza pulls at me. "Let's go."

"You want to know an agenda, Jolie, you idiot?" I yell, I've completely lost control of my temper. "An agenda is a guy that sleeps with a woman to get porn footage."

Her face falls.

"Oh, but that's okay." I shake my head in disgust. "Because he's straight and normal, so he must be a good guy."

Eliza pulls me toward the door. I get a lump in my throat, overwhelmed with emotion.

Love is love... *What a joke.*

I storm toward the door as adrenaline pumps through my system like never before.

I'm livid.

I burst out the doors of the bar in a rush, and Eliza is near running beside me to keep up.

"Nathan, don't worry about what she said. It was out of line, I'm sorry."

I stride along the sidewalk toward the car.

"Why would you let her worry you?" She cries. "We know it's not true... is it?"

I keep walking as my temper hits crescendo.

Now I've fucking heard it all.

She's questioning if I actually want her for a child. Here I am loving her with my everything, and she thinks I'm using her.

If she stabbed me in the heart it would be less painful.

And you think you know someone.

"Nathan?"

"Go back inside, Eliza." I growl. "I have nothing to say to you."

"What? Why?"

"Do you even fucking know me at all?" I cry.

She runs beside me. "I met someone you know at the conference."

I keep walking toward my car.

"His name was Zavier, and you know Zavier, don't you?"

I stay silent, my fury beyond boiling point.

"Zavier said—" She stammers in a rush.

"I know what he said!" I cry, cutting her off. "And the fact that you don't know the answer to it proves my fucking point."

"Will you slow down? I'm going to break my neck in these heels."

"I mean it. I don't want to be near you; go back inside."

"Nathan." She grabs my hand and pulls me back to a stop. "I'm sorry I spoke to my friends about it, okay? It upset me and I needed to vent."

I stare at her, lost for words, this hurts. "I asked you at least twenty times last night what was wrong, and you wouldn't tell me. Then I turn up here to be abused by your friend. How do you think that makes me feel, Eliza?"

"I needed to talk to someone."

"So, talk to me!" I yell. "Why are we together if you can't even talk to me?"

Her eyes search mine.

"You think I need an agenda to love you?" I cry out.

"I'm just scared, Nathan."

"Of what, Eliza? Of being like the rest of them? Of judging me because of who I've slept with?" I step back from her, disgusted. "Well, guess what... you should be scared because you are just like them."

Her eyes well with tears. "That's not fair."

"I'll tell you what's not fair. It's spending ten years of your life with someone, falling hopelessly in love with them, only to have them tell their friends that they think you're using them to have a child." I get a lump in my throat as I stare at her, my heart constricts.

This hurts.

I can't be near her. I turn and get into my car, slamming the door hard.

"Nathan!" she cries.

I start the car, and she throws her arms up.

"What are you doing?" She bangs on my window.

I pull out into the traffic. "Getting away from you," I mutter to myself.

Eliza

Nathan's car takes off and I watch as he disappears around the corner, the tires screeching in the distance.

Fucking hell......

I can't believe what just happened. So much for confiding in a friend. Jolie broke the friend code, big time. Furious, I turn and march back into the bar.

"What the fuck were you doing?" I cry when I find her. "How could you say that to him? I told you those things in confidence."

"I just told him the truth, Eliza. It's weird that he's suddenly come to you professing his love after all this time. Gay men don't turn straight. It just doesn't happen. Everyone knows it, not just me. Deep down, you know it, too. One day, he *will* leave you for a man. You can't fight who you really are."

"You had no right. This was between him and me. Do you know how hurt he will be?"

Jolie sips her drink and shrugs casually. "He needed to know."

"Know what?"

"That I'm watching him, and that if he hurts you, I'm going to end him."

"The only thing he knows now is what a fucking asshole I am." I cry.

"Eliza, please." She rolls her eyes as if I'm being dramatic. "You're the one who's insecure. You're the one who has all these questions about his past. Don't get angry with me for verbalising them."

My eyes fill with tears. I *am* an asshole.

I turn and march from the club and out onto the sidewalk. "Taxi!" I call as I put my hand up. A few moments later, a cab pulls in, and I jump in the back. "Smith Street, please."

The driver pulls out into the traffic, and I stare out the window in tears.

That wasn't fair.

My God, that so wasn't fair. He did not deserve that. I bounce my leg as the car drives. "Can you hurry, please?"

The driver points to the speedometer. "I'm not getting a ticket, lady."

I sit back, dejected. "Sorry." I sigh.

Twenty long minutes later, I arrive at the apartment and I take the elevator to our floor. I open the door, and I can tell instantly that he's not here.

"Nathan!" I call.

Silence.

"Nathan." I look through the apartment.

He's not here.

I take out my phone and call him. It rings out and goes to voicemail.

"Nathan." I screw up my face in tears. "Where are you?" I whisper. I close my eyes in regret. "Can you call me, please?"

I hang up and begin to pace. I keep seeing the hurt on his face, and I put my head into my hands. Oh no, no, no. I dial his number again. I listen as it rings out and I screw up my face in tears when it goes to voicemail again. I text him.

Nathan, answer your phone.
I'm freaking out.

Where are you?

A text bounces back.

Leave me alone.

Thank God. I text back.

Where are you?

A reply comes back.

I'm staying at my place tonight.

No, baby...

**Nathan, I'm sorry.
I should have talked to you.
Please come home.**

A reply bounces back.

Tomorrow.

I frown as uneasiness fills me. I reply:

I need to talk tonight.

With my heart in my throat I wait.

I can't.

He can't. What the fuck does that mean? I dial his number and it rings out again. My heart hammers in my chest, and the tears of regret roll down my cheeks as I wait for the answering machine.

"Nathan, I love you." I whisper. "I'm sorry. I'm just so scared." I pace as I think of what to say. "I'm going out of my mind with insecurity and I don't want to," I whisper as I walk to the window. I pull back the drapes and look out over the view. "It's just new and this is a transition stage, that's all." I offer an explanation. "This is weird for me, Nathe. Meeting men at conferences who put these ideas into my head is fucking weird, okay? Call me... please."

I feel so guilty that he had to hear that from Jolie.

I am fucking furious with her. How could she?

I hang up and drop to the couch. I screw up my face and I call April. Then, I cry.

———

It's early morning and still dark when I hear the key in the door. I sit up.

He's here. He's come home to talk about it.

I'm exhausted. I think I slept for an hour, tops.

He marches into the bedroom in his suit. He's ready for work already. He flicks the bathroom light on. I hear the drawers open and slam shut.

"Nathan!" I call. "What are you doing?"

I hear something fall on the floor.

"Come and talk to me," I call. What the hell is he doing in there?

Bottles fall over, and something bangs hard as he tears

through the bathroom cupboards like a mad man. "Where is it?" he calls.

"What?" I frown.

"Your fucking birthcontrol pills. Where are they?"

"What?" I frown as I climb out of bed, still half asleep. "What are you doing?"

He grabs my makeup purse and scurries through it. The makeup falls everywhere.

My new blush falls on the floor and smashes everywhere.

"You're breaking things," I cry.

He pulls out the little foil packet and studies it closely.

"What are you doing?" I whisper as I begin to panic.

"What is *this*?" He holds it in the air.

"What?"

"Where is your fucking period, Eliza?" His eyes search mine.

My face falls.

"You haven't had one since we've been together. Where is it?" He studies the packet again. "This says here you were supposed to get your period on Saturday. It's fucking Tuesday, Eliza." He screams as he holds the packet up in the air. "You're late?" The veins are sticking out of his forehead in anger. He's completely lost control.

"Nathan, calm down."

"How the fuck can I calm down?" He screams. "Heaven forbid that I should take up residency in your fucking uterus." He looks at me and shakes his head in disgust. "Or are you already pregnant? Should I go to the bar to hear about this, too?"

My eyes well with tears. *He's so hurt.* "It's coming," I whisper. "It's my first month on the pill. I swear, my period is coming. My hormones are adjusting, that's all."

He throws the pill packet at me. "Get yourself to a doctor."
He marches out and I hear the front door slam behind him.

The apartment falls deathly silent again.

He's gone.

I put my head into my hands, and my heart drops.

Fuck.

————

I sit at my desk and stare at the computer. I feel sick. My
stomach is a ball of nerves. In ten years, I've never seen Nathan
like that before. He was so angry—*so hurt.*

How do we get over this? What do I say to fix this?

And where is my period? Why *is* it late? I did everything
right. I took the pill every day at the same time. I waited the
time before I had sex. How long was it?

Fucking Jolie. I'm going to kill her with my bare hands. But I
know I can't blame her. This is my fault, and Nathan has every
reason to be furious with me.

Please, don't let me be pregnant.

This is not the way I want to have a child.

I can't be. I did everything right. The doctor told me that I
would be protected after a week, and I waited for that time. I go
through my diary and work out when I went to the doctor. I
count through on my calendar and count the days. It was actually two weeks to the day, before Nathan and I had unprotected
sex.

My phone buzzes in front of me. The name Jolie lights up
the screen. I look around guiltily, stuff it, I want to talk to her
and give her a piece of my mind.

"Hello!" I snap.

"Oh my God. I am so fucking sorry. I don't even remember what happened. Brooke called me and told me this morning."

"How could you say those things?" I whisper angrily.

"I don't know." She splutters. "Last thing I remember, we were talking about it, and then I drank too much and...God, I'm a nightmare."

"Yes, you fucking are," I bark. "Poor Nathan."

"I've already called him twice to apologize but he won't answer my calls. I'm just really worried about you, Eliza, and I don't know why but it all came out wrong."

"Do you blame him?" I whisper as I look around.

"Fuck, I'll keep trying to call him. I left him a message."

"This all could have been avoided if you weren't such a fucking idiot."

"I know. I'm going. I have to try him again. I feel terrible."

"And so you should. Goodbye." I hang up in a rush. She pisses me off.

How could she say those things to him? Adrenaline is pumping through my veins.

I try to calm myself down and go back to my pregnancy scare. Shit, this week is just horrendous. The kind you see on cable.

I type into Google. How long after starting the contraceptive pill are you covered?

The answers pop up, and I read through them. They're all the same.

The Contraceptive Pill does not protect a woman from sexually transmitted infections. Birth control pills protect from pregnancy after seven days of use but it's best to use a backup method (condoms) for the first month after taking the pill to be safe.

What?

A backup method.

A month. What do you fucking mean, a month? I begin to hear the panic as it screams through my veins like a river rapid.

The doctor told me seven days. She was positive. If I had known...

I put my head into my hands. "Oh my God."

"Excuse me?" a voice says. I glance up. "I'm here for my post-surgery consult."

The girls are all on lunch and I am covering reception. "Oh, yes." I fake a smile. I glance through the booking list. "Mia, is it?"

"You should know me by now. I've been in three times this week." She snarls.

Okay, *rude bitch.*

I type into the computer. "Sorry, I'm not normally on reception." I frown. Why has she been in three times this week? "Is there something wrong with your wound?" I ask.

"There's nothing wrong with my wound. The entire procedure was a disaster. I asked for this picture. I wanted them bigger, more natural looking." She shows me a picture on her phone. It's of an eighteen-year-old girl with perky, natural breasts. Not that I can tell, because she's had so much work done, but I think this woman is in her late thirties. She's never going to look like this.

Henry is a surgeon, not a miracle worker.

"And I can tell you now, my boobs don't look like this. I want a redo or a full refund."

"I see." I force another smile.

Seriously...fuck off, cow. I am not in the mood for your shit. I've got way bigger problems than your tits.

"Let me go and see Dr. Morgan, and I'll be right back."

She sits down on the couch and folds her arms in a huff. I walk up the hall and softly knock on Henry's door.

"Come in."

I open the door. "Hi." I close the door behind me. "Mia Schofield is here."

He exhales with an eye roll. "Yes."

"She's carrying on about her surgery." I wince. "Sorry."

"I know. This is the second time I've done them. I did them two years ago. She wanted them bigger and complained then, too."

"She showed me a picture of a—"

"I've seen the picture. Nobody is that talented." He exhales heavily and sits back in his chair. "Send her in."

"Okay."

His eyes linger on my face. "Hey, are you okay?" he asks softly. "You're not your happy self today."

"Yeah." I fake a smile.

"Still fighting with Nathan?"

I shrug. I feel so fragile that I may just burst into tears any moment.

"You know, you can talk to me at any time." He places his hand on top of mine on the desk. "I'm here for you... as a friend. I'm an excellent listener."

I smile, grateful for his kindness. "We'll be okay, it's nothing serious," I lie. "Just teething problems. It will be fine." I give him a smile and make my way back to the crazy woman in the waiting room.

"Just go in, he's waiting for you."

I watch her march up the corridor and close the door behind her.

I exhale heavily. This job sucks. I miss nursing. I miss looking after children—beautiful, sick little children who need me and are grateful for every smile. If I get offered this job at the private hospital, I'm going to take it.

I'm not cut out for cosmetic surgery. This isn't my calling.

———

I stand in the kitchen and sip my tea. I called Nathan and he said he wouldn't be long. He was short with me, and it's clear he's still furious. I don't even know what he's going to say when he gets here... or if I want to hear it.

I'm nervous as hell, and I still don't have my period.

Where is it?

I hear the key in the door before he comes into view. My eyes instantly well with tears at the sight of him. He looks like shit, and it's obvious that he didn't get any sleep last night, either.

"Hi."

"Hi." His eyes hold mine.

"I'm sorry, Nathe. I just wanted to talk to someone, and I know it should have been you." I watch him as my stomach swarms with butterflies. "You know, I was just scared to share my fears with you."

Empathy wins, and he exhales heavily. "Don't cry." He sighs as he takes me into his arms and I press my face into his shoulder as he holds me.

"I don't want this to come between us," I murmur.

"Let me have a shower and we'll talk, okay?" He brushes my hair back from my forehead and he looks down at me.

I nod, hopeful for the first time, all day. He begins to walk off and I cling to him. "Can you just hug me for a moment, please?"

He holds me tightly, and we stand in each other's arms for a long time. I'm feeling so fragile and clingy.

"I love you," I whisper.

"Do you, Lize?" he asks softly. "Or do you just think you do? Because from where I'm standing, it doesn't seem like it."

I close my eyes in sadness. "Nathe, I only told the girls what had been said to me, not that I believed it. Zavier rattled me, yes, I can't deny it. But put yourself in my shoes for a moment."

He exhales heavily. "Let me shower."

"Okay." I kiss him softly again, and he disappears up the hall.

He kissed me. There's hope.

I get back to making dinner, and I put the chicken in the oven and pour two glasses of red wine. Then, I stare at my glass and frown.

What if I'm pregnant?

I take a sip with a shaky hand, and then I pour my glass down the sink.

Fuck, this is a disaster.

The apartment phone rings. I frown and pick up. "Hello."

"Hello, Miss Bennet. It's Roy from concierge."

"Hi, Roy."

"I have a visitor here for you. He said you are expecting him."

"Who is it?"

"Robert Scott."

My eyes widen. What? Nathan must be expecting him. "That's fine, send him up."

I pour myself another glass of wine. One glass can't hurt, surely fucking not.

Moments later, there is a soft knock on the door, and I open it.

"Hello, Eliza." Robert smiles. He leans in and kisses my cheek. I know Robert from over the years. He's a nice guy. Handsome and sweet.

"Hi."

"Is Nathan home?" he asks nervously.

I frown. I thought he said he was expected. "Yeah, he's in the shower." My eyes hold his. "Does he know you're coming?"

"Um." His eyes dart up the hall to where the shower just turned off, and Robert twists his hands nervously in front of him. "No."

The hairs on the back of my neck stand to attention. ...... Something feels off.

Nathan walks up the hall in his navy, silk boxers, and he stops mid-step when he sees Robert.

"What are you doing here?" he asks.

"Um." Roberts eyes flicker to me nervously. "I wanted to talk to you... both."

I look between them.

"I wanted Eliza to hear this from me, out of respect." He shrugs. "I don't want anything underhand."

"Stop!" Nathan snaps.

"When you cut all ties this week—," Robert whispers.

"Stop, right now." Nathan growls. "I mean it, Robert."

It's as if Nathan already knows what he's going to say.

My eyes flick between them as they stare at each other. You could cut the air with a knife.

"I broke up with Liam," Robert says. "I can't be with Liam... because, I'm still in love with you."

22

Eliza

MY EYES WIDEN. *What the fuck?*

"I don't want to hear it!" Nathan snaps. "How did you know where I live?"

"Umm." Robert's nervous eyes flick to me, rattled by Nathan's cold reception. "I.... um—"

"You what?" Nathan bellows, making me jump. "How do you *fucking* know where I live?"

"I followed you home from work," Robert whispers.

"You what?" Nathan erupts.

"I just..." Robert's voice trails off, and his eyes come back to me.

"You wanted to say this in front of Eliza." Nathan sneers. "Is that it?"

Robert stays silent.

"Answer the fucking question!" Nathan bellows.

"She... she needs to know," Robert stammers. "When she said we couldn't speak anymore... she needs to know it isn't possible. She deserves to know the truth."

Nathan must have told him I don't want them speaking. I pause as I look between them.

"I'm going to go out for a while and give you both some privacy," I say quietly.

"Don't you dare go anywhere, Eliza!" Nathan yells.

My eyes widen.

"I love you," Robert says, his eyes searching Nathan's. "And I know you still love me, too."

My heart stops as I watch him. Robert's hair is dishevelled and his eyes are crazy. He seems desperate. This would have taken a lot of courage to come here and do this.

"You're too late," Nathan tells him. "I'm happy. For the first time in ten years, I'm fucking happy. You think you can barge into my home and want me back? No, you're too late."

Robert shakes his head as if panicked. "Don't say that."

"I'm tied to Eliza now," Nathan whispers as if forgetting I'm here.

I begin to hear my heartbeat in my ears, and I put my hands over my mouth. This is too much to handle. I drop my head as I process that statement.

Tied to Eliza.

Not *I love Eliza.* Not *I want Eliza. I'm tied to Eliza.*

The baby.

He's tied to me because of the baby. Emotion overwhelms me, and I don't want to be here. I don't want to hear this. I feel the need to protect myself take over. I walk out of the kitchen and into the living area.

"Eliza!" Nathan yells. "Don't you fucking leave!"

"I'm not going anywhere," I fire back. *Fuck you.* I want to be anywhere but here, listening to this.

"Get out!" Nathan yells. "Leave now, Robert."

"You've been begging me to come back to you for years," Robert cries. "I know you still love me, Nathan. It's not too late for us."

Horror dawns. *What?*

Nathan's been begging for Robert to come back to him for years?

My eyes well with tears.

"Get out!" Nathan cries. His voice cracks, betraying his hurt, and I screw my face up in pain.

He does still love him. I can hear it in his voice.

"Please," Robert begs, and I can tell by his voice that he's becoming upset.

"Don't touch me," Nathan whispers angrily, and I know that Robert has reached for him.

I close my eyes. I can feel Robert's pain.

"Don't come near Eliza again," Nathan whispers. "You wait until I'm finally happy and you think that you can show up here and upset her?"

"I'm not trying to upset her," Robert cries.

"Well, you are." Nathan yells. "And you've upset me. Get the hell out of my life, Robert. You've fucked me up for too long."

Oh God. This is bad. *This is really bad.*

Nathan never got over him. A piece of the puzzle clicks into place.

This is why he has never had another relationship. I close my eyes as I listen.

They fall silent.

What's happening?

"Please..." Nathan whispers as if pained. "Just go. Leave me be."

"I love you."

"Go!" Nathan bellows as he loses all control.

I screw up my face to stop myself from sobbing out loud, I drop my head into my hands.

"I said *go*!" Nathan yells.

"No!" I hear Robert cry, as if they're in a scuffle. "Don't do this."

I run into the kitchen to see Nathan dragging Robert toward the door by the arm. He opens the door and hurls Robert out into the corridor.

"Stay the fuck out of my life!" he yells before slamming the door hard. He marches up the hall to our bedroom.

The tears roll down my face, and I look at the back of the door.

Do I go out there and check on Robert? Is he okay?

What do I do? *What do I do?*

I hear the shower turn back on. What's he doing?

I walk back into the kitchen, and with a shaky hand, I pick up my wine and sip it.

I wince. It tastes like poison.

Everything tastes like poison... even my love.

My heart is hammering hard in my chest...what the fuck just happened?

I can't stand this. I need to see if Robert's okay. I march to the front door, open it, and I peer out into the corridor. Robert is gone.

I walk back into the apartment and into the bathroom.

Nathan is in the shower, the water falling hard over his head. His face is in his hands.

His devastation so real that I can feel it.

"Nathan," I whisper.

He remains silent.

"Are you okay?" I ask softly.

"Leave me alone," he murmurs.

I screw up my face in tears. That's not what I needed to hear. I turn and walk out into the living room and fall to the couch in tears. Can this week get any worse?

Nathan stays in the shower for over an hour, and with every minute that he's in there, a little more truth sinks in.

I'm tied to Eliza now.

I'm pregnant by a man who is still in love with his ex.

I thought he loved me.

How could I be so stupid as to fall pregnant?

Oh, fuck.

What happens now?

I have a child with him, carry on with our farce of a relationship, all while knowing that, deep down, his heart is with Robert?

Pain slices through my chest. This isn't how I thought it would go. Oh, *this hurts.*

Nathan finally appears. He's in his boxer shorts, once more, and his mask is firmly back into place.

"I'm sorry," he whispers.

I stare at the floor, unable to drag my eyes to his.

"Why are you crying?" he whispers as he sits down next to me and takes me into his arms.

"Do you want to be with him?" I ask.

"No." His eyes are sad—so much pain behind them. "I love you. I want to be with you."

My eyes search his. "Do you still love Robert?"

He stares at me, but doesn't answer, unable to push the lie past his lips.

My eyes well with tears, the lump in my throat is so big, it hurts.

"I want to be with you, Eliza."

"That's not what I asked, Nathan."

"I have a history with Robert but my future is with you. I'm sorry he came here. I'm sorry you had to hear that."

He holds me in his arms, but I don't feel loved.

I feel in the way.

I feel like his heart is breaking and he wants to go to Robert.

I feel betrayed.

"I'm going to..." I pause as I try to think of an excuse to get away from him...to get away from his hurt, "take a shower."

"Okay." He lets me go.

I walk into the bathroom, lock the door, and slide down the back of it to sit on the floor.

And all alone, I sob in silence.

I lie in bed in the darkness. I'm on my side, facing the wall.

Nathan is beside me with his back to me.

He's silent. I am silent.

There's an elephant in the room, in between us in bed.

Robert.

The air is heavy with regret, filled with lost hopes and dreams.

And an unplanned pregnancy.

"What's wrong?" Nathan whispers.

Every time he speaks to me I get a lump in my throat and it's hard to answer.

How do you verbalize so much hurt?

"Nothing," I murmur into the darkness.

He hesitates, as if wanting to say something, but he doesn't.

Eventually he says, "Goodnight."

I close my eyes as a tear rolls down onto my pillow. "Goodnight."

———

I wake alone.

Nathan has gone to work.

He didn't wake me to say goodbye. I didn't even hear him getting ready.

After crying silently in bed all night, I must have drifted into an exhausted sleep in the early hours.

I don't feel emotionally strong enough to go to work today, but what do I do if I stay home? I'll be a psychotic by the time he walks in the door this evening. He's in surgery today so I know he will be late.

I feel so alone, I need to talk to someone but my best friend and confidant is the one that's hurting me. And the worst thing about it is, he can't even help it.

I know he would never hurt me by choice.

I don't want to talk to the girls. I still feel angry with them, and I know this isn't their fault, but hearing the words *I told you so* right now will just tip me over the edge.

I have to make myself go to work. The alternative will be having a complete meltdown, and I can't let that happen.

I drag myself up and into the shower.

I'll stop at the pharmacy on the way and get a pregnancy test.

May as well get this over with.

I need to know.

————

I hit send on the final operating schedule for tomorrow.

"Hey." Henry puts his head around the door. "How's my girl today?"

I smile at Henry's casual demeanour. He calls all of us girls in the office 'his girl'.

He's not flirty or stepping over the line. He's just Henry being Henry. Weird to think back to my first impression of him now when he's actually quite endearing.

"Do you want to go out for lunch?" he asks. "I'm starved."

I look at him. "You know what? I do." I go back to typing. "Give me two minutes to finish this email."

"Okay." He disappears down the corridor, and I smile sadly.

I've all but made up my mind. I want to go back to nursing. This isn't my jam. I'm just not sure how to tell him.

I finish off my emails and grab my handbag when I notice the brown paper bag tucked safely inside.

The pregnancy test. I was going to do it at lunch.

Oh, well, I'll do it when I get home, I guess. I set off to find Henry, and twenty minutes later, we are in a sushi train across town.

"You know, I always eat way too much at these places." He says casually as he takes a plate from the train. "Because I'm eating small plates, I have this mental block where I think I can keep eating."

I smile as I grab a plate. "Me, too."

He pops some sushi into his mouth with his chopsticks.

"Well, this may very well be my main meal for the day." He shrugs casually. "So, there's that."

"Why? Didn't you end up getting back with your girlfriend?"

"No." He rolls his eyes. "I really fucked things up there."

"What happened?"

"God." He sighs, "Where do I start? When I got back from the conference, she wanted to talk." He shovels some more sushi into his mouth.

I frown as I listen. "And?"

"So...." he shakes his head as if disgusted with himself. "Of course, we end up in bed and now I don't want anything..." He rolls his eyes and makes the blah, blah, blah sign with his hand.

"You used your ex-girlfriend for a booty-call?"

He pinches the bridge of his nose. "Sounds bad when you say it like that."

"Did you?"

"It wasn't my fault. She looked hot, and my dick accidentally fell out of my pants."

"I hate it when that happens." I fake a smile. For fuck's sake, are all men completely clueless?

"Right?" He scoffs. "Me, too." He continues eating. "Anyway, now I'm the worst in the world and she's messaging me ten times a day to tell me so."

I smile sadly. It feels good that everyone has shit to deal with.

"How's your guard dog going?" he asks as he chews.

"Not so great, but that's another story."

"Why?"

"I don't know." I sigh. "We were best friends for a long time before we went out."

"How long?"

"Ten years."

His eyebrows rise in surprise. "Wow."

"And we only recently connected, and then we moved in together like two weeks later."

He winces. "Well, that was fucking dumb."

"But we practically lived together, anyway, so..."

"Yeah, but it's completely different when you're sleeping together. You should have waited at least six months before you moved in together. You're too familiar. No wonder you're fighting all the time. There's all this added pressure. You would never move in with a new boyfriend after two weeks. This is no different."

"That's exactly what it is," I reply. "It's like we're in a pressure cooker, you know? We are fighting over things I would never have imagined."

"If things don't get better, you should move into your own place for a while. Then, date again. Get some space from each other. Remember why you're in love."

I chew as I listen. "You think?"

"I know. Everyone has issues when they first move in with a partner. There's no such thing as a smooth transition, but add in the long-term friendship to the mix and it would be a nightmare. You already know each other so well, there would be no boundaries."

That makes so much sense. "So true."

And that's not the half of it, I think to myself. Throw in sexuality questions, an ex, and an unplanned pregnancy... fuck, it's no wonder we're fighting all the time. "I guess." I smile.

"Can I ask you something?" He says as he wipes his mouth with his napkin.

"Yeah."

"If you had met me in a different circumstance and you weren't with the guard dog..."

I smirk, already knowing what he's going to say.

"Would you have gone out with me?"

I dig through my food with my chopsticks. "Yeah." I smile. "I would have. You're cute in a weird kind of way."

His eyes hold mine. "Well, fuck." He raises his glass and takes a sip. "Here's to the worst timing ever."

I giggle. I really do like Henry, and I know I need to be honest. "I have a confession."

"You're going to leave him for me?" he teases with a wink.

I laugh. "No... but I am maybe leaving work."

His face falls. "Oh no, why?"

"I'm just not loving it. I'm sorry."

"Is it something I can fix?"

"I'm missing nursing, the buzz of the hospital, and I haven't decided anything yet, but I just wanted you to know in case I do decide."

He smiles sadly. "Well, that blows but I completely understand. Thanks for being honest."

We eat in silence for a while.

"What are you going to do about the boyfriend?"

"I don't know." I sigh. "Hopefully, work it out." I sip my drink. "Your idea about space from each other makes a lot of sense."

"You never know. It may very well work."

I smile, grateful for the chat. "Thanks, Henry." I wish I could blurt out all my issues, but I can't.

These are mine and Nathan's problems, and only we can fix them.

And we will...

I hope.

I sit at the dining table and listen to the clock ticking on the wall. I haven't had the guts to do the pregnancy test alone. Nathan will be home soon. I texted him an hour and a half ago, and he said he had just finished surgery and would be home about now.

I never thought I'd see the day where waiting for Nathan made me nervous. But he's acting different. He isn't texting me. He isn't looking after me. He isn't being my Nathan.

I frown at the notion. Was he ever my Nathan, or was he just on loan?

We need to talk. God, we need to talk, and I know he's still angry about what Jolie said to him the other night, but he's locked me out.

He's cold and detached.

He told me that he doesn't want Robert, that he loves me and that he wants a future with me.... but actions speak louder than words.

I keep hearing his voice as it cracked last night. He was so hurt by Robert's admission of love.

And if he didn't feel the same, it wouldn't have affected him the way it did.

I have this sinking feeling, and as much as I hate to admit it but I don't know if he would still be here if the pregnancy wasn't hanging over us. I close my eyes, it's too painful to comprehend.

I'm dreading being pregnant... but I'm dreading not being pregnant more.

If I'm pregnant, he's trapped. If I'm not,.... he's free to go... *to him.*

My eyes well with tears at the thought.

I feel sick to my stomach and have thrown up twice.

I get a vision of him and Robert living happily ever after, and me, alone and brokenhearted.

Ten years. Ten years of love and friendship. It's a lot to lose.

I angrily wipe my tears away. Stop being so negative. It's going to be fine.

He loves me—I know he loves me—but, deep down, I know he loves Robert, too. I put my head into my hands in sadness.

It isn't supposed to be like this. I'm thirty-one years old and I feel like an insecure teenager, scared that my douche of a boyfriend wants somebody else.

But then the sad reality sets in. My boyfriend isn't a douchebag. He's a beautiful man who I am deeply in love with.

Is his heart aching for someone else?

My chest constricts, how would I recover from this...if.....

The key turns in the door, and my heart somersaults in my chest. Nathan comes into view and gives me a lopsided smile. "Hi."

"Hi." I stand and go to him. He kisses me on the cheek before he brushes past me.

My heart drops at his cold demeanour.

He rattles through his briefcase and produces a brown paper bag. He pulls out a pregnancy test and holds it out for me.

"Can you take this, please?"

I stare at his haunted face as more hope about us is lost. I just want to howl to the moon. "Sure." I take it from him and walk into the bathroom.

My heartbeat echoes in my ears.

I lock the bathroom door and open the box. I wipe my eyes with my sleeve so I can try and read the blurred instructions.

How can he be so cold?

I pee on the stick, and before I look at the result, I walk back out into the living room and I pass it to him.

We stare at each other for a moment, and I screw up my face in tears.

"Don't cry," he whispers.

"How can I not?" I sob. "Look at how you're treating me."

"I'm just... we're not ready for children, Eliza."

"You know what?" I cry. "Just fucking go, Nathan. You want to, so don't let me and a baby hold you back."

I can't take this. I need to get away from him. I grab my bag and storm toward the door but Nathan jumps up and grabs me from behind.

"Don't go," He says into my hair as he holds me tight.

"What do you want, Nathan?" I whisper. "Is it me or him?"

"It's you. You know it's you."

"Then why are you acting like this?"

"I don't know," he whispers as he holds me tightly.

He holds the test up in front of us, and we both read it at the same time.

One line.

One line...

"It's negative," he whispers. "But still too early to tell." He holds me tighter.

I struggle to break free from his grip. "Let me go, Nathan." I cry.

"I can't."

"You're no good to me if you're confused," I whisper angrily.

"Don't, baby," he murmurs into my hair.

"Let me fucking go." I burst out of his arms.

"Don't you dare walk out that fucking door."

"Or what?" I cry.

"I mean it," he warns. His chest rises and falls, as if he's struggling for control.

We glare at each other. His face is full of fury, and my heart is splintered into a million pieces. "Why are you being like this?" I whisper.

He runs his hands through his hair in frustration. "I'm just fucking stressed out, okay?"

"About what?"

"You have to ask?" he cries, as if outraged.

I stare at him, my mind a clusterfuck of confusion. What the hell is going on here?

What's happening between us?

This is pointless. I'm not going to get anywhere with him tonight. I don't want to fight anymore, and I don't know what to say to make this better.

What is there to say?

"I'm going to bed." I sigh. I walk up the hall and into the bedroom, and I shut the door behind me.

It's 2:00 a.m, and I lie in the darkness and listen to Nathan's regulated breathing.

He kissed me on the cheek to say goodnight before he went to sleep.

It was a token kiss.

It was cold and emotionless. He's completely shut down on me.

I don't know what to say or do to make it better.

I want to beg him to talk to me, but then the friend in me steps in, and I want to give him the freedom and space to make a decision for himself.

I roll onto my side and stare into the darkness. Where is my period?

Why isn't it here?

Five days late. I know that sometimes early tests give a false negative result.

Nathan knows it, too.

I know what's wrong with Nathan…

He feels trapped.

23

Eliza

I WAIT in the café for Jolie and Brooke. I'm a bundle of nerves, and to be honest, these are the last two people I want to discuss this with because I already know their thoughts.

April thinks that I need to be open with Nathan and lay it all out on the table, but I feel like I need some advice from people who know us both really well.

The girls come into view, laughing and chatting as they walk through to me before they fall into their seats.

"Hi." They both smile.

Jolie leans over and kisses my cheek. "I cannot apologize for the other night enough, Lize."

I roll my eyes. "Well, thanks to you, Nathan has hardly spoken to me all week."

"What?" They both frown. "Oh no."

"We had a huge fight, and he's so hurt."

Jolie puts her head into her hands. "God, I feel terrible."

"And so you should," Brooke snaps. "I can't believe you."

"Anyway, it gets worse." I sigh. "Much worse."

They frown as they listen intently. "Nathan's ex, Robert, came back, and right in front of me, he professed that he still loves Nathan and wants him back."

Their faces fall.

"What did Nathan say?"

"He kicked him out."

"Thank God," Brooke says as she puts her hand on her chest in relief.

"But he hasn't spoken to me since."

"What?"

"He hasn't spoken to me because I think that, deep down, he wants to go back but he doesn't want to hurt me."

"You think he's confused?" Brooke asks.

"I think so... and now..." I tip my head back to the sky in despair. "I think I'm pregnant."

"Oh, fuck!" Jolie snaps.

Brooke's eyes widen in horror.

"Does Nathan know you're pregnant?" Jolie gasps.

"Yes. Well, no, because the test was negative."

"You did a test?"

"Yes. But apparently they can take a few days if the hormone levels are low."

"How late are you?"

"Five days."

"You're five days late on the pill?" Jolie gasps.

"Yes."

"Oh, fuck, you're gone. Totally knocked up." Jolie rolls her eyes.

I put my head into my hands in despair. "What do I do?"

The girls sit in silence, too shocked to reply.

"So, let me get this straight," Jolie says as she recaps the situation. "His ex came back and Nathan hasn't spoken to you since."

"Before that, actually. He hasn't really spoken to me since you said those things at the club."

Brooke punches Jolie hard in the arm. "You fucking started this shit, you bitch."

"I know." Jolie winces.

"Robert professed his love, and you think Nathan still has feelings for him."

I nod.

"But you think he's going to stay with you because you're possibly pregnant."

My eyes well with tears, and I nod sadly. "Yep, that about sums it up."

"Oh God." Brooke drags her hand down her face. "This is a fucking nightmare."

"You can't have this baby," Jolie says. "You are setting yourself up for a lifetime of insecurity."

"If I'm pregnant, I'm having it, Jolie," I bark. "And I was already insecure before any of this happened."

We sit in silence for a while as we all try to find a solution. The enormity of the situation has really sunk in, now that I've said it out loud.

"You just need to talk to him, Lize." Jolie sighs. "Only he can give you the answers."

"I know."

"He might be just stressed out." Brooke smiles hopefully.

"The thing is, what do I do? If I know that he still loves Robert, but is staying with me out of responsibility, what do I do?"

"Could you build a future with a man, knowing that you aren't his true love?" Jolie asks.

Tears fill my eyes again and I drop my head in sadness. "No. No, I couldn't."

———

I sit on the couch, curled up in a ball as I watch the minutes tick over on the clock.

It's 10:00 p.m. and Nathan isn't home from work yet. I have no tears left to cry. An emptiness has crept in and is sitting heavy in my chest. I'm dealing with a completely different man now— one that I don't know. My Nathan would never treat me like this.

Is he with him?

Nathan was gone when I woke up. I haven't heard from him all day, and my period still isn't here.

This is new territory—a dark place where I don't want to be anymore.

The end of us is near.

It's only a matter of time, I know it is.

I can feel our relationship disintegrating before my eyes, and I have no idea how to stop it, or if it's even possible. It's like we are on a collision course toward heartbreak.

Both of us are in the passenger seat, unsure who is driving.

Things are grim. They couldn't get any worse.

I scroll through Facebook and Instagram, desperately searching for a distraction but my mind is heavy.

In normal circumstances, Nathan and I would have talked through this. We'd have gone through every possible scenario by now. We would have come to a conclusion and discussed our options.

But this time, it's different.

Robert's pained words come back to me. *You've been begging me to come back to you for years. I know you still love me, Nathan. It's not too late for us.*

Problems like these don't just disappear. They come back to haunt you, year after year.

If Nathan is still in love with Robert, I will always know where his heart truly lies, and that he stayed because he didn't want to hurt me.

I know Nathan, and I know that he will never leave me. That isn't who he is.

He would sacrifice his heart for mine.

And I hate that. I hate knowing that if we are going to end, I have to do it.

He will never walk away. He would never leave me alone.

The clock ticks over to 10:30 p.m., and I drag myself off the couch and down the hall.

He knows this would be tearing me apart, and still, he stays silent.

He stays away.

I'm going to lose him.

Maybe I have already.

Nathan

I sit in the chair in the corner of my patient's hospital room, and I go through his chart again, trying to figure out what the fuck to do here.

I nearly lost him today. After surviving a twelve-hour surgery yesterday, he's fighting for survival. Justin, a twenty-one-year-old with his whole life in front of him, is unresponsive, and not coming out of it like we had hoped.

No heart transplant is easy, but it's as if his body is too tired to fight. I've sent his parents back to their hotel to shower and rest. I promised them I would stay with him until their return.

"Here you are, Doctor." The nurse hands me a cup of coffee. "Can I get you a blanket?"

"No, thanks, Emma, I'm good," I reply as I take it from her.

Her eyes linger on me. "You must be exhausted—you've been here all day."

I give a sad smile as my eyes watch Justin hooked up to all the machines, the sound of his weak heartrate echoing through the room.

Don't die.

"I'm fine." I sigh. I get a vision of him in my office last week and how excited he was to be finally getting the procedure. I had no inclination that his young body wasn't strong enough to get through it.

Don't die.

I should call Eliza. Why?

She just hurts me. The words roll though my head on repeat. How do I turn them off?

Are you in love with Eliza, or are you just looking for an incubator to make your babies?

One sentence.

One sentence to bring my entire self-worth to a screaming halt.

Just one sentence is all it took to see myself how her and the rest of the world see me. As they will always see me.

My past will never be in my past. It will never be done.

I will always be the man with an agenda—a man who wants her for her uterus.

Eliza knows me better than anyone. At least, I thought she did.

She broke something inside of me and I'm trying to get it back. I really am.

I'm calling out to my heart to drop it, but it just can't.

How do you ignore the most hurtful thing you've ever heard?

How do you pretend to yourself that it doesn't matter that she thinks I would use her to have a child? How do you force yourself to drop something that means everything to you?

What if she's pregnant?

I put my head into my hands as my elbows rest on my knees as Jolie's words come back to me. I let the poison roll over me and sink into my soul again.

What are you planning... to give her five years and three kids, and then go back to your ex, while your best friend raises your kids alone?

How could she think I want Robert when she is my entire world?

Doesn't she know me at all?

How could she go to a bar and say these things when I begged her for an answer all night? How could she? I get a lump in my throat just thinking about it. How could she even think such a thing?

The piercing sound of a flat line echoes throughout the room, and I jump to my feet and hit the call button.

"Justin," I cry. "Justin, no!" I tear his blankets down to get access to his chest as nurses come running from all directions.

"Stay with me, Justin," I whisper. "You stay with me."

.   .   .

Nathan's alarm goes off at 5:00 a.m., and I watch him stir. I've been watching him since he got home and fell into an exhausted sleep. He didn't get home until two hours ago.

His eyes find me in the darkness, and I smile softly. "Hi."

"Hi."

I reach over and cup his face in my hand. "Where were you last night?"

His eyes drop to the blankets. "I lost a patient."

My face falls. "I'm sorry." I know how hard this hits him.

"Me, too," he whispers sadly.

He tries to sit up, and I reach for him. "Nathe."

He turns back to me.

"Can you just...?" I shrug softly. "Hold me for a minute."

His face softens, and he takes me into his arms. We cling to each other. It's as if the tighter we hold on, the more we can chase the demons away.

"I love you," I whisper. "So much. You know that, don't you?"

"I love you, too," he murmurs into my hair.

I want to tell him that we can work this out—we need to try harder—but I don't want to force him into anything if his heart is aching for another.

I need to let him go.

I pull back to look into his big, blue eyes, and they seem so sad. I brush the hair back from his forehead. "Are you okay?" I whisper.

"I will be." He leans in and kisses me softly.

When will he be okay? *When he leaves?*

We kiss again and again, and it's filled with regret and sadness.

It's an emotional overload for both of us.

He rolls over on top of me and falls between my legs as we

kiss. Our bodies desperately need the comfort of each other. Needing the connection that's been missing. He slowly slides the side of his shaft through my lips... but I'm dry.

So, dry. A first.

"You'll need something."

He reaches over and grabs some lube from the top drawer. He massages it in, and then he slowly rises above me and slides in deep.

Our breaths catch, and we stare at each other.

His body is deep inside mine.

I stare up at him as emotion overwhelms me.

"I love you," I whisper.

"I love you, too," he murmurs back, but there's an emotion behind his words.

Something that I can't put my finger on.

Regret? Anger? Is it sadness?

Is this goodbye?

He rises above me on straightened arms, and he spreads his knees on the mattress as he slowly begins to ride me. He closes his eyes, as if to block me out, his body unable to be slow and tender. He needs the release, not the intimacy.

I bring my legs up. *Is he thinking about him?*

Does he feel guilty for fucking me?

My eyes fill with tears, and when he sees them, something changes in his demeanour.

A feeling runs between us. Animosity.

He slams in hard, and I wince.

He's angry, and I scrunch up my face as he gives it to me hard.

He's angry that I'm making him do this... that he has to go through with the betrayal.

I scrunch my eyes shut as he fucks me. There's no emotion. There's no love.

He's shut down—blocked me out. He's thinking about someone else.

This is a seminal transfusion.

He slams me one, two, three times, and he holds himself deep.

"Come." He winces, as if in pain.

I clench down hard, but there's no chance of coming. This is breaking my fucking heart.

How could I possibly be aroused?

He hisses and holds himself deep. I feel the telling jerk of his cock from his orgasm.

He moves slowly as he completely empties himself, and I stare up at him through my tears.

It's like I don't even know him anymore.

He rolls off me and puts the back of his forearm over his face as he lies on his back.

That felt wrong to him too. He's rattled.

What just happened?

How could a love that was so beautiful become so cold?

So hurtful.

"I've got to go to work." He gets out of bed in a rush.

I close my eyes, unable to even look at him. This cut gets deeper every day.

I don't know how to save us.

———

I walk out into the courtyard at work. It's now 10:50 a.m., and I know Nathan should be in between appointments. I dial his number.

"Hello," he answers.

"Hi." I can't even hear his voice without tearing up. I'm an emotional fucking wreck here. "I just, um..." My voice trails off.

"Are you okay?"

"Yeah." I don't even want to tell him, but I know I have to. "My period arrived."

He doesn't say anything, and I frown as I wait for his answer.

"Did you hear me?" I whisper.

Silence.

"Nathan?"

"Okay, thanks for letting me know," he says, devoid of emotion.

I frown, what does that mean? Is he happy, sad?

"I've got to go," he says.

"Okay."

He hangs on the line, and I close my eyes. I can't take this. I can't stand losing my best friend. It's like watching a car crash in slow motion. Nobody should have to bear this pain.

"I finish early today. I'll pick you up from work," he says.

I smile, hopeful that this is an olive branch. "Yes, alright."

I go back to work, and my brain starts to tick over and over the last few days.

Robert. His coldness.

No baby.

If I just had my old apartment, I could give us both some breathing space—give Nathan some time to think. Give myself some time to try and regain some confidence. I don't know who I am anymore, but I've never felt so insecure and weak. This isn't who I am. This is unlike anything I've ever faced—unlike anything most women will ever face.

I don't know how to compete with his past.

I can't.

A woman can't compete against a man. Not if it's a man he truly wants.

No amount of love can change that, and there is so much love between us.

I exhale heavily, knowing we moved in too quick.

But then, neither of us could ever have imagined that this would happen.

That Robert would come back and open old wounds. Damn that fucking asshole for ruining everything.

At least now with no pregnancy, I have options, and so does he. Nathan isn't tied to me.

His words, not mine. I was never tied to Nathan. I was there by choice.

I begin to wrack my brain for a solution—one where we can try and salvage the damage that has been done this week. I'm not even sure where the damage has come from, because Nathan is saying that he wants me... but he's not acting like it.

He's acting like a man who is confused. A man who needs time to work out what he wants in life. And I know that Nathan, and I said in the beginning that our friendship is the most important thing, but the goalposts have been moved again, and we both know that it's all or nothing now.

We couldn't be friends; not with feeling the way that we do about each other.

And I would rather die than have to be witness to his life with Robert.

———

I'm waiting on the sidewalk when Nathan's Tesla pulls into the curb.

"Hi." I smile as I get into the car.

"Hello."

We pull out into the traffic, and it's there again.

This awkwardness between us. I have this overwhelming feeling that like I'm forcing him to stay against his will. I was hopeful, now that the pregnancy thing was over, that things would return to normal.... Guess not.

I turn the radio on, and we drive for a while, not speaking. A song by Evanescence comes on. *My Immortal*. I've never really listened to the words before, but it fits our situation perfectly.

We both stare out of the windscreen as the sad words sing out. It's like it's talking directly to my soul.

> ***And if you have to leave,***
> ***I wish that you would just leave.***

That's exactly what I feel is happening to us.

I watch Nathan as he drives, void of emotion, a shell of the man that I love, and I know what I need to do.

I'm not going to let us hate each other.

I'm going to give him the space that he needs. Soon, I will know if he loves me or not.

Either way, I need answers.

———

It's 8:00 p.m., and we're sitting on the couch in silence. We had take-out, and I feel sick to my stomach.

I frown as I try to work out how to broach the subject. "So, um... you know how I told you I wasn't liking my new job?"

His eyes come to me. "Yes."

"I've thought of a solution that might... help us both."

"What's that?"

"I applied for a job at the private hospital and I got the email today that said I was successful."

He nods as he listens. "Okay."

My eyes search his. "The job's in New York."

"What?" He sits up abruptly. "What do you mean, it's in New York?"

"It's only four days a week. And it would give us some time, you know."

"Time for what?" he snaps as he stands and marches into the kitchen.

I run after him like a puppy. "You can sort out your baggage with Robert, and then we can start afresh. We moved in together too quickly, Nathan."

"What?" he explodes. "I don't have any baggage with Robert."

"Yes, you do, Nathan. You've been distant ever since he came here."

His eyes hold mine.

"And I know you would never leave me... so."

His face falls as if having an epiphany. "So, you're going to step aside *for him*?"

My eyes fill with tears. "I can't compete with Robert. What do you want me to do?"

"I want you to fight for us, goddamn it!" he cries. "Why can't you compete with Robert? Tell me why?" He demands.

"If you want a man..." My voice breaks. "I can't compete."

His face falls, and he steps back from me as if I've just delivered a physical blow. "And there it is again," he whispers.

"What do you mean?"

"You are the last person." He sneers in a whisper. "That I ever thought would judge me based on who I've loved in the past. That would gauge my capability to love based on what you think it should be." His face falls. "I thought you knew me."

"That's not what I mean."

"You're never going to drop this." He shakes his head as if totally convinced.

"Nathan."

"There's always going to be this seed of doubt in your mind. I'll never just be the person who loves you. I'll always be a guy who gave up men for you." His eyes fill with tears. "Love is love... *until it isn't.*"

My eyes search his. "That's not what I mean."

"That's what you said," he whispers.

"I can go to New York and... and give us both some time... maybe," I stammer.

"I don't need time!" he cries. "I need you!"

"I know you don't see it at the moment but we need this time apart. I'll be home every week, and we can make it work. It's just a few months and then I'll be back. We got together so quickly. It was a whirlwind, and I need to know that I've given you the space to contemplate your future."

"No."

"Nathan."

"I said *no*. You go to New York and that is it. We are fucking done."

"Stop it!" I yell. "Listen to my reasoning."

"I'm done listening to you, Eliza." He picks up his keys.

"Where are you going?" I cry in a panic.

"Out."

"When will you be home?"

"After you go to New York."

"Nathan." I sigh.

"I'm done." His eyes hold mine.

"Don't say that."

His eyes meet mine. "I loved you with all of my heart." He turns toward the door. "Goodbye, Eliza."

My face falls along with my tears. Nathan walks out the front door and doesn't look back.

It clicks shut with a final bang.

24

***

Eliza

I SIT and stare at the paper in front of me with the pen in my hand.

What can I possibly write to make sense of this? I just want him to understand, although I'm not even sure myself.

I'm just going to lay it all out on the table. He can decipher it as he wishes.

> *Nathan.*
>
> *Timing hasn't been kind to us, my darling.*
>
> *We met ten years ago by, what I thought at the time, was an accident.*
>
> *It was anything but an accident. I believe it was fate.*
>
> *I was meant to meet you, to be by your side as a friend for ten years. We were meant to fall in love, and in a perfect world we would have ruled that world together.*

But I have doubts, and not about my feelings for you, because they are set in concrete. I will love you for all of eternity.

My fears are for you.

You see, Nathan, I know how much you care about me, and I know that any man who sleeps beside a woman for a long period of time will develop feelings for her. You were blindsided by your attraction to me, and in the end, you couldn't fight it. We moved quickly and fell in love, and the days I spent in your arms are the happiest times of my life.

But things fell apart, and I'm broken-hearted, battling to get through the days. So, I'm going to explain things from my perspective. I'm not saying I'm right and you're wrong or vice versa. I'm just trying to find a solution to this mess.

And being honest with each other seems like the only thing we haven't yet done.

When you went to Stephanie when you had feelings for me, it broke something between us.

The trust I had in my best friend was lost.

I tried to get it back, but it never recovered. I was insecure about her, and then in Majorca, you told me that the biggest regret in your life was leaving Robert. It made me wonder if you'd ever gotten over him.

A feeling that stayed with me throughout our time together.

We came back to San Fran and moved in together immediately, I never resolved my Stephanie and Robert fears. This was entirely my fault, not yours. I blame myself for not talking to you and trying to resolve this earlier. I didn't want to be the insecure girlfriend. I thought you deserved better.

Then I found out that you spoke to Robert every day, and obviously still cared for him. That, coupled with the fact you were friends with Stephanie all along and had lied to me about it, left me feeling so betrayed and only fueled my fears even more so.

While being desperately in love with you, my insecurities were spiralling of control.

Then, I met Zavier at the conference.

He was lovely, and we clicked straight away. I knew from the first moment that I talked to him that you and him were lovers. I wasn't upset about it. I can see why. He's beautiful.

We met, we spoke, and he told me about the two of you, and I understood. He said you were a wonderful person and he wished us the best. But at the end of the conversation,when I told him about our friendship for ten years, he said that it made a lot of sense.

All week at the conference, I wondered what he meant by it, and on the last day before I flew home to you, I asked him to elaborate as to what he meant.

He said that perhaps he thought you wanted children and your body has started to crave mine to fulfill its destiny. He also said that you had told him that you were still in love with Robert.

I was beyond devastated.

Crushed that perhaps we had fallen in love under false pretences, and that, no matter how much we loved each other, your love for Robert was never going to go away.

I was selfish, too proud to tell you my fears, and I talked to my friends instead of you. I thought I could handle my insecurities myself. I didn't want you to see how badly I was struggling with us.

Because us was so, so beautiful, and you deserved better.

Maybe when you love someone as much as I love you, fear is always present. An evil, waiting in the wings to steal happiness.

I drop my head as a tear rolls down my cheek. God, this really is it for us. I blink to try and focus, and I begin to write again.

Then Robert came to you and professed his love, and seeing your reaction to him, I know it hurt. It's obvious that you still love him.

You wouldn't talk to me. You withdrew. Even through a pregnancy scare, we were distant. I died a little every day without you. At a time when I needed you the most, I was completely alone, faced with the possibility of having a child with a man who loved another.

I understand why—you didn't want to hurt me by leaving. That's not who you are.

Nathan, my darling, I'm giving you the time you deserve.

I love you so much—I love you more than life itself—and I could never keep you held to me, knowing that your heart is aching for someone else.

As your best friend, I need to sacrifice my happiness for yours.

Hopefully, we will find a way back to each other and you will come to me in New York.

I will wait for you. I will love you from across the country and pray that you return to me.

But I understand if you can't, and I wish you all the happiness you deserve.

Please remember how much you are loved, and make the decision that is right for you.

I'll be okay.

Always,
   Eliza
   xoxo

———

"Last call for flight 756 to New York."

I sit in the boarding lounge of the airport. I've been here for five hours. I couldn't sit and wait in that apartment a moment longer.

Nathan hasn't been home for three days. I guess, if I was questioning whether I was doing the right thing, Nathan has answered me, loud and clear.

He wanted me to stay and fight for us, but there are two people in a fight and I can't do this alone.

I wouldn't want to.

He needs to show up, too. He needs to see where I am coming from, and that shutting down on me isn't the answer.

Now, on reflection, I get his point. I see what he is upset about. But he's wrong thinking that this is all in my head. I was there. I saw it with my own eyes how upset he was when Robert came to him, and I know he doesn't understand any of this now, but hopefully, in time, he will.

Our love was too fast, too passionate, and too blinding with its beauty.

I smile sadly. Boy, *was it beautiful*. Nathan and I together, when things were going good, was a fairy tale.

It doesn't get any better than what we had, and if he can throw it away so easily without even showing up for the fight then I guess I did us all a favor by leaving.

"Last call for flight 756 to New York," sounds over the intercom once more and I exhale heavily.

It doesn't make it hurt less.

I want the happy ending. I want the fairy tale where he runs through the airport to stop me from leaving. I glance up in the hope of seeing him. I long to see him frantically running to stop me from ruining everything.

But he's not here.

He hasn't been here since Robert came. Maybe even before that.

He checked out on me when I needed him to stand up and tell me what I had done wrong.

And he said that I had a prejudice. But maybe the complex is his, not mine.

I'm not saying I'm in the right, but any woman who found out that their partner had spoken to his ex every day for ten years, and that he had always begged them to come back to him, would be rattled. Add to that, the ex came back professing his love, and the boyfriend has hardly spoken two words to you since. It's not rocket science.

I *am* doing the right thing.

We need space. We need time.

I need him.

My eyes fill with tears.

"Last call for flight 756 to New York," repeats over the intercom.

I stand, and with one last longing look over San Francisco airport, I drag myself on the plane. It feels like my world is ending, and maybe it is.

Maybe this is the stupidest fucking thing I've ever done.

He didn't come.

———

The text comes through from Jolie, and I scroll through the selections she's sent to me:

Furnished apartments.
One bedroom, furnished, great location.
Week to week, no lease.
And btw, Santiago is a prick.
Had a gangbang last night with four girls.
He's gone.

I smirk, thank God, that's over. I mark it down to go and look at it. I don't want to be locked into anything long term.

I'm in a café, and I've been in New York for three days. I'm staying at a hotel. I don't start work until next week but I just had to get out of San Fran... *away from him.*

The dust has settled, and the tears have stopped. I'm getting angry now.

How could he do this to me?

I thought after he read the letter that things would work out, or I would at least hear from him for closure. I was sure the letter explained everything: my thoughts and hopes and dreams for us. My undying love for him and how much I cherished what we had.

I thought he would have called, if not as a lover, but as the best friend he's always been. Nathan has always been my biggest supporter, the friend who loved me through anything.

Except his own pride, apparently.

Is he okay? What if something has happened to him?

Stop it. Stop worrying about him.

I called Alex the day I left. I explained that we had broken up and asked him to watch over Nathan for me. He promised me he would, but is he?

Is Alex looking after him? My stomach twists. I know that nobody looks after Nathan as well as I do.

He needs me.

But then I remember that maybe he doesn't, maybe this is his ticket out. And just maybe, he's happy that I left. I let my mind go to the dark place it likes to visit at 3 a.m. and I wonder if he's called Robert. He called him as a friend for all these years, yet he can't even check in on me now.

I'm alone in a city where he knows that I know nobody.

It hurts to realize that he doesn't care, and even if he does, he's too proud to call me anyway.

I fear the worst for us, I thought he would've called me by now and we would talk and work this out without being blinded by each other. I thought that once sex was taken off the table, he would be forced to open up to me. I honestly believed that he would need to look at things through my eyes.

Guess I was wrong.

The more time that passes, the sadder I get.

I thought the day I left San Fran was the worst day and that it couldn't possibly get any worse. I was wrong. Losing a little more faith in someone every day is insidious.

The toxic poison of lost dreams and hopes is seeping into my bones.

The taste of disappointment runs through my veins.

I'm questioning everything: who I am, who he is, if he ever loved me. Perhaps I imagined the whole thing because no one could ever be this cold to someone they truly cared about. Ten years together, and now it's like we never existed.

I didn't just lose my love. That would be bearable. That would be recoverable. I lost my best friend. I lost a part of myself. My identity as a person has somehow been altered. I need to get it back because I don't want to live in a world where my best friend doesn't care.

A man comes into the café carrying a bunch of roses, and he orders a coffee. He's in a suit and looks professional.

I watch him with a sad smile. Are those for his wife? Is it their anniversary? I watch him talking and laughing with the cashier. He seems so happy.

I blink to stop the tears. I would give anything to feel happy again.

I'm sick of fucking crying.

I've been doing it for nine days now since this all began.

This isn't who I am.

Nathan

I close my eyes as I put the key into the door.

I hate coming home.

Coming home to an empty house is the worst kind of torture. It reminds me of what I don't have. It hits me straight in the face as I walk in the door to a cold and lonely apartment without the aroma of a home-cooked meal or Eliza's infectious smile.

The house is deathly silent.

I throw my keys on the sideboard and go straight to the bar to pour myself a scotch—my only friend and constant companion. I've found if I drink enough, I can sleep.

With a shaky hand, I sip my scotch as I walk out into the kitchen with the bottle, Eliza's unopened letter sits on the bench where she left it. It's taunting me, begging to be read.

It's this little game I play with myself every night. I call it the wheel of torture.

I sit at the counter, drink in hand, as I stare at the letter. It taunts me with words unsaid.

But I can't read it. I will never read it.

Because she didn't love me enough to stay and fight, and I loved her too much to let her go.

But she went anyway.

So, it doesn't matter.

I tip my head back and drain my drink before I pour another immediately. I feel the heat of the spirit rolling down my throat.

I'm done with love. I never want to feel this bad again.

I get my laptop and I open it up to click on the history.

Find My Phone.

I switch it on and type in Eliza's phone number. I watch the little red dot light up the screen. It blinks, the beat strong and consistent.

She's in her hotel.

My chest tightens as I watch it. Her phone is a hotline to my heart. It brings back everything, and I see her laughing and smiling up at me. I see us making love and lying together naked. I remember the happiness I felt in her arms.

With a shaky hand, I refill my glass and drain it. Then, I do it again. I just want to sleep. I want to wake up and not feel like this.

I close my eyes as her betrayal washes over me.

It's cold, bitter, and it hurts like hell.

One month later: September

I sit at the bar and stare at the screen on the wall.

I'm in a dark place.

Twenty-nine days without her. Twenty-nine days in a cage of living hell.

I miss her.

I miss who I am when she's beside me.

Happiness.

The elusive emotion.

I'm angry that my life has turned out the way it has.

I'm not talking to Robert for purposely hurting Eliza. I'm not talking to Eliza for purposely hurting me.

I've never felt so alone and I don't know how to pull myself out of this.

I know I need to. This can't go on. Every day, I tell myself that this is the last day I will let myself feel like this, and yet, every day I wake up and do it again.

I exhale heavily as the noise from the bar bustles around me. I'm lost in my pity party for one.

"Hi there," a voice from behind me says.

I turn to see a man standing there. "Hi."

He gestures to the stool beside me. "Mind if I take a seat?"

I shrug. "Sure."

He sits down and orders a drink. "I'm Anthony."

"Hi." I raise my eyebrows as I stare straight ahead.

Fuck off, Anthony. I am not in the mood to talk shit tonight.

The bartender puts Anthony's drink down in front of him, and he takes a sip. "Do you have a name?"

"Nathan." I turn my attention to him.

He smiles as he sips his drink as his eyes linger on my face. He has dark hair and an athletic physique.

"Are you always so rude?" he asks me.

I exhale heavily. "Apologies. I've just had the worst month of my life. Not really in the mood for talking."

"That makes two of us."

I nod and continue to stare straight ahead. "Well, you seem to be talking just fine." I sigh.

He chuckles. "I could talk underwater. What happened to you?" He lifts his scotch to his lips.

"Girlfriend left me." I glance over at him. "You?"

"Boyfriend left me."

I nod, and we both exhale heavily as we get lost in our own thoughts.

"So, if you're not in the mood for talking, why did you come out?" he asks.

I shrug. "Trying to drag myself out of this hole. I'm sick of being home alone. You?"

"Same." He smiles over at me. "I guess I was looking for someone to take my mind off my problems."

His eyes hold mine, and the air buzzes between us.

He puts his hand on my thigh and slides it up my leg. "I was hoping to run into someone like you," he whispers.

"Is that so?"

"Do you want to go back to my place?" He shrugs. "We can... talk... in private."

My eyebrow rises. "Naked?" I ask.

"That's what I was hoping for."

We stare at each other as the air between us swirls with something dark and familiar.

The chance to not feel—to block everything out.

A reprieve from reality.

I drain my drink and slam it down on the bar. "Let's go."

Eliza

October

"Eliza, go home." Miranda, my boss, smiles. "You have three whole days off. What are you going to do?"

"Nothing much. Go to the gym, walk in Central Park, food shopping. Same stuff, different week."

Miranda laughs. "Well, enjoy the sunshine. The weather is supposed to be beautiful this week."

"Thanks." I grab my bag from my locker. "See you on Friday."

I walk up the hall toward the elevator. I love this job. I love this hospital. I feel really at home here. This is my tenth week in New York. I've made a few friends from the gym and I'm trying to keep myself busy.

I had no idea what I was signing myself up for when I moved across the country. Thinking back, it was so incredibly brave... or just plain stupid.

Either way, my plan didn't work.

I haven't heard from Nathan since the day I told him I was thinking about leaving.

So much for giving him space to sort his feelings out. I really thought we were more than this.

I exhale heavily and make my way out into the bus bay. I cross my arms and wrap my jacket around me. It's dark and cold. Every day, it's like I play this little game with myself. How long can I act happy before I crack and have a complete meltdown?

Tears threaten, constantly. It just takes one thing to trigger a memory, one song, the tiniest little thing, and I'm back in Heartbreak Hell, as if it just happened.

It's hard to pretend that the love of my life hasn't ripped my fucking heart out.

I'm losing hope. I thought it would take Nathan two weeks, at the most, to miss me.

I guess not.

The bus pulls up, and I climb on and show the driver my pass. I take a seat by the window and stare as the scenery goes rushing by.

I feel like I'm living in a detached state, hovering way above and watching myself from the sky. Living life as normal, while dealing with an insidious disease.

A frostbitten heart.

Every day, it freezes a little more and I lose another piece of myself. It's like the Antarctica and my heart is an iceberg, slowly melting and dripping into the sea.

Never to be whole again.

I keep reminding myself that I'm one of the lucky ones. I'm working and financially independent. There are no children involved. I'm free to move on with my life.

But if I had a baby, I would have a piece of him.

One that I could keep.

I inhale deeply as I close my eyes and repeat my mantra.

No tears. No more tears.

I thought I was braver than this. I don't know why this break up has messed me up so hard but I'm going to pull myself together. I really am.

I have to.

"Is this seat taken?" a man asks.

"No." I shuffle over to make room for him, and he takes a seat.

The bus travels along the road, and I stare up at the moon.

It's big and round and I wonder if Nathan is looking up at it, too.

I get off the bus and arrive at my building. I see a familiar face, and I run to her.

April has surprised me, and I jump into her arms.

Feeling the safety of her love brings down my walls, and I find myself crying into her shoulder.

"It's okay, baby. I'm here now. I've got you," she whispers as she holds me tightly.

And for the first time in so long, I feel safe. April's here.
I feel loved.

Nathan

November

I copy the number from my computer screen into my phone,
and I wait as it rings.

"Hello, Laser Clinic," the chirpy voice answers.

I swivel in my chair. "Hello, I would like to make an
appointment for a consultation, please. I'll need the latest in
the day or after business hours, if possible."

"Of course, what is the consult in regards to?"

"Tattoo removal."

I can hear her typing into her computer. "And what and
where is the tattoo you want removed?"

"Lower right side, rib cage, and it's of three birds."

"Okay, did you want them fully removed?"

"Yes, completely gone."

"And how long have you had them for?"

I frown as I think. "About five or six months."

"Oh, so they are relatively new?"

It feels like a lifetime ago since I got them. "I guess."

"And reason for the removal?"

"Come again?" I frown. Nosy fucking bitch. Why does she
need to know this shit?

"I mean, is there a problem with the tattoo, such as infe-
rior workmanship, etcetera?"

"Ah," I pause as I choose my words carefully. "No, I... they aren't what I thought they would be. I just need them removed immediately."

"Okay, I can book you in on the twenty-third of this month."

"There's nothing sooner?" I frown.

"No, I'm sorry. That's our first available late appointment. We can do 6:00 p.m.."

Maybe I should call someone else? I exhale heavily. I want it done tonight. Fuck it. I don't want to be reminded of what I don't have every day when I look in the mirror. "Yes, that's fine." I sigh.

"Okay, great, we will see you then. Do you know our address?"

I look at the website. "You on Pitt Street?"

"That's right. We will see you soon."

"Thank you, goodbye."

My intercom sounds.

"Yes, Maria?" I say.

"Dr. Mercer, have you got the dictation on the reporting that you want done this afternoon?"

"It won't be long."

"Sir, I need it if you—"

"I am well aware, Maria," I snap, cutting her off. "Please, just do as I ask you to do, when I ask you to do it. I don't want to hear your opinion." I bark.

"Yes, Doctor."

I roll my eyes. I'm sick to fucking death of her busting my balls.

"We also need to go through your schedule for the next two months."

. . .

"Not today."

"I need it today. Your waiting list is out of control, and I need to know when I can make appointments."

I close my eyes in frustration. God, give me strength.

"Maria?"

"Yes, Doctor?"

"When I say not today, I mean not today. Do you understand what that means or do I need to bring you out a copy of the English dictionary?"

"Yes, Doctor."

"Goodbye." I push the intercom with force. Fucking hell, that woman is nagging me to death.

I press the button on my voice recorder and begin to go through my recorded notes. There's a knock on the door, and it opens before I can say anything.

Maria comes in with a cup of coffee and a piece of chocolate cake. She places it in front of me, and I narrow my eyes. "What is this?"

"Cake, to sweeten you up." She fusses around and cleans my desk, leaving me to sit back and watch her.

"Move," she orders as she goes to wipe my desk down.

I sit back to give her space. I watch her for a few minutes. "Are you finished?"

"Nearly."

"Well, hurry up." I sigh. "And stop nagging me."

"You stop being a grumpy ass." She neatens the magazines.

I smirk. She's got me. I am a grumpy ass. "How do you put up with me, Maria?" I ask.

"It is not without difficulty, sir."

I chuckle.

She keeps fussing about. "Eliza is doing well in New York."

I sit up. "What? How do you know?"

"I called her today. I needed her help with a program she installed for us on the computer."

"Well,... w-wh... what did she say?" I stammer.

"That she is enjoying New York." She keeps wiping my desk. "She asked how you were."

"What did you tell her?"

"I told her that you were miserable."

"Why would you say that?"

"Because you are. Only you are too stupid to see it."

"Get out of the way." I swat her away from my desk. "I'm not paying you to give out your opinion, Maria, especially when it's deluded. Stay out of my business."

She stops and puts her hands on her hips. "Look me in the eye and tell me you aren't miserable, Nathan."

"You know, some employers fire staff who overstep the line." I huff.

She smirks and puts her hand on my shoulder as she walks past me. "Yes, sir."

"Get out and stop patronising me." I turn back to my computer.

Maria gets to the door and turns back. "Oh... and Dr. Mercer?"

"For God's sake, woman, what is it?" I growl.

"Eliza is still single."

My eyes hold hers, and I clench my jaw. "And why would I need to know that piece of information, Maria?"

She shrugs casually. "Just an observation, sir."

I roll my eyes. "Unfucking-believable," I mutter under my breath.

"Yes, I thought so, too. A woman as beautiful as Eliza? I was positive that she would have been snapped up by one of those hot businessmen by now."

I point to the door. "Out! Or so help me God, woman."

The door closes, and then she pokes her head back around. "Eat your cake."

"Get out!"

She smiles and goes to say something else. I stand and storm to the door to close it on her face.

Fuck me. That woman is annoying.

———

It's 1:00 a.m., and I find myself here again.

The Escape Club.

The place full of beautiful women where anything goes.

Even my memories disappear, if only for a short time. At least it's a reprieve.

"Hello, sir." The beautiful brunette smiles.

My eyes drop down her almost naked body and back up to her face. I feel the pulse in my cock as it comes alive with hunger.

"I'm Mahalia. How can we help you tonight?"

"I'd like a private room, please." I hand over my membership card.

"Of course." She smiles. "You know where to go?"

"Up the stairs and to the left."

"Yes." She rises up on her toes and kisses my ear. My hand goes to her behind, and I drag her over my cock.

"It's good to see you again, sir," she whispers.

I smirk as her hot breath dusts the skin on my neck.

There's something so refreshingly freeing about fucking for fun.

I turn to walk up the stairs before I turn back to her. "Oh, and Mahalia?"

"Yes, sir?"

"I'd like two girls tonight. Brunettes."

She smiles darkly. "Of course, sir." She types something into her computer and then her eyes come back to mine. "Enjoy."

The air buzzes between us.

"I always do."

———

I stand under the shower with the hot water running over my head.

I exhale heavily and close my eyes in regret as I drag my hands down my face.

Here we go again.

The comedown after the high.

No matter when I fuck, who I fuck, or how hard I fuck, it always comes to a crashing halt.

I feel like shit for days.

Because it wasn't her, and I cheated again.

Only I didn't cheat because we aren't together.

I just don't know how to get my heart to understand that.

I rest my forehead against the hard, cold tiles. Regret runs through my soul.

Let me go, Eliza. Let me go.

25

Eliza

December

THE TABLE IS full of laughter and chatter. I watch on as April talks to our grandfather. I'm so happy she could come home for the holidays. It's Christmas day, and I am back in Florida. I should have really been working, but the thought of spending the holiday on my own was all too much.

This is my first Christmas alone. Normally, Nathan has come to my house or I have gone to his family's.

This year, it's different.

Nathan's parents called me this morning to say Merry Christmas. They said they wished I was there. I wonder if they even know that we were together.

I never told them, and Nathan's mom has visited me in New York twice for lunch and never once has Nathan been mentioned. I had to bite my tongue the entire time so I didn't blurt out and tell her what a jackass her beloved son is.

Well, that's not true. He's not a jackass... just to me.

I'm doing a little better—feeling proud of myself for staying strong.

I got a promotion at work and am settling in more. I've met three really nice girls, and we have started hanging out and doing things. I even got asked on a date this week by a security guard at my building. I mean, I'm not going or anything, but it gives me hope, you know?

Maybe there is life after Nathan Mercer.

Surely a lesson that hurt that bad has to teach me something, and what doesn't kill you only makes you stronger, right?

I smile sadly as I sip my wine. I thought it was going to kill me for a while there.

I had an ache in my chest that just wouldn't go away. It's funny you know, I always thought that my grand love story was going to have a happy ending. Never once did I think that, once I fell in love with my soul mate, it wouldn't work out.

I know that eventually I'll meet someone else, but I can't imagine ever loving someone as much as I loved Nathan. It's like I'm grieving a death.

But it's the death of who I thought I was—of who I thought my best friend was.

A death of all my hopes and dreams.

My phone dances on the table, and the name Henry lights up the screen. I smile and get up from the table.

Henry Morgan has surprised me. He's kept in contact, and we've become friends. He's called weekly to check in on me. He's uncomplicated, refreshingly open, and I do enjoy talking to him.

"What do you want?" I answer with a smirk as I walk out onto the deck.

"Merry Christmas, old bag."

I giggle. "Let me guess: you're home alone, desperate and dateless."

He chuckles. "Why else would I be calling you?"

"I thought as much." I smile. "Merry Christmas, Henry."

"Was Santa good to you?"

"Ha." I laugh. "The old bastard forgot where I lived."

"Yeah, me, too. I was hoping to wake up to a sack of hot Christmas fairies under my tree. The ones with two vaginas."

I laugh out loud. "I haven't heard of those kind of fairies."

"Yes, only the very good get them."

"Ah, that explains a lot. What are you doing today?" I ask.

"With the fam. You?"

"Same, I go back to New York on Wednesday."

"I have some time off. Can I come and visit?" he offers.

I scrunch my eyes shut. He's asked me this before, and I don't want to go there with him. I know what's going to happen if he comes to visit me. Our conversations skate along the edge of flirting often.

"Not yet," I reply. "I'm not ready for visitors yet. You'll have to stick to your Christmas fairies for a while."

He chuckles. "Okay, your loss. You can't really compete with doubled-pussy fairies, anyway."

I laugh. "Undoubtedly."

"Eliza!" my mother calls. "Dessert."

"I've got to go."

"Okay, I'll call you next week."

· · ·

I smile. "Bye, Henry. Merry Christmas."

"Bye, Lize. Have a great day."

Nathan

January

"Hi, there," the sexy voice behind me rasps. "Where have you been?"

I turn, surprised. "Stephanie, hi." I force a smile.

"Have you been avoiding me?" she purrs.

I chuckle. "I couldn't even if I tried."

"This is true." Her sultry eyes hold mine, and I know she has something on her mind. Stephanie always has something on her mind. And, yes, I have been avoiding her like the plague.

"What are you doing tonight?" She goes up onto her toes as if distracted. "Do you want to get a drink?"

"Ah." I raise my eyebrow in frustration. "I thought we already established this." I exhale heavily. I need to just come out and say it...*again*. "That's not a good idea, Steph."

"Why not?"

"I told you already. I'm not into you that way."

"She's not coming back, Nathan." She snaps.

"I know."

"So, let me get this straight. You won't sleep with me because you don't want to upset *her*." She puts her hand on her hip in a huff. "But you're not even together anymore. Isn't that slightly ridiculous?"

My temper bubbles close to the surface. "Listen, not that it's any of your business," I whisper angrily. "It's true, Eliza will never know if I slept with you. But I'll know. Since you are a trigger for her, I'm not fucking going there." I glare at her. "I have told you this, time and time again. I am not having this conversation with you anymore." I become exasperated. Her constantly trying to get into my pants is really beginning to piss me off. "Get it through your head. Do you fucking understand?"

"You owe her nothing. I can please you in ways she never could."

"Goodbye, Stephanie." I turn away from her. "Keep this up and I don't even want to talk to you anymore as a friend. It's getting ridiculous."

She grabs my arm, leans in and whispers. "Let's have a party for three with your ex!"

"Let's not." I roll my eyes. "And I don't sleep with him, either."

"Because of her?"

"Yes. Because of her." I whisper angrily. "Robert and I are just friends. That has been well and truly established since I..." My voice trails off. Why am I explaining myself to her? "Goodbye, Stephanie."

I walk down the corridor and into my office. Fuck.

How in the hell did I ever think that woman was attractive?

I need a vacation.

Eliza

February

"Happy Birthday, Alex." I smile down the phone.

"Ah, my favorite girl." He laughs. "Thank you, Lize."

I miss this guy. "How are you?"

"I'm good, how are you?"

"Great," I lie.

"How's New York?"

"It's good. It took a while to get used to but I'm getting there."

"When are you going home to San Fran?"

"Ah..." I hesitate. "Soon."

"Mom said she saw you last week. She makes up excuses to come to New York and have lunch with you, you know."

I laugh. "Oh, I love her. She makes my week when she comes to visit."

"Have you spoken to Nathe?"

"No." I sigh. "I haven't heard from him."

"Have you called him?"

"No."

"How long has it been?"

"Six months or so." My heart constricts at the mere mention of his name. "Is he okay?" I hold my breath as I wait for his answer.

"He misses you."

I close my eyes. "Has he said anything?"

"He won't let me talk about you at all. I have no idea what's going on with him. He goes fucking psycho if I even mention your name."

"Is he seeing anyone?" I ask nervously.

"Not that I know of."

"I left him a letter." I exhale heavily. "I honestly thought we would work this out, Alex."

"What did the letter say?"

"Why I left, and how I was giving him space to finalize his past. I told him that I would be here waiting for him with open arms when he did."

"Can I ask you something?"

"Yes, of course."

"Why didn't you two go to couples therapy?"

"What do you mean?" I frown.

"Well, you had so much to lose, and he was seeing a therapist at the time, so why didn't you ever go and see the quack with him and get professional help with all this shit? You're both so stubborn that you can't see the woods for the trees."

I frown. "I never thought of that."

"Well, I was thinking about you the other day, and I wondered."

"Who is his therapist?" I ask.

"Elliot someone."

"Yes, I remember." Hmm, I think for a moment. "I'm going to look this doctor up and maybe call him."

"It can't hurt. And hey, why don't you call Nathan while you're at it?"

"I've nearly called him a million times." I smile.

"So...why didn't you?"

"You know why we broke up, right?"

"Yes, it's the tragic version of *Pride and Prejudice*." He sighs.

"Why would you say that?"

"Well, your prejudice and his pride."

"I don't have a prejudice." I frown.

"Yes, you did."

"How?" I scoff.

"Well, you feared he was going to go back to a man."

"That's a legitimate fear, Alex."

"If he was straight and you met him, would you fear that he would go back to another woman?"

"Well, no... but, that's different."

"That's how Nathan sees it... in black and white."

"That's not... that's not a prejudice, Alex."

"Isn't it?" He pauses for a moment. "Did you treat him the same as you would have treated a straight boyfriend?"

My heart sinks. I didn't. I was led by fear. "Look, I know I wasn't the innocent party in this. We both handled things badly. But I tried to save us."

"How?"

"The letter. I begged him to work things out and come find me. He never did, Alex. What was I supposed to do? Call him every day and beg until he gave in? He needs to want this, too. There are two of us, and I've made my wishes known."

He exhales heavily. "You two are fucked up."

"Tell me something I don't know." I smile sadly. "But you're right; I'm going to call Elliot and see if I can have a phone appointment with him. Maybe he can give me some clarity or direction. I mean, I know it's too late for Nathe and me, but maybe he can help me learn from my mistakes and move forward."

"That's a great idea."

"It's so nice talking to you." I smile. "Can you do me a favor?" I ask.

"What's that?"

"Can you check on your brother for me? I really worry about him."

"Okay. I will."

"Call me anytime if you need me."

"I will." He pauses. "Take care, babe."

"You, too. Happy birthday."

He chuckles. "I'm getting fucking old."

"It's true, you are."

"Bye, Lize."

"Bye, Alex."

May

"Knock, knock!" I call.

"Eliza." Neil rushes to hug me. I've finally given in and come to visit Nathan's parents in Vermont. "Come, come in." He ushers me into the house. "It's been too long since you came home."

Home. This isn't my home, this is Nathan's. Ugh, this was a bad idea. I shouldn't have come.

"Come in, love," Phyllis says as she pulls me in for a hug. "I've made us a cake." She squeezes me in an embrace. "It's so good to see you."

I smile into her shoulder. "You, too." I look around the familiar home. "What's new?"

"We have three new calves." Neil smiles proudly.

"You do?" My eyes widen. "Oh, let's go see them."

"I've been saving their births for your visit." He gives me a cheeky wink, and I laugh.

"So, you can actually save births now?" I tease as I link my arm through his and we make the way out the back door.

"For you, my darling," he taps my hand on his arm, "I would do anything."

. . .

It's late afternoon and nearly time for me to drive my rental car back to New York. Nathan's parents want me to stay the night but it feels off.

We are sitting around the kitchen island counter, having a last cup of coffee before I leave.

"Oh, you didn't tell me about your vacation in Hawaii." I gasp as I remember.

Nathan's mother's eyes nearly pop out of her head. "Oh my God, we had the best time, Eliza. Hawaii! You need to go."

"Yes, I know, I've been. Nathan and I went years ago, remember? You went with the Hendersons, right?"

"Yes. Oh, boy, we're not travelling with them again. All they did was fight and bicker the entire time."

"Really?" I frown. What in the hell do sixty year olds fight about on vacation?

She rolls her eyes. "Every little thing was a drama."

"That woman's a bitch," Neil admits. "Glad I'm not married to her, that's for sure."

"Moaning and whining all the time about every little thing." Phyllis sighs.

I laugh. Who knew people were still bitching at that age? I learned something today.

"Go get the photos for me to show Eliza, Neil," Phyllis says. "I just had some developed last week."

"Where are they?" he asks.

"They're in an envelope in the top drawer. I haven't put them in the album yet."

He toddles off, and I sip my coffee. "We went to this one restaurant one night and it was so good," Phyllis continues.

Neil passes me the envelope of photos, and I begin to go through them as Phyllis tells me every little detail of their ten-day itinerary.

I look at each photo and turn over to read the back. Phyllis always writes the location and date that the photo was taken on the back of every photo. She's done it for forever. I keep flicking through the images when I get to one of Nathan. He's at the beach, wearing only board shorts, standing knee high in the ocean.

My chest tightens at the sight of him. It's been so long.

Wait. Did he go with them? I turn the picture over and read the back.

Nathan, Ibiza, December 28th

What?

Nathan went to Ibiza for New Year. Are you kidding me?

Phyllis keeps rattling on, and I keep flicking through the images. Another image of Nathan comes up, and it's obvious that Phyllis has forgotten these are mixed with hers. It's a picture of Nathan on a deckchair, at the beach, shirtless. He's laughing and reaching for the camera.

Nathan, Ibiza, December

Who took this photo?

I stare at it for a moment. He looks so relaxed. My heartbeat begins to thump hard in my chest and I flick through the images again. I get to the next image, and my heart drops. It's a picture of Robert.

On the same beach as Nathan.

I turn the image over and read the back for confirmation.

Robert, Ibiza, December

Wow.

I sit back in my seat.

And there it is, in black and white. Well, not black and white. More like bright and beautiful colors.

I think back to December, and while I was lying on my couch in the fetal position, crying, he was in Ibiza with Robert.

They *are* together.

It wasn't in my imagination at all. All this time, I was blaming myself, thinking that maybe I had overreacted.

I fake a smile as if unrattled, and I flick through the rest of the images on autopilot. I don't want to know anymore.

I want to get the hell out of here because I'm pathetic, and he's nothing but a fucking asshole.

I gave him time to sort himself out, and I thought that maybe his heart was broken, too—that maybe he was coming back for me.

What a joke.

I hand the photos back and stand. "I have to go."

"Oh." Phyllis' face falls. "You sure you don't want to stay the night, love?"

"I can't." I smile as I walk toward the door. "I'm sorry." I hug Neil. "Thanks for today." I close my eyes as I hug him really tightly. I know that this will be my last hug with Neil. I'm never coming back here.

I'm not giving Nathan Mercer one more fucking tear.

I give Phyllis a hug, and my eyes well with tears. It sucks that I have to lose these two people, too. "Okay." I quickly brush past them to get outside. "Goodbye!" I call as I walk to the car.

I don't want them to see my face. I don't want them to know that I know.

I get in the car and start the engine with a rev as I fake a smile and wave. I put the car into reverse, and without looking back, I drive out of the driveway and out of Nathan Mercer's life.

I'm fucking done.

———

It's Tuesday and my finger hovers over the name:

Henry Morgan

It's time. I need to move on. And I know just how to do it. I dial his number.

"Hey. What do you want?" he answers with an obvious smile.

"Are you still coming to the conference in New York on Friday?" I blurt out before I can reconsider.

"I am."

"Let's go out Friday night."

"Ah." He chuckles. "Finally, I've been waiting for you to want to see me."

My eyes close. He's such a flirt. "Well, I do, so hurry up and get here."

Nathan

I'm sitting in the waiting room, looking around at the people sitting and waiting. What are they all doing here?

An elderly woman, a young man, a couple in the corner.

They all look so put together, as if nothing could possibly be off in their lives.

And then, there's me. The perfect illusion.

Expensive suit, good-looking by society's standards,

financially independent, fit and healthy. A heart surgeon at the top of his game. No procedure on the operating table scares him, but then he's also someone who drives around the block ten times every night before he can muster up the courage to go into his apartment.

That guy hates going home because it reminds him of her.

Home isn't home anymore, and nothing is what it's supposed to be.

I'm fucked up. I'm fucked up, bad.

And I'm really trying to pull myself out of this, but every day without Eliza, I feel like I lose a little more of my sanity. Things are going from bad to worse.

Everything is coming to a head, and I'm not sleeping again, which is dangerous in my profession. I'm taking sleeping tablets to get in four to five hours a night, and even then, my body fights it.

I inhale sharply. I've come to a new therapist today. I'm not getting anywhere with Elliot. I want a new perspective. One from a female.

The door opens, and a woman walks out into the waiting room. "Nathan?"

I stand. "Yes."

She gives me a kind smile. "This way, please." She shakes my hand. "My name is Amanda."

"Hello, Amanda." I nod.

She holds her hand out. "Please, take a seat."

―――

"Is the room satisfactory, Mr. Mercer?" the girl from reception asks.

"Yes." I smile.

"Your luggage will be up in a moment." With a kind nod, she heads toward the door.

"Thank you."

The door clicks, and I look around the penthouse.

I'm in Majorca, in the same apartment that Eliza and I spent our vacation together.

I walk out onto the balcony and stare out over the sea. The breeze whips at my hair, and a flood of memories wash over me like a warm bath.

I smile, I feel at peace here. It's like I can feel the closeness that Eliza and I shared. It lingers in the air like a wonderful perfume.

This is a special place, and I came here to try and find some clarity. This heartache isn't going away. If anything, it's getting worse by the day. I was positive that it would be fine, and that everything would pan out as it was supposed to. But it doesn't feel like that. It's like I'm fighting against fate.

With every breath that I take, I feel it. The weight of what I have lost is a heavy load to carry.

Follow your gut.

The age old saying is supposed to lead me in the right direction. But unfortunately, my gut has left the building, along with all rationality.

Recently, it's like everything has come to a head. I keep going over and over that last week we were together, and how I reacted to Robert's admission of love.

I was shocked, for sure. But I constantly told Eliza it was her that I wanted.

I exhale heavily. Did she see it differently to me? I told her that I didn't want him. I told her I loved her. I told her how I felt.

But she left anyway.

I close my eyes in regret. I don't even know who was in the wrong anymore.

I was positive it wasn't me, but I know Eliza, and I know that she would have called me, if only as a friend, if I were not to blame.

I watch a seagull. It flies over the ocean and lands on the sand. Music starts up somewhere in the distance, and another wave of fresh memories roll in.

I remember us dancing out here in the moonlight to the distant melody.

I open a beer and take a seat in the deckchair, and I put my feet up on the ottoman as my mind repeats the mantra, *Where did we go wrong?*

Five days later

I sit on the balcony and stare at the unopened letter in my hand. I read the words on the front of it.

My darling Nathan.

It's those exact words that have kept me from opening it.

She's going to try and soften the blow as to why she left— justify it in some way—and I don't want to hear it. She needn't waste her breath, because the cold, hard fact is that she just didn't love me enough to stay. No pretty words can take that away.

Amanda's, my new therapist, words come back to me with her advice: *If you don't open the letter, you won't ever move on.*

She thinks that because I don't know all the facts, my mind is holding onto the heartache, and holding me captive along with it. She thinks there's a reason I couldn't have my tattoo removed.

I throw the letter onto the table in front of me, and I sip my beer as I stare at it and then place it back down.

This fucking letter has been taunting me for six months.

I twist my hands together on my lap as I brace myself.

Fuck this. I pick it up and tear open the seal.

Nathan.

    Timing hasn't been kind to us, my darling.

———

I walk into Majorca airport and up to the reception desk, on a mission.

"Hello." The receptionist smiles.

"Hello, my name is Nathan Mercer, and I am booked on a flight to San Fran this morning?"

"Yes."

"I would like to cancel it, please."

Her eyes come to me in question.

I need to see her. "I'm changing my destination. I'm going to New York."

26

Eliza

I HIT APPLY, and I smile with a sense of accomplishment.

I'm going home, back to San Francisco, and back to my old life.

Sans Nathan, of course, but I'm not staying in New York and hiding from heartache like a coward anymore.

I'm okay, and I'm strong enough to be in the same city as him now.

I've rented an apartment in my old neighborhood, and I'm looking forward to catching up with my old friends. I'm going back to my beloved hospital, and I'm starting again.

I can't believe I let a relationship rule me for so long. Even in grief, it controlled my thought patterns.

I mean, I know why I left.

But, I had to clear the last ten years from my hard drive and it was successful. It has finally been erased. Took its time.

There's no denying that the six weeks in Nathan's arms were beautiful and soul changing. In the end, though, it was tragic.

But it was just six weeks, and for every week we were together, I spent a month grieving its loss. Six weeks in love. Six months to recover.

I go to the bathroom and look at myself in the mirror. I reapply my lipstick and fluff up my hair.

Henry Morgan is in town, and tonight, we are going on a date.

I'm not nervous. I'm excited.

For the first time in a long time, I'm thinking about me and my needs. I'm wearing a fitted black dress that has a low neck-line and long sleeves. The skirt is tight, and it falls to just below my knee. My sky-high, strappy stilettos seal the deal.

I smile as I turn and look at myself in the full-length mirror. I rearrange my boobs in my bra and push them up.

I look good. I look like myself. Who I really am, before all this victim of heartbreak crap. I grab my purse and my keys, and I head out.

I'm meeting Henry at the bar of his hotel.

I smile to myself as I ride down to the ground floor in the elevator. Here I go.

Bring it.

Nathan

I get into the cab. "Where to?" the driver asks.

"The Four Seasons, downtown, please."

"Sure thing."

He pulls out into the traffic and I look out the window. I love New York. It has a buzz that can be found nowhere else on Earth. I watch on as the cab drives through the suburbs, into the city.

I go over what I want to say tonight. It's all I've thought about for a week. I have prepared a speech in my head. She might be working, but that's okay.

I'm closer to her than I have been in six months, and I can wait till tomorrow if I have to.

I click on the Find My Phone app—my constant companion over the last six months. I used to have it as a necessity as Eliza lost her phone every second day.

But now the necessity is for a different reason. Purely indulgent. It tells me where she is, tells me when she's working, and it calms me that she's safe. I've spent more time watching Eliza's little red dot over the last six months than I have anything else.

The dot is closer now—so much closer—and hope fills me as I wait for it to find her. I watch it blink as it searches, and then it flashes as it locks on. *There she is.*

It's moving. She must be in a cab.

I smile as I watch it, feeling closer to her already.

I'll drop my bags at the hotel and shower, and then I'm going to find her.

My eyes roam over the passing traffic as we enter the city.

Eliza. I'm coming, baby.

Eliza

I walk into the bustling bar and glance around. It's packed with suits. There are literally men everywhere I look. I feel a buzz of excitement as I feel eyes rest on me. It's like I finally have an open for business sign on my forehead.

"Eliza."

I look over and see Henry approaching me, and I break into a broad smile. He pulls me into a hug and holds me tight.

"It's so good to see you." He holds my hand as he steps back to look at me. "Dear God, woman, how have you gotten hotter?"

I laugh.

"Let's go," he says as he drains his glass and puts it down onto a nearby table.

"You don't want to stay and have a drink here?" I ask.

"No, Eliza." He replies flatly. "Every man and his dog is eyeing my date."

I smile bashfully. Oh shit. He thinks it's a date, too. Now, nerves really do dance in my stomach. "Okay."

He leads me out of the bar and onto the busy sidewalk. "I thought we could go to a restaurant on Fifth. I've been before, and the food and cocktails are incredible."

"Okay, I'm easy."

He chuckles with a wink, and I roll my eyes.

"You know what I mean." I scoff.

He puts his hand up and hails a cab. Moments later, we arrive at our destination. He helps me out of the cab and then we walk down eight stairs, and in through the grand, black front doors. This place looks exclusive, and the restaurant is below street level. Large windows look up at the busy surroundings. It's dark and moody, and just... wow.

"Hi, I had a table booked for Morgan."

"Yes, of course. This way, sir." The server leads us through, and we sit at a table near the front windows. Candles flicker on the table, and she hands us our menus. "The house specials tonight are the seafood platter, a mushroom gnocchi with arugula and walnut pesto, and then we have a snapper in a garlic sauce with honey-roasted vegetables. Our dessert specials are a freshly made macadamia crunch ice cream with chocolate coated strawberries, and then the chocolate parfait."

"Thank you." I smile. "Sounds good."

"What would you like to drink?" she asks.

I frown over to Henry. "Wine?"

"I don't drink wine," he says, distracted by the menu in front of him. "You get whatever you want. I'll have a beer, thanks."

I fake a smile. I'm so used to me and Nathan having the same tastes in everything. "I'll have a margarita, please."

"Okay." She smiles and takes off toward the bar.

Henry's mischievous eyes come to me. He takes my hand across the table. "Have you missed me?"

I giggle. "No."

That's not a lie. I haven't missed him at all, and to be honest, I'm beginning to wonder why I'm even here. I'm not feeling any chemistry. It's like I'm here with my brother.

Ugh...*focus.*

"So, tell me about New York." He smiles.

I put my hands up. "Here we are. I love New York."

"You're enjoying it?"

"Very much. I'm coming home, though, next week."

"What?" He frowns.

I laugh at his shocked face. "I'm moving back to San Fran."

"What brought this on?"

"My contract was up here and... " I pause as I think of the right wording. "It's time."

"So, what does the guard dog think about that?"

I roll my lips. *Don't go there.* I rearrange the napkin on my lap. "Nathan and I broke up," I say.

"Yes, I know. That's why you left." He smiles sarcastically as he sits back. "Can't say I didn't see it coming."

"Here you are." The waitress puts our drinks on the table in front of us.

"Thank you." I take a sip of my margarita and I inwardly wince. Fuck, that's strong. It tastes like hand sanitizer. What kind of tequila is this? "Why do you say that?" I ask as I fight the urge to shiver in disgust. How the hell am I supposed to drink this rocket fuel?

"His over the top jealousy of you."

I watch him and take another sip. Oh hell, this drink is bad. Real bad.

"He was obsessed with you."

I smile sadly. I was obsessed with him. "Oh, well, that's in the past." I need to change the subject. "Tell me about you. Are you still booty-calling your ex?"

He chuckles. "No. I found a new booty-call girl, though."

I laugh. Henry and his honesty. No man says that on a date. "You have? Is she hot?"

"So hot." He takes my hand, picks it up, and kisses my fingertips. "Not as hot as you."

I get an internal running commentary of what Nathan's dry reply to that statement would be, and I smile. "Well, I'm flattered."

He winks, totally oblivious to his comment, and I drop my head and smile.

Oh man, who was I kidding? I don't like Henry Morgan.

He's a twit.

Over the next four hours, I listen to Henry ramble on, and while he's a great guy and a lovely friend, I'm feeling nothing.

Zero connection.

But I don't think he's feeling the same because he keeps

kissing my hand and talking about the places he wants to take me when I get home.

Oh jeez, how do I get myself into these situations?

"I have to get going soon." I smile. "I have an early shift in the morning."

"A nightcap at my hotel first?" He smiles hopefully.

"Ah." I frown. "I'm not..." I pause as I try to think of the perfect wording for my let down. "I'm not really ready for a nightcap, Henry."

"Oh." His face falls. "Really? I was totally feeling it."

I giggle in surprise. "You were?"

"Totally." He smiles playfully. "Wait till you kiss me good-bye. Then you'll change your mind."

"Oh, I will, will I?"

"Yeah." He raises his hand to the waitress for the check. "You'll be begging to be nightcapped by me."

"Okay, let's see what you've got." I laugh as I play along.

Ten minutes later, we walk out of the restaurant and out onto the street. There's a cab rank just outside, and we walk to it. He takes my hand in his and turns me toward him. He tucks a piece of my hair behind my ear as we stare at each other. I want to know if there is anything here. I need to know once and for all.

"Is this where you kiss me goodbye?" I ask.

He leans in and his lips slowly take mine. His hands rise to my face, and he kisses me deeper. A little tongue, a little angst, and a whole lot of nice.

He kisses me again, and my eyes close.

Okay, maybe we *could* work with this.

He kisses me again. "Come back to my hotel," he whispers against my lips.

His words snap me out of the moment, and I come back to reality with a thud. "I can't."

I step back from him. He grabs my hand so I can't totally escape and smiles over at me. "I'll see you when you get back then?"

I nod.

He steps forward and kisses me again. It's soft and tender, and his lips linger over mine.

"I have to go." I turn and open the door of the closest cab, and he waves and then gets into the cab in front of me.

"Where to?" the cab driver asks as we wait for Henry's cab to pull out.

"Forty-second, please." I look out of the window, and straight into the stare of Nathan.

He's standing against the wall, his hands in the pockets of his oversized coat.

He's glaring at me. I can feel his fury as if it is a tangible force.

Oh fuck.

He was right behind us the whole time.

Henry.

Of all the times.

I drag my eyes from his. Is it a coincidence that he was here? Anxiety takes over. "Just... just drive please," I stammer to the driver.

He gestures to the congested road in front. "Traffic, lady."

The door of the cab opens, and Nathan gets into the back-seat beside me. He slams the door behind him.

"What are you doing?" I snap.

"Henry Morgan?" he whispers angrily. "You're with Henry

fucking Morgan?" He gasps. "I've been heartbroken for six months to find out that you ...." The veins are sticking out of his forehead. "To find out you've been with him all along." He's furious.

"What? No." My face falls. Why is, *I've been heartbroken for six months* the only thing I heard in that sentence? "Go home to Robert, Nathan." I snap.

"What?" He erupts.

"You heard me."

"We need to talk."

"You're five months too late Nathan. Go away." I glare at him, and then I turn to the driver. "Can you kick this man out of the cab, please? He's uninvited."

"Are you kidding me?" Nathan whispers angrily.

The driver holds his hands up. "Come on, lady, what do you want from me?"

"Right. That's it." I get out of the cab and begin to march up the sidewalk on a mission.

I don't know what I'm doing right now, but I do know that I don't want to be sucked into Nathan's world again. I've only just gotten out of it, and I can't let myself go back there.

He hurt me too fucking much.

I hear the cab door slam behind me, and I know that Nathan is hot on my heels.

He grabs my arm and spins me toward him. "Eliza. Stop."

"Go away." My emotions boil over and my eyes fill with tears. "Just... just leave me alone."

"I read the letter."

"Huh?"

"I read it this week."

My eyes bulge from their sockets as I completely lose my cool. "What?" I shriek. "Are you two years old?" I turn and march off into the crowd again. I'm too angry to even talk to him. He only just read it! I can't even deal with this man.

He calls me from behind, "Eliza!"

"Go home to Robert, Nathan. I don't want to talk to you." I march on.

He grabs my arm and pulls me back to face him. "Jesus Christ, woman, will you listen to me for one fucking minute? I'm not with Robert. I was never with Robert."

"I saw the pictures of Ibiza, Nathan."

He frowns, as if confused.

"At your mother's. I saw the photos." I splutter, "How can you still lie to me after all this time? Did our friendship mean nothing to you at all?"

"We were on a Contiki reunion trip with twenty other people, Eliza. Separate rooms and very limited speaking. There is nothing with fucking Robert, like I told you." His eyes search mine. "You left me for Henry Morgan?"

"No." I sigh. God, how this must look? "That's the first time I have seen Henry since I left... not that it's any of your business."

"You kissed him?"

"Yes." I throw my hands up. "I kissed him, all right."

"What else have you been doing?"

I stare at him, and a pull toward him overwhelms me. He's so familiar.

So loved.

"Lying on the couch crying over you, Nathan." My eyes fill with tears at how pathetic I must sound. "So stay the fuck away from me, okay?"

His face falls and he pulls me close. "Baby."

"Don't." I struggle to break out of his arms, and he holds me tight against my will. "Let me go." I struggle, and finally break free. I push him hard in the chest and he stumbles back. He shakes his head, knowing that I've completely lost my shit.

"I just want to talk." He splutters.

"You're too late."

"I can't move on until we do."

He wants to move on.

My strength returns. "Fine." I drop my shoulders as I prepare for war. "Let's talk. You have exactly ten minutes." I march into the closest bar and take a seat at a high table. He tentatively sits down beside me. The waitress approaches.

"We will have two margaritas with Agave top-shelf tequila, please," he says.

I clench my jaw. I hate that he knows my drinks. "I don't want to drink with you." I bark.

"Fine. I'll drink both." He snaps.

The waitress raises her eyebrows as if surprised by my bitch antics, and I clench my jaw. I give her my best, *You don't know the whole story* look.

He's a jerk, okay?

I twist my fingers on my lap. I don't want to blurt out nasty things so I'll just stay as quiet as I can.

His eyes come to mine, and he smiles softly. "It's good to see you, Lize."

I clench my teeth shut and give a curt nod.

It's so good to see you.

His brow furrows as if he's searching for the right thing to say. "You've lost a lot of weight."

"Couple of kilos. I've been going to the gym."

He fakes a smile and scratches his head.

"You wanted to talk, so talk," I say.

"Did you mean it? The letter?"

I shake my head as disappointment fills me. "I can't believe you didn't read it until now."

"Neither can I." He sighs. "I just... ." his voice trails off.

"You just, what Nathan?"

"I didn't handle things as well as I could have."

"You think?"

We stare at each other, and I know that this is it: my moment of truth where I need to say all the things I didn't say before. I have so many regrets, and I need to be honest now, or forever hold my peace.

"Neither did I, Nathe. This isn't all your fault. I'm to blame as well." I shrug sadly. "I shouldn't have left a letter. I should have said it to your face."

"Can you say it now?"

"It's too late." I sigh. "It won't mean the same now as it did then so just forget it."

We stare at each other and sadness rolls over me. It really *is* too late for us.

There is nothing left to say that can erase the hurt between us.

He takes my hand in his and rests it on my thigh. "Please." He closes his eyes as if steeling himself to hear it. "Eliza, you said you'd wait forever."

I get a lump in my throat. Seeing him in the flesh brings it all back. The happiness, the heartache, and everything in between.

"I wanted you to know that I understood that you needed time, and that as your friend, I wanted to give it to you."

His eyes hold mine. "Why would you say that?" he asks softly.

"Because I was watching you struggle."

He squeezes my hand in his as if prompting me to speak openly. "How was I struggling?"

"Nathe." I smile over at the beautiful man in front of me. I know it's too late for us but I still adore him. "You were going along as normal, and then all of a sudden you got these feelings of attraction for me. And you acted on them almost instantly."

"No, I didn't."

"Oh, what, you waited a few weeks?"

"That was a long time not telling you, Lize."

"Anyway, my point is that once we were together and in love —and I do know that you loved me—it was full speed ahead. But I also knew that you wouldn't leave me, and that, even if you had feelings for Robert, you would never have left me for him. That's not the kind of person you are."

His brow furrows as we stare at each other.

"I wanted to give you a choice, Nathan."

"Why?" He whispers.

"Because ten years being your best friend has taught me one thing: your happiness was more important to me than our relationship." I get a lump in my throat. "I could never let you give up your happiness for mine. I loved you too much for that."

He drops his head.

"And then you wouldn't talk to me when I was terrified that I was pregnant."

He closes his eyes in regret.

I squeeze his hand. "It's okay, Nathan. I understand."

His eyes shoot back up to mine. "You understand what?"

"I know why you had to force me to leave you."

"Eliza, I never meant to make you leave me. Just the opposite." He pauses for a moment as he collects his thoughts. "When Jolie said those things to me... " His voice trails off.

"What?" I prompt him to continue.

"I don't know." He shakes his head as if unable to articulate himself. "Something happened."

"What do you mean?"

"I didn't shut you out because I wanted Robert. I was devastated by you. I wasn't able to...." He cuts himself off.

I squeeze his hand in mine. "What Nathe?"

"How could you think that I would use you for children?" His eyes search mine. "How could you possibly think that? You know me. Better than anyone else, you know me."

Oh God, he's still hurt about this.

He clenches his jaw. "I couldn't get my head around it, Eliza. I still can't. It was the most hurtful thing that anyone has ever thought of me."

Guilt fills me. "Nathe, I knew that deep down. I was looking for a reason. I wasn't afraid of you. I was afraid of me. I knew that I wouldn't be okay if we didn't work out. And I was right, I wasn't."

We stare at each other, and deep regret swirls between us. He dusts his thumb back and forth over the back of my hand. "So, you're with Morgan now?"

"No." I roll my eyes. "Tonight, was the first time I've seen him since I left. You're with Robert?" I ask.

"I'm not with Robert!" he snaps, annoyed. "How many times do I have to fucking tell you that?"

"But you've been with Robert?"

"Not physically, no. I've seen him but not how you think."

"What does that mean?"

"Ibiza was a nightmare. We were never going to work if we got back together. That was done ten years ago. And besides, we fight every time we see each other now."

"Why?"

"Because he came to our home to upset you and it worked. You left me."

"What about Stephanie?"

"I haven't touched either of them, I swear on my mother's life," he growls in frustration.

"Who have you been with?" I know I shouldn't ask but the masochist in me wants some pain.

"You don't want to know the answer to that question." His eyes hold mine.

That means a lot of people.

I get a lump in my throat and drop my head. This is why we can't be together.

I'm weak as fuck when he's around.

He cups my cheek in his hand and brings my face up to his. "But it cemented something for me."

His eyes search mine.

"It's you Eliza. It's always been you. And I know that my love for you started out platonic, but you have owned me since the day we met."

We stare at each other and, God, I want to take back the last six months. I want to throw myself into his arms and kiss and make up.

But I need to have some backbone and stand up for myself. "What are you saying, Nathan?"

"I love you. I will always love you."

I stare at him.

"I want us to try again."

"No." I shake my head, the hurt all still too raw to even contemplate it. "I can't."

"Why not?'

"Because I can't depend on you like I did. It's not healthy to be as we were, and of course, we failed. It was a car crash waiting to happen. We know each other too well, Nathan."

"That's impossible."

"I don't want to get back together."

He frowns, and I see a glimmer of his temper hovering just below the surface. "You can't know each other too well." He spits. "That's ridiculous."

"I want to be friends," I announce. "I'm moving back to San Francisco next week."

"You're moving home?" he asks hopefully.

"No, I've got my own apartment."

He sits back in his seat, affronted. "Well, this is nice, isn't it?"

"What's that supposed to mean?"

"I come here and lay my heart out for you, and you reject me again anyway."

"What?" I snap. "Don't you dare get angry with me for not jumping back into your arms." I pick up my drink and take a huge gulp. I'm getting angry, too, now. Does he think I should jump into his arms at the snap of his fingers? "While you've been fucking yourself better, I've been devastated. So, forgive me for not wanting to jump back into bed with you, Nathan."

He rolls his eyes. "How long are you going to throw that in my face for?"

"You know what?" I stand in a huff. "I'm not. That was the last time." I turn and storm out of the bar. Who the hell does he think he is?

Nathan Mercer is still an asshole.

27

Eliza

I MARCH UP THE SIDEWALK, toward the cab rank.

"I can't believe I wasted my time even talking to him," I mutter as I storm along. "Comes back here, says a few pretty words, and thinks I should drop to my knees and suck his second-hand dick. How many people has he fucked while we were apart? I'm done. So fucking done with him." I'm banged hard on the shoulder by a man walking past me. "Ouch."

"Sorry," he calls.

I keep storming and see the cab rank up ahead. There are two people waiting in line but no cabs. It begins to sprinkle with rain.

"Oh, great, this is just what I need."

How many times are you going to throw that in my face?

I narrow my eyes as my blood begins to boil, and this is exactly my point.

Nathan Mercer is a selfish fuckface who only cares about himself.

"Eliza!" he pants as he reaches me. He must have been running to find me.

I cross my arms in front of me. "Go away, I have nothing to say to you."

"What?" He breathes heavily. "We haven't finished talking."

"Yes, we have."

The rain begins to get heavier, and I roll my eyes. Is this for real? It hasn't rained for weeks, and the one fucking night I'm out without a cab, it decides to come down.

"Why can't we try again?" he asks.

"Because you're an entitled asshole, that's why." I snap.

"How am I entitled?" He gasps.

"You break my fucking heart, turn up here and demand I come back to you at the snap of your fingers."

"You said you loved me."

"I said I loved you back then, asshole."

He narrows his eyes. I know he doesn't like being called an asshole. Well, too bad, because he is. "So, you don't love me now?"

"No." I stare straight ahead. "I don't, actually."

"Liar."

"Just go away, Nathan."

The rain begins to really come down.

"Are you fucking serious?" I cry to the Gods. I storm over to stand under an awning, and I take out my phone.

"What are you doing?"

"Calling an Uber. What does it look like?"

"Why are you being such a fucking bitch?" He whispers angrily.

I lower my phone and glare at him. "Your mouth is too big for your own good."

His eyes bulge.

"You're an ostrich." I go back to my phone.

"What does that mean?"

"It means"—I huff—"that you bury your head in the sand, and that your eyeball is bigger than your fucking brain."

"Listen." He sneers, and the rain really begins to pour down now, bouncing up from the sidewalk and hitting us as we stand under the awning. It's loud, and we have to yell to hear each other. "Okay, I asked you to come back to me. That doesn't make me fucking stupid."

"No. What makes you stupid is the fact that you think I would come back to you like this."

He frowns and opens his mouth to say something, and then shuts it again. I've got him.

I book my Uber, and put my phone back in my handbag.

"What do you want from me?" he asks.

"Nothing."

"So how do we fix this?"

"I don't want to fix this."

He puts his hands on his hips. "I'm one minute away from dragging you back into the fucking bar, Eliza. Tell me how to fucking fix this?" He growls in frustration.

"I'm not looking for a boyfriend, Nathan. You can be my friend but that's it, and with your track record, I'm not even sure I want you as that."

"What's that supposed to mean?"

"It means I've been in a city where I know nobody for six months, and you haven't fucking checked on me once. You're a shitty friend, that's what."

He clenches his jaw as he glares at me.

"But that's okay. I know you were busy." I flick my hair over my collar as I stare straight ahead. I'm going for an Oscar here. I'm being overdramatic but to hell with it. He deserves it.

"Meaning what?"

My blood pressure rises to boiling point. "Let's just say that your last six months look very different from mine."

"Okay, right." He throws his hands up in frustration. "So, let's put each other through another six months of hell then, shall we? Because proving a fucking point is so much more important than being happy." He yells as he loses control of himself.

I roll my eyes. "Go away."

"I am away. I've flown all this way to see you and you won't even talk to me."

"And there it is again." I smile to myself with a shake of my head. "Unfucking believable."

"What?" he yells. "What's that supposed to fucking mean?"

"It's all about you, Nathan. Everything is all about you. For once...," I yell, "just fucking once, can you put my wishes before your own?"

"What *do* you want?"

"I want to be friends. Listen to me when I speak. I can't say it any clearer than that. I want to be friends."

"I don't want you as a fucking friend, Eliza. I want you as my wife!" he shouts.

What?

He steps back as if shocked that he just said that out loud.

"Well, that's not happening," I say quietly. "Because at the moment, I only want a friend. Having *you* as a husband is the very last thing on my mind."

His eyes hold mine.

"Friendship. Take it or leave it," I say.

He clenches his jaw. "Leave it."

"Like I knew you would." The Uber pulls up. I get in and slam the door.

Nathan stands on the sidewalk, his face is murderous, and he glares at me as the car pulls out into the traffic.

I'm not even joking. Nathan Mercer really is an asshole.

———

Sleep: the wonder drug. I wish they sold it in bottles.

I walk down the sidewalk and smile. I'm feeling weirdly relaxed today.

I don't feel regret. I don't feel anxious at all about Nathan's and my fight last night.

I feel in control. I feel like myself. Liberated, even.

Being a bitch is empowering.

I've been to the gym this morning. I did my last grocery shop, and now I've just bought another two cheap suitcases to take my extra things home.

I walk into my building and take the elevator to my floor. My phone pings with a message in my handbag. It's probably the girls about tonight. I have my farewell dinner tonight at a restaurant, and I'm looking forward to it.

The elevator doors open. I wheel the empty suitcases down to my apartment and dump them next to my door. I take out my phone to see the text. It's from Nathan.

Okay, fine.
Friends.

I twist my lips to stop myself from smiling. I reply.

Thank you.

Another text bounces in.

Can we have lunch?

I roll my eyes. Great. I throw my phone onto the couch and don't reply. I flick the kettle on. Another text bounces in.

**Friends eat lunches together,
you know?**

I narrow my eyes. What will I reply with? I put my phone down again. God, he's going to play on the friends thing now, isn't he? Another text bounces in.

This is your last chance to have lunch with an ostrich before he flies out this afternoon.

I smile at his ostrich analogy. Okay, he's going home. There's no chance of me giving in, and he gets it.
I text back.

**Fine.
Where do you want to meet?**

A text comes back.

What do you feel like?

Hmm, he's being nice today.

Meet me at Hugo's on 42nd in an hour?

A reply comes straight back in.

Sounds good.
See you then.

I walk into Hugo's at 1:00 p.m, and Nathan stands when I arrive. He's at a table near the window.

"Hello." He puts his hand out to shake mine.

I look at his outstretched hand. Nathan has never shaken my hand apart from the first day we met. Oh God, here we go.

I shake his hand and fake a smile. "Nice to see you again so soon, Nathan."

"Likewise, Eliza." He smiles sweetly.

I take a seat, and he sips his coffee. "You ordered already?" I ask.

"Yes, " he replies casually. "And I told them that we'll split the bill."

"Okay, good, that makes it easier." I pick up the menu and look at my choices as I try to hide my smirk. This is him *being friends*. "What are you having?"

"The lasagne."

Of course, he would have that.

I look through the choices. "I'll have the salad. Lasagne is too heavy for me."

"You don't like lasagne anymore?" He asks dryly.

"Too heavy," I repeat casually. "Leaves me with a bitter aftertaste."

He stares at me flatly, and I bite the side of my cheek to stop myself from smiling.

Game on, asshole.

"Well, my taste buds haven't changed." He rearranges the napkin on his lap. "Obviously."

"I can't imagine they would with your gorging at the all-you-can-eat buffet." I close the menu. "The germs in those places are off the charts... or so I've heard."

He catches his bottom lip with his teeth to stop himself from saying something snarky. He sips his coffee, and I really have to concentrate on not smiling.

"How was your hotel?" I ask.

"Fine, thanks." He sits back and crosses his legs. He's wearing faded blue jeans and a navy jacket with a gray shirt underneath. His honey hair is messy and long on top, and his jaw is so square that he belongs on a modelling shoot.

Why does he have to be so gorgeous?

"Are you ready to order?" the waitress asks as she approaches us.

Nathan gestures to me.

"I'll have the chicken salad and a Diet Coke, please." She slowly writes down my order and turns to Nathan. She looks up at him, and once she sees his face, she smiles goofily and tucks her hair behind her ear as her cheeks turn to a rosy pink of flirtation.

Oh jeez....

A trace of a smile crosses Nathan's face when he sees her reaction to him. "Hello," he says in his deep voice.

"Hi." She gushes.

His eyes hold hers intently. "What do you recommend?" His eyes glance to her name badge. "Tiffany, what a beautiful name. May I call you Tiffany?"

She smiles as if she's just won the lottery. "Of course, you can."

"What's good here?"

"Um." She hunches her shoulders in excitement that he wants to talk to her, and I roll my eyes. Dear God, nothing's changed. He still has a fan club everywhere he goes.

Unable to help myself, "He'll have the lasagne." I cut in.

Oh hell, shut up.

Tiffany's eyes flicker to me and then back to Nathan. "You want the lasagne?" she asks.

Nathan's eyes hold mine, and he smiles like the cat that got the cream. Damn it, I just played right into his hands with my little jealous outburst.

"Yes, that sounds delicious." He smiles. "I might have a glass of wine, too. Would you like a glass of wine, Eliza?"

"Nope." I'm not drinking with him. That's a recipe for disaster.

He smiles as he looks through the drink menu. "How sad that she won't drink with me, right, Tiffany?" He peruses the choices.

Tiffany giggles on cue, and I want to vomit in my own mouth.

"I need to keep my wits about me." I fake a smile at Tiffany.

Nathan's eyes rise to mine. "Why is that?"

"Well, I'm going out tonight. I don't need a head start." That's not actually a lie. I really don't want to get drunk. *I also don't want to end up in bed with you...* but that's a secret I will take to my grave.

"Oh, I see." His eyes scan the drinks menu. "I'll have a glass of the Henschke, please."

"Is that all?" she asks.

"It is." He smiles. "Thank you, Tiffany."

She goes up onto her toes, and then with a bashful smile, she takes off to the kitchen.

I stare at him flatly, don't say it, don't say it. "You're very friendly today, Mr. Mercer." I internally kick myself for saying it.

"I'm always friendly, Eliza, what on earth do you mean?"

"No, you are impatient and grumpy."

He smiles. "I've changed since we last spent time together."

"Oh, you have, have you?"

"Yes." He looks around the restaurant like he's Mary fucking Poppins and butter wouldn't melt in his gorgeous mouth. Too bad I know that it does.

"Do tell, what's changed?" I ask.

Tiffany arrives back with our drinks and puts them on the table in front of us. "Thank you." He smiles as he raises his glass to me. "Bottoms up." He takes a sip.

I raise my eyebrow as I watch him, unimpressed that he's drinking our favorite red wine, and I'm not.

"I'm more empathetic now," he tells me.

My eyebrows rise in surprise. "Really? Has this change happened today?"

"No, why do you say that?"

"Well, you were especially self-absorbed last night."

"Hmm." He sips his wine, and I can almost see his lips twitching as he tries to hold his tongue. "I've worked on that."

"Who with? Your therapist?"

"Here's your bread." The waitress puts the bread onto the table, and she looks between us with a huge smile.

Oh, for Pete's sake, *get lost Tiffany.*

Nathan butters his bread. "Do you want some?" he asks me.

Don't say it... don't say it... don't say it.

"How many men have you slept with since we broke up?" I ask. *Shut up, shut up.*

"None."

"None?"

"Nearly one, but I didn't go through with it."

"What does that mean?"

"We left a bar with the intention of having sex, but once I was outside, I realized I didn't want it and I left. That's not my... I'm not into it."

"How many women?"

"None that count."

"Nathan." I snap.

"Why would you want to know that?"

"Because I need to know. I want to have all the facts in front of me."

"Why?"

"I just do."

His brow furrows as if doing an internal risk assessment. "Four."

Hmm, not as bad as I imagined. "Who are they?"

"What the fuck does it matter?" He whispers angrily.

"You want me to process everything. This is me doing that."

"I have no idea. They work at the strip club."

I sit forward in disgust. "You had sex with prostitutes?" I whisper.

"You would rather have me spend the night sweet-talking someone?" He gasps as if outraged. "It was a physical urge I had to scratch, so I took care of it in the most mechanical way that I knew how to."

"So, you went to the strip club on four occasions, and..."

"Twice."

I frown. "You did the four girls twice?"

He looks around. "Keep your fucking voice down," he whispers. "I went to the strip club twice and had a threesome with two girls both times."

My mouth falls open and I sit back. "Wow. Go you."

I stare at him for a moment, and it's official. I must be tapped. A normal woman would be outraged, but this information has me strangely mollified. He wasn't intimate with anybody. It was *just* sex.

"I nearly called your therapist last week," I admit.

"Why?"

"I just wanted to check if you were okay." *Shit, shut up, shut up.*

He sits forward, as if excited. "You were worried about me as recently as last week?"

"That was before I found out you went to Ibiza with Robert."

"On a platonic group holiday. Don't make it sound like something it wasn't, Eliza."

"Hmm." I sip my Diet Coke. "I don't care what you do anyway." I lie.

He gives me a slow, sexy smile as his eyes hold mine. "I know."

He's so onto me.

I sip my drink as I look around. This was a bad idea.

Our meals arrive, and we eat in silence for a while. He's completely at ease, while I'm deep in regret about my little slip up about asking who he slept with. Why did I ask that? Now he knows I care.

"You know, my mother knows everything," he says.

I frown as I chew. "What do you mean?"

"She knows that we fell in love, and she knows that we broke up."

My mouth falls open. "But she's never said anything. I must have seen her ten times, and I speak to her every second day."

"Because she was afraid that if you knew she knew, things would be weird between you. She was scared that you were going to leave her, too."

I put my hand over my heart. "That makes me so sad. I would never leave her."

He raises an eyebrow. "Just me, then."

"I was forced to leave you, Nathan, it was never by choice."

"Well, it doesn't matter now." He bites his lasagne off his fork. "We are just friends, after all."

"Precisely."

His eyes hold mine, and I know he's trying to make me crack without actually saying anything.

"Where is your new apartment in San Fran?" He changes the subject.

"In my old neighbourhood, around the corner."

"It's okay?"

"Yes, smaller than my last one but it will be fine."

He twists his lips as he listens. "How long is your lease?"

"Twelve months."

"Twelve months?" He snaps in an outrage.

"Yes," I reply calmly. "Is that a problem?"

"No." He bites the food off his fork with force. "Why would it be?" he asks through gritted teeth.

I inwardly smile, and we eat in silence, once more.

"What time does your plane leave?" I ask.

"Five."

"Okay, you probably should get going soon," I reply happily.

He stares at me, deadpan. "I should."

"You should ask your friend Tiffany for the bill."

"I will." His bottom teeth catch his top lip, and I know he's trying desperately to hold his tongue. "I mean, there's no reason to stay in New York tonight, is there?"

"No." I shrug. "There really isn't."

He narrows his eyes. "I guess I'll see you around then."

"Yeah, maybe." I shrug casually, as if I don't have a care in the world.

"Where are you going tonight?"

"Out with my work friends for dinner and drinks. It's my farewell dinner. I'm really looking forward to it."

His eyes hold mine, and it's really hard not burst out laughing at his attempt to hide his tantrum from me. I can read him like a book.

"Well, have a safe trip." I stand.

"We need to split the bill."

Nathan doesn't split bills. This is the first time in ten years I have ever heard him say that to anyone. "Okay, great. How much do I owe you?"

"Sit back down while I work it out." he whispers angrily.

"What's wrong with you?" I ask innocently.

"Nothing."

"Really? Because you look like something is wrong."

"Nothing. Is. Wrong." He growls.

I smile. "I'm glad you've changed and are now so empathetic. This is a real improvement, Nathan. This will be great for your new relationships going forward."

He glares at me and I think I have a new favorite hobby—goading Nathan Mercer is fun.

Come on, fight me. I dare you.

I take my money from my purse and put it onto the table. "It was lovely seeing you."

He narrows his eyes.

I put my hand out to shake his, and he squeezes it so hard, he nearly breaks my fingers.

"Have a safe trip home," I say.

"I will." His eyes hold mine. "Have a nice life."

"I will." I smile sweetly.

We walk out the door, and into the street, and he turns toward me. "Got anything you want to say to me?" he asks.

"Goodbye." I smile.

I turn to walk down the street, and I close my eyes with pride.

I did it. I stuck to my guns.

———

The table all erupts into laughter, and I snort my drink up my nose. It's been the best night. We had dinner and are now sitting around a large table in a busy cocktail bar.

There are twenty-seven of us in total–mostly people I work with and a few of their husbands. I'm going to miss these guys.

"Oh Lord, have fucking mercy." Louise gasps. "Look at that fine specimen at the bar."

We all glance over to see who's she talking about, and my mouth drops open.

Nathan, *my Nathan,* is standing at the bar.

What the hell is he doing here?

"Holy shit, he's ridiculous," Annie says. "Do you reckon he's a model or something?"

The girls all sit and stare at him with a running commentary on what he could do to them.

He's standing against the bar with his elbows resting on it as he talks to the barman. He's wearing black jeans that fit in all the right places, his tight ass firmly in view and a black shirt that shows off every inch of his broad shoulders. His strong forearms are bare and displaying his designer chunky silver watch. His hair is messed up to perfection and, God, the girls are completely right. He looks fucking hot.

"Actually, I know him," I announce.

"What?" They all gasp.

"He's my friend from San Fran. His name is Nathan."

"What the hell?" Annie hits me on the leg. "Go... bring him to us!" she demands.

I giggle as I stand and go to the bar.

He turns toward me as I approach him, "Eliza." His gaze drops to my toes and back up to my face. "What are you doing here?"

"I was just about to ask you the same thing."

He sips his drink as his eyes dance with mischief. "Are you following me, Bennet?"

"I thought you went home."

He licks his bottom lip as his eyes darken. "Change of plans."

28

Eliza

"AND WHAT ARE THEY?" I ask.

He turns to the bar as the waiter approaches. "Two top shelf margaritas, please."

"Sure thing," the waiter replies and gets to work making our drinks.

"What's the change of plans, Nathan?" I repeat.

"Well..." His brow furrows as he sips his drink. "Obviously, I'm still here."

"I can see that. Your stalking knows no bounds."

"It's a necessary evil."

"Why?"

"I'm working on something that I can't really talk about yet." He shrugs as he looks over at my table of friends. He gives them a smile and wave. I glance over to see them all watching us. Oh jeez, we have an audience.

I turn my attention back to him. "Why not?" I ask.

"It's a work in progress. I haven't had enough time to carry out the ground work yet."

"Which is?"

"To become completely irresistible to you." He smirks against his glass, and his eyes dance with mischief. "Although, it shouldn't be hard."

I struggle to keep a straight face. "Oh, really?"

"Why? Don't you find me irresistible?"

"Not in the least," I reply, deadpan.

He gives me a slow, sexy smile, "Well, there you go. My point proven."

That's a lie. He is completely irresistible and then some.

Stop it.

"So, when do I get to hear about this plan?" I ask.

"After you introduce me to your friends."

"You know you're not actually invited tonight."

"Do you want me to leave?"

I shrug. "No."

He smiles softly. "Good, because I don't want to go."

We stare at each other, and it's there between us, the crackle in the air. That spark of possibility. An attraction I can't deny.

"Come on," he says, pulling me out of my little daydream. "Let's go meet your colleagues."

"You're just my friend, remember?"

"How could I fucking forget? How long for, anyway?"

"Until I say so. With your track record . . ."

"Why does it matter now?"

"Because it does, that's why. If you think I'm trusting you not to do that again on a whim, you are sadly mistaken." I weave through the tables, leading the way until we get to my friends.

"This is Nathan," I introduce him. "We are friends from San Fran."

"Hello." He smiles at everyone.

"Take a seat," I say.

He pulls out his chair and sits opposite me. "How is everyone?" He smiles at them.

They all break into chatter with him. A new hot guy at the table seems to be very exciting.

I sip my drink as I watch him. He's being friendly and nice, answering all their questions and trying really hard to make conversation.

So un-Nathan-Mercer-like.

"So, what do you do, Nathan?" Annie asks.

"I'm a cardiologist," he says.

I can almost see the girls' eyes lighting up.

"And do you have a partner Nathan?" someone asks.

"Yes, I do. A beautiful girlfriend, very much in love." He smiles.

I watch him command the table as everyone hangs on his every word.

"How long have you been with her?"

His eyes flicker to me. "Ten years."

My heart swells.

"Ten years?" Annie gasps. "And you haven't married her yet?"

"Ah." He smiles and drops his head, as if embarrassed. "We took the long way around. Maybe one day."

His eyes come back to linger on me.

"If I can talk her into it," he adds, we stare at each other across the table.

What am I doing?

I love him. He loves me...

But I don't trust him, and the hurt still lingers.

I don't want to jump back into a relationship. I can't go through that again.

I just can't.

But then...

"What's your favorite hobby, Nathan?" someone else asks. This is like a really bad dating app. Who cares about his hobbies?

"Horse riding," he answers without missing a beat.

I bite the inside of my cheek to stop myself from laughing. He's never been horse riding in his life.

He raises his eyebrow across the table at me, and I know he means sex.

I smile against my glass. That's actually true. Sex is definitely his favorite hobby.

Three hours later, Nathan has talked to everyone in the club, and his friendliness is at an all-time high. I've never seen him trying so hard to be nice. He's standing at the bar, ordering drinks, and I go and stand beside him. I've had more than enough of his top shelf margaritas, and I'm feeling very relaxed.

"So, Mr. Mercer."

"Yes." He gives me a slow sexy smile. "That's my name."

"Are you going to tell me your plan?"

"That depends."

"On what?"

"Well, you have to agree to it before I tell you."

I laugh. "Do you really think I'm that stupid?"

"I'm hoping so." He takes a sip of his drink.

"Tell me the plan."

"Well..." He inhales sharply, as if he's steeling himself. "You only want to be friends?"

"Correct."

"But I only want you. "

We stare at each other as the air crackles between us.

"So... I've come up with a compromise, so to speak. I think this will suit us both."

"Which is?"

"I'm really not sure how you are going to react to this, and it could completely backfire here."

I roll my eyes. "Just spit it out."

He hesitates for a moment. "How would you feel about being friends with benefits?"

I stare at him, dumbfounded.

"But you know it would just keep me... well, both of us, really... physically satisfied while you..." He trips over his words.

"While I what?"

"Decide on our future."

I stare at him, what in the world? This is the last thing that I was expecting him to say.

"No pressure. No expectations," he continues. "Just living in the moment for a while." He shrugs as if this makes complete sense.

I roll my lips to hide my smile. "So, you want to use my body as a booty-call?"

"No... I want you to use my body as a booty-call."

"And what body part are you going to be benefiting me with?"

"Right now?"

I nod as our eyes lock.

"My tongue".

I raise my eyebrow.

"I want to lay you out, spread those pretty thighs apart and lick you up. It's been way too long since you came on my tongue."

I get a visual of Nathan's head between my legs, and I get tingles down there. *That'll do it.*

"Hmm, interesting concept," I reply dryly, as I act uninterested.

He smirks. "I think so."

"No expectations?" I raise my eyebrow.

"Not a one."

"No promises?"

"Orgasms are the only sure thing."

"Hmm." My mind begins to run at a million miles per minute. This could be the perfect plan. I get to have him, but I'm not tied down if things go pear-shaped.

"What about other people?" I ask.

"What about other people?" He replies.

"Would you be sleeping with other people?"

"Well, seeing how I've been alone for six months and haven't, I don't see that happening."

"Have you forgotten the strippers?"

"No. But I wish you would," he mutters dryly. "Can you wipe that from your memory bank?"

"Unfortunately, not." I sip my drink. "The other people is a deal breaker for me. I don't want a public booty-call."

He smiles broadly, knowing he nearly has me. "No other people."

"Hmm." I sip my drink as we stare at each other.

The air crackles with possibilities.

"So?" I watch on as in slow motion his tongue darts out and

swipes out over his bottom lip. My sex clenches as I imagine it licking my most sensitive parts.

"What do you say?" he prompts me.

"I suppose you can have a trial."

"A trial?" he asks in surprise. "What the fuck does that mean?"

"I mean, if I'm offering a booty-call position, you can try out for it. No promises, though."

"You're wrong. There is one promise." He steps forward, and he drops his lips to my ear. His breath dusts my skin. Goosebumps scatter up my back at his close proximity. His hand drops to my waist, and he squeezes me hard. "I promise to fuck you so damn good, baby, you won't be walking for a week."

Play it cool.

"We'll see," I reply.

"We going?" he asks.

I nod. "I suppose."

He grabs my behind and pulls my body hard up against his. "Go and tell your friends that you have to go because you have a cock to ride."

I giggle. "Who said romance is dead?"

"This is a booty-call, Eliza. Romance has nothing to do with it."

"You like saying those words, don't you? You said it ten times already."

"Booty-call," he mouths with a smirk, and I smile up at him.

It does sound kind of good.

He bends and his lips take mine. There's a little tongue and a little suction, and a big flood of arousal between my legs. He turns me away from him and slaps me on the behind. "Hurry the fuck up."

· · ·

I close my eyes as I put the key into my front door with nerves flooding my system.

It's been a long time since I've been touched.

Since I've touched him.

Nathan stands close—so close that I can feel the heat from his body radiating through mine. He pulls my hair to one side and kisses my neck with an open mouth. He grazes his teeth on my earlobe and I close my eyes. He bites me again and again, and my nipples harden. He splays his hand over my stomach and pulls me back onto his erection. Teeth sink into my neck, and my eyes flutter with arousal.

Oh hell.

I feel a dull ache between my legs. He feels big... good.

As hard as a fucking rock.

I feel his lips move to my ear as I stand facing the door. His breath quivers on the inhale, as if he's barely hanging onto control.

"Open the door, Eliza," he whispers.

I turn the key, and he pushes me forward and kicks the door shut with his foot.

His eyes dart around my tiny studio apartment, and then come back to rest on me.

Thump, thump, thump goes my heart.

He seems different, more intense, more aroused. *Just more.*

He sits on the end of the bed and leans back on his outstretched hands. "Take your clothes off. Now."

Jeez.

"Are you serious?"

"Do it."

I slide my dress over one shoulder.

His eyes dance with fire as he watches on.

Then, once over the other shoulder, I slowly wiggle it

down over my hips. It falls and pools on the floor around my feet. I stand before him in lacy black panties and a matching bra.

"All of it."

I put my hands on my hips in protest, and he raises an impatient eyebrow. "Eliza."

Oh hell, I'm not sure about this booty-call thing. It seems to be going all his way.

I swallow the lump in my throat and reach around to unlatch my bra before I toss it to the side.

He gives me a slow, sexy smile, and he gestures to my panties with his chin. "Take them off."

Be the best damn booty-call he ever had.

With my eyes locked on his, I slide my panties down over my hips and step out of them.

He licks his lips as he inhales sharply. He stands, and in one quick movement, he takes my nipple in his mouth and bites me hard. I whimper as he moves to my other breast. He bites that, too, and he grabs my breasts aggressively.

"Fuck, I love your tits." He growls around my nipple. His dark eyes are locked on mine. I can see his tongue as it flicks over my hardened nipple. He's totally lost to his arousal and it's fucking hot.

Oh hell, I tip my head back to the ceiling, and I shudder hard. *Calm down, calm down.*

I swear, I'm going to come.

He throws me on the bed and spreads my legs. Then, he stands over me, his eyes roaming over my open, pink flesh.

Let's get straight to it then.

I feel like I can hardly breathe. Is there any air in here?

His shirt is lifted off, revealing his broad shoulders. His stomach is rippled with muscle, and he has a scattering of dark hair across his chest. A trail of hair picks up at his navel and disappears into his black jeans.

Dear God, he's beautiful—more beautiful than I remember.

"Touch yourself," he murmurs with his eyes locked on my sex. "Spread those pretty little lips and touch yourself for me."

My back arches off the bed. Oh man, I forgot how intense Nathan is in the bedroom. He's off the charts.

I run my hand down over my clavicle, and then over my breasts, moving lower... lower.

His dark eyes watch on.

I spread my lips with my fingers, and a trace of a smile crosses his face. He's holding his breath. "That's it," he whispers. "Go deep, baby."

Fuck.

I slide my finger into my sex, and he unfastens the top button of his jeans aggressively.

"Two," he commands.

I slide two fingers in, and he inhales sharply as his eyes flutter closed.

"Fuck yourself." He slides his jeans and boxers down his legs.

His cock is rock hard as it hangs heavily between his legs. Thick veins run down its length, and its head is engorged and a beautiful shade of dark pink.

Ready to fuck.

Spurred on by the sight, I begin to work my sex. My legs are open, and fucking hell, I'm going to come without him laying a finger on me.

"That's it, baby. Harder." He hisses.

He takes his cock in his hand and begins to stroke himself. I can see all the muscles in his shoulders and chest as he works himself, and my back arches off the bed.

He jerks himself hard as I watch on in awe, and pre-ejaculate drips from his end. He leans over me and smears it across my lips.

I go to take him in my mouth, and he pulls away from me.

"My turn." He drops between my legs and spreads them wide. He kisses my sex softly, and his thick tongue darts out and licks me, making me buck beneath him.

Dear God.

"Oh, I've missed Tiny," he purrs, and I smile goofily at the ceiling. He spreads me with his fingers and licks me again. Before long, he is eating me deep, using long, hard licks where his tongue flutters deep within me.

I shudder as he holds my legs back and begins to eat me with his whole face. His whiskers, his nose, his lips... he's all in, as if branding himself with my scent.

The sensation is just too much, and I shudder. He bites my clit and I cry out as an orgasm rips through me. "Ah!" I whimper.

He takes his time and licks me more, cleaning me up. Now it's deeper, more sensual, and his eyes are closed. This feels so intimate.

I've missed him.

I forgot what it felt like to be worshipped, and I scrunch the sheets beneath as my legs hang in the air.

"Nathan," I pant.

His eyes open, this time they are dark. With his eyes locked on mine, he nibbles my clit as my arousal begins to build again.

"Nathan!" I beg. "Fuck me!"

He smiles against my sex. He's loving this even more than I am.

He stands and rolls a condom on, and then he comes over me. He lifts my legs and puts them over his shoulders. Oh shit.

"Careful," I whimper.

"Your body loves my cock, Eliza. She sucks him in."

He pushes forward, nailing me to the mattress, and I whimper beneath him. "Easy," I beg.

He stays still, and my sex ripples around him as she adjusts to his size. Fuck, he's a big man.

"Kiss me," I breathe.

His eyes close and his lips take mine as we both get lost in the moment.

Our kiss is deep, passionate, and everything that we've missed about each over the last six months.

This is it. This is what I've missed. This feeling that no one else has ever given me.

We stay still, his body deep in mine as we kiss tenderly. It's as if we have all night to kiss—all night to enjoy each other.

"I'm going to move, baby," he breathes.

I know this is supposed to be a cheap booty-call, but all I can feel between us is tenderness.

Love.

I nod as I hold his face in my hands. I need him close to me.

He slowly slides out. My knees are up against his chest, and I feel the burn. "Oh." I wince.

"Too good." He breathes as he takes my lips in his. "Let me in, baby; open up." He slowly circles his hips as he tries to loosen me up. I feel a glimmer of arousal.

"That's it," I whisper.

He smiles down at me and repeats the delicious movement. I get a rush of cream and open right up. We both feel it, and he slides in easily. "Yessss," he purrs.

I giggle, excited that my body has decided to let me play.

He spreads his knees wide and begins to thrust slowly. We kiss as a sheen of perspiration dusts our bodies.

"Nathe," I whimper as I hold his face in my hands.

"I know, baby," he pants as he lifts my legs higher. He straightens his arms and goes deeper. "I know." His mouth hangs slack as his pumps gets harder and harder. I watch his beautiful face as it contorts, and I rise onto my elbows to kiss him.

We fall still for a moment as we kiss, as if forgetting we are in the middle of hard fucking. Our tongues tenderly slide together.

"I missed you," he murmurs against my mouth.

My heart melts. "I missed you more."

Something cracks inside of him, and he tips his head back and slams in hard. "You have to come. You have to come," he moans. "You have to fucking come."

"Ahh!" He pulls out and, once again, his mouth is on my sex. He flicks his tongue over my clitoris. My chest rises and falls as I try to catch my breath. My hands are on his damp shoulders.

I moan. "Oh..." I twist to get away from his onslaught.

He was going to come and he didn't want to before me. He wants to make sure I come, too. He's always the perfect lover.

Every single time.

This is too intimate, too real, *too perfect.*

I'm going to come.

"Nathan!" I cry. "Get back on top of me. Now!"

He slides in deep again, and I moan as I clench down hard and come in a rush.

Nathan's eyes roll back in his head as he watches me, and he lets loose with deep, hard pumps. The bed begins to hit the wall with force. The sound of our skin slapping echoes throughout the room.

His moan is deep and guttural, and he holds himself deep as he comes in a rush.

We move together slowly to completely empty his body into mine, and then he falls onto his elbows and kisses me tenderly. We smile against each other's lips.

My man is home.

I wake hours later in a state of exhaustion. Nathan and I have been at it for hours, until we couldn't physically do it anymore. We fell asleep in each other's arms in a state of bliss. I lean up onto my elbows. It's dark, and Nathan is now out of bed and dressing.

"What are you doing?" I ask.

"I've got to go."

I frown. It's still dark out. "What, why?"

"I'm on an early flight."

"Oh." My heart sinks. "Okay."

He sits on the side of the bed and smiles as he brushes the hair back from my forehead. "You were incredible."

I smile goofily at him.

"We should do it again sometime."

What?

My dream instantly dissipates.

Oh, the casual thing. He's playing the game. *Of course he is.*

I roll my lips to try to hide my smile. "Yeah, I'll think about it," I reply casually.

He stands in a rush, annoyed by my answer.

I roll over onto my side and put my back to him. "Can you lock the door on your way out, baby?" I scrunch my face into my pillow, knowing full well that he will be going postal on the inside.

"I'm going," he says.

"Yeah, I know." I smile into my pillow. He wants me to

demand that we get back together. Well, too bad, I'm not. I wasn't joking the other day, being a bitch really is fun.

"Don't call me, I'll call you." He huffs.

"I wasn't going to. Have a safe flight," I say casually.

He hesitates, and I know he wants to lose his shit. "I'm going," he repeats.

"Yeah, okay. God, I'm trying to sleep here, Nathan."

He inhales sharply, and he marches out the door. It slams behind him.

I roll onto my back and smile goofily at the ceiling. Holy shit.

Who am I?

29

Eliza

I EMPTY the last of the boxes and look around my little apartment. I love it.

It feels like home already. I flew in last Sunday and have spent the week unpacking and settling in. I rejoined my old gym and caught up with my friends. I start work on Wednesday.

It's Sunday night, and I haven't heard from Nathan all week. I wanted to get settled and not call him the minute I landed in San Francisco. I need to be independent and, damn it, I'm going to try my hardest to do it.

I do really want to see him, though. He's all I can think about, and I can't tell you the number of times I've nearly called him. I told myself all week that if I hadn't heard from him by Sunday, I can call him. Tonight is the night.

My phone dances across my coffee table, and the name Phyllis lights up the screen.

Nathan's mom. "Hello," I answer.

"Hello, darling, how is my favorite girl settling in?"

"I'm great. Feels good to be back home." I look around at my surroundings. "My apartment is so cute. Wait till you see it."

"Have you started work yet?"

"No, I start on Wednesday."

"At Memorial, right?"

"Yeah." I smile, and a strange thought comes to mind. Has she been spying on me for Nathan? He did say she knows everything and yet, never once has she made out that she has.

Hmm. I wonder if he asked her to check on me for him.

"How are you?" I ask.

"Good, good. Nothing new here. Back to you. Have you caught up with all of your friends?"

"Yes, I've been out to dinner every night this week."

"Oh..." She seems taken aback. "Have you seen Nathan at all?"

And there it is. She knows I haven't. "Not yet. Hopefully soon."

"You should let him know you're in town. He would love to see you."

"Yeah, I was going to call him tonight, actually."

"Oh, great." She gasps as if her work is done. "Well, I'll let you get off the phone then so you can call him."

"He's probably busy."

"No, he has nothing going on." She snaps as if frustrated.

I smile broadly. Why, you sly, old fox. "Okay, I might. I'll see how I feel."

"Well, you should just go over there."

"I'll see." I bite my bottom lip to stop myself from laughing out loud. How didn't I see her fishing for information before?

She hesitates, and I know she's wondering how to ensure I call him. "He'd love to see you."

"Yes, I'll call him. I promise."

"Great. Goodbye, dear."

I hang up and giggle. His mother is in matchmaking heaven. I fall onto the sofa and scroll through my phone. What will I text him?

Hmm, what says friends with benefits without expectations? I scroll through as I think. I know.

An idea comes to me, and I get the giggles as I type in an emoji.

I wish I could see his face when he opens this. I text him.

?

I hit send and burst out laughing.

My phone pings almost immediately.

Tonight?

I smile like a school girl as I type in my reply.

Yes, please.
xoxo

I wait for his reply. I imagine him on his couch, pondering his reply.

What's your address?

I jig on the couch and type in my address, and then another message bounces in.

About 8:30 p.m.?

I jump from the couch in excitement.

Sounds great.
xoxo

I glance at my watch. Oh shit, that's only an hour away. I need to shower and wash my hair. I glance down at my legs. I need laser. This won't do. I need to be irresistible and downright fucking hot.

I make my way to the bathroom and get my razor out. Hmm, it's not in my makeup bag. I tear through the bathroom cabinet. None.

"Shit. Where are all my fucking razors?" I haven't seen any since the move. Did I throw them all out?

Surely not?

I march into my bedroom and begin to look through my toiletries like a mad woman. You don't send someone an eggplant and then turn up hairy.

I can't believe I sent someone an eggplant. I giggle at the prospect. What the hell? I've hit a new low.

I keep looking for a razor on a mission. "Fuck it."

I go back into the bathroom and tear the cupboard apart and then sit on the floor in a dilemma.

I have two options: run to the store two blocks away and grab a razor, or turn up looking like a gorilla.

"Store." I grab my keys and run out the door in a rush.

An hour later, I pour myself a wine. The last hour has felt like running a marathon. I felt like I was in the Amazing Race or something. The closest store was out of razors, so I ran to the one six blocks away, got caught in the rain, my shoe got caught in a drain, and I fell over and bruised my knees. I ran all the way home and shaved my legs and all my bits, then I discovered that I'm out of hair conditioner after I've already washed it. So now I look like a fuzzy bear... but at least my body is as smooth as a baby's bottom.

Just how he likes it.

I sip my wine. He had better appreciate all of this preparation.

There's knock on the door and I hunch my shoulders up in excitement.

He's here.

I tighten the cord on my silk robe I'm naked underneath it, aiming to be a sex kitten. I open the door in a rush.

My face falls when I see a man standing there. "Delivery for Eliza Bennet."

"Oh." I frown. "It's very late."

The delivery man widens his eyes. "And urgent, apparently."

It's a big box, hmm. "Okay."

"Please sign here." He hands me over his screen. I sign it and go back inside.

I shut the door and look at the large, pink box.

"What in the world?" I slowly take the lid off and peer into the box. It's a cane basket, filled with eggplants.

I burst out laughing. "Are you serious?" Oh my God, only him. There's a small white envelope, too. I open the card and read it.

You ask,
I deliver.

x

I take an eggplant out, hold it in my hand, and I laugh.
Only Nathan.

Nathan

I smile against my wine glass as I imagine Eliza opening the box.

Well, it serves her right for being a smartass.

I glance at my watch, willing to bet any money that she turns up here. I know her better than she knows herself, and I know that she won't not see me if she has made up her mind to do so.

I sip my red wine and roll it around my mouth when there's a knock at the door.

I smile and stand up. *Right on cue.*

I open the door. "Yes?"

She's standing in the foyer, wearing her cream, silk robe. She has an overnight bag with her. Her long, dark hair is down, and she smiles, revealing her beautiful dimples.

"Eliza!" I act surprised.

She rises onto her toes and kisses me quickly. "That wasn't the kind of eggplant I had in mind, Nathan."

"Oh, really?" I raise a brow and my eyes drop down her body as the crisp smell of soap teases my senses. "Did you catch a cab here wearing only that?"

"Uh-huh." She marches past me, into the apartment. "The driver had a semi."

I smile. "I don't doubt it." I close the door and watch her as she looks around.

"I forgot how beautiful this apartment is."

I look around as I try to see it through her eyes. "Wine?" I ask.

"Yes, please."

I go the kitchen and pour her a red wine, refilling mine, too. "I've only just come back," I admit.

She sits up on the counter like she always does, and I stand between her legs.

"What do you mean?" She lifts the glass to her lips, and my cock clenches in anticipation as I watch her. Wonderful memories of her sitting on the counter just like this flood back like a tidal wave.

I need her back.

"I didn't come here for a long time. I stayed at my old apartment," I continue.

"Why not?"

"I don't know. After I had the meltdown, I didn't want to come back."

Her face falls. "You had a meltdown?"

I nod. "I had to take a couple of weeks off work."

She drops her head and stares at the floor for a moment.

"What?" I ask.

"It makes me sad that I wasn't here for you." She grabs my

528

T-shirt and pulls me in for a kiss. It's slow and sensual, and it wakes up all those intimate memories of us. "Have you spoken to anyone about this meltdown?" she asks softly as she pushes the hair back from my face.

"No." I kiss her again, my tongue sweeping through her open mouth.

Fuck, *the way she kisses.*

"I'll come with you, if you want." She watches me for a moment. "Don't you want to know why?"

"I don't want to think about it. And I know why. I was under a lot of stress."

"Baby." She kisses me again. "You also have some unsettled issues. *We* have unsettled issues." She kisses me again as if to soften the blow. "I'll come to the therapy session with you if you want. I'd like to get to the bottom of our problems. I want to fix them."

I smile down at my beautiful girl, and hope fills me. Maybe we are going to be all right.

"You'd do that?" I ask.

"Of course, I would."

I stare at her for a moment and narrow my eyes. "Did you already fuck the eggplant?"

"What?" She smiles. "Why would you say that?"

"Well... you're being all sweet and Eliza-like. Kind of how you are after you've had the crazy fucked out of you."

She bursts out laughing, and I smile as I watch her. "You don't actually fuck the eggplant." She smiles. "It's a figure of speech, Nathan."

"Yeah, you do," I tease. "The eggplant goes into Tiny while I fuck your ass."

Her face falls. "Wait... what? Since when?"

"Everyone knows that."

"I thought it was just like a funny thing people sent."

I grab a handful of her hair and pull her face back to meet mine. "You really should do more research on your emojis before you send them out."

"Obviously." She smiles as I kiss her. "I should have asked for a dick pic instead."

She's joking, and I'm joking, but I can't hide my feelings.

I want her back. I want us back.

I kiss her softly. "Why would you want a dick pic when you could have the real thing for forever?"

We fall serious as we stare at each other and an ocean of closeness swims between us. "Nathe, you know I love you, right?" she whispers as her eyes search mine.

"Then come home!" I kiss her softly to plead my case. "Please, come home. I can't live without you for another moment."

"We need some time apart to readjust. I just want to date for a while."

"How long?"

"I don't know. I can't push it. You understand, don't you? You broke my heart, Nathan. I have to take my time with this. I just can't switch it back on."

I stare at her but can't push words of acceptance past my lips, they will just be a lie.

I don't want another second apart.

I clench my jaw to hold my tongue. I want to scream and yell and fight and argue my case... but I know that me throwing a tantrum is only going to push her further away. I exhale heavily. I have to wait this out and use my head or I *will* lose her forever.

"I can make an appointment with a therapist if you want?" she offers.

"I'll do it."

"Do you want me to come?" She asks softly.

I shudder at the thought of her hearing something that I don't want her to. "No, I want to go alone."

"Okay." She smiles up at me and kisses my lips. "We should probably move into the living room."

"We should?"

"Uh-huh." She jumps down and leads me out into the living room. She sits me down on the couch. She takes a cushion and puts it on the floor between my legs.

My arousal begins to ignite as I watch her. She puts her hair into a bun, and then she drops to her knees in front of me.

"What are you doing?" I rasp.

She unzips my jeans and pulls them open with a sharp snap. "Worshipping my eggplant." She takes me in her mouth, and her tongue ripples around my cock.

I tip my head back and spread my legs wide. "That's it," I whisper.

She smiles around me and cups my balls as she flicks her tongue over my end.

I feel a fire start within me. I watch as her cheeks hollow when she sucks.

Eliza gives the best head jobs on Earth. There's nobody hotter than her.

I clench my jaw to try and hold myself back.

She begins to work me hard with her hand, and pre-ejaculate beads. She moans softly when she tastes it.

Her eyes darken as she watches me. "Fuck my mouth," she breathes around me.

I exhale heavily and take her head in my hands as I slide my cock deep down her throat. "I will, baby. I will."

Eliza

Nathan's alarm goes off and I smile sleepily. I'm wrapped in his arms, feeling like a goddess. Something has changed between us. We didn't fuck last night; we made love.

Sweet, tender love. I know Nathan's body was made for fucking but his heart was made for loving, and I loved it hard last night. The closeness between us is back, and with every kiss, every touch, I lose a little more of the hurt we caused each other.

He hits snooze on his phone and then he kisses my temple.

"Play hooky with me today," I say quietly.

I feel him smile behind me. "Don't tempt me." He kisses me again before climbing out of bed and disappearing into the bathroom.

I hear the shower turn on, and I doze back off to sleep. It's so nice having nowhere to go and nothing to do. I could get used to this lifestyle.

Nathan walks back into the bedroom only a few minutes later, making me stir. He's wearing his navy suit, he's all dressed up and he smells delicious. He sits on the side of the bed and leans down to kiss me again.

"I'm going, baby."

I smile sleepily up at him. "Okay."

He brushes the hair back from my forehead. "Don't go back to your place. Stay here." He kisses me softly. "We can have dinner together tonight."

I wince as I remember.... Oh shit.

"I can't tonight." I pull him down on me and kiss him. "Tomorrow night."

"Why not tonight?"

"I have plans." My sleepy relaxed state begins to dissipate.

"What plans?"

I frown. "I'm... I'm having dinner with Henry."

"What?" He jumps to a standing position. "Over my dead fucking body."

"It's only to tell him that I'm not interested in him." I lie back down and close my eyes. It's too early for this shit.

"You haven't told him that you aren't interested yet?"

"I haven't spoken to him, so I'm sure he already knows, but when he asked me to dinner tonight, I thought that telling him in person was the decent thing to do."

He marches out into the living room and I put my forearm over my eyes, what is he doing now?

He storms back in and shoves my phone in my face. "Call him."

"What?"

"You call him now and tell him that we're back together."

"Nathan."

"Fucking *call him!*"

I get out of bed. "I'm not calling him. He was a good friend to me while I was in New York. I owe him the respect of telling him in person."

"No."

"We are not back together yet, Nathan—cut it out. I'll go to dinner and tell him, and then I'll come back to stay here with you afterward."

"No."

"You don't have a choice." I march into the bathroom. I sit down to go to the toilet, and he marches in.

"I saw you kiss him, remember, Eliza? I know what he wants!"

I roll my eyes at his dramatics. "Do you mind?" I gesture to me sitting on the toilet. "I'm kind of busy here."

"Cancel. I mean it."

"Will you get the hell out while I go to the bathroom?" I yell. "Give me some fucking privacy."

He storms out.

So much for waking up in my dreamy love bubble this morning. I finish up and wash my hands. I brush my teeth and try to tame my just-fucked hair with my fingers.

God, I'm a mess.

I walk out to find Nathan pacing. The veins are sticking out in his forehead.

"I'll get ready here. You can drive me there and pick me up, but *I am* going," I say calmly. "The choice is yours, Nathan. I'm not taking your bullshit. You know I don't want him."

"He wants you."

"I don't care." I bark. "I want you!"

His face softens. "You want me?"

"You know I do." I mutter dryly. "Stop acting like the victim here."

He exhales heavily, his jaw still ticking in anger. "You'll be here when I get home?" he asks.

I straighten his tie as I stare up at him. "Yes." I kiss him. It's like taming a fucking tiger being with this man. "And I'll get ready here. You can drop me off, and then I'll call you when it's time to pick me up."

He stares at me, still unhappy about it.

"Nathan, trust me, having this conversation is the last thing I want to do tonight. But I've been avoiding his phone calls, and he's been good to me. I need to do this in person."

He exhales heavily. "Fine."

I smile up at my beautiful man and dust my hands over his broad shoulders.

"You're kind of cute when you're jealous." I smile as I run my fingers through his whiskers.

"Fuck off." He pushes my hand away. "Well, what am I going to eat tonight?"

"Whatever you've been eating while I was gone. You're a big boy now. I'm sure you can make yourself some toast."

He rolls his eyes. "Goodbye."

I kiss his lips, and he pulls away and turns for the door.

"Have a nice day, dear." I smile sweetly.

"Impossible!" The door bangs closed, I smile and climb back into bed. I snuggle in and close my eyes. Things are looking up.

———

What was I thinking?

This was the stupidest of all stupid ideas.

I glance over at my irate cab driver-slash-friends-with-bene-fits-slash-jealous, psycho boyfriend. Nathan grips the steering wheel with white-knuckle force as he glares at the road.

We had a fight over me wearing a dress. Apparently, it was too sexy. I wasn't allowed to have a glass of wine while I was getting ready because I need my wits about me, and now he's trying to tell me how long I have to eat.

He pulls the car up in the parking bay and looks across the road, into the restaurant. "I'll just wait here in the car," he grumbles.

My eyes widen. "Go home, or I am not coming to your house tonight. Cut it out, Nathan. You are acting like a child."

"And you are acting like you don't give a fuck."

T L SWAN

"About what?"

"About me."

My heart sinks. I can't imagine him leaving me to go out to dinner with someone else.

"I'm going to be quick, okay? An hour and a half, tops." I lean over and kiss his lips. "And you are not acting like a friend with benefits," I remind him.

"Because we are not fucking friends with benefits." He growls. "We're back to-fucking-gether."

"How many times can you say fuck in one sentence?" I huff.

"Don't push me, Eliza." He whispers angrily, his eyes look like they are about to explode.

I open the door. "I won't be long." Without looking back, I cross the street and walk into the restaurant.

Henry is sitting at the back. I smile and make my way over to him. He stands and kisses my cheek.

"Hey there, stranger."

"Hi." I fall into my seat.

"Would you like some wine?"

"Sure."

He fills my glass, and I glance over toward the front window. Did Nathan leave?

He'd better have.

"So, here you are, back in God's country." Henry smiles.

I chuckle. "I am."

"How have you settled in?"

"Oh, really good. My new apartment is great and I joined my gym again. I don't start work until Wednesday. What about you? What's happening?"

He rolls his eyes. "Where do I begin?"

. . .

Over the next hour, I laugh and chat with Henry. There isn't anything between us and he knows that. We are just friends. Actual 'just friends', not like the kind of friends Nathan and I are.

We're mid way through our main meals when my phone beeps with a text in my handbag. I discreetly slide it out and put it onto my lap so I can read it. It's from Nathan.

You have ten minutes or I'm coming in there to break his fucking neck.

30

Eliza

OH GOD, here we go.

I begin to eat quickly, is he serious?

I need to get out of here before he busts through the doors like The Hulk.

"So..." Henry smiles. "Why haven't you been answering my calls?"

I swallow the food in my mouth and it scratches my throat.

Oh God. I hit my chest to try and dislodge the chicken.

"I... I think we are better off as friends, don't you?"

"No, why?" He stares at me intently.

"I don't think we... you didn't feel a connection with me. I know you didn't, and neither did I."

"If we gave it some time, I know we would work."

He's not going to let me go without a reason, and I know I have to just come out and say it. "The truth is, Henry, that I got back with Nathan."

He rolls his eyes. "I thought as much."

"Why did you think that?"

"I saw him in New York."

My face falls. "You saw him on the sidewalk?"

"No, I saw him in the restaurant. He was sitting at the bar for our entire date."

My mouth falls open as I imagine poor Nathan watching me laughing, giggling and flirting all night.

"Oh God." I drag my hand down my face. "I'm sorry, Henry. I didn't know he was there, and I most definitely wouldn't want to make you uncomfortable."

"I know." He smiles as his eyes hold mine.

I put my head into my hands. "This is a disaster. I didn't know he was there, I'm so sorry. We talked that weekend, and we've since decided to try again."

"I knew it." He gives an annoyed shake of his head. "That's fine, I understand."

I take his hand across the table. "Thank you for understanding."

"Can I ask you something?"

"Of course."

"What do you see in him?"

I smile softly. "I know how he comes across to the outside world."

"Like a lunatic?"

"I'm not perfect, either, and this time, I know it's going to be different between us. We are going to make it work. It's only new but I think there's hope, you know?"

"How are you going to make it work?"

I look over and see Nathan pacing outside on the sidewalk. I smile at the beautiful rageaholic that he is before I turn my attention back to Henry.

"I've no idea." I pick up my purse, take out some money, and I put it onto the table. I stand and kiss Henry's cheek, and then I put my hand on his shoulder as I walk past him toward the door. "You're a good friend, Henry."

He smiles. "Good luck!" he calls. "You're going to need it."

I giggle to myself. That is the understatement of the year.

I walk toward the door just as Nathan bursts through, and I point to the street outside. "Out," I mouth.

He stands still, his chest is rising and falling as he struggles for air, he looks like he's about to explode. I walk past him and out the door. With one last warning glare at Henry, he turns and follows me.

The car is still parked in the same spot across the road where he had dropped me off...*of course it is.* I should have known he wouldn't leave.

"You took too long." He stammers as he storms to the car. "I hope you have a defibrillator in your handbag because I'm about to have a fucking heart attack, Eliza."

I chuckle as I walk across the road. *This man kills me.*

"This isn't funny." He growls.

I try to open the car door but it's still locked. "Open the door, Nathan."

He opens the door and we both climb in. I look over at his poor, tortured face.

I've put this poor bastard through hell. "Take me home."

He starts the car.

"To my place."

He stops what he's doing and glares at me. "Oh, so you are going to carry on about this?"

"No, I'm going to get some clothes to bring to your house, you moron."

He watches me as if scared I'm about to run. I guess the old me would have.

"I understand why tonight bothered you." I lean over and kiss him. "I never have to see Henry again. I get it, and it's over now."

He frowns, as if surprised. "You do and it is?"

"Yeah." I smile as I run my hand over his two-day growth. "You know what, Nathe? We have to stop carrying on like idiots and start talking to each other. If this is it for us—and we both know that it is—and we want to plan a future together, we won't make it unless we communicate better and grow the fuck up. No more tantrums, no more leaving, no more jealousy, no more spying on people in restaurants."

His face falls.

"Yes, I know about you in New York. No more secrets, and no more fucking bullshit, Nathan."

He smiles softly, as if he's hopeful, too.

"Do we have chocolate at home?" I ask.

"No."

"Well, you better stop at the store then." I sit back and pull my seatbelt over my shoulder casually as if I have this conversation every day. "Hadn't you?"

He stares at me for a moment, and then a slow, sexy smile crosses his face. "I love you, Eliza."

"I know." I smile as I pick up his hand and kiss the back of it before cupping it around my face. "And I love you."

We did it. We got through an argument like adults.

He pulls out into the traffic and I smile as I look out of the window. And just like that, I feel the tectonic plates slide into place. The bullshit between us is over.

We can finally start afresh and look at each other through untainted glasses.

We love each other so much. We have put each other through so much.

And for what?

The games end now.

I walk out of the elevator like I'm a rock star. I'm at Nathan's office, and after our little fight last night—or should I say, lack of fight?—I have a spring in my step.

I have hope for us. Actually, that's not even true. I don't have hope. I know. The time apart wasn't for nothing. It did us both good.

This is it for us. We *are* going to make it.

I walk into the reception area, and Maria lets out an audible gasp. "Eliza." She jumps from her chair and rushes to hug me.

I laugh out loud as she nearly knocks me off my feet. "Hello."

"Oh my gosh, you're back?"

"Yes, I am." I laugh as she holds me at arm's length. "Is he free?" I ask.

"He is." She smiles as she continues to hold me.

"Maria, why aren't you this pleased to see me each morning?" Nathan's distinct voice asks from behind me.

We turn to see Nathan leaning on the doorframe, watching us. He's in his dark charcoal suit, wearing a pale blue shirt and a dark blue tie. He looks every bit the gorgeous, pin-up CEO.

My heart swells. "Hello, Dr. Mercer."

"Hello, Eliza." His eyes hold mine. He's different today. That twinkle is back in his eye. "Maria, you will be relieved to know that Eliza is back in charge of my schedule. Please converse with her on all my engagements from here on in."

"Yes, Doctor." Maria smiles goofily.

"Can you organize a month off with her at some point?" he adds.

I frown in question.

"Are you going away?" Maria asks as she looks between us.

"Yes." His eyes find mine, with the best 'come fuck me' look I have ever seen. "Back to Majorca."

My heart swells.

"Any special occasion?" Maria fishes.

"Maybe." He raises an eyebrow and chucks his chin toward his office. "Block me out for half an hour, Maria."

"Yes, Doctor."

I walk to him. He puts his arm around me, pulls me close, and kisses my temple as we walk toward his office. I nearly fall over in shock. Nathan has never touched me before in front of his employees. I didn't even know if they knew we were together for that brief six weeks. It seems like a lifetime ago now, though. So much has happened since then.

"Awe, you two are so cute!" Haley calls from behind us.

"Back to work!" he barks. "I'm sure you've better things to do."

"Not really!" she calls back.

He pulls me into his office, and his lips find mine as he kicks the door closed behind us.

I giggle into his kiss. "I'll come and see you every day if this is the reception I get."

"Or you could just work for me all the time?" His tongue sweeps through my open mouth.

"You're wrecking it," I murmur. "Stop talking."

He falls into his chair and pulls me down onto his lap. We

kiss again and again, and I can feel his erection beneath me. "Let's go into my consultation room," he breathes.

"No chance."

His hand slides over my breasts and he kneads them hard. "Why not? We're breaking all the rules here, anyway," he whispers into my ear.

"Nathan, no," I whisper. "We're not having sex with all those people just outside the door. What if they come in?"

"Then they'll have something to look at." He bites my neck, and goosebumps scatter my arms. His phone dances across the table, and the name Amanda lights up the screen. "I have to take this." He nips me with his teeth again. "Hello?"

"Nathan, it's Amanda." I can hear what she is saying as clear as day.

"Hello."

"I forgot to email you the transcript of our session."

"Oh." He frowns. "Okay."

"What's your email address?"

His eyes find mine. "Actually... can you send it to Eliza?"

"Ah, Nathan, this is wonderful progress. Yes, I would love to. What's her email address?"

He tells her my email address before he nips my neck with his teeth again.

"Okay, perfect, I'll send it now."

"Oh and, Amanda?" He smiles wistfully. "Thank you. You've helped me... more than you know."

"You're most welcome. It's been my pleasure."

I don't know who she is but whatever she said to him has healed something. He hangs up, and I don't ask who it is. I don't care.

"That was my new therapist," he says.

I smile, surprised that he offered information without me pushing for it.

Who is this man, and what has he done with my Nathan?

"A woman. How very liberated of you."

He chuckles. "She's sending the recording of our session to you."

"Why?" I frown.

He shrugs and nips my neck again. "You said no more secrets."

I smile as I stretch my neck to give him access. "I did, didn't I?"

"Although, this may just prove how fucked up I really am."

I giggle as I kiss him. "I love your fucked up." We smile against each other's lips.

"I forgot to tell you," he says. "This weekend, I'm getting a kitten."

I frown. "A what?"

He shrugs as he tries to act casual.

I've been trying to get a cat for years and he would never let me. "You told me you were allergic."

"Maybe not." He smirks.

"You don't like cats."

"But you do."

My mouth falls open. "Nathan Mercer, you wouldn't stoop so low as to get a kitten to make me move back in with you, would you?"

He raises an eyebrow and gives me that 'come fuck me' look again.

I whisper, "Diabolical."

He chuckles and I stand, leading him into the consultation room by his hand. "You have seven minutes to fuck me."

He slams me up against the wall, and his lips drop to my neck. "I only need five."

———

I struggle with the grocery bags as I let myself into Nathan's apartment.

I wanted to come back and make a special dinner for us. I've missed cooking for him. It's 2:00 p.m., and after my R-rated lunch date in the consultation room, I'm buzzing.

Everything just feels so different this time.

Like it's meant to be.

I drop the shopping bags in the kitchen and put my favorite play list on.

I open the fridge and see a bottle of our favorite wine. It's too early for wine.

Why not?

I smile broadly as I take it out, you know what? Fuck it. After the shitty six months I've just had, I'm letting myself just be for a while. If I want a glass of wine at 2pm....then damn it, I'm having it.

I pour myself a glass and smile as I take a sip. I can hardly wipe the goofy smile from my face. I'm not getting ahead of myself or anything but this feels promising.

I make my marinade, and I baste the beef and wrap it before I put it into the fridge to cook later. I peel the apples and put them on the stove top to breakdown. I'm making Nathan's favorite apple pie for dessert. Next, I'll make the shortcrust pastry. I forgot how wonderful it is to cook for someone. The music plays through the apartment, and I smile to myself as I dance and chop. My mind goes over our little lunchtime rendezvous.

I go over the last few days and how me not falling into Nathan's arms in New York worked out well. I have my own apartment and my independence now. I don't feel pressured or insecure. I feel like me—like how I'm supposed to feel.

And him asking his new therapist to send me the transcripts is a big deal. Nathan has always been so secretive.

Actually, I wonder if she sent them. I dry my hands on a tea towel and grab my phone to check my emails.

Amanda Beynon Therapy Transcripts.

I click on the first one and hit play. I stand my phone up against the window sill so I can listen as I continue with my pastry.

I hear a rustling, and I turn up the volume on my phone as I concentrate to hear them.

"Hello, Nathan," a female voice says. "I'm Amanda."

I listen intently as I spread the flour over the counter, they must be shaking hands.

"Hi. Nathan Mercer."

"Please take a seat. Lay it back until you're comfortable."

I smile as I visualize Nathan lying on her office chair.

"What brings you here today?" Amanda asks.

"Um." He hesitates. "I'm... I'm not ... doing so well."

I frown and stop what I'm doing so I can concentrate. The hairs on the back of my neck stand to attention.

"Tell me about what's going on," she replies.

"I, ... I had." He stops.

My heart drops, he's struggling to talk.

"Take your time," Amanda says softly. She's kind and caring, I can hear it in her voice.

"I just..." He pauses again. "I broke up with my girlfriend and I don't seem to be able to move on."

"Okay, I see. How long ago did this happen?"

"Six months."

I frown. Wait. Is this from before we reconnected?

"Have you seen her since?" she asks.

"No."

Oh shit, it *is* before we saw each other again.

"I see." She listens for a moment. "And why did you end your relationship?"

"She left me." He sighs sadly.

"Why was that?"

"She didn't love me enough to stay."

"What's her name?"

"Eliza."

"Did Eliza tell you that?" Amanda asks.

"Yes, and she moved to New York to get away from me."

My heart drops.

"Were there any issues between you?"

"A million," he replies, monotone, I close my eyes as I am transported back to the darkness.

"Tell me about Eliza," Amanda says softly.

I hold my breath "She's the most beautiful person I know. Selfless and sweet."

"You sound very close."

"She's more myself than I am," he replies softly.

My eyes fill with tears.

"What happened between you?" she asks.

"We were best friends for ten years and I was with other people. Men."

"How do you identify your sexuality, Nathan?"

"Pansexual," he replies without hesitation.

My eyebrows rise. Wow, he seems definite on that answer now.

Progress.

"But while we were friends, I fell in love with her."

I smile softly.

"How long were you together?"

"Six weeks."

"How long were you in love with her before that?"

"Ten years.

I sip my wine, fascinated by what I'm hearing.

"Although, I didn't realize it for a long time."

"And how did you finally come to that realization?"

"I couldn't bring myself to have sex with anyone else. I only wanted to be with her."

"So, you were having sex with her the entire time?"

"No, we were platonic friends. But I would rather go without sex than sleep beside someone else. In the end, I couldn't betray her. Not even if I had wanted to."

"Sleeping beside her was important to you?"

"She was the best thing in my life."

I close my eyes in regret. *Why didn't he just talk to me.*

"What was the catalyst for your breakup?" Amanda asks.

"She thinks that I only wanted to be with her so that I could have children."

My heart sinks, and the apple hisses in the saucer on the hotplate. "Shit." I snap as I lift it off the heat.

"How did that make you feel?" Amanda asks.

Silence...

"Nathan," she urges. "Tell me how that made you feel."

"I don't want to talk about it."

"Aren't you here to sort this problem out?"

"I... I can't talk about it," he stammers. "I have to go."

549

I frown as I listen. What? He's going to just walk out?

"Sit back down, Nathan," she demands.

Silence.

With a shaky hand, I sip my wine.

"I would like to talk about it if we can," Amanda says.

"I can't." Nathan stammers and I can hear the stress in his voice. "I tried."

Nerves dance in my stomach.

"Who did you try and talk to about it?"

"Eliza," he replies softly.

"What did Eliza say?"

"She fobbed it off—said I was overreacting," he whispers.

God, I did.

"She was more worried about my ex."

"What about your ex?"

"He told her that he wanted me back, the day after I found out what she thought of me."

"How did that make you feel?"

"I was too upset about Eliza to care about Robert. He's irrelevant."

"You don't feel the same about him?"

"No. Eliza knew that. I told her many times I didn't have feelings for him."

"Does Eliza know how much she hurt you?"

Silence.

"Did you talk to Eliza about how you felt?" Amanda prompts.

"I couldn't." He pauses. "I didn't want to be near her."

"Why not?"

"Because I loved her with everything I had and still, it wasn't enough."

I get a lump in my throat.

Fuck.

"I don't know why I couldn't talk to her, but I couldn't. I still can't. I just... can't talk about it to anyone, even though I want to. I don't know. It's fucking weird."

"Nathan." Amanda pauses. "Have you ever heard of burnout?"

"Like stress, you mean?"

"Burnout is the experience of physical, emotional, and mental exhaustion, often caused by long-term involvement in emotionally demanding situations."

"What does that mean?"

"Could it be, Nathan, that you shut down on Eliza because you were battling with yourself over your love for her, and you had been for a long time?"

What does she mean by that?

Silence.

"Is it possible that Eliza verbalized your deepest fear?"

After a while, he softly says, "I already knew."

"You knew what?" Amanda asks.

"Deep down, I knew she would think that I only wanted her for a child."

"Why?"

"Because I don't fit into society's box and she does."

"How does that make you feel?"

"Sad."

"Because...?" Amanda prompts.

"Because as much as I want to believe in it, love isn't love."

My eyes fill with tears.

"Out of everyone in the world, Eliza knows me better than anyone, and if she doesn't believe in my heart," he whispers sadly, "nobody ever will."

The tears break free and roll down my face.

"Oh, Nathe," I whisper. This was before he read my letter.

He actually believed I didn't love him.

Amanda goes on to say something else but I don't want to hear any more.

I can't stand it.

I fumble with my phone and turn it off. Then I throw my phone out onto the couch in the living room.

I pour myself another wine so fast that it sloshes over the side of the glass. My heart is racing in despair. Enough is enough.

No more pain.

I sit at the kitchen counter and wipe my eyes. Nathan will be home soon.

I've cooked his favorite dinner and dessert. I've showered and primped and now I just feel so sad.

So guilty, and *so, so stupid.*

Nathan and I broke each other's hearts because we couldn't communicate. Now that I've heard those transcripts, it's opened back up my emotions, and everything feels so real and raw.

I can't stop crying.

I've listened to them all and I can feel his pain. I imagine him heartbroken and going to a stripper for sex. I can't stand it.

I hear the key in the door, and I quickly wipe my eyes.

"Hey!" he calls happily. He walks around the corner, sees me, and his face falls. "What's wrong?"

His silhouette blurs. "I'm so sorry, Nathe," I whisper.

His brow furrows in confusion.

"Love *is* love." I wince through my tears. "I should never have left."

He stares at me for a moment.

"Can you forgive me?" I whisper.

He rushes to me and wraps me in his arms. "It was my fault. I should have told you."

"No—"

"Ssh," he cuts me off as he kisses my lips. The emotion between us is so strong that it tears my heart wide open.

"I'm moving back in, no more games," I murmur as he kisses me. "I'll never leave you again."

We cling to each other, and he drops his head to my neck as he holds me tightly.

And it's still there, the pain in his grip.

The person who he loves the most left him because he was different to anyone else she knew.

What kind of person does that?

"I'm sorry, I'm sorry," I whisper again and again as I hold him.

He pulls back to look at me, and he wipes my eyes as he smiles. "Stop, it's over, and we're never going back there. It's time to move on from both of our issues."

I smile up at him as I push the hair back from his forehead. "I love you, Nathe. More than anything, I love you. Tell me how to make this up to you."

"I love you, too." He holds me cheek to cheek and smiles. "There is one thing you can do," he says softly.

"What's that?"

His eyes meet mine, "Marry me." His eyes twinkle with a certain something.

My heart stops.

"Are you serious?" I whisper.

"Too soon?" He closes his eyes, as if he's filled with regret. "Oh, man, I was supposed to wait..."

"For what?"

"For me to plan something romantic and perfect that you would never forget." He kisses me softly. "But I can't wait any longer." He kisses me again. "I love you too much."

Our kiss deepens and, oh, I couldn't love this man any more than I do, and yet I know tomorrow, I will.

"What do you say, Lize?" He smiles softly. "Do you want to be my wife?"

"You bet, I do."

He picks me up and twirls me round as we both laugh. We kiss again and again. Who is he kidding? How could there be a more romantic and perfect time than now?

"Dinner smells fucking amazing. What is it?" he mumbles against my lips.

"Eggplant soup, followed by eggplant lasagne, and then eggplant pie for dessert."

He glances over to the oven with a look of disgust. "Are you serious?"

"Deadly."

His eyebrows rise in surprise. "That isn't the type of eggplant I had in mind, Eliza."

I laugh as I pull him in for another kiss. "Well, some fool delivered me sixteen eggplants so we have to use them." I tease.

He chuckles and he squeezes me tightly. "You ask, and I deliver."

———

We lie in the darkness on our sides, staring at each other.

Tonight has been monumental for us.

We got engaged, made love, and then we had dinner. After that, we made love again and again, took a deep, hot bath together, and now, as the dust of heartbreak settles, we're talking. And not just skimming around subjects, either. It's like our commitment has changed things and we are opening up to each other like never before.

Married.

The feeling of intimacy between us is like nothing I've ever felt.

"The butt plug thing," I whisper.

Nathan watches me. "What about it?"

"I thought you wanted to have anal sex with me... because you missed it."

"What?" He frowns. "Why would you think that?"

"I don't know." I shrug. "Why would I have thought any of the things I have thought?"

"I wanted it for you."

My eyes search his as I run my fingers through his stubble. "What do you mean?"

"Babe... ." He pauses as if getting the wording right. "You are so perfect, but so... naive, sexually."

"You think I'm vanilla?" I whisper, wide-eyed.

He chuckles. "Your vanilla just happens to be my favorite flavor." He kisses me quickly as if to soften the sting.

I bite my lip as I contemplate this theory. It never occurred to me that I'm sexually vanilla. I always thought I was techni-colored, fucking fantastic flavor.

"You said you a wanted a bad man to teach you bad things."

"So, you tried to deliver, and I read into it the wrong way." I sigh heavily.

God......what a colossal fuck-up.

"It's fine. I get why you did." He smiles and tucks a piece of hair behind my ear. "It's okay, we don't have to do that. I never want you to do anything that your uncomfortable with."

I stare at him, and this is it: the moment where I define what we will be. "I want to."

I kiss his neck and then my lips brush lower onto his chest. I take his nipple into my mouth and nip it with me teeth. "I want to be everything that you need."

"You already are. You're not ready for that yet.

"So get me ready."

His eyes hold mine as I drop between his legs. He inhales sharply and opens them in invitation. I lick the tip of his dick as the air crackles between us. "Are you up to the challenge?" I lick him again. "Can you train me to fuck me how you want to? My husband deserves so much more than vanilla."

He smiles darkly as he grabs my hair in his two hands and slides deep down my throat. "I'll see what I can do."

Our story isn't neat and it doesn't fit into any boxes. We are complicated and messy.

Fucked up and tainted.

But...

This is love.

Our Way.

The End.

EPILOGUE

Three weeks later

Eliza

I HOLD my hand out and stare down at the perfect solitaire diamond on my ring finger. We picked up my engagement ring today. Nathan designed it and had it made especially.

"I am literally loving myself sick." I swoon.

Nathan smirks as he sips his beer. "Couldn't tell."

I'm sitting on the kitchen counter, and we're just about to go out for dinner and drinks to celebrate.

"Can you take another photo of me?" I ask.

He takes out his phone, and I hold my hand up. "Make sure you get my ring."

He rolls his eyes. "You've made me take five hundred photos of that ring today." He takes a few photos.

"Take some more." I put my hand on my face. "Make it look casual so my ring stands out."

He drops his phone and looks at me, deadpan. "Nobody sits on the kitchen counter with their hand on their face, Eliza."

I smile goofily. "Nobody else has a ring this perfect. This is the ring of my life, Nathan. Get with the program." I stare at it lovingly. I'm not even joking. This is the best engagement ring I've ever seen.

He chuckles. "It had better be the ring of your life."

I pull him closer by his shirt, and I kiss his big lips. "I just love it. I just love you."

"I have another surprise for you," he says as if remembering something.

"And what would that be?"

His eyes dance with delight, and he takes off into the bedroom. "Now!" he calls. "Stay with me on this one."

I kick my feet around in excitement. When he says that, it's usually something sexual. The man is a deviant. He's had me wearing butt plugs all week for my, and I quote, *'training'*.

He reappears with a black box wrapped in gold ribbon. He passes it over. "Don't freak out."

"Okay...." I open the box and stare down at the black egg. I frown. "What's this?"

"A little bit of fun."

I stare at it as I pick it up. It has a latex texture. My eyes rise to meet his. "And what do you do with this?"

Nathan smiles darkly and spreads my legs. He rubs his fingertips over my panties. "You wear it."

"Where?"

He puts his finger into the side of my panties, and he slides his two fingers deep into my sex. "Here."

My eyes flutter closed. "I'm already wearing a butt plug, Nathan," I remind him. He put it in this afternoon as he went down on me.

I swear to God, this man is going to fuck me to death.

He smiles as he takes my lips in his. He sucks on them as his tongue does that twirling thing it does so well. "They go together, babe," he breathes.

Arousal heats my blood. "How much longer am I in this training stage?"

He rubs the egg over my panties. "Wear this tonight, and it will be the last session."

My eyes widen. "You want me to wear it... out?" I gasp. We've only played around at home before. This is next level crazy.

"Why not?"

I shrug. "Because..." I pause as I search for the right wording, "it's rude, Nathan."

He chuckles as he slips the egg under my panties and rubs it back and forth through my wet lips. "That's the point, babe."

"You want me to wear a butt plug and an egg thing... inside my body... at the same time, while we go to dinner?" I rasp.

"Yes." He nods, smirking. "I do."

My eyes widen. "Nathan."

"Humor me." He laughs as he pulls me closer for a kiss.

"This could be disastrous," I murmur against his lips.

"Or just fucking hot." He spreads my legs and puts them up on the counter. He slowly slides the egg deep inside my body.

My eyes close. "Ohh..." I whimper as my body sucks it in. I'm already teetering on the edge of an orgasm from his plug.

"How does that feel?" He rearranges his hard dick in his pants.

I frown and squirm as I try get used to the sensation. "Full."

He bites his bottom lip as he watches me. "Just how I like it." He rubs my sex through my panties. "Let's go. If we stay here any longer, you're getting it good."

He takes my hand and drags me off the counter. Something tells me I'm going to get it good, anyway.

An hour later, Nathan and I are sitting at a table in our favorite bar. It's bustling, and I just want to stare at my ring.

"I'll get us another drink, babe. Margarita?"

"Yes, please."

Nathan disappears to the bar, and I feel a flutter inside.

Oh... what's that?

It was like my body contracted around the egg. I feel my face heat, and I look around.

God, Nathan is next level dirty. I smirk as I sip my drink. If all of these people in this club knew what I have going on under this dress, they would be appalled.

Or impressed. I'm undecided where I stand on it. All I know is that there is a lot of stuff going on inside of me right now, and it's fucking hot.

I feel a flutter from deep inside again, and I frown as the air leaves my lungs.

What *was* that?

Is my body contracting around it? I drain the last of my drink as I feel a flutter again. Goosebumps scatter up my arms. Every time my sex contracts around the egg, I get a sharp jolt of pleasure from my behind. I drop my head, overwhelmed by the sensations. Everything feels magnified down there. *Thump, thump, thump...* pumps the pulse in my sex.

Fuck.

Nathan sits back down at the table and passes me my drink. "Thanks." I pick it up and take a huge gulp.

I feel a vibration, and I close my eyes as arousal begins to take over. What's going on here?

"Everything all right?" Nathan asks as he takes a sip of his drink.

"I just..." There's another flutter deep inside, and my eyebrows rise by themselves. "Holy fuck," I whisper.

"Mercer," we hear someone say.

"Oh my God, Cam?" Nathan laughs out loud, and he stands to shake a man's hand. "Eliza, this is my friend Cameron Stanton," Nathan introduces me. Nathan seems very pleased to see this man, whoever he is.

"Hello." I wince as I clench my sex to stop the flutters.

"Hi, there." Cameron smiles.

"What are you doing here, man?" Nathan laughs.

"Oh, Ash has a family reunion thing going on. I'm just here to pick up a bottle of wine. She's out in the car. I was going to call you tomorrow to try and catch up."

God, this guy is gorgeous, tall, dark, and handsome. But of course his good looks could be due to the fact that I'm halfway through fucking an egg right now, and even the salt and pepper shakers seem attractive.

Nathan and Cameron fall into conversation, and the egg begins to pulse. *Thump... thump... thump.*

Ooooh, fuck.

My legs begin to open by themselves. Oh no, I'm going to come.

I sit back and grip the edge of the table with both hands as perspiration dusts my skin.

I glance up, and Nathan's eyes are locked on me. He bites his bottom lip and then gives me a sexy wink before he continues talking to his friend.

Wait. What? Is he doing this?

He puts his hand into his pocket, and then the egg begins to pump faster. Oh my God.

He *is* doing it.

My body begins to contract as it rides the waves of pleasure, and it's all I can do to keep a straight face and act normal.

This is so...

My eyes are trying so hard to roll back in my head as my chest rises and falls. I struggle for air, and I grip the table with white-knuckle force.

The egg pulses harder and harder, and my behind is contracting along with it.

I need to get to the bathroom. I can't come here in front of Nathan's friend.

Oh, hell.

Nathan is a bad, bad man.

My eyes widen as I drop my head. Will I make it to the bathroom?

Nathan smiles as he watches me. He's loving this, *the bastard.*

"Yes, sounds good. Breakfast. The four of us," Cameron says. "Lovely to meet you, Eliza. See you both tomorrow."

I give him a flustered wave, and Nathan falls back into the seat beside me. "Sorry about that." He leans over and kisses me. I grab the back of his head.

"Are you doing this?" I wheeze.

He smiles playfully. "You mean this?" He fumbles around in his pocket, and the egg begins to vibrate, hard, drilling me *there*.

I struggle to keep my legs closed. "Oh, God," I breathe.

Nathan kisses me. His teeth catch my bottom lip as my sex contracts. "You like that, baby?"

"Take me home," I whisper as the room begins to spin out of control. "Take me home. Take me home. Take me home," I chant.

He pulls me closer for a kiss and I can't hold it for a second longer. I shudder as I come hard. Nathan smiles against my lips and kisses me through it. My heart is beating hard and fast in my chest.

What the hell? I just had an orgasm... *in public.*

"You're completely insane." I tip my head back and smile at the ceiling in disbelief.

Holy shit, Nathan Mercer is everything I never knew I needed, and then some.

I'm marrying this man. What the hell? I can hardly believe it.

The reality of us and our messed up, beautiful story blows my mind, and I laugh out loud as I hold up my hand. "Do you want to see my ring again?" I ask.

"No, Eliza." He smirks and picks up his drink. "I don't."

We crash through the door at midnight, our lips are locked. We've reached a new level of desperation.

Nathan has had me on the precipice of orgasm all night, and I'm quite sure that his new favorite toy is that remote control. He's teased me, we've danced and laughed, and he got me talking a new level of dirty as I felt his rock-hard dick through his jeans. God almighty, I am good to go. I want something that only he can give me.

"Now," I beg against his lips. "Now, Nathan." I'm so aroused that I've lost all control. "Fucking give it to me."

He inhales sharply and pulls me into the bedroom. He stands me at the foot of the bed, and he turns to me with seductive eyes.

He reaches up under my dress, removes my panties, and he lifts my foot to rest on the bed. He then slowly takes out the egg, and my body contracts with disappointment. I like that little thing.

Maybe I have a new favorite toy, too.

His hand moves to the butt plug, and he twists it as his eyes hold mine.

My chest rises and falls. "I need this, Nathe, I need this," I whimper.

I'm not joking, I really do. His aim was to get me ready. Not only am I ready, I'm fucking desperate. He's right, my body has adjusted and it has woken something up inside of me. It's dark and forbidden, and something I never thought I would crave.

He slowly twists it as he takes the plug out, and my body contracts. "Ohh." My body shudders from the loss.

Nathan takes my face in his hands and kisses me hard, his lips tenderly taking mine in a tantric dance of seduction. My body contracts once more, close to orgasm. "Nathan, please," I beg, he's been teasing me all week, and I just can't take it anymore.

He smiles darkly, as if impressed.... and my heart swells.

He takes off my dress and bra, and positions me exactly how he wants me on the bed. I'm lying on my side, my legs curled up.

I hear him take off his clothes, as well as the top drawer

open and close. I hear the click of a bottle. Lube... fuck, this is it.

He nestles in close behind me, and I feel his lips at my ear. "I'm going to warm you up, baby."

"No more warming up. I'm fucking cooked."

He chuckles as his fingers massage the lube *there.*

I close my eyes at the sensation. Feels good.

Who knew I would ever like this?

"Hurry up," I demand.

I feel his lips smile against my shoulder, and he pulls the blanket up over us, as if to protect me and keep me warm—to wrap us up from the outside world.

Oh, I love this man.

His lips fall to my ear. "Once we start, we don't stop. There is no stopping midway, okay?"

I nod.

He lifts my top leg over his forearm, and I feel his tip at my opening, "Kiss me," he breathes.

I turn my head, and his lips take mine as he pushes forward. He goes in a little way, and I smile against his lips. Oh, yes, I like this.

He meets resistance, and he pushes forward some more. My brow furrows. Ouch.

"Kiss me, Eliza." His tongue brings me back to the moment.

"Nearly there, babe." His voice is husky, and his breath quivers as he fights for control. I smile as his lips dust up and down my neck and then lifts my leg a little farther and pushes hard. My body resists, and I scrunch my eyes shut.

Oh fuck, that smarts.

"It's okay, it's okay," he whispers. He repositions me so that I roll more onto my stomach, my leg still lifted in his hand. "Are you okay?" he breathes.

I smile with a pant. Even during his thick arousal, he's worried about me.

"I'm just going to go, okay?"

I nod, and he pushes forward hard and drives me into the mattress. My body has no choice other than to accept him.

My eyes roll back in my head. Oh, good God, that's deep.

"Ssh," he soothes as he falls down over me. "It's okay, baby." He kisses me, and it's tender, beautiful, and everything just feels right. Like I'm meant to be here, learning this with him.

I scrunch up my face as emotion overwhelms me.

"Are... are you hurt?" he whispers in a panic.

"No, Nathe." I smile against his lips. "I'm perfect. You are perfect."

We kiss.

"I love you," I say against his mouth.

This is a beautiful moment between us.

His eyes flutter closed, and he puts his hand on my lower stomach and slowly brings my body back onto his. He stays still to let me accept him.

His teeth go to my neck, and he softly bites me up and down. I get a flutter of arousal. "Yes," I whisper.

He moves me some more, and my body seems to accept his and loosen right up.

"That's it," he whispers. "That's it, babe." His fingers drop to my clit and he slowly begins to circle over it as he pulls out and slowly pushes in again.

My head drops back to his shoulder as a wave of pleasure shoots through me. "Yessss," I hiss.

I feel him smile behind me, as if realizing that he's just unlocked the Holy Grail, and he pushes forward hard, more confidently this time.

I let out a deep moan as my body begins to ride him. "Oh God, Nathe... that's good."

He smiles and pulls out, and then he slides back in with more force. Each pump becomes more measured, deeper, more fucking amazing.

"Give it to me... harder," I pant.

He repositions me onto my knees and spreads my legs. With my hipbones in his hands, he pulls out and pushes back in. I smile because I'm doing it.

I'm actually doing it, and it's good. What have I been doing all this time?

I begin to push back against him, and he moans. *He likes that.*

I like it, too, and I begin to ride him, circling my hips while he hisses in appreciation.

"Come on." I push back against him.

"Oh... fuck," he growls, as if the last of his control has broken and he pulls back and slams in hard. The air is knocked from my lungs, and I smile into the mattress.

Here we go.

Then we are hard at it, our skin slapping together as we connect. I feel like I'm in a porno or something.

This is so surreal.

He reaches around and runs the tips of his fingers over my clit, and I contract hard around him. Oh God, yes.

"Come for me," he moans. He's close. I can hear the edge in his voice.

He circles his fingers again, and I shudder deep within as I come hard around him.

He lets out a guttural groan and holds himself deep. I feel the telling jerk of his cock deep within me, and we fall to the mattress.

We pant for a moment, and then Nathan turns my head and kisses me over my shoulder. His body is still deep inside of mine when he smiles against my lips.

"Look at you, Miss Give It To Me Harder."

I giggle, feeling very pleased with myself. "I know, I'm like a porn queen or something."

He chuckles and kisses me again. "You really are."

We kiss for a long time, and then he slowly pulls out and my body contracts, grieving his loss. He rolls me toward him and brushes the hair back from my forehead.

"Do you know how much I love you, Eliza Bennet?" He stares at me.

I smile, because I do. "Yes." I kiss him again. "You know that, now that we've done that, you have to marry me."

He laughs out loud. "I guess I can manage that. Eliza Mercer has a certain ring to it."

Three Months later - Majorca

April pulls my veil down over my face with a huge smile.

"You look amazing, Lize."

"Thanks." I stare in the mirror at my reflection. I'm wearing a fitted, strapless white dress that's embedded with crystals. My hair is down with big, soft Hollywood curls, and I feel like a princess.

It's my wedding day, and we are at the Sea View Rustic in Majorca. It's a beautiful resort perched on the clifftop over-looking the Mediterranean Sea.

Our closest friends and family have flown in and, oh, I'm nervous.

"It's time," my dad says.

I turn to him.

"You look so beautiful, darling."

Butterflies dance in my stomach. "Thanks, Dad."

April hands me my bouquet. "Are you ready to get married?" She smiles.

"I am." I take it from her. "Let's do this."

We walk out of the bridal suite and make our way outside where I can hear the violin music playing. There's a large area along the clifftop lined with white chairs. All of our friends are lined up, creating an aisle. At the end of the ledge is the Des Galliner, an open, stone, circular arbour that is over six hundred years old. I can see the priest, Nathan, and Alex waiting for us there.

"This is it." Dad smiles.

I nod.

The violinist begins to play the wedding waltz, and everyone turns toward us. Nerves dance in my stomach, and I exhale heavily as we begin to walk toward the end.

Nathan turns to me, and he smiles softly. My eyes fill with tears.

There's nothing to be nervous about.

He's wearing a black dinner suit, and his honey hair is messed up to perfection. But it's his heart that is calling me to run down this aisle.

He inhales deeply as I walk toward him, and I know he's feeling emotional, too.

We are so in love.

We arrive at the end of the aisle, and dad takes my hand and passes it to Nathan. He gives me a slow, sexy smile before he softly kisses my cheek. "Hi."

"Hi."

"You look beautiful."

I beam with happiness, and we turn toward the priest.

"We are gathered here today...," the priest begins.

Nathan's eyes never leave mine, and he has this mischievous grin on his face.

He can't believe this is happening. Me neither, actually.

I hunch my shoulders together in excitement, and Nathan chuckles.

It's like we are in our own little world, oblivious to what is being said around us.

We are interrupted from our little daydream with the words, "Do you, Eliza, take Nathan Mercer to be your lawful wedded husband, from this day forward, to have and to hold, in sickness and in health, for as long as you both shall live?"

I smile at my beautiful man as his eyes fill with tears. "I do." I slide the wedding ring on his finger.

"And do you, Nathan, take Eliza Bennet to be your lawful wedded wife, from this day forward, to have and to hold, in sickness and in health, for as long as you both shall live?"

"I do." He smiles as he slides the wedding ring on my finger.

I giggle in excitement and he bites his bottom lip to stop himself from laughing.

"I now pronounce you man and wife. You may kiss your bride."

Nathan lifts my veil back, and to the cheers of our family and friends, his lips slowly take mine as we smile against each other.

We made it...

Our way.

Five years later

I stir the gravy on the hotplate, and a text comes through on my phone:

I smile and text back.

Please!

I put my phone down and continue with dinner. Twenty minutes later, I hear the key in the door.

"Daddy!" I hear Ashton cry.

"Dada." Gracie struggles to get down from my arms, but she toddles in a run toward the front door. I smile as I turn back to my stirring.

Daddy is the favorite person in the house. His homecoming is a huge deal every night. Ashton is four, and Gracie is eighteen months old. We live in our apartment through the week, so that we are close to the hospital for Nathan. For the weekends, we bought a farm an hour outside the city. Life, for us, is hectic... and so happy.

I hear Nathan laugh out loud, and then I hear Ash scream in excitement.

He's getting tipped upside down by his feet out there like he does every night.

I hear Gracie squeal in excitement. She's getting tipped back and kissed on her neck right now. Ha, no wonder him getting home is so exciting.

He's the fun one.

"Snoopy, no." I hear Nathan gasp.

I smile as I stir, every single night without fail, Snoopy, our cat, likes to brush up against Nathan's dark suit pants, leaving the evidence of fur for his affection, much to Nathan's horror.

"Snoopy, no." Ashton says as he steps in to be dad's bouncer.

Nathan walks around the corner with his children in his arms. He smiles softly when he sees me.

"Hey, babe."

"Hi." I beam. I still get a physical reaction to my husband. Nothing is hotter than Nathan Mercer in his suit.

He kisses me, his lips lingering over mine, and the kids struggle to get out of his arms. He puts them down, and they run off.

"How's my girl?" His hands run down over my heavily pregnant stomach.

"Good." I smile against his lips. "Huge."

He chuckles. "And fucking hot." He pulls my hips toward him. Nathan Mercer has a new fetish. He's officially obsessed with my pregnant body.

I'm all hormonal and horny, so we are a good match. Although, I'm quite sure that married pregnant people are not supposed to act like we do. We're bad.

His tongue tenderly explores my mouth as he kisses me, and I feel my feet rise up from the floor.

"I got you something today." I smile.

"I'm fucking starving," he says, distracted. He turns and looks into the oven and then realizes what I said. "You did?"

I hand it over proudly. I did good with this present. I wrapped it and everything

"What is it?" He holds it to his ear and gives it a shake.

"Just open it."

He tears the wrapping off, and his eyes widen. "Eliza," he whispers.

I giggle. It's the latest book from his favorite author, Giraldi.

I ordered it in, especially. It doesn't hit bookstores until next week.

"I haven't read a book in so long." He stares at it in awe. "I can't wait to read this this weekend."

"I know. You deserve this book, honey." I love that he's so excited. He doesn't get time to read anymore. With work and the kids and me, he falls into bed in an exhausted heap every night.

He opens the front page and sees the message I wrote.

Truer, Madder, Deeper.
Forever.

He holds the book over his heart and smiles. "Thank you." He kisses me softly. "I love it—so thoughtful."

Gracie comes running into the kitchen and holds her arms up for Nathe. He picks her up, and she reaches for his book.

"Careful," he says as he passes it over. "Very special," he whispers.

She hurls it, and it goes flying across the room and lands straight into the sink full of the dishwater I have a pot soaking in.

"Ahh." His hand dives in after it and pulls it out. It's soaking wet, and water flies everywhere. It slops onto the counter, completely ruined.

He looks at me, deadpan, and puts Gracie down. She runs off into the living room, totally unfazed.

I put my hand over my mouth and burst out laughing. "She's one," I remind him.

"She's good at it." He puts his hands on his hips and stares at his beloved book. "Are you fucking kidding me?"

"Do you want some wine, Daddy?" I smile to soften the blow.

He closes his eyes as he holds in his tantrum that he desperately wants to have. "Yes. Yes, I fucking do."

The End.

Read on for an excerpt from Mr Masters....

MR MASTERS EXCERPT

AVAILABLE NOW

Prologue

Julian Masters

ALINA MASTERS

1984 – 2013

Wife and beloved mother.

In God's hands we trust.

Grief. The Grim Reaper of life.

Stealer of joy, hope and purpose.

Some days are bearable. Other days I can hardly breathe, and I suffocate in a world of regret where good reason has no sense.

I never know when those days will hit, only that when I wake, my chest feels constricted and I need to run. I need to be anywhere but here, dealing with this life.

My life.

Our life.

Until *you* left.

The sound of a distant lawnmower brings me back to the present, and I glance over at the cemetery's caretaker. He's concentrating as he weaves between the tombstones, careful not to clip or damage one as he passes. It's dusk, and the mist is rolling in for the night.

I come here often to think, to try and feel.

I can't talk to anyone. I can't express my true feelings.

I want to know why.

Why did you do this to us?

I clench my jaw as I stare at my late wife's tombstone.

We could have had it all... but, we didn't.

I lean down and brush the dust away from her name and rearrange the pink lilies that I have just placed in the vase. I touch her face on the small oval photo. She stares back at me, void of emotion.

Stepping back, I drop my hands in the pockets of my black overcoat.

I could stand here and stare at this headstone all day— sometimes I do—but I turn and walk to the car without looking back.

My *Porsche*.

Sure, I have money and two kids that love me. I'm at the top of my professional field, working as a judge. I have all the tools *to be* happy, but I'm not.

I'm barely surviving; holding on by a thread.

Playing the façade to the world.

Dying inside.

Half an hour later, I arrive at Madison's—my therapist.

I always leave here relaxed.

I don't have to talk, I don't have to think, I don't have to feel.

I walk through the front doors on autopilot.

"Good afternoon, Mr. Smith." Hayley the receptionist smiles. "Your room is waiting, sir."

"Thank you." I frown, feeling like I need something more today. Something to take this edginess off.

A distraction.

"I'll have someone extra today, Hayley."

"Of course, sir. Who would you like?"

I frown and take a moment to get it right. "Hmm. Hannah."

"So, Hannah and Belinda?"

"Yes."

"No problem, sir. Make yourself comfortable and they will be right up."

I take the lift to the exclusive penthouse. Once there I make myself a scotch and stare out the smoke-glass window overlooking London.

I hear the door click behind me and I turn toward the sound.

Hannah and Belinda stand before me smiling.

Belinda has long, blonde hair, while Hannah is a brunette. There's no denying they're both young and beautiful.

"Hello, Mr. Smith," they say in unison

I sip my scotch as my eyes drink them in.

"Where would you like us, sir?"

I unbuckle my belt. "On your knees."

Chapter 1

Brielle

Customs is ridiculously slow, and a man has been pulled into the office up ahead. It all looks very suspicious from my position at the back of the line. "What do you think he did?" I whisper as I crane my neck to spy the commotion up ahead.

"I don't know, something stupid, probably," Emerson replies. We shuffle towards the desk as the line moves a little quicker.

We've just arrived in London to begin our year-long working holiday. I'm going to work for a judge as a nanny, while Emerson, my best friend, is working for an art auctioneer. I'm terrified, yet excited.

"I wish we had come a week earlier so we could have spent some time together," Emerson says.

"Yeah, I know, but she needed me to start this week because she's going away next week. I need to learn the kids' routine."

"Who leaves their kids alone for three days with a complete stranger?" Em frowns in disgust.

I shrug. "My new boss, apparently."

"Well, at least I can come and stay with you next week. That's a bonus."

My position is residential, so my accommodation is secure. However, poor Emerson will be living with two strangers. She's freaking out over it.

"Yeah, but I'm sneaking you in," I say. "I don't want it to look like we're partying or anything."

I look around the airport. It's busy, bustling, and I already feel so alive. Emerson and I are more than just young travellers.

Emerson is trying to find her purpose and I'm running from a destructive past, one that involves me being in love with an adultering prick.

I loved him. He just didn't love me. Not enough, anyway.

If he had, he would have kept it in his pants, and I wouldn't be at Heathrow Airport feeling like I'm about to throw up.

I look down at myself and smooth the wrinkles from my dress. "She's picking me up. Do I look okay?"

Emerson looks me up and down, smiling broadly. "You look exactly how a twenty-five-year-old nanny from Australia should."

I bite my bottom lip to stop myself from smiling stupidly. That was a good answer.

"So, what's your boss's name?" she asks.

I rustle around in my bag for my phone and scroll through the emails until I get to the one from the nanny agency. "Mrs. Julian Masters."

Emerson nods. "And what's her story again? I know you've told me before but I've forgotten."

"She's a Supreme Court judge, widowed five years ago."

"What happened to the husband?"

"I don't know, but apparently she's quite wealthy." I shrug. "Two kids, well behaved."

"Sounds good."

"I hope so. I hope they like me."

"They will." We move forward in the line. "We are definitely going out at the weekend though, yes?"

"Yes." I nod. "What are you going to do until then?"

Emerson shrugs. "Look around. I start work on Monday and

it's Thursday today." She frowns as she watches me. "Are you sure you can go out on the weekends?"

"Yes," I snap, exasperated. "I told you a thousand times, we're going out on Saturday night."

Emerson nods nervously. I think she may be more nervous than I am, but at least I'm acting brave. "Did you get your phone sorted?" I ask.

"No, not yet. I'll find a phone shop tomorrow so I can call you."

"Okay."

We are called to the front of the line, and finally, half an hour later, we walk into the arrival lounge of Heathrow International Airport.

"Do you see our names?" Emerson whispers as we both look around.

"No."

"Shit, no one is here to pick us up. Typical." She begins to panic.

"Relax, they will be here," I mutter.

"What do we do if no one turns up?"

I raise my eyebrow as I consider the possibility. "Well, I don't know about you, but I'm going to lose my shit."

Emerson looks over my shoulder. "Oh, look, there's your name. She must have sent a driver."

I turn to see a tall, broad man in a navy suit holding a sign with the name Brielle Johnston on it. I force a smile and wave meekly as I feel my anxiety rise like a tidal wave in my stomach.

He walks over and smiles at me. "Brielle?"

His voice is deep and commanding. "Yes, that's me," I breathe.

He holds out his hand to shake mine. "Julian Masters."

What?

My eyes widen.

A man?

He raises his eyebrows.

"Um, so, I'm... I'm Brielle," I stammer as I push my hand out. "And this is my friend, Emerson, who I'm travelling with." He takes my hand in his and my heart races.

A trace of a smile crosses his face before he covers it. "Nice to meet you." He turns to Emerson and shakes her hand. "How do you do?"

My eyes flash to Emerson, who is clearly loving this shit. She grins brightly. "Hello."

"I thought you were a woman," I whisper.

His brows furrow. "Last time I checked I was all man." His eyes hold mine.

Why did I just say that out loud? Oh my God, stop talking.

This is so awkward.

I want to go home. This is a bad idea.

"I'll wait over here." He gestures to the corner before marching off in that direction. My horrified eyes meet Emerson's, and she giggles, so I punch her hard in the arm.

"Oh my fuck, he's a fucking man," I whisper angrily.

"I can see that." She smirks, her eyes fixed on him.

"Excuse me, Mr. Masters?" I call after him.

He turns. "Yes."

We both wither under his glare. "We... we are just going to use the bathroom," I stammer nervously.

With one curt nod he gestures to the right. We look up and see the sign. I grab Emerson by the arm and drag her into the bathroom. "I'm not working with a stuffy old man!" I shriek as we burst through the door.

"It will be okay. How did this happen?"

I take out my phone and scroll through the emails quickly. I knew it. "It says woman. I knew it said woman."

"He's not that old," she calls out from her cubicle. "I would prefer to work for a man than a woman, to be honest."

"You know what, Emerson? This is a shit idea. How the hell did I let you talk me into this?"

She smiles as she exits the cubicle and washes her hands. "It doesn't matter. You'll hardly see him anyway, and you're not working weekends when he's home." She's clearly trying to calm me. "Stop with the carry on."

Stop the carry on.

Steam feels like it's shooting from my ears. "I'm going to kill you. I'm going to fucking kill you."

Emerson bites her lip to stifle her smile. "Listen, just stay with him until we find you something else. I will get my phone sorted tomorrow and we can start looking elsewhere for another job," she reassures me. "At least someone picked you up. Nobody cares about me at all."

I put my head into my hands as I try to calm my breathing. "This is a disaster, Em," I whisper. Suddenly every fear I had about travelling is coming true. I feel completely out of my comfort zone.

"It's going to be one week... tops."

My scared eyes lift to hold hers, and I nod.

"Okay?" She smiles as she pulls me into a hug.

"Okay." I glance back in the mirror, fix my hair, and straighten my dress. I'm completely rattled.

We walk back out and take our place next to Mr. Masters. He's in his late thirties, immaculately dressed, and kind of attractive. His hair is dark with a sprinkle of grey.

"Did you have a good flight?" he asks as he looks down at me.

"Yes, thanks," I push out. Oh, that sounded so forced. "Thank you for picking us up," I add meekly.

He nods with no fuss.

Emerson smiles at the floor as she tries to hide her smile.

That bitch is loving this shit.

"Emerson?" a male voice calls. We all turn to see a blond man, and Emerson's face falls. Ha! Now it's my turn to laugh.

"Hello, I'm Mark." He kisses her on the cheek and then turns to me. "You must be Brielle?"

"Yes." I smile then turn to Mr. Masters. "And this is..." I pause because I don't know how to introduce him.

"Julian Masters," he finishes for me, adding in a strong handshake.

Emerson and I fake smile at each other.

Oh dear God, help me.

Emerson stands and talks with Mark and Mr. Masters, while I stand in uncomfortable silence.

"The car is this way." He gestures to the right.

I nod nervously. Oh God, don't leave me with him.

This is terrifying.

"Nice to meet you, Emerson and Mark." He shakes their hands.

"Likewise. Please look after my friend," Emerson whispers as her eyes flicker to mine.

Mr. Masters nods, smiles, and then pulls my luggage behind him as he walks to the car. Emerson pulls me into an embrace. "This is shit," I whisper into her hair.

"It will be fine. He's probably really nice."

"He doesn't look nice," I whisper.

"Yeah, I agree. He looks like a tool," Mark adds as he watches him disappear through the crowd.

Emerson throws her new friend a dirty look, and I smirk. I

think her friend is more annoying than mine, but anyway... "Mark, look after my friend, please?"

He beats his chest like a gorilla. "Oh, I intend to."

Emerson's eyes meet mine. She subtly shakes her head and I bite my bottom lip to hide my smile. This guy is a dick. We both look over to see Mr. Masters looking back impatiently. "I better go," I whisper.

"You have my apartment details if you need me?"

"I'll probably turn up in an hour. Tell your roommates I'm coming in case I need a key."

She laughs and waves me off, and I go to Mr. Masters. He sees me coming and then starts to walk again.

God, can he not even wait for me? So rude.

He walks out of the building into the VIP parking section. I follow him in complete silence.

Any notion that I was going to become friends with my new boss has been thrown out the window. I think he hates me already.

Just wait until he finds out that I lied on my resume and I have no fucking idea what I'm doing. Nerves flutter in my stomach at the thought.

We get to a large, swanky, black SUV, and he clicks it open to put my suitcase in the trunk. He opens the back door for me to get in. "Thank you." I smile awkwardly as I slide into the seat. He wants me to sit in the back when the front seat is empty.

This man is odd.

He slides into the front seat and eventually pulls out into the traffic. All I can do is clutch my handbag in my lap.

Should I say something? Try and make conversation?

What will I say?

"Do you live far from here?" I ask.

"Twenty minutes," he replies, his tone clipped.

Oh...is that it? Okay, shut up now. He doesn't want a conversation. For ten long minutes we sit in silence.

"You can drive this car when you have the children, or we have a small minivan. The choice is yours."

"Oh, okay." I pause for a moment. "Is this your car?"

"No." He turns onto a street and into a driveway with huge sandstone gates. "I drive a Porsche," he replies casually. "Oh."

The driveway goes on and on and on. I look around at the perfectly kept grounds and rolling green hills. With every meter we pass, I feel my heart beat just that bit faster.

As if it isn't bad enough that I can't do the whole nanny thing... I really can't do the rich thing. I have no idea what to do with polite company. I don't even know what fork to use at dinner. I've got myself into a right mess here.

The house comes into focus and the blood drains from my face.

It's not a house, not even close. It's a mansion, white and sandstone with a castle kind of feel to it, with six garages to the left.

He pulls into the large circular driveway, stopping under the awning.

"Your house is beautiful," I whisper.

He nods, as his eyes stay fixed out front. "We are fortunate."

He gets out of the car and opens my door for me. I climb out as I grip my handbag with white-knuckle force. My eyes rise up to the luxurious building in front of me.

This is an insane amount of money.

He retrieves my suitcase and wheels it around to the side of the building. "Your entrance is around to the side," he says. I follow him up a path until we get to a door, which he opens and lets me walk through. There is a foyer and a living area in front of me.

"The kitchen is this way." He points to the kitchen. "And your bedroom is in the back left corner."

I nod and walk past him, into the apartment.

He stands at the door but doesn't come in. "The bathroom is to the right," he continues.

Why isn't he coming in here? "Okay, thanks," I reply.

"Order any groceries you want on the family shopping order and..." He pauses, as if collecting his thoughts. "If there is anything else you need, please talk to me first."

I frown. "First?"

He shrugs. "I don't want to be told about a problem for the first time when reading a resignation letter."

"Oh." Did that happen before? "Of course," I mutter.

"If you would like to come and meet the children..." He gestures to a hallway.

"Yes, please." Oh God, here we go. I follow him out into a corridor with glass walls that looks out onto the main house, which is about four metres away. A garden sits between the two buildings creating an atrium, and I smile as I look up in wonder. There is a large window in the main house that looks into the kitchen. I can see beyond that into the living area from the corridor where a young girl and small boy are watching television together. We continue to the end of the glass corridor where there is a staircase with six steps leading up to the main house.

I blow out a breath, and I follow Mr. Masters up the stairs.

"Children, come and meet your new nanny."

The little boy jumps down and rushes over to me, clearly excited, while the girl just looks up and rolls her eyes. I smile to myself, remembering what it's like to be a typical teenager.

"Hello, I'm Samuel." The little boy smiles as he wraps his

arms around my legs. He has dark hair, is wearing glasses, and he's so damn cute.

"Hello, Samuel." I smile.

"This is Willow," he introduces.

I smile at the teenage girl. "Hello." She folds her arms across her chest defiantly. "Hi," she grumbles.

Mr. Masters holds her gaze for a moment, saying so much with just one look.

Willow eventually holds her hand out for me to shake. "I'm Willow."

I smile as my eyes flash up to Mr. Masters. He can keep her under control with just a simple glare.

Samuel runs back to the lounge, grabs something, and then comes straight back.

I see a flash.

Click, click.

What the hell?

He has a small instant Polaroid camera. He watches my face appear on the piece of paper in front of him before he looks back up at me. "You're pretty." He smiles. "I'm putting this on the fridge." He carefully pins it to the fridge with a magnet.

Mr. Masters seems to become flustered for some reason. "Bedtime for you two," he instructs and they both complain. He turns his attention back to me. "Your kitchen is stocked with groceries, and I'm sure you're tired."

I fake a smile. Oh, I'm being dismissed. "Yes, of course." I go to walk back down to my apartment, and then turn back to him. "What time do I start tomorrow?"

His eyes hold mine. "When you hear Samuel wake up."

"Yes, of course." My eyes search his as I wait for him to say something else, but it doesn't come. "Goodnight then." I smile awkwardly.

"Goodnight."

"Bye, Brielle." Samuel smiles, and Willow ignores me, walking away and up the stairs.

I walk back down into my apartment and close the door behind me. Then I flop onto the bed and stare up at the ceiling.

What have I done?

It's midnight and I'm thirsty, but I have looked everywhere and I still cannot find a glass. There's no other option; I'm going to have to sneak up into the main house to find one. I'm wearing my silky white nightdress, but I'm sure they are all in bed.

Sneaking out into the darkened corridor, I can see into the lit-up house.

I suddenly catch sight of Mr. Masters sitting in the armchair reading a book. He has a glass of red wine in his hand. I stand in the dark, unable to tear my eyes away. There's something about him that fascinates me but I don't quite know what it is.

He stands abruptly, and I push myself back against the wall.

Can he see me here in the dark?

Shit.

My eyes follow him as he walks into the kitchen. The only thing he's wearing is his navy-blue boxer shorts. His dark hair has messy, loose waves on top. His chest is broad, his body is...

My heart begins to beat faster. What am I doing? I shouldn't be standing here in the dark, watching him like a creep, but for some reason I can't make myself look away.

He goes to stand by the kitchen counter, his back is to me as he pours himself another glass of red. He lifts it to his lips slowly and my eyes run over his body.

I push myself against the wall harder.

He walks over to the fridge and takes off the photo of me.

What?

He leans his ass on the counter as he studies it.

What is he doing?

I feel like I can't breathe.

He slowly puts his hand down the front of his boxer shorts, and then he seems to stroke himself a few times.

My eyes widen.

What the fuck?

He puts his glass of wine on the counter and turns the main light off, leaving only a lamp to light the room.

With my picture in his hand, he disappears up the hall.

What the hell was that?

I think Mr. Masters just went up to his bedroom to jerk off to my photo.

Oh.

My.

God.

Knock, knock.

My eyes are closed, but I frown and try to ignore the noise.

I hear it again. Tap, tap.

What is that? I roll towards the door and I see it slowly begin to open.

My eyes widen, and I sit up quickly.

Mr. Masters comes into view. "I'm so sorry to bother you, Miss Brielle," he whispers. He smells like he's freshly showered, and he's wearing an immaculate suit. "I'm looking for Samuel." His gaze roams down to my breasts hanging loosely in my nightdress, and then he snaps his eyes back up to my face, as if he's horrified at what he just did.

"Where is he?" I frown. "Is he missing?"

"There he is," he whispers as he gestures to the lounger.

I look over to see Samuel curled up with his teddy in the

diluted light of the room. My mouth falls open. "Oh no, what's wrong?" I whisper. Did he need me and I slept through the whole thing?

"Nothing," Mr. Masters murmurs as he picks Samuel up and rests his son's head on his strong shoulder. "He's a sleepwalker. Sorry to disturb you. I've got this now." He leaves the room with his small son safely asleep in his arms. The door gently clicks closed behind them.

I lie back down and stare at the ceiling in the silence. That poor little boy. He came in here to see me and I didn't even wake up. I was probably snoring, for fuck's sake.

What if he was scared? Oh, I feel like shit now.

I blow out a deep breath, lift myself up to sit on the edge of the bed, and I put my head into my hands.

I need to up my game. If I'm in charge of looking after this kid, I can't have him wandering around at night on his own.

Is he that lonely that he was looking for company from me —a complete stranger?

Unexplained sadness rolls over me, and I suddenly feel like the weight of the world is on my shoulders. I look around my room for a moment as I think.

Eventually, I get up and go to the bathroom, and then walk to the window to pull the heavy drapes back. It's just getting light, and a white mist hangs over the paddocks.

Something catches my eye and I look down to see Mr. Masters walking out to the garage.

Wearing a dark suit and carrying a briefcase, he disappears, and moments later I see his Porsche pull out and disappear up the driveway. I watch on as the garage door slowly closes behind him.

He's gone to work for the day.

What the hell?

His son was just found asleep on my lounger and he just plops him back into his own bed and leaves for the day. Who does that? Well, screw this, I'm going to go and check on him. He's probably upstairs crying, scared out of his brain. Stupid men. Why don't they have an inch of fucking empathy for anyone but themselves?

He's eight, for Christ's sake!

I walk up into the main house. The lamp is still on in the living room and I can smell the eggs that Mr. Masters cooked himself for breakfast. I look around, and then go up the grand staircase.

Honestly, what the hell have I got myself into here? I'm in some stupid rich twat's house, worried about his child who he clearly doesn't give a fuck about.

I storm up the stairs, taking two at a time. I get to the top and the change of scenery suddenly makes me feel nervous. It's luxurious up here. The corridor is wide, and the cream carpet feels lush beneath my feet. A huge mirror hangs in the hall on the wall. I catch a glimpse of myself and cringe.

God, no wonder he was looking at my boobs. They are hanging out everywhere, and my hair is wild. I readjust my nightgown over my breasts and continue up the hall. I pass a living area that seems to be for the children, with big comfy loungers inside it. I pass a bedroom, and then I get to a door that is closed. I open it carefully and allow myself to peer in. Willow is fast asleep, still scowling, though. I smirk and slowly shut her door to continue down the hall. Eventually, I get to a door that is slightly ajar. I peer around it and see Samuel sound asleep, tucked in nice and tight. I walk into his room and sit on the side of the bed. He's wearing bright blue and green dinosaur pyjamas, and his little glasses are on his side table, beside his lamp. I find myself smiling as I watch him. Unable to help it, I put my hand out and push the dark hair from his forehead. His bedroom is neat and tidy, filled with expensive furniture. It kind of looks like you would imagine a child's bedroom being set out in a perfect family movie. Everything in this house is the absolute best of the best. Just how much money does Mr. Masters have? There's a bookcase, a desk, a wingback chair in the corner, and a toy box. The window has a bench seat running underneath it, and there are a few books sitting in a pile on the cushion, as if Samuel reads there a lot. I glance over to the armchair in the corner to his school clothes all laid out for him. Everything is there, folded neatly, right down to his socks and shiny, polished shoes. His school bag is packed, too.

I stand and walk over to look at his things. Mr. Masters must do this before he goes to bed. What must it be like to bring children up alone?

My mind goes to his wife and how much she is missing out on. Samuel is so young. With one last look at Samuel, I creep out of the room and head back down the hall, until something catches my eye.

A light is on in the en-suite bathroom of the main bedroom.

That must be Mr. Master's bedroom.

I look left and then right; nobody is awake. I wonder what his room is like, and I can't stop myself from tiptoeing closer to inspect it.

Wow.

The bed is clearly king-size, and the room is grand, decorated in all different shades of coffee, complimented with dark antique furniture. A huge, expensive, gold and magenta embroidered rug sits on the floor beneath the bed. The light in the wardrobe is on. I peer inside and see business shirts all lined up, neatly in a row. Super neatly, actually.

I'm going to have to make sure I keep my room tidy or he'll think I'm a pig.

I smirk because I am one according to his standards of living.

I turn to see his bed has already been made, and my eyes linger over the velvet quilt and lush pillows there. Did he really touch himself in there last night as he thought of me, or am I completely delusional? I glance around for the photo of me, but I don't see it. He must have taken it back downstairs.

An unexpected thrill runs through me. I may return the favour tonight in my own bed.

I walk into the bathroom. It's all black, grey, and very modern. Once again, I notice that everything is very neat. There is a large mirror, and I can see that a slender cabinet sits behind it. I push the mirror and the door pops open. My eyes roam over the shelves. You can tell a lot about people by their bathroom cabinet.

Deodorant. Razors. Talcum powder.

Condoms.

I wonder how long ago his wife died. Does he have a new girlfriend?

It wouldn't surprise me. He is kind of hot, in an old way. I see a bottle of aftershave and I pick it up, removing the lid before I lift it up to my nose.

Heaven in a bottle.

I inhale deeply again, and Mr. Master's face suddenly appears in the mirror behind me.

"What the hell do you think you're doing?" he growls.

To continue reading this story, it is available on Amazon now.

AFTERWORD

Thank you so much for reading and
for your ongoing support
I have the most beautiful readers in the whole world!

Keep up to date with all the latest news
and online discussions by joining the Swan Squad VIP
Facebook group and discuss your favourite
books with other readers.
@tlswanauthor

Visit my website for updates and new release information.
www.tlswanauthor.com

ABOUT THE AUTHOR

T L Swan is a Wall Street Journal and #1 Amazon Best Selling author. With millions of books sold, her titles are currently translated in twenty languages and have hit #1 on Amazon in the USA, UK, Canada, Australia and Germany. Tee resides on the South Coast of NSW, Australia with her husband and their three children where she is living her own happy ever after with her first true love.

Made in the USA
Las Vegas, NV
06 March 2025

19151773R00353